The Price of Freedom

A Novel of the American Revolution

Martin R. Ganzglass

A PEACE CORPS WRITERS BOOK

ALSO BY MARTIN R. GANZGLASS

Fiction

The Orange Tree

Somalia: Short Fiction

In the American Revolutionary War Series

Cannons for the Cause

Tories and Patriots

Blood Upon The Snow

Spies and Deserters

Treason and Triumph

Non-Fiction

The Penal Code of the Somali Democratic Republic (Cases, Commentary and Examples)

The Restoration of the Somali Justice System, Learning From Somalia, The Lessons of Armed Humanitarian Intervention, Clarke & Herbst, Editors

The Forty-Eight Hour Rule, One Hand Does Not Catch a Buffalo, A. Barlow, Editor

Cover Image: *Washington's Grand Entry into New York, Nov. 25th 1793* Chromolithograph by Thomas Sinclair from an original Drawing by Alphonse Bigot

For My Grandsons

Treason and Triumph
A Peace Corps Writers Book.
An Imprint of Peace Corps Worldwide

Copyright © 2018 by Martin R. Ganzglass
All rights reserved.

Printed in the United States of America
by Peace Corps Writers of Oakland, California.

No part of this book may be used or reproduced in any manner whatsoever without written permission except in the case of brief quotations contained in critical articles or reviews.

For more information, contact www.peacecorpsworldwide.com
Peace Corps Writers and the Peace Corps Writers colophon are trademarks of PeaceCorpsWorldwide.org

This novel is a work of fiction. The historical figures and actual events described are used fictitiously. All other names, characters, places and incidents are products of the author's imagination. Any resemblance to living persons is purely coincidental.

ISBN 978-1-950444-02-1
Library of Congress Control Number
2019944863

First Peace Corps Writers Edition, July 2019.

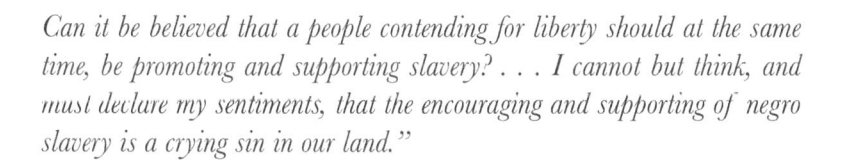

Can it be believed that a people contending for liberty should at the same time, be promoting and supporting slavery? . . . I cannot but think, and must declare my sentiments, that the encouraging and supporting of negro slavery is a crying sin in our land."

Jacob Green, Presbyterian Minister, 1778.

Part One
The Limits of Liberty

Chapter 1 - Family Matters

Sarah Cooper sat in a quiet corner of the Knox's warm kitchen, humming softly to herself. Reaching down she gently rocked the wooden cradle and loosened the blanket swaddling her newborn son's small body. With his eyes closed, one could not see they were grey green like hers, though he had Adam's high forehead and broad nose. Maybe, she thought, that was due to nursing and his nose would be less flat, more like hers, over time. It did not matter. To her, he was a beautiful baby.

She had never seen Adam so happy, so filled with love for her and adoration of their little boy. When Adam chose the name Emmanuel, Sarah had not proposed her own father's name. He was most likely Willis Parks, the master of the Tidewater Virginia plantation where her mother was enslaved. How else had Sarah acquired the color of her eyes and her lighter skin? She knew of at least four pregnancies her mother had endured to breed more slaves for Parks. And that was before Sarah was sold to Reverend Penrose of Hackensack, New Jersey, seven years ago. She had not seen her mother since.

She banished these gloomy thoughts by remembering Adam dancing around the room, embracing Emmanuel, so tiny in his father's muscular arms, telling him he would teach him to catch the biggest fish, weave the tightest nets, forge the strongest hooks, carve the best oars, tar the finest hull, row the fastest dory, until laughing at her husband's exuberance, she told him to stop before their son became frightened by the torrent of his words.

With the arrival of their son, she and Adam were enjoying the most joyful and blissful time of their lives. General Knox, Lucy and their two children were temporarily residing in a spacious solid brick home, for the duration of Mrs. Knox's pregnancy. She was due the beginning of December. Adam, a Master Sergeant and a member of General Knox's staff was assigned a small attic room for himself, Sarah and their child. She surmised Mrs. Knox had her hand in this. Sarah was Mrs. Knox's favorite baker and now the nanny for Henry, their sixteen-month old boy. On occasion Sarah took care of little Lucy, bringing the five-year old girl down to the kitchen and letting her help make the dough or place the cut and cored fruit in the pies.

Sarah enjoyed baking and the friendship with the cooks and other servants in the house, although most were white. She liked the steady wages she received in hard coin but missed being an independent businesswoman, providing baked goods for the social events of other prominent Philadelphia families. The offer to serve the Knoxes was one she could not refuse. She owed them. It was the General who had proposed to Adam the dangerous bargain that had made her a free woman. In return for engaging in a year long spying mission, Knox agreed to arrange for the purchase Sarah's freedom. When Adam had thwarted the plot to kidnap General Washington from the Ford Mansion in Morristown, General Knox swiftly made good on his promise. The precious papers certifying her freedom signed by Reverend Penrose, along with a letter verifying her status signed by General Knox himself, were hidden beneath her clothes in their locked trunk, in their small room in the attic.[1]

Not that she had felt unwanted in Mr. and Mrs. Jeremy Absalom's home where she had lived since coming to Philadelphia before Adam arrived from Yorktown. However, there was no comparison between the home of a respectable, elderly free black couple, living at the edges of the established boundaries of the city and the Knox's elegant residence located in the center of the bustle of Philadelphia and the social swirl that occurred within the house.

Besides, the Knoxes had been most generous, giving Sarah and Adam a crib, some baby clothes and most importantly, prevailing upon Dr. Rush, when he came to examine Mrs. Knox, to look at Emmanuel as well.

She was surprised to see Jeremy Absalom enter through the rear door of the kitchen, rather than coming down the three steps from the dining room. Then she realized, as a black man, even a free one, he knew not to come to the front door of the Knox's residence to ask for admittance to see her. Jeremy was a tall man, now stooped with age and requiring the use of a cane. She wondered what compelled him to come this distance over the rain-slicked cobblestones to visit her. With preparations underway for the dinner meal, the kitchen was full of commotion. She waved at him and quickly skirted the large oak table in the center, heaped high with uncut vegetables. Sarah helped him off with his coat and hat, hung them on a hook near the fireplace to dry and offered him a chair near the cradle.

"Ah, this is your son," he said sighing, as he settled himself against the hard wooden seat and bent stiffly down to peer in. "His name is Emmanuel," he said more as a statement than a question. "There are not too many black men named Emmanuel," he said softly. "Most are given the names of ancient Romans by their masters to show how clever and educated they are in the classics." His voice, although low so only Sarah could hear, had a bitter edge to it.

"I heard a sermon once, a long time ago," Absalom continued, looking up at the beamed ceiling as if the words would descend from heaven through the roof. "This preacher taught that Emmanuel meant 'God is with us.' At the time I was not yet free. My every day's existence under the threat of the whip and the constant hard labor with little sustenance, convinced me of the very opposite." Again the note of bitterness.

"But now, I see free blacks in an army fighting for independence from a brutal tyranny, your own husband, himself freeborn, who risked all to purchase your freedom and," he nodded toward the cradle, "your own infant babe."[2] His tight lips formed a grim smile, although his eyes betrayed a greater joy. "A second generation born free. I think perhaps I was wrong all these years." He exhaled deeply, placing both hands on the knob at the top of his plain worn cane and rested his chin upon them. "I hope your son's name is a prophecy for a better life for him." He sat there lost in thought, his clouded eyes staring at the brick wall behind the cradle.

Abruptly, remembering the purpose of his visit, he straightened in the chair and glanced around the room, taking note of the white cooks and servants close to them. "I have received a letter that I believe pertains to you. I would have preferred to meet with you in private, but this will do." Absalom bent forward and brought his head closer to Sarah's.

"An acquaintance of mine, Peter Williams, a Sexton at the John Street Methodist Church in New York City, has written to me."[3] He paused and waved one hand dismissively. "Not only to me but others as far south as Baltimore and north to Boston, where there are significant populations of free blacks. Peter is a religious man with many friends within our communities," he added by way of explanation. What had this black Sexton written that affected her, Sarah thought apprehensively. Mr. Absalom was telling the story at his own pace however and would not be rushed. She rocked the cradle and hoped Emmanuel would not interrupt him by waking.

After another lengthy pause, Absalom picked up the thread, this time speaking even more softly. Sarah leaned forward straining to hear him above the voices of cooks and servants, the banging of pots and pans, the thwock of a cleaver cutting a haunch of meat, the constant coming and going and slamming of pantry doors.

"Sexton Williams has in his employ at the Church, two Negroes who fled Virginia, and reached the British lines on the coast. Fortunately, they were able to stow away on a British ship that made its way to New York City. One is a woman, perhaps close to fifty years of age, the other is a young boy, maybe fourteen or so." He rocked from side to side as if seeing the two Negroes in his mind. "The boy has a brand burned on to his forehead for attempting to run away before." He sniffed deeply, taking in the cooking aromas filling the kitchen and nodded appreciatively.

"He must have spirit since it did not deter him from trying again. This time he succeeded."

Absalom pulled his chair closer so that the two were now almost head to head and placed his hand on Sarah's bare forearm. "According to Sexton Williams, the woman is looking for the whereabouts of a daughter named Sarah, the only one of her daughters sold to someone in the north."

Sarah could contain herself no longer. "Please tell me the woman's name."

"Lettia. The boy, who is her son, is called Jupiter," he said with disgust. "They do not use their master's name but it was Parks."

Sarah cupped both of her hands over her mouth and nose. Her eyes filled with tears. "It is my mother. My poor, poor mother."

"Sarah," someone called. "Mind the breads and cakes in the oven."

She rose, wiping her hands wet with tears on her apron. "It is my mother," she said, repeating the phrase over and over as she made her way to the side of the hearth to remove the loaves from the Dutch oven.

When she returned, Absalom was rocking the cradle and peering down at Emmanuel who had awakened and was staring up at him with a furrowed brow. The infant made tiny sucking noises, unsure whether to cry or smile. Sarah picked her son up and held him tightly.

"Adam and I will find the money and bring them here. I will take care of her. And my brother can be put to work. Will you write your friend? Tell him to inform my mother I am in Philadelphia, married and a free woman. Will you help us? To be reunited with her after all these years," she said through tears of joy. "It is another blessing for us." In her mind, Sarah already saw her mother settled in somewhere in town, a room of her own, or in the Knox's kitchen, helping out, staying warm in the winter, minding her grandson.

Absalom sighed and shook his head slowly. "Sarah, my child. Even in Philadelphia where the devout Friends and influential patriots have strong anti-slavery sentiments, slave catchers and bounty hunters prowl the wharves and streets. These are evil men.

Your mother and brother are not safe here. I am sorry to say they are only free in British occupied New York."[4]

"Then, I will go to her," Sarah said defiantly. One or two of the servants looked at her curiously, having heard her loud declaration. Emmanuel whimpered and nuzzled her bosom. If she were still nursing when she left for New York, she would have to take the little one with her. Adam would help her plan the journey. He would know how to reunite her with her mother and brother and get them to safety.

That night, exhilarated by the knowledge her mother had escaped the plantation but somewhat apprehensive about what to do next, she lay in the darkness in their narrow bed. Her mind was filled with fragments of plans - how to travel, where to hide the money she would need, what warm clothes to bring - when Adam softly closed the door to their small room. The bed creaked as he sat on the edge, removed his boots and placed them, one at a time on the floor, making every effort not to wake Emmanuel. She kissed him on his cheek and nestled on his shoulder, her mouth a few inches below his ear.

"Mr. Absalom brought news today of my mother. She is in New York City. One of my brothers too," she whispered. "I plan to go to them."

Adam brusquely sat up. "You cannot," he said.

"Shh. You must whisper or you will wake the baby. And others will hear." She pointed to the wall behind them through whose planks came distinct sounds of snoring and snippets of conversation.

"I am whispering," he retorted loudly.

"Adam. You are not. Since the mortar bomb, you hear neither me nor yourself. You are speaking loudly," she hissed firmly. As if to prove her point, Emmanuel whimpered a few times and then, more fully awake cried demandingly. Sarah swung her legs out of the low bed and gathered her son in her arms to nurse him. Adam placed his pillow behind her back and affectionately stroked her bare arm.

"I am sorry," he said, drawing a sharp shh from Sarah.

"We cannot talk here," she said quietly, almost directly into his left ear. "Think of how I may be reunited with my mother, free from the fear of slave catchers in Philadelphia. I will wake you at four when I rise to begin my baking. The kitchen will be empty and your loud voice will disturb no one." She felt his rough hand under her chin. He kissed her gently to show he was not angry with her, and rolled over on his right side with a grunt.

Sarah was in the kitchen measuring flour from the earthenware crock, when, with a loud crash, Adam entered and dropped the armful of logs he had carried in from outside.

"I will build up the fire for your oven," he said.

"Now that you have shaken the very floor boards," Sarah admonished him, "first see to our son." If my mother were here, she thought, she would be cradling Emmanuel or shuffling around the kitchen cooing and reassuring him. Angrily, she pounded the rye dough before shaping it into a loaf, recognizing her frustration improved her kneading.

"There is no safe place for your mother within our lines," Adam said. "That is the cruel fact of it. I have thought this over. Once she has left New York City, if she comes south to Philadelphia, she must pass through New Jersey and a wide swath of patriotic slave holders, like your former master, Reverend Penrose."[5] He spat out the man's name with disgust. "They have a common interest with your mother's master in seeing that runaway slaves are returned to their rightful owners. I know from my year among Colonel Tye's Black Brigade." He lifted his son from the cradle and took long stomping strides around the room. "The boy must learn to cope with normal noise," he said by way of explanation.

"If your hearing does not improve, your own voice will be noise enough."

Adam ignored her. "Traveling north may be better but there will always be the threat of being seized by slave catchers. The coastal ports are more dangerous because she could be spirited away quickly with none to give chase."

"If she and my brother were with us and the Army near West Point, and they did work of some kind in our encampment, would she not be safe there?"

Adam stopped short in his circling of the room and gave her an angry look. "At Yorktown, I have seen His Excellency reclaim two of his own slaves who ran away from Mt. Vernon," he said bitterly. "If a slave catcher came to West Point and demanded your mother and brother be returned to their master, I doubt that General Washington would hesitate a moment in granting that request." [6]

"But how would they know where to find my mother?"

"Sarah. People are envious of others happiness. Or greedy. At Yorktown, my brother soldiers turned into gangs of runaway slave hunters for a guinea. "No," he shook his head vehemently. "I tell you, she will never be safe within our lines."

"Then I will go to her. I will bring her money and decent clothes before the harsh winter sets in. I will see her and give her comfort."

"Sarah, that is not possible. There is our babe whom you are nursing to consider. It is dangerous. The wife of a member of General Knox's staff behind British lines. You could be arrested as a spy." He shook his head vehemently. "I will not have it."

"Oh, so you say you will not have it, do you?" Sarah turned around to confront him, her hands on her hips above her apron. "And yet, you do not offer any plan for me to even see my mother." She saw the hurt in his eyes and something of the helplessness he felt. "Adam. You risked your life because of your love and desire to see me free," she said more softly. "Can you deny me the same right to take some risk to give my own mother hope and comfort?"

"I will find a way," Adam said as other servants began to file into the kitchen. "Trust me Sarah. Trust me." Sarah pretended to be preoccupied with the loaves of rye and wheat bread she had placed in the oven. Adam held Emanuel with one arm and carried the cradle in the other to its usual corner near the hearth. He would talk to Will about what could be done. Perhaps they could somehow communicate with Willis Parks and negotiate for the purchase of Sarah's mother and brother. It would take time. And how would they accumulate the money? He had not been paid for months and if the soldiers were paid by Congress, it would be in worthless paper.

Parks would definitely not accept Continentals for his two slaves.

Perhaps, Lettia and her son could escape from New York once the army moved north. It may prove the best alternative. Somehow, he could protect them in the encampment. Sarah's plea moved him. She looked to him for help. He would do anything for her. For the moment, he was confused and did not know what to do.

—⚏—

Elisabeth heard the front door close slowly as Will returned from poring over the records at the Office of the Commissary of Prisoners near the State House. For days he had been frustrated. The signed paroles of officers and entries pertaining to the common soldiers, more than 8,000 in total, had not been sorted or even organized by regiment. It was late afternoon and Henry, their eighteen-month old son, lay asleep on the bed. Downstairs, she heard the cook bustling about the kitchen. The aroma of what smelled like a meat pie wafted through the house. A good meal for this cold November evening. The Lewises would be home soon but for the moment she was thankful she and Will would be alone. He had regained some of the weight he had lost from the fever that twice sickened him at Yorktown, but he still had a haunted look about him. Only their son could bring a smile to his face, that beaming youthful grin she yearned to see as his normal countenance.

Will was halfway up the steps when Elisabeth came from their bedroom. "Henry is still sleeping," she said leaving the door ajar and motioning for them to go to the parlor just beyond the first floor landing.

She sat in the chair closest to the door and reached her hand out on the plain pine side table. He put his hand over hers eager to tell her his news.

"The clerks have finally located John's records. After I saw him at Surrender Field at Yorktown, my brother escaped when I was laid low with that cursed fever. John signed his parole on October 20th and took passage on a sloop that left for New York on the 31st." Will removed his hand and pounded his fist into his cupped hand.

"Had I been healthy, instead of lying incapacitated in a hospital in Williamsburg, I would have grabbed him by his fat throat and choked him until his eyes bulged."

"Will," Elisabeth said, alarmed at the vicious look of hatred on his face. "This is so unlike you."

He looked at her, puzzled by her objection. "I had hoped he was with the part of the defeated army that went north by land to the prison camps at Winchester or Frederick. If he had, I could have plucked him from either camp and finally avenged his attack on you. Now," he said, his voice heavy with regret and resignation, " I must wait until General Washington mounts his campaign and we retake New York."

Elisabeth did not know how to approach her husband, obsessed with revenge and thoughts of killing his brother. John had assaulted her in the last days when the British occupied Philadelphia. That was more than three years ago, four this coming spring.

"Will. Do not torment yourself so," she said gently. "John did me no harm. The memory of that encounter has long since been obliterated by the joy of being married and our darling son. I was more scarred by our lengthy times apart than the danger of the few minutes in his clutches." She permitted herself to lie for the good of her husband's well-being. Sometimes, less frequently than before, she did think of John's fingers closing around her throat while she gasped for air, his pock-marked face inches from her own, and the look of malice and triumph in his eyes.

"You do not understand," Will said shaking his head. "My brother assaulted you in this very house." He gestured toward the entranceway where John had struck Elisabeth and knocked her to the floor. "I am reminded of this every moment we are here. I promised you I would kill him if I ever met him and I will fulfill that promise. It is a matter of my honor."

"I do not care one whit for revenge or your honor, Will Stoner," she replied more angrily than she intended. "After all these months of separation, and constant anxiety over whether you are alive, dead or hopelessly maimed, I only care about our family, our son, and being together. Dear Will, do you not see, that is all that matters."

Tears streamed down her cheeks. "This war will be over soon. Everyone thinks so. I pray there will be no battle for New York. There may be peace without another campaign such as Yorktown" she said hopefully. "Then, your brother will be no more to us than an unpleasant memory. We will enjoy the hard won benefits of peace and independence from Britain. Think of that Will. Together, as the vows we took – until death do us part- a peaceful normal life, not torn apart by war."

Will stood up and held her against him. She sobbed quietly as he kissed the top of her head. "I am sorry Elisabeth. Both for upsetting you and failing to avenge you at Yorktown. I cannot seek him out now that he is safely behind enemy lines. However, unlike you, I am eager for the battle to drive the British from New York and the opportunity to find my brother and kill him." He stroked her hair, the blond curls straightening through his fingers. "As I said, it is a matter of honor. Something women do not understand," he said instantly regretting his brusque tone.

Elisabeth pushed his arms away and dabbed her cheeks with her sleeve. "Think of what you say, my dear husband. What good is your honor if you leave me a widow and Henry without his father. You would condemn me to a miserable existence, my memory of you obscured by my tears of grief. I look forward to a peaceful life as a family. You look to war and revenge. I fear who you have become." His eyes revealed how deeply her words had hurt him. She almost embraced him again but bitterness and anger restrained her from doing so.

As she ascended the stairs to their bedroom she decided she would speak to Mrs. Knox and prevail upon her to talk to her husband. General Knox who was like a father to Will. Perhaps he could convince Will to cease his desire for vengeance and recognize the blessings of the family he had.

—⚋—

They were four miles from Middletown Point near the shores of Raritan Bay. After Colonel Dayton had given the soldiers of the

3rd New Jersey Regiment six weeks furlough, it had taken Corporal Caleb Wade and Private Matthias Vose almost five days to trudge the less than forty miles from Trenton. The closer they got to the coast, the worse the devastation in the countryside. They passed apple orchards wantonly cut down, the stumps like gravestones in neat rows, overgrown with ivy and weeds. Here and there were burned homes with fire-blackened gaping windows, pieces of broken and charred furniture strewn about, the stout oak upright beams of roofless barns poking up from their stone foundations. In some of the small towns, empty shells of looted homes lined the road, plundered and ravaged by raiding Loyalist bands, based on Staten Island and known to be still active in these coastal areas.

Vose had mostly recovered from his bayonet wounds received at Yorktown during the failed British counterattack. He still limped from the gash in his thigh and lacked stamina to walk more than eight hours a day.

This afternoon, Caleb, who until now had been considerate of his friend's weakness, urged him to keep going. The grey sky threatened a cold rain or perhaps even sleet and snow, and he had no desire to sleep in the open that night. More than the risk of adverse weather, Caleb was anxious to get to town and find Catherine Vinson, Corporal Traynor's sister. When Traynor died, Caleb found a letter from his sister in his haversack. Written in August, Catherine informed her brother his wife Polly had died in childbirth. Their newborn daughter had barely survived. Who knew if the babe still lived? He feared that he would be the first to tell her of her brother's death. Even worse, he dreaded discovering that Traynor's infant daughter had followed her mother to the grave. He was not sure why this made a difference to him. Sickly newborns usually died within weeks of being born. He knew neither Traynor's wife nor the babe. Yet, following Traynor's senseless death after the British surrender at Yorktown, he wished for the little girl to survive, to learn from her aunt how her father had fought and died and what a good man he had been.

Traynor had been the one to comfort Caleb after the executions of the mutineers at Chatham. And it was Traynor in whom Caleb had confided that Reverend Avery's sermon had cleared his mind and given him hope that the Lord was still with him.

Caleb had taken those words to heart and given up his drunken ways. His calmness of spirit amazed those who knew him before – quick to anger, always ready for a fight or to drink himself into a stupor and, when the occasion presented, to plunder from Whig and Tory alike.

Wade was a big man while Vose was short and stocky. By draping Vose's arm over his shoulder, Caleb was able to take much of the weight off of his friend's bad leg. In this ungainly up and down hobble, they reached the outskirts of the town. They passed what they took to be the remains of the Church, the weathered rubble of blackened bricks and splintered wood adjacent to a cemetery where few gravestones remained upright. Those buildings that seemed occupied, judging by the dim candlelight filtering through the repaired ill fitted doors and window frames were clustered close to the creek. In the cold evening darkness, Caleb could still make out a few long storehouses and piers and a stone millhouse with its water wheel tilted at an angle off its shaft. Sounds of voices and shouting came from a tavern just off the wharf. Despite Caleb's scowl, Vose licked his lips and gestured they should go there. Seeing no other choice or anyone around to ask for the Catherine Vinson home, they mounted the narrow porch, passing under a faded sign denoting the establishment as "The Safe Harbor."

Inside, several men were boisterously eating and drinking around a long wooden table. The proprietor, distinguished by a stained, worn leather apron motioned for the others to make room for the two newcomers on the benches. Vose sat down on one end, easing his wounded leg out. Caleb took both of their muskets and stood them upright in the corner.

"Welcome to The Safe Harbor," the man said. "I am Enoch Hawkins and you two appear to be soldiers in our cause. Continentals are most welcome here. We need extra men in case the filthy Loyalist bastards come raiding again." Caleb appraised the militiamen at the table and the muskets, one rifle and two fowling pieces stacked against a wall.

"Do you have sentries posted," he asked noting the nine men seated at the bench.

"Oh we do," one of them answered. "Along the creek and fifty yards up the road in both directions," he said, pointing first one way and then the other. Caleb thought it strange they had not encountered any sentries near the burned church. Perhaps these militia thought sentry duty meant hiding amongst the bushes and shrubs. He hoped they had imbibed less than those at the tavern. Based on the amount of beer being quaffed, Caleb doubted that these nine would be able to be roused and fit to serve.

Hawkins looked curiously at Vose with his bad leg stretched out before him and then at Wade still standing. "Who are you? You are not from our township and few others without business come through here. We have suffered severely from raiding bands of Loyalists. Even the Pine Barrens raiders have ventured this far north on occasion."

His comment provoked a series of curses from the militia. "Every one of those whoreson's bastards should rot in hell," one man shouted, draining his mug and slamming it down on the table.

"These Loyalists, some of whom are former neighbors," Hawkins continued, "not only do they plunder our crops and stores, but seek to capture prominent militia and merchants amongst us to exchange for those we have caught and imprisoned."[7] He wiped his hands on his greasy leather apron waiting for Caleb or Vose to respond.

"We are of the 3rd New Jersey Regiment," Caleb said. "We were furloughed by our Colonel in Trenton after marching up from Yorktown and I am . . ." The word Yorktown immediately elicited a cacaphony of "huzzahs," toasts to General Washington and cheers of "victory is ours" and "death to the British."

The tavern owner motioned for a young boy to bring a chair for Caleb and he himself brought two tankards of beer. He sent the boy back into the kitchen for food plates, loudly declaring that the heroes of Yorktown deserved the finest the tavern could offer. With a false show of modesty, he accepted the approval of his generosity from the militia men.

"Now. Tell us, what the siege was like," Hawkins asked.

"How loud were all those cannons?" another asked.

"And the surrender of the whole British army," one of the drunken militiamen added.

Vose grinned, pleased to be the center of attention and pointed to his stretched out leg. "I myself was wounded by a British bayonet in a counterattack before we beat them back. 'Twas the day after they hoisted the white flag to discuss terms."

Wade let him go on. What was the harm in letting him have his moment of glory and describe it the way he wanted rather than the way it was. Vose was a good man deep down. Best not to embarrass him by telling he was drunk at his post when their position was overrun and had bawled like a baby when they retook the parapet, afraid his superficial wounds were fatal.

Vose was a good story teller. He described the thunderous constant cannonades, the night sky lit up by flares and the fiery tails of mortar bombs. Although he had been in the hospital in Williamsburg and not present at the surrender, he had heard the story enough times from Wade and others in their Company to accurately describe the sullen, defeated British soldiers, drunk and straggling in lines down the road toward Surrender Field, the Hessians more precise and disciplined, the British officers on their horses, putting on their sneering and contemptuous faces to hide their shame. Wade was thankful Vose did not describe the aftermath, their Regiment's guard duty in the ruins of Yorktown and the death of Corporal Traynor.

The next morning Caleb left Vose at the tavern regaling a new group of militia with his stories of the splendid victory. With Traynor's haversack on his back and the pouch with the dollars in the inner pocket of his breeches, he followed the tavern keeper's directions, about half a mile down the road through town. The cold morning mist off Matawan Creek had lifted revealing Middletown Point, with its shabby homes, generally untended fields, broken fences and half sunken wharfs and tilted piers as a once prosperous community repeatedly ravaged by war.

Thin tendrils of smoke rose from the chimneys of a few homes, indicating despite their decrepit appearance, they were indeed inhabited.

Wade counted three houses past the scarred three-story brick mansion, with a pile of shattered weathered furniture trashed and left from several raids ago. He stopped before a rundown two-story stone house with a sagging porch, several missing shutters, and a low, shingle sided shed with an empty corn crib in front. A long branched sycamore with several dead limbs grew at the junction of the shed and the house.

His mouth was dry and his mind filled with dread as he knocked at the door. He was no good at this sort of thing, telling someone her brother had died. And what about the baby? Caleb took a deep breath. He owed it to Traynor who had stood by him in his time of need. He swung the haversack from his left shoulder and held it in front of his chest, like a supplicant making an offering and shifted his weight nervously from one foot to the other.

A scrawny boy came around from far side of the porch. Wade guessed his was six or seven and judging by his rolled up breeches and an ill-fitting shirt, he was wearing an older brother's hand me downs. He was carrying three large turnips. His bare feet were caked with mud.

"Are you a soljur?," he asked, staring up at Caleb, still holding the haversack in his hands.

"That I am," he replied with a smile. "Is your mother home?" The boy hesitated trying to decide whether this was information he should give to a stranger, but succumbing to Caleb's smile, nodded and pointed to the front door.

"Will you take me to her?" Caleb asked cheerfully although his tongue felt it was covered in cotton and his hands were clammy with anxiety.

The boy nodded and scampered up the porch and pushed the door open with his shoulder. Caleb was aware of how loud his footsteps sounded on the floor slats.

"Mother. There is a soljur here to see you," he announced in a high-pitched scream.

"Bring him in here and shush now Thomas or you will wake the baby."

The boy pointed to the light at the end of the narrow hall, his thin arm lost in his shirt sleeve. Caleb ducked low to avoid banging his head on the doorframe and entered, his shoes clomping on the worn wooden floor boards. A low fire burned in the hearth. An iron pot hung from a hook and the smell of freshly baked bread filled the room. The woman was cutting potatoes and carrots with a large kitchen knife. Thomas put the turnips down on the oak block table and stood next to his mother. She was a big woman with a long jaw and wispy brown hair streaked with grey and drawn back under a dirty cotton puffed cap. He stared at her, trying to recognize a family resemblance to Corporal Traynor. Perhaps the eyes, he thought, more oval than round. Her dress, patched here and there, was frayed at the hem and sleeves. Her blouse, once of good linen and quality was now the worse for wear.

Caleb stood frozen in place, the image of Traynor's eyes staring up at him, blood burbling from his mouth, the eyes at first wild with panic and then unseeing. He realized she was waiting for him to state his business.

"I have not come for any mischief," he blurted out, as if that was an appropriate thing to say first. "Are you Catherine Vinson?" Caleb asked, removing his tri-corn and glancing around the kitchen. There was a cradle, against the wall, not too close to the hearth but close enough to benefit from the heat of the fire and stones.

"I am," she replied. "And who are you?" she asked suddenly with alarm as Caleb turned, strode quickly to the cradle and knelt down to peer at the infant within.

"Is this little Polly? Please God grant that this is Corporal Traynor's newborn babe."

"Tis indeed my brother's daughter, named after her mother who passed in childbirth this summer. Again who are you to know this?" she asked anxiously, clutching the kitchen knife firmly in one hand held in front of her.

Caleb did not answer. He began sobbing, holding on to the edge of the cradle with his big hands and repeating over and over again, "She survived. Thank God she survived."

He rose and wiped his nose on his sleeve and then, consumed by another urge, knelt down again, leaned into the cradle and kissed the baby's forehead.

"I served with your brother in the 3rd New Jersey," he explained as he stood. "We were in Lieutenant Phelps' company. He was my Corporal." Caleb could see in Catherine Vinson's eyes she now knew why he was here. "Is this your son?" She nodded.

"Then let me tell you about your brother and his uncle," Caleb said nodding to the boy. He remained standing near the cradle, as if his words would reach the baby and she too would learn about her father. He started with himself, his role in the execution of the mutineers and Traynor's comforting him when Wade's only thoughts were of suicide. He told of her brother's bravery at the battles of Springfield and Connecticut Farms and of the construction of the siege trenches and patrols of no man's land between the lines at Yorktown. Finally, he came to the part he dreaded the most. It seemed easier because he knew Catherine already understood her brother was dead. Caleb described how senseless Traynor's death had been, after the surrender when there was nothing remaining to be done but patrol Yorktown and maintain order, and how he had died in his arms.

While he talked, Catherine methodically cut vegetables, avoiding Caleb's eyes but absorbing his words. Thomas stood next to her, gripping the table hard with both hands, his mouth open, his eyes wide. Occasionally, without being told, the boy would carry the vegetables to the hearth and drop them into the pot.

Caleb handed her Traynor's worn haversack with the three leather straps and buckles. Inside, was an extra linen shirt and threadbare stockings, as well as Catherine's August letter to her brother. She took it, sat down on a chair near the fireplace, lay it gently on her lap and stared at the contents, idly rubbing the fabric of the shirt.

"I thought with no word from James he was dead or dying. I knew in my heart little Polly would be mine to raise."

Caleb let her sit in silence before bringing the leather pouch from his breeches' pocket. "There are twelve dollars in pieces of eight. Money due to your brother." He put the pouch in her hand and closed her fingers tightly around it. "It is yours now. I vowed before God I would deliver it to you."

Catherine nodded and tucked the pouch in a pocket under her apron. She made a small grimace of a smile. "This will see us through the winter and beyond but I would rather have him standing here in this kitchen holding his little daughter."

She sat silently for a while longer, stroking Traynor's shirt. "Where is he, my brother?" Her voice broke before she recovered. "Buried as a Christian I pray."

"He is buried in a Church cemetery in Yorktown. It is on a bluff overlooking the York River. It is a pretty place," he added to comfort her. Caleb did not tell her there had been no Minister reading the biblical text over Traynor's grave. No, the Regimental Chaplain had given one sermon for the many soldiers being buried within the low brick walls of the cemetery that day. Yet, all of those interred had their names read out and thus, Wade accepted the Chaplain's prayer as being for each of them and all of them.

"Where is your husband?" Caleb asked, wishing not to dwell on the thought of Traynor's body, wrapped only in his blanket being lowered into the grave. There was not enough wood available to make coffins for everyone. Barely enough for the officers, he had heard.

"He and my older son are on a sloop trading up river. They will return in a few days."

"I will be gone by then. Tell them about your brother's service in our cause. And be sure to tell little Polly about her father. Promise me that." Catherine nodded her agreement.

"Mother. Does this mean Uncle James is dead?" Thomas asked, looking from Catherine to Caleb.

"Yes, Thomas, it does."

"So we will never see him again?" the boy inquired trying to comprehend the concept of death.

"No, Thomas, you will not," Caleb answered. "That is why I have come. To tell you about the soldier your uncle was and how bravely he fought and believed in our cause. These are memories you will keep and in that way, your uncle will be with you as you grow." These were more thoughts and words than he expected to say but now that he was past telling Catherine her brother was dead and seeing little Polly and knowing she was alive, he felt less anxious or tongue tied. "Your uncle was my friend and brother soldier and I too will remember him."

With the corner of her apron she wiped away the first tears she had cried since Caleb had come. A small wail from the crib meant that Polly was awake.

"Would you mind if I held the child?" Wade asked. "Only for a little while."

Catherine nodded and Caleb reached down and took the swaddled bundle in his arms, readjusting her knitted cap against the draft. He walked around the kitchen cooing to her, telling her he knew her father and he would be so proud she was such a pretty girl and a good baby.

"More than soft words, she probably is in need of food," Catherine said, handing him a wooden bowl of bread soaked in milk. "Feed her slowly now, in small bits. She is not yet six months," she cautioned him. "Then stay and share our dinner with us."

Caleb ate with them, one hand spooning the hearty vegetable stew, the other cuddling Polly who had fallen asleep in his arms with her tummy full. Catherine talked about how the town had fallen on hard times, caught in a never-ending cycle of raids and resistance. The large brick mansion had been owned by the Burrowes family who owned a complex of corn mills, storehouses and some sloops that carried their cargo up the creek to the Raritan and beyond. John Sr. was captured by the British in a raid when the Redcoats burned the Scots Presbyterian Church to the ground, captured Reverend McKnight, as well, she added. They heard later the Reverend died on a British prison ship in New York harbor. "Before," she said, "the Loyalists raided for forage, food and supplies. Now they seek only revenge and hostages to exchange for Loyalist raiders caught and threatened by the noose of the Whig's hangman." She put her head in her hands and sighed. "When will it end? When can we live in peace again?" she asked, not expecting Caleb to answer.

"It will end when we drive the British from our land," Caleb responded. "The Loyalists will either leave with them, or live amongst us again as our neighbors."

Catherine shook her head. "Too much blood has been spilled in this county for us ever to be neighbors in peace again. That is why they strike at us with such anger. The Loyalist raiders know they can never get back their homes and farms and so attempt to destroy us all."

"Perhaps you are right and then again, perhaps the Lord will find a way to heal your hearts."

Catherine laughed bitterly "These are strange words from a soldier."

Caleb shrugged and smiled, slightly embarrassed. "I have seen enough of death to last my lifetime. I hope for the Lord to guide me to live as a good Christian once there is peace." He was about to tell her of Reverend Avery's sermon but thought he would sound foolish. "I am at The Safe Harbor. Tomorrow, before my companion and I leave, I will come by again to say goodbye."

It was dark when he left. He stood on the porch for a moment, thinking the memory of holding little Polly and her cherubic face looking up at him would give him solace in the days to come when Traynor's absence would eat at his well-being.

That night he lay stretched out next to Vose who had drank too much and smelled of rum and vomit. They were five to a bed in a loft Hawkins had rented to them for a shilling each. Listening to the snores and farts of the others, Caleb thought maybe when the war was indeed over and some years had passed he might return to this town and visit with little Polly. The thought of seeing her grown pleased him. He drifted off to sleep with visions of warm sunlight, a young girl running alongside the creek waving to his sloop as it arrived, although why he would arrive by ship instead of overland puzzled him. His family's farm was more than seventy miles to the northwest near the New York border, inhabited by his widowed mother and two younger brothers whom he had not seen since enlisting in '77.

Caleb awoke with a start to the roar of the discharge of muskets and shouts from the road below. He was the first out of bed, cursing himself for leaving his musket on the rack below in the hall of the tavern. The door to their room flew open and three men, armed with pikes and pistols burst inside. One held a lantern high to make sure there were no weapons. Caleb's first thought was the five of them could overwhelm the intruders. Then, he noted the hammer on the lantern man's pistol was cocked and assumed the weapons were primed and decided against it.

"Up you bloody scum and be quick about it or be prepared to meet your Maker." Prodded by the pike points they were forced to leave their boots and hurried down the narrow stairway. Vose stumbled, his bad leg giving way, almost knocking all of them down. Below, in the main room, Hawkins and several of the militia aroused from their sleep near the hearth, were surrounded by more than fifteen men, irregularly dressed and armed with an array of muskets, fowling pieces, pikes and swords. A few others were busily commandeering the barrels of rum and beer and any bottles of liquor they could find.

Their leader, dressed in a dark brown hunting coat, a sword hanging from his side and a black tri-corn on his head, paced back and forth, urging his men to hurry. He had a round face, with narrow eyes and one scarred dark eyebrow arched in a permanent inverted V.

"You take everything I own, John White" Hawkins said glumly.

"That is Captain John White to you Enoch Hawkins," he replied, "and it is your liberty that is also forfeit." With that he ordered all the captured men, including Hawkins outside. Caleb kept close to Matthias, supporting him as best he could as they were marched, in their bare feet, in total darkness ahead of the three wagons loaded with the Loyalists' plunder from the surrounding countryside and The Safe Harbor. As they passed Catherine Vinson's house, Caleb was relieved to see that the door was closed and no light came from within. He prayed she, Thomas and Polly had not been molested. Once beyond the town, they trekked on in silence, following a road for somewhat less than an hour, prodded along when their pace slowed by the raiders with pikes. As best Caleb could tell, they arced inland from the creek but then bent back toward it. Ahead, he thought he could distinguish two masts of a sloop, arising from a sleek dark hull and heard the gentle lapping of the waves.

Guarded by the Loyalist raiders, the dozen or so captives formed into lines from the reeds and muddy shore to the narrow gangplank and transferred from one to the other the barrels of rum, bushels of rye, oats and wheat, tubs of butter and cheese and baskets of cabbages and potatoes. Caleb, because of his size and strength was among those unloading the wagons and carrying barrels to the prisoners waiting at the foot of the gangplank. He had been separated from Vose who he last saw on board near the hatch cover. White was standing on the deck, his sword unsheathed waving it about as he directed some of the tubs and barrels to be stored on deck and others below.

With their vessel loaded and now riding low in the water, several raiders took axes and smashed the wagons' axles and wheels to render them useless. The others, using their pikes forced the prisoners up the gangplank. Caleb was half way up when the dark was pierced by the flash from a line of muskets, followed by the roar of the explosions, the whistle of balls through the air and shocked cries of wounded raiders.

Wade threw himself backwards off the plank, as if he had been shot, and fell into the shallow ice cold water. Holding his breath, he swam under the hull and surfaced several feet beyond in the darkness. Then, as quietly as he could, he slowly stroked away from the stern and in the direction of the way they had marched, angling in toward the reeds. Crouching in the mud, he saw another volley and then another from the darkened shore line. He estimated there were at least forty men on shore who had ambushed the raiders. White had managed to weigh anchor and get the sloop underway, her bow pointed toward the open water. A few sporadic musket shots followed her departure and then all was quiet.

Clambering through the weeds, Wade emerged dripping wet into the chill air and walked slowly toward the campfires that now illuminated the place where the raiders' sloop had been moored. As he approached, confident this was a militia unit, he called out, through chattering teeth, he was a friend, a Continental captured by the raiders who had escaped. He was taken in hand by a sentry who escorted him to a place by the fire and gave him a blanket to wrap around his wet clothes. There were others who had also run away, Hawkins among them. Anxiously, he looked around for Vose, checking the faces of the ten or more rescued prisoners grouped around the fires.

"We are fortunate," Hawkins said to Caleb. "The ones they have taken will end up in New York City prisons or worse, held in those pestilent ships on the East River."

He felt remorse and grief for having insisted that Vose accompany him to Middletown Point so that Caleb could meet Traynor's sister. It was his undertaking not that of Vose. And now, he was responsible for his friend's capture and imprisonment in such foul conditions it was known few survived the cold, the sickness and starvation. He took small comfort, when, at the break of dawn they returned to the town, there was a plume of smoke and a glimmer of a candle burning in the window of Catherine Vinson's home.

Chapter 2 - New Opportunities

Newly promoted Captain John Stoner of Brigadier General Timothy Ruggles' Loyal American Associators, formerly attached to the Queen's 17th Light Dragoons, sat contentedly on his horse overlooking the southeastern end of Gravesend Bay. The collar of his red wool cloak was turned up against a cold December wind but he did not mind the chill. Better the cold of a New York winter, cured by a roaring fire in snug quarters with a willing wench, than the disease- ridden swamps of Charlestown or Savannah. He watched with smug satisfaction as the four transports, wallowing low in the water with their cargo of Dragoons, horses and supplies, emerged through the narrows into lower New York Bay. Their escort of two fast frigates, masts almost bare of sails to keep pace with their slower, ungainly charges, led the way toward the open waters.

He hoped this was the last he would see of the Dragoons, the haughty Lieutenant Chatsworth and their conceited Colonel, always talking of the glories to be gained on the battlefield, of honor to be won, of showing courage under fire. He was sick of their condescending manner as upper class British officers, with their estates in England and relatives who attended the royal court, or went to the latest plays in London. It was an incessant irritant to John, like a scab constantly being picked at. They treated him like a country bumpkin because of his manner of speech and his origins in rural Schoharie, New York. Although he had tried to hide his fear when he rode with the Dragoons on the forays he could not avoid, they suspected him of cowardice and disdained him for it. What sane man would eagerly seek a battlefield death, he thought. No! Let them go south and die of some dreadful fever, shivering their last in shit stained straw. Let them be buried in a soggy soil that would cast their bones to the surface after the first heavy rains. They could choke on their vomit in their death throes and find their honor it that. Good riddance to them all, John thought.

John had taken the first opportunity to be paroled to New York after his rebel brother recognized him at the surrender of the British Army at Yorktown. He had no intention of ever leaving the city again. He would never place himself in a position where he could be captured and Will would find him. In the unlikely event the Americans mounted a direct assault on the city, he felt confident they would be repulsed by a combination of the army and the fleet. If not, money would be his salvation, enough to bribe a merchant captain to let him on board and escape where his brother could not follow.

Smugly, he thought not only was he avoiding danger but also accumulating wealth in such amounts to secure his future and to overcome any slights, insults or feelings of inferiority when dealing with snobbish British officers. He had seized opportunities and taken advantage where others more timid would have hesitated. He had parleyed a contrived meeting with General Benedict Arnold into becoming a trusted provider of personal security to both the General and his charming wife, Peggy Shippen Arnold. The General himself, had entrusted John with protecting his family in his absence and made available funds to do so, some of which ended up in his pocket, when Arnold first was given command of a force to fight the rebels in the south and later when he sailed north to attack New London.[1]

The arrival of Prince William Henry in the early fall had been a God-send to John's coffers. Playing on the need for maximum security for the heir apparent to the throne, John had convinced Major Pritchard of General Clinton's Intelligence Staff of the need to supplement the official guard of dragoons, grenadiers and troops,

New Opportunities

with an undercover army of agents, spies and informers. Once given the official go ahead, and with money no object, he proceeded to hire such a surreptitious force. His books, which he dutifully brought with him when he briefed Pritchard carefully showed each agent, spy and informer by a code name, next to a precise record of his monthly stipend. The pompous Major carelessly dismissed John's offer to review the books with the sanctimonious sentiment that gentlemen did not need accounts to verify their word. Well and good John had thought and increased the ghost entries so that almost half were non-existent employees. Their pay in guineas, pounds and shillings ended up in the hidden compartment at the bottom of John's trunk, securely padlocked at the foot of his bed.[2]

Now, John thought, he was to visit the honorable Judge George Duncan Ludlow, at the good Judge's invitation, It was John's main purpose for his trip on a wintry day away from the diversions of the city, although watching the troop transports carrying the Queen's Dragoons south was an added pleasure.

John had met Judge Ludlow, whose official title was Master of the Rolls and Superintendent of the Court of Police of Long Island, at the print shop of the Royal Gazette where he had gone to post an advertisement.[3] James Rivington, the printer had introduced them, although John never discovered why the good Judge was there. Rivington had invited the two of them to his newly opened private coffee-house.[4] Patronized mainly by Loyalist Officers, it was a more welcoming venue for John, where most spoke in the accents of the colonies instead of the clipped inflections and tones of superiority of titled British Army Officers.

It was a cold, ten-mile ride to Judge Ludlow's estate, east of Hempstead through the rich, flat farmlands of the Island. There were few other travelers on the rutted road. John engaged his mind by turning over the possibilities of why the Judge thought he could be useful. Surely, it could not be to provide security, although John's reputation in that field was well known within certain circles. By the time he arrived it was dusk. He was ushered by a liveried black servant into the library. A roaring fire, two high comb backed Windsor chairs and a side table with a brandy bottle and glasses gave the promise of a hospitable evening. Although John was familiar with the luxury of the homes of General Clinton and Benedict Arnold, he greedily noted Judge Ludlow had indeed done well for himself. Much of the furniture, the desk, cabinets and tables were of mahogany with brass fittings. The chairs themselves were of dark walnut with thin wooden spokes of ash. John thought, this life style was not beyond his reach, if he was prudent. He would not revert to his old gambling habits that had lost him large sums at the faro tables, egged on by Chatsworth and others. This time he would avoid the temptation of gambling and the elusive promise of quick riches. He would make his money steadily through different schemes to secure his future.

"Well, well, John. So pleased you are able to visit and spend the night." Ludlow gestured for Stoner to take a seat. He turned to the servant at the door. "We will have a late supper. For now see that we are not disturbed."

The Judge was of a slight, almost frail build with narrow shoulders that reminded John of a stalking crane. He had the body of one unaccustomed to physical labor with thin arms and calves that looked spindly in his silk stockings. His head was capped by a shock of lifeless brown hair, with a raggedy edge straggling down his neck and over his collar. As Ludlow settled in the armchair, John noted he rested his feet on an ottoman. The chair was too deep for the Judge's feet to reach the floor. Feeling somewhat superior, John sat back in his chair and casually crossed his legs.

"Be a good fellow and pour us some brandy," Ludlow asked, motioning with his skinny fingers toward the side table. "My wife is at some soiree in Manhattan, accompanied by my son. I pleaded I had business to attend to and we will get to that in good course, John. All in due time."

"You are alone in this large house by yourself?" John asked, his eyes taking in the mahogany furniture, the shelves filled with books, the silver serving trays and brass sconces.

"I know your abilities in protecting the famous and powerful," the Judge said, smiling as if he knew more than John realized. "Your service to General Arnold and his little family, is just one example.

Moreover, General Ruggles has spoken to me of your discretion and abilities in shall we say sensitive situations." His thin-lipped smile was more calculating than sincere. "No need to trouble yourself with worry," he said dismissively. "In addition to the servants, there are more than forty armed soldiers recruited from Loyalist ranks, who enjoy extra pay and supplemented rations for the privilege of living in quarters on my estate."

He raised his glass to John and took a sip of brandy. "You were at Yorktown with Lord Cornwallis. A terrible disaster, terrible – and the blame lies entirely with General Clinton. His indecisiveness and excessive caution, dare I say timidity in failing to send relief troops and supplies or in having the army evacuated in a timely fashion led to this catastrophe." He carried on at length in this fashion, alternately criticizing Clinton and praising Cornwallis while offering his opinions on a military strategy to end the war with Victory for the Crown. Finally, as if remembering Stoner was present, he paused. "Are you of the same opinion, John?"

Stoner sipped his brandy, appreciating the sensation as the liquid filled his mouth and felt with pleasure the heat as it went down his throat. It was a fine brandy, better than any he had tasted in New York. It was difficult to know from the Judge's lengthy monologue what opinion John was supposed to agree with.

"Every day we looked to the York River and beyond for signs of the British navy, bringing reinforcements and munitions," John replied. "Properly supplied, we would have swept the French and the Rebels before us. Cannon fire from the fleet would have overwhelmed the enemy's artillery." He emptied his glass and poured himself another, forgetting to refill the Judge's. "Instead, we were low on ammunition, starving and subjected to a constant bombardment, day and night." John thought by conveying his suffering, which actually had not been that severe at Gloucester Point, he would engender sympathy in the good Judge and make him more favourable toward him in the discussions to follow.

"So, I have heard," Ludlow murmured, impatiently holding out his glass for John to refill it. "If only General Clinton had sent our General Arnold south to Yorktown as head of a relief force instead of a diversionary attack on New London..." he left the sentence unfinished, as if envisioning a crushing victory over the allied French and American forces.[5] John had no wish to break the Judge's silence and, putting on a solemn face, pretended to be lost in memories of the miseries he had suffered at Yorktown.

He politely endured the Judge's detailed exposition of how the Army in New York, if used properly and with aggressive leadership, currently lacking in General Clinton, could crush the small Rebel force in New Jersey and then make a major thrust up the Hudson Valley and wipe out Washington and the rabble once and for all. This from a man John thought contemptuously, who had never endured enemy cannon fire, or the deadly sniping of Rebel long rifles. The loss of the army at Yorktown was like the loss of a finger, Ludlow observed, while the arm, the more than twelve thousand trained and well-equipped men in barracks in New York City, remained strong, ready to strike the final blow. Not to mention the Navy, Ludlow added that would sweep the French fleet from seas from Providence to Savannah. "The French are no match for the Royal Navy," he concluded.

The French had beaten the British navy off Chesapeake Bay, John thought. That was why we rotted, trapped and under constant bombardment in that pestilent swamp of Yorktown. He held his tongue. He was starving by the time the good Judge himself presumably hungry, rang a bell and signaled for supper to be served.

The Judge dominated the conversation over plates of thick slices of cold beef and roast chicken, cut into quarters, the skin crisp and imbued with rosemary and sage, warm bread served with crocks of butter and cheeses, supplemented by glasses of Madeira. He offered more of his views on military strategy and how the Cabinet in London must hold firm and prosecute the war to a successful conclusion. It was only after the servants had cleared the plates and left them with the brandy and a few pleasant trifling sweets, that the Judge came to the point of his invitation.

"I will be frank with you, John. From my inquiries I know you to be a clever man and one of character and discretion. Most importantly from my perspective, you are an outsider. By that I mean not one employed by me as Superintendent of the Court of Police."

John nodded. "I thank you for the compliments you have paid me. I hope to live up to your expectations and accomplish whatever service you expect of me." He recognized he had struck the right tone by the Judge leaning forward in his chair and eagerly clasping John's hands.

"As Master of the Rolls and Superintendent of the Court of Police of the Island, I exercise vast powers, that afford me opportunities to be paid for approvals, permissions, supplies and the like."

John listened, forcing himself to maintain a bland expression as Judge Ludlow explained the various schemes and businesses he directed and benefited from. First, there was the extensive smuggling between Long Island and Connecticut across the Sound. Manufactured goods from Britain and Ireland, legitimately imported into the city, found their way by various means to the eastern end of Long Island where they could be shipped across the Sound and sold in Connecticut for enormous profits. However, Ludlow said with a smirk, no goods could leave New York without a permit, issued by the Court of Police. Conversely, firewood much in need in the city, was smuggled in from Connecticut to be sold in New York, again requiring a permit to be brought into the city.

"As Superintendent, I also approve the confiscation of rebel lands, houses and property. The land and houses, once divided, are rented out to distressed Loyalist refugees from New Jersey, with the rent collected by employees of the Court of Police." The Judge went on to describe numerous licenses he issued, that were required to operate taverns, smiths and mills, as well as a duty imposed on peddlers and hawkers.[6]

"Finally," Ludlow said, dropping his voice, "there is the business of Negroes. Those who are legitimate slaves of Loyalists on the Island remain slaves, if their owners certify them as their property. Some slaves die or run away. Our Loyalist plantation owners are understandably in need of labor to plant and harvest their crops and tend their herds of sheep and cattle. All necessary to supply our army with flour for their bread, meat, fruit and vegetables for their mess halls. They are inclined to claim another, perhaps a slave who escaped to our lines with a promise of freedom, and certify this new slave as originally theirs."[7] The Judge rubbed his hands together as if absolving himself of any wrongdoing for the greater good. "I accept the certification for a fee and do not question too closely whether or not the slave was originally a free black within our lines. However, some of these plantation owners seek to avoid paying the fee by not reporting the acquisition of a new slave." He sighed as if their petty cheating was another burden he had to bear as Superintendent.

John waited patiently, not yet clear on what the Judge expected of him.

"I have given you an account of the inner workings of the Court of Police. I am surrounded by employees who skim at every opportunity, turn a blind eye to smuggled goods going out or coming in without a permit, for their cut of course, rents recorded as paid in full but paid only by half, if that, with a cut going to the person I charged to collect them." He sighed. "Then, there are those unscrupulous plantation owners who seek to avoid paying for a mere certificate of ownership."

He pointed a bony finger at John. "You John, with your network of informants, agents and spies, I know you employ in the service of others, will be my eyes and ears to end this skimming and duplicity that deprives me of my rightful portion. You will make enemies among my employees of the Court and the smugglers who are used to paying a bribe and reaping, nay taking the profits due to me."

"I have no fear of enemies," John replied boldly, thinking of the few stout ruffians he would need to hire as bodyguards.

"I will pay you well for your endeavors. I have heard from Major Pritchard you keep scrupulous accounts of your network's employees. Thus, you are well positioned to sniff out false entries of rents, licenses and fees, booked but uncollected."

Oh, you will pay, John thought. First in the percentage you will give me for uncovering the skimming and then in the payments I will take from those I apprehend but do not expose to you.

Later that night, lying under a thick quilt on a mattress so soft, he seemed to be floating on a bed of feathers, John laughed, at first quietly and then loudly guffawed, risking that the Judge might hear and find it peculiar. That Major Pritchard who was too supercilious to even presume to look at John's books, the very pages containing a record of John's own skimming, had vouched for their veracity to the learned Judge was such a delicious irony it was a shame he could not tell anyone. Still silence was a small price to pay for a very profitable evening.

—⚏—

Private Matthias Vose waited until the worms from the sea biscuits floated to the top of the water in the battered iron pot. They were fat, white slug like creatures. After two weeks in the cold, dank brick prison in lower New York, surrounded by so much death and agony, the sight of worms in his food did not perturb him. Cupping his hand, he scooped them out, quickly dropped them on the stone floor and crushed them under his thin-soled shoe, taking satisfaction from the squishing sound they made.

The men who had been imprisoned the longest, said the building once was a sugar house, storing the sugar and molasses from the British West Indies before it was refined into rum. It might have been constructed as a prison in mind. The massive six-story building, the largest in the city, had bars on all the small, arched windows with neither shutters nor panes of glass. The mid-December snows blew threw the open windows and covered the floor of their cells, twenty men crowded into a room, lying on vermin infested straw.[8]

Every night, on their floor alone, three, four, or five men died, carried out in the early morning to the death carts and wheeled away to unmarked graves in shallow ditches. They died of the bloody flux, fevers, and a few of madness, their wild stares and outraged screams, finally subdued by death itself. Sometimes they were sewn into their blankets awaiting burial. Often, the living stole or bid on their threadbare blankets, filthy with vomit, shit and blood. It was another layer of cloth for the living to keep out the cold, although it deprived the deceased the last meager vestige of the dignity of being buried in a shroud.[9]

Vose shuffled over to the fire in the center of their cell to wait his turn to warm the salted pork and moldy dry biscuit in the fetid water that comprised his soup. It was his only meal of the day. He hunched over in an attempt to gather in some of the warmth from the small fire that burned under the iron tripod. The man in front of him, turned, recognized him and taking his elbow urged him forward.

"You took a beating standing up to Sergeant Waddy. As mean a bastard as ever wore a redcoat" he growled, his voice husky with phlegm. "You give us all a bit of hope."

Vose nodded in appreciation. After a week of prison life, a burly British Sergeant, invalided from active duty, urged him to join a British regiment. They tried to recruit all new prisoners. He offered the chance for clean clothes, decent food and pay. Laughing maliciously in front of the others, Waddy assured Matthias it was the only way to escape a certain death from disease or starvation. Too many prisoners ahead of him on the list, he boasted. Some captured in '79. Vose would be dead before he would be exchanged, the Sergeant smirked, while poking Matthias in the chest.[10]

He had stood erect and almost nose to nose with Waddy. With as much contempt as Vose could muster, he spit out the words – "I was with our army at Yorktown. Why would I join a defeated enemy that straggled out in broken ranks like beaten dogs to surrender, having lost its honor on the battlefield." The enraged Sergeant had caned him about the head and shoulders but it was worth it. Matthias would do it again. In the frigid darkness of that night he told his fellow prisoners, some of them too far gone to hear him, about the battle of Yorktown and the surrender ceremony. Aching but satisfied he had done some small act to lift their spirits, he had drifted off to sleep. When he awoke in the bitter cold of the morning, two of his cellmates awaited the death cart.

Now as Vose bent hunched and stared into the thin gruel in his pot over the fire, he was overwhelmed with despair. This was only his third week in prison. How would he ever survive? The very stench of the place was unbearable. The slop buckets and tubs for piss and shit were overflowing. Men expended the little energy they had, scratching maniacally at the vermin that infested their hair, their armpits and their crotches. The sight of soldiers, the ones who had been here the longest, their teeth falling out, bleeding from the gums and eyes, frightened him. He knew their fate awaited him. He stifled a whimper, seeing himself as any one of the wretches lying weakly on their pallets of straw, shivering in the cold, their sunken eyes and gaunt faces staring uncomprehendingly about them, or others gnawing on a piece of leather from their torn shoes as if it was a roasted turkey leg.

His friend, Caleb Wade, would tell him the Lord was with him. Not in this hellhole. Not with death all around, with men dying in agony, screaming for their mothers, or the spittle bubbling from their mouths just before the final rattle in their throats, or giving up all hope and succumbing to the relief of never awakening again. He himself would go mad in this place. He must escape. That thought possessed him as he heated his pot, slurped down the warming liquid, bit through the gristle of the knuckle of the moldy pork he had been allotted, and sat with his back against the frigid stonewall. It would be two more days before they again received their meager allotment of firewood to heat the cell.

In the morning, his mind was more alert than it had been for days, focused on his determination to escape. The British brought ten more prisoners into their cell. Laughing, the two guards told the men not to worry about the over-crowding. It would resolve itself soonest if some of those already there died more quickly.

The prisoners in Vose's cell had divided themselves into squads of six each for the purpose of sharing ten minutes of comparatively fresh air at the one window. Matthias was in the third squad and when it was their turn, instead of gazing up at the grey winter sky and enviously watching the sea gulls soar freely, he stared down at the small exercise yard surrounded by a close board fence nine feet high. They were on the fourth floor but even from that distance he could see one of the boards joining the far corner was askew with a gap of about half a foot, between its end and the ground. When his squad's turn came the next hour, he confirmed indeed there was a small space. Convinced more than ever that he must attempt to escape while he still had the strength to do so, he thought he would need a tool to pry the board loose. His personal possessions had been taken from him upon his capture. All he had was his little iron pot and a wooden spoon. The spoon was not strong enough but the pot's handle could serve as a pry bar. But how could he carry it into the exercise yard, if and when the British allowed them out.

For two days he mulled the problem over but no solution came to mind. Late in the afternoon, on the third day, when the winter darkness shrouded the room, the massive oak door creaked open and three men, only slightly less emaciated than the prisoners, carrying bundles of clothing, warily entered.

"Clothing collected from several of the churches," Sergeant Waddy announced. "A Christmas gift to you scurvy scum." He pointed with his swagger stick further into the room. "Drop them there and let these rebel bastards fight for it." There was movement among the standing prisoners as they began to jockey for the best position to grab what was offered.

Vose was at the back wall, shielded by the men and the darkness from the Sergeant's sight. "By squad," he shouted. "First Squad, forward." The prisoners upon hearing the command, shuffled into their familiar lines, a few of them, helping the ones lying on the thin straw pallets to stand and partake in the division. When it was his squad's turn, Vose picked a patched coat, far too large for him, with no buttons and a tear on one shoulder that revealed the cotton batting underneath. It would do, he thought suppressing a smile.

That night, the men, more animated than usual, talked among themselves as to whether there would be extra rations or fuel for Christmas Day, although no one was quite sure when that was. Matthias prayed they would be granted access to the exercise yard. The next day, snow blew through the window all morning. By midday, those who could were standing and stamping their feet, wrapped in their newly acquired rags, trying to keep warm.

New Opportunities

One of the men passing by the window noted there were prisoners in the yard. "From what level are you?" he shouted down. "Ground floor," came the reply. Vose heard and calculated how long it would be. The British would probably allot thirty minutes for exercise. If the group below was the last room on the first floor, Vose's cell would be let out in more than two hours. Good. It would be almost dusk, unless the Redcoats arbitrarily postponed their turn until the morrow. He paced the cell vigorously, careful not to step on those lying listlessly on the floor, praying it would continue snowing and their chance would come.

It was late afternoon when the key turned in the lock, the door swung open and Sergeant Waddy with two sullen guards who obviously did not relish the outdoor duty, entered the cell. "By order of the Provost, you traitorous scum are given the privilege of exercising in the yard for thirty minutes. Twenty-five men at a time. Line up in two rows, and I hope you freeze your arses off and catch a fever to dispatch you all to hell."

Vose picked up his pot, wrapped it under his coat. The Sergeant and one of the guards led Vose and his cellmates down the slippery stone steps and out into the yard. Several of the men, those with the strength to do so, shuffled around the perimeter of the fence, while others huddled in bunches closer to the entrance. The two guards stood just under the doorframe, protecting themselves from the falling snow. Vose hobbled along the fence and each time he passed the corner where the gap was between the wide board and ground, he felt more confident. As he walked, he urged some of the men to join him, imitating how the British had sullenly shambled out to surrender at Yorktown and telling them details of the ceremony –how General Washington and his senior staff had sat calm and dignified on their well-groomed horses, the drunks among the British ranks and the grim precision of the Hessians. This time when he reached the corner he slowed down and then pretending to stumble, dropped down on one knee, pulled the kettle from underneath his coat, put the handle between the board and post just above the gap and pried it back. It gave easier than he thought it would. As fast as he could, he crawled on his stomach through the narrow opening he had created and he was out on the cobblestoned pavement.

Vose ran as fast as he could in a crouch, keeping close to the walls of the adjacent Church. At most, half of the exercise time was left before Sergeant Waddy and the guards would do a head count as the men returned to their cell. He knew the Hudson River was to his left. His plan was to reach the shore, steal a boat and row himself across to the New Jersey side. Best to stop running, shamble slowly and not call attention to himself. He hoped there was no curfew or, if there was it was not yet time to be imposed. His confidence increased as he got closer to the river. No more brick and stone buildings lined the streets. The houses were much poorer, made of salvageable wood and planks, slapped together, some with no windows or small windows covered by leather flaps or scraps of fabric. The muddy streets were strewn with the contents of chamber pots and garbage, some of it frozen and mercifully covered by the falling snow. Elsewhere there were fresh, foul smelling mounds of shit and piss. In the darkness he tried to avoid them, not always successfully. The many people about looked as ill-kempt and shabby as he did, Loyalist refugees from New Jersey who had been driven from their homes and farms. He was thankful his torn, ragged overcoat covered the remnants of his uniform. If they discovered he was a Continental and escaped prisoner, the best he could hope for would be a beating before they turned him in.

There were fewer people on the streets as he got closer to the river. He scrabbled down a narrow alley and heard the water lapping against the stone breakwater. In his eagerness to reach the water, he almost blundered into four British sentries warming themselves around a fire on the shore. Vose flattened himself against the cold, snow- covered ground and crept backwards on all four. His kettle under his coat clanked against something hard. One of the sentries looked up in his direction. Then, apparently satisfied it was nothing, turned and held his hands to the fire. Cushioning his precious metal pot against his coat, Vose retreated back up the alley and headed further north.

New Opportunities

Every time he approached the water he encountered British sentries. Their fires dotted the shoreline at irregular intervals. He decided to make one final attempt and turned once again toward the river where the southern end of the Common merged like a sharp knife into a broad street. The wind off the river rattled the walls of the hovels around him and the ice in the frozen mud cracked beneath his feet. He cringed against a rough wood wall as several drunken sailors emerged from a shack, loudly berating the whore inside for cheating them. Hoping against hope, he kept to the darkness and cautiously looked around the corner. The river, an immense wide ribbon of blackness, lay beyond a dilapidated pier. Perhaps, there was a rowboat hidden and tied up beneath it. As he crept out from the safety of the shadows, shivering from the cold wind, he saw the flames of another sentry fire. The soldiers were positioned near the last row of hovels facing the river, with a clear view of the rocky shoreline and the piers jutting out, like so many frozen fingers toward the water.

Reluctantly, Matthias abandoned his plan of stealing a boat and rowing to New Jersey. It was now completely dark. He resolved to retrace some of the way he had come and head across the city toward the East River. There, he hoped, he might be able to find farmer or local willing to ferry him across to Brooklyn. By now, he was weak from hunger and numb from the cold. Every step he took was an effort. The moon had risen, casting light on the main north-south streets. After scurrying across The Broadway, he squatted in the dark shadows of unlit buildings, gathering his strength. He heard a low growl behind him and turning confronted a large snarling black dog, teeth bared and slowly stalking toward him. In desperation, Matthias grabbed the handle of his kettle, took two steps and swung it just as the mongrel leaped. The dog yelped in pain as the iron hit his head, turned tail and ran whimpering down the alley.

Matthias, panting from the exertion, held the kettle in one hand and with the other pulled his coat closed and hobbled down the street. The snow had stopped but there was a crust on the surface so every step he took could easily be heard. He was dazed and disoriented. Only his determination not to be recaptured, kept him moving east. He had heard tales of worse prisons than the sugarhouse where they sent prisoners who tried to escape. He knew he would never survive those conditions, designed not to break men's spirits but to kill them. Finally, in the remaining darkness of the night, overcome by exhaustion, frozen in his extremities, with an enormous hunger gnawing at his insides, he collapsed under some brambles, in sight of the wharves on the Manhattan side of the East River.

He was awakened in the early morning by the not so gentle prodding of a cane against his side. Wearily he opened his eyes, too weak to resist or fight any longer. Matthias groaned as he sat up, and with his numb fingers brushed the frost in his ill-kempt hair and beard. A white haired gentleman with ruddy cheeks and a bulbous nose stared down at him. His hat was tied to his head with a scarf and another wrapped twice around his neck to ward off the wind from the river.

"Who are you? What is your name?"

Tired, his mind numb from starvation and exhaustion and groggy with sleep, Matthias blurted out, "Private Matthias Vose of Colonel Elias Dayton's 3rd New Jersey Regiment. I have escaped from the sugar house prison."

The man grunted in reply and for a moment, Matthias thought the old man would bring the cane down on his head. Instead, he reached down and helped Matthias up. He was surprising strong for an elderly man. "I am Cornelius Fleming. Come, we must get you out of sight before the Redcoats arrive to begin their morning perusal of goods crossing the river."

Firmly holding Matthias under his arm he quickly escorted him along the stone wall of a storage house. They both ducked under the doorframe and Matthais saw he was in a low dark room with but two windows on each side and one small rectangular one high up at the far end. A pile of untanned cow hides filled part of the dank space, along with assorted barrels, bushels of turnips, cabbages and potatoes and some odds and ends of furniture.

New Opportunities

"You have quite a stink to you," Fleming observed, using one gloved hand to brush off any odor that might have adhered to his own fine black outer coat. "Take one of those hides for warmth, a few of these vegetables and hide in a dark corner. Tonight, we will move you in my wagon to more comfortable quarters, a hot meal and perhaps even a bath."

"I am grateful to you . . ."

Fleming raised his hand to stop Vose from saying anything further. "Show your gratitude once we have smuggled you to Brooklyn and the Island and from there across the Sound to Connecticut, by rejoining your Regiment. It will be a wasted effort and unnecessary risks taken by many, if you were to desert," he added gruffly, as he left, closing the door tightly behind him. Matthias heard Fleming throw the bolt and snap the padlock shut.

He was too exhausted to object to being thought of as a soldier who would desert. Dragging one of the hides, he stumbled toward the far wall in the darkest corner, and curled up like a dog seeking secure shelter from a thunderstorm. He dreamed he was back with the 3rd New Jersey soldiers, racing down The Broadway, with Caleb Wade at his side, driving the panic-stricken Redcoats before them to liberate the gaunt diseased men in the sugarhouse prison.

—⚘—

Sexton Peter Williams looked at his young pupil before him, crossing and uncrossing his muscular legs, his brow furrowed which accentuated the oval brand on his light brown skin. His skin color and his grey green eyes betrayed his former master's seed, making the branding of his own son all the more evil to the Sexton.

The light blue painted plaster covering the ballast stonewalls, the circular benches indicative of the Methodists' commitment to community, and the faint ticking of the clock, given to the Church by John Wesley himself, always served to calm him. He wondered how to communicate this feeling to Jupiter, hunched over in front of him, shaking his head as he wrestled with the letters in a simple reader.

The boy was smart and well spoken, the Sexton told himself. He had spent months teaching Jupiter to speak correctly. The grammar was mostly right with a strong southern pronunciation. But the boy was full of unbridled energy. No, it was more rage and anger, at those who had abused him as well as those who tried to control him, even for his own benefit. What was so hard about learning to read, Williams thought. He wanted to prepare this young man for opportunities for a better life, a life full of possibilities once he was free after the war was over. After the victory at Yorktown, the Colonies will certainly win their freedom from the Crown. The Sexton almost laughed out loud at this thought. He himself was still a slave of a devout Methodist who believed he was doing God's work by assigning Williams to work at the Chapel. Still, Peter knew and fervently believed that God would set him free. How and in what manner was God's plan for him, his humble servant.

"That is enough for today, Jupiter," Williams said, recognizing that forcing the young man to agonize over his letters any longer would only make him more rebellious.

"Go to Master Talbot's fish market on Dock Street. The good gentleman has promised us a few pounds of fish and heads for our Church. Be sure to thank him for his generosity." He noticed Jupiter's frown. "On my behalf of course. And be civil to him Jupiter," he commanded sternly. "He is feeding your mother, and you and the others we shelter here who are in need. There is a basket in the pantry," he called to Jupiter's hastily disappearing back.

Grateful to be released from his lessons, Jupiter bounded down the few steps of the brick church into the cold December afternoon. He hated this frozen city, with its snow, too little firewood to warm one while inside, its darkness and gloom, the cold, wet morning fog, the wind blowing off one river or the other. If he could have his freedom in Virginia, he would be back there in a blink of an eye. First, he would kill Master Parks for mistreating his mother, selling off his brothers and sisters, lashing him on more than one occasion and branding him when he had been recaptured. He wrinkled his nostrils, recalling the smell of his own burning flesh. Shooting Parks would be too quick a death for the man who, although his father, and had inflicted such pain on them all. Maybe he would carve him with a butcher knife first and bash his brains in with a stone. That done, he would take one of Parks' fine horses and gallop into the warm sun and feel the wind against his skin. In his daydream, he had no idea what he would do afterwards, but the thought of riding with the sun warming his neck and arms pleased him.

Even with his scarf wrapped around his ears, he felt the cold winter's bite and strode briskly with one hand cupped over his ear, the other grasping the reed basket. He turned onto Dock Street and the bitter wind from the East River chilled his bare hands and face. He wished his frayed coat had pockets, like the Sexton's, or gloves that he had seen white gentlemen wearing when he was sent to the better part of town.

He ignored the drunks swaying in the door frames of the shabby, low taverns, crossed the wet cobblestones and approached the many stalls on the river side of Dock Street. Gulls squawked from their perches on the poles that held up the canvas roofs or hopped along the pavement, pecking at flecks of raw flesh and scales. Jupiter had been here before and found Mr. Talbot's with a sparse crowd of female servants chattering and haggling as they examined what was left this late in the day. By now, the better fish, the winter flounder, fluke and sea bass were gone. There were a few eel still left, lying still in a sand filled crate and a two or three ugly dogfish, their spines wilted in death. He knew it was his place to wait until the women had made their purchases before approaching Talbot. The fishmonger nodded in recognition and pointed to a bucket underneath his stand. Jupiter squatted down and immersed his bare hand into the ice cold water and pulled out heads of the finer fish sold earlier in the day. They had been gutted and cleaned by Talbot for his better class of customers, for an extra pence or two,. Once his basket was almost full, he waited, until the man added the one remaining and unsold dogfish to the offering.

"Give the good Reverend and Sexton Williams my greetings," he said, wiping his hands on his linen apron, smeared with fish blood and innards. He turned his back and was taking down the canvas and probably did not hear Jupiter's mumbled thanks over the wind and noise of the street.

It was dark as Jupiter hurried south on Dock Street. There were few people about although the noise from the dimly lit taverns and flop houses indicated they were crowded. The fish heads and dogfish would make soup for a few days to feed the twenty odd destitute former slaves the Methodist Church sheltered. He was hungry and the hot soup would warm him up. As he rounded the corner, he heard heavy footsteps behind him. Turning, he saw two burly men, walking rapidly behind him. He moved into the street to get out of their way, dodging around a man pushing an empty handcart toward the wharf. As he resumed his way, one of the men grabbed him by the elbow, and yanked him into a narrow dark alley. Jupiter shouted and struggled to break free. He was struck on the back of his head by something hard and immediately lost consciousness, dropping the basket to the cobblestones.

"He is the third one this month," one of the men said, sticking the wooden belaying pin into his pants band while the other propped the young black against the wall. "Captain Stoner is doing very well for himself."

"Matters not to me how well he does," the other ruffian said. "As long as he pays us what he promised. Remember, we do not see a single silver coin until he is delivered on the Island." They pulled a slouch hat over Jupiter's head and holding him up between them, as if supporting a drunken friend, headed to the sloop on the East River.

Chapter 3 - Home in Albany

To Elisabeth, Albany seemed small and quaint with its Dutch gabled houses instead of the three-storied Georgian homes of Philadelphia. The town of her birth, sitting on a bluff overlooking the Hudson, now struck her as more of a river trading post than a city. To her well-traveled eye, Albany lacked all that Philadelphia offered - the bustling city market, the industry of the wharf area, the candlelit ballrooms, the dining halls of the fine taverns, the theaters, the sense of being in the center of political power around Independence Hall. It had barely one-tenth the number of people of the American capital, and of its four thousand inhabitants, four hundred were slaves.

Still, she admitted to herself, it was good to be home. To bring her husband home to her family and to present their son Henry to her parents and brothers; to have him adored, coddled, tossed in the air and chased screaming in delight around the house, everyone ignoring or tolerating a mischievous two year old. Agnes, the family cook, who had not seen Elisabeth for five years, wept with joy when they first arrived. The little girl she had helped raise was now a married woman with a family of her own. She cuddled Henry to her ample bosom, and almost knocked Will over with a rapturous hug.

"You were a young, unwashed teamster boy in my kitchen wolfing down everything within reach when I first laid eyes on you,

And now look at you," she beamed. "An officer in the Continental Army." Her eyes scanned his worn blue army coat, torn and patched, his breeches with buttons missing, his grey colored stockings. Elisabeth smiled fondly at her old nurse and knew immediately, Agnes would take charge of refurbishing Will's uniform, if she had to bleach the dirt out barehanded. Elisabeth hoped her father would speak to his tailor and perhaps the proper blue woolen cloth could be found and a new coat made, with clean white facing stiffened with a linen lining, shiny brass buttons, silk stockings for dress wear, and ribbed woolen ones for warmth. She hoped they would not be needed for yet another winter campaign.

Elisabeth was at peace, this first week at home, sleeping next to Will in her old room, with Henry angelically curled up in the crib that had served numerous Van Hooten children. There was no more talk from Will of somehow sneaking into New York to find his brother. Nor threats of revenge or satisfaction of honor. And when she told him, they were expecting another child, his eyes had filled with tears and he had held her as tightly and warmly, as when their love was new and wondrous.

What a pleasure it was, she thought, to once again be surrounded by the familiarity of her childhood home, her father's library with the luxury of many books to choose from, and well made candles, hard with enough beeswax, for reading in the late winter afternoons. Will was on furlough, as were many of the other officers. Captain Hadley was with Mercy, their son and her family in Morristown. The General himself was with Lucy Knox and their newborn baby boy in Philadelphia.[1] She assumed Will's friend, Master Sergeant Cooper, his wife Sarah and their own little boy were also in Philadelphia. Mrs. Knox had found Sarah to be of much assistance and would want her nearby to bake for her teas and dinners.

It was mid-February and the Hudson was frozen. On clear cold mornings, Will hitched Big Red to one of the family sleds. With Henry bundled up on his lap, peering out from within his father's winter army coat, they rode up and down the ice, going as far north as the bend in the river and then prancing down toward the boat docks. On such mornings, Elisabeth sat in the parlor reading a book of poetry, trying not to worry about the ice cracking and the river swallowing up her husband and darling son. It seemed so long ago when Will had first arrived in Albany in '75 with the noble train of artillery, coming down from Ft. Ticonderoga. He had driven her and Agnes across the Hudson, hauling a cannon behind. Strange she thought, how anxieties over her husband's safety in wartime led to seemingly senseless fears in times of tranquility.

The war was far away and yet, despite the aura of peace and quiet from the snow-covered hills, Elisabeth could not but feel an uneasiness, a premonition of what she did not know nor want to put a name to. Her fears were unmoored to any particular facts or threats of danger. Will would not understand. Nor would her own mother, who having seen so little of the world, maintained a pleasant blissful happiness within the boundaries of Albany. Mrs. Catherine Van Hooten prattled on endlessly about Elizabeth Schuyler's wedding to young Colonel Alexander Hamilton more than a year ago. The party at the Schuyler's Mansion, a massive square two-story building with a tall rounded portico entrance, opening into a fifty foot long hall, had been the social highlight of her mother's life. The trays of delicacies, the wondrous dishes served, the fine wines, the gowns of the ladies, her own gown adorned with imported silk and lace, the elegant music, the dashing officers in their pristine uniforms, she described all in detail as if the wedding at "The Pastures" had taken place last weekend.[2]

Even if Elizabeth had been able to get a word in edgewise, she would not have wanted to diminish her mother's joy by describing the events she herself had attended in Philadelphia. Yet, she had to admit, her mother was a provincial lady of means, oblivious to the disruptive currents swirling around her of war and politics, far more threatening than those of the Hudson in flood.

Elisabeth could not enjoy such tranquility born of lack of experience. She had lived under British occupation in Philadelphia while spying for General Knox and played the role of coquette on Captain Montresor's arm while desperately pining for Will. With Mercy Hadley she had attended to the maimed, the horribly wounded and diseased soldiers of the Army and seen the feigned madness of Peggy Shippen Arnold and the near catastrophe of General Arnold's betrayal of West Point. She had too great a familiarity with the turmoil caused by revolution and war to be able to retreat to a state of blissful calm.

She reread the melancholy lines of the poem again.

No warning giv'n! Unceremonious fate!
A sudden rush from Life's meredian joys.
A wrench from all we are! from all we love!
What a change
From yesterday! Thy darling hope so near,
Long labourd prize!) O how ambition flushd
Thy glowing cheek! ambition truly great,
Of virtuous praise.
And Oh! ye last, last, what (can word express
Thought reach?) ye last, last silence of a friend. [3]

Shaking her head to clear the dark thoughts from her mind, she closed the book with a snap and placed it none to gently on the side table. This will not do she told herself. To overcome her fears, she needed to confide in someone who like her, had a husband in the army.

First she would write Mercy, with whom she could discuss things frankly. She went to the study, found paper and a quill on her father's elegant, walnut desk and lifted the silver lid with the pine cone design. The ink inside the crystal container had congealed in the cold. Leaving the unspoiled white quill, she took the container downstairs to the kitchen. Agnes chattered away, bubbling over with praise for her handsome husband and their adorable son, while Elisabeth carefully poured some hot water into a pot and immersed the inkwell halfway in it, careful to keep the water from flowing over the top. The kitchen, warm and friendly, with the hubbub of preparations for the afternoon's big meal, restored Elisabeth's equilibrium, banishing her thoughts of foreboding.

There was a commotion at the back door and Will and Henry burst into the kitchen, their noses and cheeks red with cold. "This young man is in dire need of hot cider to warm his innards. We have been sleighing the river and now that we have attended to Big Red, he is entitled to his reward." He pulled Henry off his shoulders, losing his tri-corn in the process, and placed him firmly on the floor.

"You should not have kept him out so long," Elisabeth admonished gently, unwinding the too long scarf from around Henry's neck and shoulders. She paused for a moment, thinking of the scarf she had made for Will when he was wintering at Valley Forge and she was in British occupied Philadelphia. Please Lord she thought. Let this be the last winter of the war.

Agnes grabbed Henry in her arms and sat him down on the hearth and handed him his own small mug of mulled cider, cautioning him to sip it slowly. "Hot," Henry said, blowing over the lip of the mug. "Hot," he repeated, pursing his lips and puffing with short breaths. Agnes gave the boy half of a warm bread muffin being readied on a tray for dinner and slathered it with clotted butter. Henry licked the butter off first before stuffing it into his mouth. "He has his father's appetite," she said to Will as she handed Henry the other half.

Following the meal in the long dining room with twenty or so seated around the table, the dozen or so men adjourned to the library. Will was the only one in uniform. The wealthiest and thus more filled with their own self importance, seated themselves closest to the fireplace, with the others spread out around the room. Those of Dutch heritage brought out their meerschaum pipes and the air filled with the fragrant aroma of tobacco. Will never drank much and politely refused the insistent efforts to refill his glass with Madeira wine. One was enough after the two glasses at dinner, and anyway, he preferred beer or cider laced with rum. The talk was of the booming real estate business, in Albany and in the upper Hudson Valley and the growth of Albany as a commercial port.

"Tis only a few sailing days from New York," one said, stating the obvious which they all knew. "By cultivating more land and growing more crops, we expand our markets, not only with Britain but with other countries of the continent."

"No more restricted trade," another added, "to limit our profits."

"Why is trade restricted?" Will asked. His question drew a smirk from Bleecker.

"Why, we were only permitted to export to the mother country," Bleecker replied in a tone implying Will should have known that. Will recalled during dinner he had briefly been introduced to Pieter Bleecker a merchant and member of some governing city body. "Business will be good again, after the war. Even better," Bleecker said triumphantly, "I will ship to The Netherlands or France, Spain or Spanish Florida, wherever I can get the best price."

"You speak as if the war is already over and our independence assured," Will answered, from beyond the circle of chairs, an edge of bitterness in his voice. "There are more than fifteen thousand British and Hessian troops in New York City and much of the British Navy in New York harbor. Whilst you plan your commercial schemes, our Army is short of winter clothing, blankets and shoes, the men wear tatters, starve and go unpaid for months. How long do you assume this Army will hold together to protect you merchants before it disintegrates, or mutinies and marches on Congress demanding the pay and rations they were promised upon enlistment?"

"I and these other men of substance in this room have contributed much money to the cause," Bleecker responded huffily. From his seat in the wing-backed chair to the right of the fireplace, he appraised Will quickly, first with a look of curiosity and then the lids flicked and Will felt he had been dismissed. Bleecker's cheeks, normally ruddy and now enhanced by the glow of the flames in the hearth contrasted with his surprisingly pale forehead. His furrowed brow and tight lips indicated he regarded Will challenging his views as an impertinence.

"The Officers from here - Generals Schuyler and Ten Broeck, to mention but two - have excelled in fighting in our Revolution. What do you, a mere Lieutenant know about the strategies of war and state of our Army?"

Will's impulse was to respond angrily but he restrained himself.

He was aware of Luykens Van Hooten, his father-in-law, watching him from across the room. Will placed his glass on a side table and grasped the worn facing of his army jacket.

"Sir," he began, addressing Bleecker with a slight inclination of a bow. "I have worn this jacket in every battle from Trenton in '76 and '77 through Yorktown. Surely you do not think it is patched and frayed because I have refused to accept a new one? No junior officer of the Continental Army has received as much as a new clean linen shirt for over five years. We have not been paid for three, unless you count paper Continentals,which I am certain you as men of business would not accept." He paused and looked around the room before continuing in a calm but firm voice. "I have seen soldiers with nothing but rags on their feet leave bloody footprints in the snow as they marched to battle. I myself have visited soldiers in hospitals where there was no firewood to keep the wounded warm, nothing but straw for bedding, no blankets and little food."

He raised his glass to Van Hooten."Elisabeth and I have been fortunate to have financial support from her family." He smiled at his father-in-law in gratitude. "Other Officers have not. Their destitute wives beg for their husbands to send money to sustain themselves or to resign their commissions and return home and engage in work that will feed and clothe them. General Knox, in whose Regiment I am privileged to serve, has told me General Washington has pleaded with Congress to provide the funds to support the Army. That some States authorize money for their own individual Regiments or militias does not provide Congress with the necessary funds to pay the soldiers of the Continental Army." He lowered his voice still calm but firm of tone. "When I enlisted in '76 I was a young lad and gave no thought to our slogan 'Join or Die.' If it means anything in this, the sixth year of the war, it means financing the Army through Congress, not as individual States. Or," he waved his hand in dismissal, "we will remain colonies of the Crown and our Revolution will fail."

His comments were met by stunned silence. Bleecker, his face flushed by the heat of the fire and Madeira turned to Van Hooten with a smirk. "Your young son-in-law apparently believes himself to be learned in political philosophy as well. It has been my experience that youth rush to hasty conclusions and do not understand the implications of their opinions. If we succumb and trade the absolute authority of the Crown for the absolute authority of a Congress, we have only traded one arbitrary ruler for another." He vehemently shook his head. "I for one, trust my freedoms to our State Legislature and the militia we have raised to support to protect our security." Several others nodded and raised their glasses in agreement.

"And I," Will replied evenly, "have seen militias from the New England states turn and run from a Hessian bayonet charge and flee the field when a British eight-pounder sends a ball in their direction. It was the Continental Army that captured Burgoyne at Saratoga and that same Army forced Cornwallis to surrender at Yorktown. That army gentlemen, is the bulwark to protect your freedom. And as for my political philosophy, it stems from John Locke's Second Political Treatise, a book given to me by General Knox, who firmly espouses its principles."

Bleecker waved his hand in dismal and redirected the discussion to the more comfortable subjects of trade and land holdings while they imbibed more wine. Another hour or so passed before several of the guests rose to leave. Van Hooten motioned for Will to remain in the library.

After bidding his guests good night, he returned and he and Will took chairs next to each other before the fire. "A few of the men here tonight, Pieter Bleecker included, are members of our Committee of Correspondence. They rule Albany in the absence of an elected City Council and are persons of influence in our community."

"Was it wrong of me to speak so frankly before Bleecker and the others."

Van Hooten smiled at Will, his coal black eyes twinkling with delight. "Not at all. You acquitted yourself well. It does them good to hear different views. They are well-intentioned although I admit more motivated by profit than patriotism." He tapped his fingers together studying his son-in-law. "I would like to invite you to a meeting of the Committee." Will began to protest, but

Luykens waved off his objections. "It does our cause no good for the seriousness of the distress of our Army to be ignored. You must speak, as directly and forcefully as you have tonight, views I do agree with myself."

In the firelight, like a tailor assessing a client for a fitting, Van Hooten skimmed his eyes over Will's overall appearance.

"However, we must have you properly attired for such an event. A new jacket and a proper pair of breeches and stockings. Of course, a tri-corn, without the musket ball holes," he added, "although it does lend gravitas to your presentation. I am proud of you Will."

"Thank you, sir."

They sat in silence for several minutes, Van Hooten gazing into the fire.

"You must know by now I deliberately asked General Knox to assign you to me when we traveled across Long Island recruiting sympathizers to our cause, before the British landed on the Island. It was an opportunity to take your measure as a man, since you were courting my youngest daughter."

Will nodded, studying his father-in-law. He had aged over the half dozen years, his face more lined, the skin beneath his neck not as firm. However, his eyes still retained that intensity which had initially frightened Will when they first met. "I thought as much," he said. That had been in '76 before the defeat at the Battle of Brooklyn and the long retreat through New Jersey.

"Remember our escape from the Dragoons at The Rising Sun?" his father-in-law continued. "It was your brother John who was with them and would have given us away. We almost became prisoners of the British, if not for the quick thinking of your Mariner friend."

"Adam is now a Master Sergeant with General Knox's Regiment. We have been together in several battles, including Yorktown where he saved my life from an unexploded mortar bomb in the trenches. I encountered my brother twice over the years. I have vowed to kill him when we meet again," he blurted out.

Van Hooten looked at Will. "Bleecker is a fool for thinking

the young know nothing. War alters the normal association of age with knowledge. He is also a hypocrite having fawned all over young Colonel Hamilton, only a year or two older than you, at the wedding dinner at the Schuyler Mansion."

At his father-in-law's urging, Will told of first meeting John in the aftermath of the Battle of Princeton when his brother was fleeing with the British baggage train, and then seeing him at Surrender Field at Yorktown, both times wearing the uniform of a British Officer.

"That does not explain why you have taken a vow to kill him," Luykens observed, fixing Will with a penetrating look.

Reluctantly, Will related John's assault on Elisabeth in Philadelphia, her rescue by Edward Lewis, their Quaker friend, and Elisabeth's insistence that Will not seek out his brother in New York for revenge or satisfaction of honor. "She says my honor matters less than my duty to her and our son."

Van Hooten's nodded, his expression grim. Will wondered whether he had been wise to describe the details of John seizing Elisabeth by her throat and attempting to squeeze the breath out of her.

"Elisabeth is both resilient and strong of character," her father said. "If circumstances bring you and your brother to meet once again, on the battlefield to liberate New York, then you should fulfill your vow. However, you have Elisabeth and your son to consider, as well as your happiness now as a family and in the peacetime that will surely follow this war. Do not permit revenge to cloud your judgment. It is not worth what you may lose. Of that I am certain."

Will sighed and nodded his head in agreement. "I have reluctantly reached the same conclusion, tho' I admit sometimes I envision killing John and feel pleasure in the imagined deed. I will wait for the appropriate time and not seek him out."

"Good," Van Hooten said patting him on the knee. "The advice of your wife is more purely motivated than mine. It stems from her deep affection for you and her commitment to honor her vows and remain as your wife until death do you part. That does not mean you should hasten the end by impetuously seeking out death."

"Do not worry. I will give her my word and now to you as well." Will smiled. "Elisabeth is definitely strong willed and vehement in expressing her views. She follows her father in that regard."

Van Hooten snorted at the compliment. "That she does," he said bidding Will good night. Will tried to silently climb the stairs to their bedroom but the creaking steps and the wide wooden planked floor of their room announced his presence.

"You have been with the men a long time," Elisabeth said pointing to Henry asleep in his crib, his rear end high in the air and his head facing away from the candle. "The ladies were becoming impatient and were ready to leave. Mother and I were at our wits' end as to how to entertain them. I suppose the well off gentlemen have filled your head with business schemes and money to be made."

Will shrugged. "I may have spoken too bluntly to Pieter Bleecker and others of the Army's need to be paid. I almost demanded they send monies directly to Congress instead of equipping local militias that are as useless on the battlefield as a sponge bucket with no bottom."

Elisabeth raised a hand to her mouth, stifled a giggle and motioned for Will to sit beside her on the far side of the bed, away from their sleeping son.

"Your father thought I acquitted myself well. He and I engaged in a long talk after all had left. He wants me to address the Committee about the Army's dire situation."

"Mama will be most impressed. As she was last week when a courier from General Schuyler's staff delivered a letter addressed to me from Mrs. Knox. It must have arrived with the dispatches from Philadelphia."

"I assume that letter had nothing to do with military matters."

"Of course not." Elisabeth leaned her head on Will's shoulder. "Lucy, Julia Rush, Dr. Benjamin Rush's wife and others in Philadelphia have been zealously raising funds for our soldiers.[1] Perhaps," she continued, "we will collect money from the wives of those prosperous merchants I met tonight. Of course to supplement the funds you will persuade the Committee to send to Philadelphia." She poked him in the ribs to emphasize her teasing.

"Your father also intends to make me more presentable with a new uniform."

She motioned with her hand he was speaking too loudly. "All the young ladies of Albany will be envious of me," Elisabeth whispered, "to have such a handsome husband escorting me about town." She took the holder and softly blew the candle out.

Will pulled off his boots and placed them quietly on the floor. "I do not relish being trotted out to perform like an actor in some play," he said irritably. He removed his breeches and clothed only in his nightshirt, lay down next to Elisabeth. She snuggled on his chest and kissed him gently on his neck. "A decent uniform does not change you. You are a strong voice for our cause. As you spoke to those merchants at our wedding dinner in Philadelphia you will speak with conviction to this Committee. Remember, dear Will, how General Knox complimented you then on your well-chosen words. He was proud of you then as I always am."

Will told her how her father had recalled the spy mission on Long Island. "Your father has a way of probing for every significant fact," Will mused. "Believe me, I did not intend to. I told him of my brother's assault on you in Philadelphia."

He felt the tension in her body as she tightened her grip on his hand.

"You have my word, my dear Elisabeth. Only if we meet on the battlefield."

"I pray there will be no more battles and the speculation of peace becomes a reality."

They lay together in silence, Will's breathing becoming quieter as he drifted off to sleep.

In the darkness with her eyes wide open, Elisabeth regretted ever having told Will the details of that morning in Philadelphia. Unconsciously, she rubbed her fingers along her cheek where John had struck her and slid her hand to her throat. It was four years ago and it haunted Will more than her. Now her father knew as well. Silently, she prayed for peace. Once the war ended, the British would leave and John Stoner with them. Her fear of Will being maimed or dying on a battlefield, or being killed seeking out his brother, would diminish and with time would trouble her mind no longer.

—⚘—

Jupiter knew, by counting the sunrises, it was the third day of his enslavement on the plantation. He still bore a large knot on the back of his head that hindered him less than being hobbled by a stout two foot long rope around his ankles. That was to keep him from running away, the big Negro called "Prince," told him. It would come off soon enough, once the overseer was confident Jupiter would not attempt to escape.

He did not even know where he was. The flat fields around the slaves' shacks behind the three-story red brick house were covered with snow. In the distance, he could see woods, the trees bare of leaves, their branches beckoning to him to come, seek shelter and freedom beyond.

In three days, he had walked only as far as the barns and the pig stys. This place was unlike the plantation he had been born on and worked his entire young life. Here, there were only eighteen slaves who toiled outside the house. His former master, Willis Parks, owned more than one hundred on his Tidewater tobacco plantation. All Jupiter knew how to do, was plant and tend the tobacco plants, harvest and cure the leaves, bundle them up in hemp bags and load them on the wagons. Until he and his mother had escaped and arrived in New York City, he had never been off the Parks plantation, never even ridden a wagon to the river where the bags of tobacco were loaded on shallow draft sloops and taken down to the bay.

The first day, finding himself alone, tied to a post in a slave shack, he had rocked back and forth on his haunches, despondent, waiting for someone to come. When the others returned from work, he eagerly told them he had been kidnapped and assumed they would help free him. They knew from the way he talked he was not from around this plantation, wherever it was. He told them he was originally from the South, and with his mamma had come to

New York, was free behind British lines and worked with Sexton Williams at the John Street Methodist Church. They ignored him, except for Prince who told him he was here now and would have to work just like the rest of them, beginning tomorrow.

When the other slaves discovered he had never tended to animals and could not help with milking of the cows or feeding the cows, sheep and pigs, Jupiter was given a shovel and a wheelbarrow. He shuffled around the barn, cleaning up the cow shit and dumping it behind the barn. His fingers became numb from the cold winter wind and his thin jacket barely kept his body warm. Hampered as he was by the rope hobble, it was difficult for him to climb the ladder to the loft, where he discovered it was relatively warm among the bales of straw. Here he took his time, separating the sheaves, lugging them to the edge and tossing them down from the loft. Slowly, he spread the clean straw in the stalls he had mucked out, and thought despondently of what had happened to him. It was too late to tell Sexton Williams how he hungered to be learning to read in a warm dry room, listening to his teacher's gentle corrections.

The next day, Jupiter and a short stocky slave named Yast went with Prince to the pig sty. Prince carried a large mallet and Yast, two saws and a small axe. Jupiter carried a heavy length of thick rope, a wooden tub and an old cloth bag. At first, he thought they were going to build something, although he saw no wood or nails.

Prince explained they were going to kill a pig, pointing to a large hog. To Jupiter it looked like it weighed more than the three of them together. They entered the sty. The frozen mud was like stone and hurt Jupiter's feet, still hobbled around the ankles. The three of them moved forward with their arms out and boxed the pig in a corner. Prince, motioned for Jupiter to stand back and nodded to Yast who held an eight inch knife in his hand. Prince walked slowly, talking softly to the pig until he was within arms length. The animal looked cautiously at him through its tiny eyes, its nose sniffing for a scent of danger. Prince took two swift steps forward and struck it with the mallet in the middle of its skull. The pig dropped immediately. Yast rushed forward grabbed the pig by the snout, lifted its jaw and made a deep cut across its throat. Blood gushed from the wound in pumping spurts into the mud. Jupiter, moved back against the flimsy wall of the pig shed as the dying hog thrashed uncontrollably on the ground. They waited while the pig bled out, and then at a nod from Prince, Yast placed two large logs of wood under the shoulder and haunch so the body was tilted down and the belly exposed.

Prince ordered Jupiter to grab the hind leg and hold it up. He did as he was told, feeling the hard bristles and the warmth of the flesh beneath. Yast inserted his knife under the skin and deftly cut midway up the haunch before making a complete circle above the hoof. He did the same on the other hind leg and then, with Jupiter again doing the lifting, repeated the process on the front legs. While Prince and Yast skinned the rest of the legs and began working on the body, they gave Jupiter a saw and instructed him to cut off the hoof just above the first joint.

Jupiter squatted down in the frozen mud, his toes and fingers numb from the cold. He grabbed one foot and slowly drew the handsaw back and forth where Yast had indicated. A trickle of blood appeared in the cut flesh. He sawed through the white bone and dark red marrow, put the severed foot in the bag and cut off the other hind leg. Prince and Yast had skinned the pig on the upper side and stood watching Jupiter as he worked on the two front hooves.

"You damn slow," Prince said. He grabbed the saw from Jupiter and in a few strong strokes had cut off both feet and tossed them to Jupiter. Prince knelt in the bloody, frozen mud. He took his knife and inserted it between the hog's hind legs. Jupiter watched as the big man placed the fingers of one hand inside the cut and moved along with his knife in the other until he reached the chest.

"Yast. Get the hoist." Yast beckoned to Jupiter. The two of them carried the eight foot high triangular shaped wooden frame from around the back of the shed. Jupiter stumbled and almost caused Yast to drop it. Yast cursed angrily as he regained his balance. Jupiter said nothing thinking he would never get used to this cold, the frozen ground, the bitter winds, the snow and ice. "What's that on your forehead?" Yast asked as they awkwardly maneuvered the hoist around the corner of the shed toward the sty.

"My former master branded me for runnin away."

"You ain't goin run away from here."

Jupiter did not see why. At the plantation in the Tidewater, Master Parks kept dogs for hunting and for chasing down runaway slaves. Here there were no dogs, just geese that swarmed around the yard adjacent to the house and honked noisily when anyone approached. He was sure he could outrun a goose, he thought smiling confidently to himself.

They set the hoist behind the half skinned pig and tied the thick rope that Jupiter had been given to carry around the two hind legs. Using the block and tackle, the three of them lifted the hog off the ground. Jupiter, numb from the cold stomped his feet and tried to warm his fingers by tucking his hands under this armpits. He watched as Prince and Yast finished skinning the rest of the carcass. Prince made one long deep cut along the belly, a quick cut near the throat, another near the tail and the pig's guts fell to the ground.

Jupiter filled the empty tub at the pump and brought it around, staggering from the pump to the sty, his long arms stretched out holding the two handles of the tub. He could easily have carried the tub filled with water. The weight was not the problem. It was his legs being tied together that slowed him down and caused him to spill so much water. By the time he returned to the skinning site, the tub was only half full. Prince barked at him to clean up the guts and organs. Cautiously, he lifted the slimy white intestines, the dark heart and the red lobed liver and pushed them under water. His fingers felt as if they would fall off in the icy water and he found himself, to his own disgust, rubbing them in the still warm organs of the slaughtered pig.

It was late in the day when Prince and Yast completed skinning and cleaning the pig. Yast had sawed off the head and Prince was splitting the carcass in half, when the overseer, Mr. Marsh sauntered over. Jupiter rose from squatting over the tub and straightened his stiffened back and tried to ease the frozen tightness in his shoulders. This was the first time he had seen the overseer up close. He was a thick chested man, with big hands. Even in his high boots he was shorter than Prince but well fed, with a vigorous stride. His face

Home in Albany 75

reminded Jupiter of the toughs he had seen in the wharf area where he had been sent on errands – rough, weathered, and confident.

"Hang it out overnight to chill and tomorrow you can cut it up as usual. Ham roasts, ribs and chops for Mr. Harand's kitchen and the rest for salt pork in barrels. Be sure and save the lard. The cooks need it." He spoke in clipped tones. Jupiter noticed that Prince and Yast had bowed their heads when Marsh arrived and avoided looking directly at him. Why was that, he thought. Both Prince and Yast had knives. And there was the axe and the mallet. They could kill him in an instant and free all of them. Jupiter wanted to shout – Kill him. Gut him like the hog. Hit him with the mallet.

As if his thoughts had reached Marsh, the overseer turned and looked at Jupiter, who straightened his back even more, noting with surprise he was about as tall as Marsh.

The overseer looked him up and down, noting the long arms, lack of fat around the middle and stout legs. Jupiter thought if Marsh stepped forward and tried to examine his teeth, as he had seen slave buyers do in Virginia, he would punch him in the face. "Was he any help at all?" Marsh said, staring Jupiter down and directing his comment to Prince's bowed head.

"Some, Mistah Marsh. He be good in time," Prince responded, his eyes still downcast.

"Well," Marsh said. "Give him what he can do for now. We will need him as a field hand this spring and summer."

Prince nodded. "Yes, Mistah Marsh."

"And take that rope off. He is not going to run away." Marsh started to walk toward the red brick house in distance. As if it were an afterthought, he turned and pointed at the tub. "Those guts in there. And the feet too. Prince," he commanded. "You decide how to divide up with the others. You Negroes will be eating good for a week."

Jupiter did not think the innards and four feet would feed eighteen slaves for a full week. He realized Marsh had the power to decide whether or not they got the throwaways. If he had said nothing, Prince would have left the tub and the bag and returned to the slave shacks empty handed. Why did Prince accept this?

The next two days, the three of them prepared barrels of salted pork. Prince and Yast cut the carcass into one pound pieces, while Jupiter rolled the ten gallon oak barrels from the storage shed to the pig sty and tended the three fires with large copper pots on tripods filled with brine solution. He hauled split logs from the woodpile to keep the fires going, separating those that were frozen together with the small hatchet they had given him.

He said little and listened to the talk of Prince and Yast through the day. He learned that Mr. Harand was their master, he and his wife had three daughters and Prince's woman was one of the house servants. The salt came from the coast, although he did not learn where that was. When Prince mentioned New York City, Jupiter could barely conceal his excitement. The barrels, once they were filled with alternating layers of salt and pork, the meat covered with salt brine and the lids fitted tightly in place, were destined for the British ships in New York harbor. It was idle chatter between Prince and Yast – how many of the barrels would fit on a wagon, they went back and forth on how many wagons and many oxen they would have to bring from the barn. It would take two days over frozen rutted roads to reach the river. Jupiter thought, if he could be a helper on one of those wagons, he would swim across the river, if he must, to get to New York.

It was late in the afternoon when they fastened the lid on the last of the barrels. Prince, Yast, and Jupiter rolled the barrels up a worn wooden ramp on to first one wagon and then another. Jupiter was beside himself as they tied the upright barrels tight in two rows and then lashed them to the sides. It was dark by the time they finished and there were no oxen hitched up. Jupiter determined tomorrow he would ask Prince to be a helper to one of the drivers.

When he approached Prince first thing, the big slave laughed at him. "The wagons are gone. Left early mornin. You think you will have an easy day, huh. There's stumps to be burned out for the new field. That's your work today." As they crossed the road to the flat field dotted at the end with a row of remnants of once tall oaks, Jupiter looked longingly at the fresh wagon wheel tracks in the slush heading west. Now, he thought, at least he knew the direction.

That night he ran away. He followed the road and the ruts toward the river, the city and his freedom. Confidently, he walked all night. At dawn he headed off the road, through a field to a copse of trees and thick hedges. Hungry, he fell asleep and was startled awake by the whinny of a horse in the distance. Other travelers on the road, he thought, and fell back asleep. He vaguely heard the crunch of boots on the frozen crust of snow and then, suddenly the pain of a lash across his shoulders. Another lash across his back. The third wrapped around him pinning his arms. Whimpering, he struggled to his feet to be confronted by Mr. Marsh. Without a word, the overseer knocked him to the ground with one punch, bound his wrists together and pulled him across the snow to the road. Then, tying the loose end of the rope to one stirrup, he rode back in the direction of sun in the sky in the east, at a pace too fast for a walk but not so fast that Jupiter would be dragged.

Back at the plantation, Marsh ordered Prince to give Jupiter twenty lashes "and to lay them on good." Prince did his job well. Another slave threw a bucket of salt water on his flayed back. The overseer ordered the other slaves not to give him any balm or "such salve," to ease his lacerated flesh.

That night, Jupiter lay in the far corner on the cold dirt floor of the slaves' hut. He moaned constantly from the intense pain of his flayed flesh.

The next day he was put in ankle chains. He hobbled around the barn barefoot, stepping in and shoveling out the cow shit, clanking from stall to stall from morning until nightfall. When he slept he was chained to a thick wooden peg driven deep into the dirt floor. He could not even go outside to relieve himself and awoke in his own filth. For the first time in all his years of being enslaved, he wished he were dead. The other slaves, those who had been on this farm for a long time, huddled around the hearth and their cooking pots and ignored him. He knew they regarded him as trouble. He had done nothing to earn their sympathy or compassion.

Jupiter thought about them and their refusal to run away. Freedom was nearby. At Master Parks' Virginia plantation there was nowhere to run away to. At least until the British came and offered freedom to slaves who entered their lines. Here, the British were across the river. Why not flee to freedom that was so close?

Although he suffered physically from his lacerated back, his mind was clear. On one sleepless night, trying to turn this way and that to ease his back, he recalled there were slaves in New York City, working on the wharves, in warehouses and as house servants. They were behind British lines but were not free. Sexton Peter had said they belonged to those who supported the British. Only slaves of those in rebellion to the Crown were granted freedom. Now he understood. Master Harand's plantation was owned by a Loyalist. None of the others could run away for there was no freedom for them.

Jupiter had no way of keeping track of time, now that he could not measure the end of a week by the worship on Sunday, when he would mop the floors and help Sexton Peter clean the church afterwards. He guessed more than two weeks passed before they removed his ankle chains. It was a small step and he reveled in the freedom of movement once again. At the end of the day, he washed his clothes in the cattle trough and returned to the slave hut shivering in the cold but smelling cleaner. He took his bowl and squatted down near the fire. One of the slaves he did not know elbowed him further away.

"Leave the fool alone," Yast said gruffly. "He aint no damn good for nothing anyways. An maybe we will be punished for not stoppin him runnin away." He stared across the relative warmth of the hearth and gestured with his empty bowl. "Din't think about getting us in trouble. Dumb shit and stink like one too."

When it was his turn, Jupiter ladled out the gruel, noting the few pieces of gristly pork in his bowl, chewed the hominy bread and listened to the talk of the other slaves. Spring was coming and they would be out in the fields, plowing and planting wheat and corn, and clearing new pastures for the cows and sheep. The plum, peach and apple trees would need pruning. There was talk of cutting down oak trees and milling them into barrel staves.

Jupiter did not understand much of what they were talking about. He had only planted and harvested tobacco. That was all he knew. He did not know about plowing or planting grains. It was all strange to him. No matter. He would escape when it was warmer. He had been slowed by the snow and slippery ice that coated the roads and enabled Marsh to track him down. He knew the road west led to the river and beyond that the city. He would bide his time and try again. He would steal a knife and this time if he did not succeed, he would kill himself. He would not return to the Harand plantation and live out his life as a slave again.[5]

Chapter 4 - Escape to Connecticut

It was mid April and, on either side of the road, the pastures of clover and wheat were a bright, verdant green. Matthias Vose sat on the wagon seat, feeling the hard plank through his woolen breeches. Rivulets of sweat ran down his shirt as the mid afternoon sun warmed his back. Next to him, Edmund Carpenter, a farmer and tavern owner smartly snapped the reins on the brown haunches of his team of oxen. They were heading east a few miles to deliver logs to a neighboring farm. There, Vose would be sheltered for as long as necessary before moving closer to Long Island Sound and the welcoming shores of Connecticut.

Since arriving in the town of Brooklyn two months ago, he had been moved from house to farm by a clandestine group of patriots and sympathizers. Sometimes he stayed at a church, sometimes in a barn, but he always kept out of sight. In Brooklyn, Hessians arrogantly strode the streets harassing the civilians and brawling drunk among themselves.

His rescuers had taken his Continental Army jacket, tri-corn and breeches and burned them. Now, he wore an old brown felt crown round hat and a pair of ankle high leather shoes, one with a tarnished buckle, the other with a worn piece of rawhide holding the flaps over the tongue. Even if he did not have a bad leg, he would not have been able to run very far or fast. He had kept his Regimental buttons though, tucked deep inside the linen pocket of his pants.

Matthias was aware he must play his part. He was Edmund's distant cousin from New Jersey, come to help on the farm and in the tavern. Others in Carpenter's family would vouch for him. However, on this well-travelled road out of Brooklyn in broad daylight, he felt extremely vulnerable.

Carpenter, although not generally a talkative man, sensed Vose was ill at ease. He kept up a running account of the hardships the people had endured since the British occupation. "First, they cut down the saplings for fuel. Next, they took our locust fences. Our cattle now wander everywhere, getting lost and trampling down our crops." He waved his arm to either side. "We have no certainty of whether we will have hay and grain to harvest or to feed our livestock in the coming winter." Matthias nodded in sympathy. His host was a robust man, maybe forty years old, with leathery skin and a wide mouth that revealed many of his teeth were missing. "If t'were not for my tavern, my family would starve what with the levying, taxing and the impressment of our horses, oxen and cattle."[1]

He took off his hat and wiped his brow, looked up at the wisps of clouds in the blue sky and said vehemently, "T'is God's very own decree that our people shall be free. Thanks be to Providence the Hessians are no longer quartered amongst us." Matthias listened as Edmund told of the six who had lived with his family. "They took possession of our kitchen, lashed up their hammocks, cooked our food, and hung about smoking, drinking and playing cards and dice the live-long day. The Sabbath meant nothing to them. Indeed, it afforded them a more favorable time for stealing and pillaging when most of us are attending divine worship."

"They are no longer with you?" Matthias asked anxiously, fearful of being in close contact with enemy soldiers on a daily basis and forgetting Carpenter had already thanked God the Hessians had left.

"No. They were ordered back to Staten Island and from there to do their evil deeds of plundering and pillage across the Hudson. I hope General Washington and you Continentals show them Yankee lead and steel." Vose smiled in agreement, thinking of his brothers in arms and especially Private Caleb Wade. How joyous would be their reunion when Vose finally returned to their regimental camp, wherever that may be.

    The clatter of hooves shattered Matthias' reverie. The sight of a single light horseman, helmeted in his bright red jacket, cantering toward them turned his blood cold. The dragoon reined his horse in front of the two oxen.

    "Make haste. Unload your wagon of this wood and follow me. We have forage ahead to take to our camp. Your wagon will serve."

    Edmund held the reins tightly in his hands and objected. "If the forage is ahead, may we proceed with our wood, unload it there and then carry your provisions to your camp."

    The dragoon took affront when Carpenter did not obey immediately. "You will do what I say now or I will cut both of you down." To emphasize his threat, he unsheathed his sabre and waved it in the direction of Carpenter and Vose. Then, seeing the men hurriedly clamber down from the wagon ready to do his bidding, the cavalry man ordered them to get back on the wagon and to hurry down the road with their load of wood.

    The light horseman trotted alongside them, urging them to move faster, all the while brandishing his saber. "Quite full of himself," Carpenter muttered to Vose as the horseman rode ahead a little.

    In about a mile they came upon a large shed at the edge of a field. Two dismounted dragoons lounged about, their horses calmly grazing on the fresh spring clover. Carpenter removed his hat and with it covering his mouth grumbled, "T'is Mr. Pettison's summer crop that will not grow to fruition." Their mounted escort pointed toward a weathered wooden shed, before joining his companions in the shade of a large oak at the corner of the field. Edmund reluctantly drove his oxen along the path to the front. There, they unloaded the wood they had laboriously stacked in the morning in two piles on either side of the entrance. Carpenter led the oxen into the shed. Vose caught a glimpse of a silver flask being passed among the three dragoons before he entered the relatively cool dimness of the shed.

The tired beasts stood patiently in the shelter, munching on hay scattered on the ground.

Edmund looked up at the roof and grunted. "No loft and open at both ends. Probably just a run in for the horses when there are storms" he said. To one side there was a harvest sledge half-filled with cut hay from last summer. Fresher hay and straw lay in mounds on the floor. Edmund grabbed Matthias by the arm and pointed to a thin dark stain leading to the back of the shed. "T'is blood," Carpenter said, following the line out and a short way into the field. The trampled grass indicated the wounded person had fled in the direction of the woods. As they returned, they noticed a pitchfork, cast aside with the prongs up and blood smeared on the long ash handle. It was lying in the milkweed growing alongside the shed.

"I hope it was not one of Mr. Pettison's sons who is wounded. This is his pasture. The hay is still here because the British have taken most of his horses. I hope the moldy crop poisons the cavalry's mounts." He motioned for Vose to begin loading their wagon with the bad hay in the sledge first. With each pitchfork full, a white cloud of stale dust filled the air, causing both men to cough violently. Working quickly, they covered it with newer hay taken from the center of the shed until the wagon was loaded higher than its sides.

"We should kill them," Vose said vehemently thrusting the pitchfork deep into the hay load. Edmund shook his head. "The cavalry would take horrible retribution upon the community if three of their own went missing. Pettison's farm would be the first to go up in flames and not even Providence could protect the rest of us from the dragoons' vengeance." He put his arm on Matthias's shoulder. "No. We will take this load to where they direct us and proceed to my inn for the night. I will send a lad to make inquiries at the Pettisons. Tomorrow, you will accompany me here and we will take the wood to where it was intended."

In the morning, as they drove back to the shed to reload the wood, Carpenter told him the Pettison boy had lost three fingers. "He is lucky the dragoons did not cut him down for resisting. Mr. Pettison will complain to their commanding Colonel, but nothing will come of it," he said grimly.

To Vose's surprise, after they had delivered the timber to the farm as promised, they continued east instead of turning back.

"I still am of the opinion we should have killed them," Vose said. Edmund grunted but said nothing.

They traveled on in silence through the midday, stopping once to relieve themselves, until Matthias felt compelled to ask, "Where are we going?"

"T'is time to move you closer to The Sound," Edmund replied. "Tonight, we will sleep at the Oakley farm. They are of the Society of Friends. Josiah Oakley is a mild, patient and pious man. He will bring you to Huntington."

"And then?" Matthias asked anxiously.

"From there it is but a short way to the coast and a whaleboat to take you across The Sound to Connecticut. Once across, you will rejoin your regiment and fulfill your expressed desire to kill Redcoats."

"You misjudge me if you think me a bloodthirsty man. I have been in enough battles and seen enough gore to satisfy everyone on this entire Island," Vose said, spreading his arms to encompass the land on both sides of the road. "I have been in a British prison and seen men die of starvation and disease. I wish to punish them for their cruelty and, now, for the brutal maiming of the Pettison boy."

Edmund acknowledged Matthias' statement with a nod and grunt. "Josiah Oakley is firm in his faith and is known for his judicious advice. He is called by one and all 'The Peacemaker.' In his own way, he helps our cause although his religion tells him to aid neither side. It will not be well for you to talk about bloody revenge in his presence." With that, Edmund closed his lips firmly around a stem of hay and it was clear he would say no more. No other words passed between them that evening and he left before dawn.

Vose spent the next few days splitting wood, helping Oakley's two sons clear the well, replacing a wagon axle and shoring up the stonewall of the root cellar. His labor was welcomed. At each evening meal, Josiah bowed his bald head, fringed by grey-white hair, and led them in a prayer of thanks to God for their meager dinner.

Vose joined in, his arms outstretched and linked with other members of the family.

All of the Oakleys went to the Meeting House on the Sabbath, leaving Vose alone on the farm with work to be done but sternly prohibited by Josiah from doing any of it. Early Monday morning, Josiah and Vose hitched up the team of oxen, and headed east with a basket of freshly baked bread and pies for the Searling family in Huntington. Both were in their shirt sleeves, Josiah protected from the sun by a broad brimmed black hat, Vose by his round brown felt hat, stained by the sweat from his brow. He yearned for his worn tri-corn, long since lost and hoped he would soon be wearing one and a uniform again.

Josiah let the oxen meander at a slow pace. Matthias was impressed at how Josiah controlled the oxen by a series of different sounding clicks, and not by any snapping of the reins or cracking a whip. Unlike Edmund, Josiah was a loquacious person. He talked mostly about the many colors of the flowers in the meadows, the kinds of sweetbriar, thorny berry branches and creeping vines lining the road, marking by their floppy stance, where they once had grown on wooden fences. Josiah did not say it, but Matthias knew the British or the Hessians had pulled the fences down for firewood.

Josiah pointed out the different stands of trees, locust, oak, maple and ash. Even the stumps in the orchards drew his praise for the green shoots emerging from the cut trunks, rather than a comment on their wanton destruction by the occupying troops. He commented on the many species of birds that came to his farm in seasonal waves, the wild ducks and geese that populated his pond and the rest of the island in the fall, flew south and miraculously began reappearing in the early spring. Or the barn swallows that neighbored with him year round, nesting high in the rafters and flitting around at dusk capturing all manner of insects.

"Tis the hand of God, my son. The wonders of nature around us and the abundance of the earth, are evidence of the Divine - the Creator of all living things." A broad smile of pleasure and peace crossed his narrow face. Matthias would have described his face as severe. But when Josiah spoke his face was marked by a continual expression of serenity and grace.

Vose held his tongue, but thought what a timid and useless man Josiah was for this neighborhood ravaged by war. What good was his kind spirit to prevent enemy troops pillaging at will, seizing young men for forced labor, burning and trampling crops and leaving his neighbors with little to feed themselves and their families when winter came.

They traveled for several miles, with Josiah continuing to praise the verdant land and the wonders of nature, all as evidence of God's beneficence. Mathias was half listening when he saw a church spire in the distance. "Is that Huntington?" he asked.

"Indeed, tis Huntington and the Anglican church steeple you see. We believe it is by deeds one fulfills God's will on earth, not by creating buildings in His name," Josiah said in a mild rebuke to those who had built the church.

The road narrowed around a bend and straightened like a brown, dusty arrow on the ground pointing toward the tall, slender steeple, and the town still hidden from view by trees. A gentle breeze blew toward them. It prompted Oakley to note the whiff of salt water and expound on the bounty of the shore and sea. It was in the midst of Josiah's description of the schools of fish and abundance of clams, mussels and eels within easy reach of the shore when Matthias noted two red dots on horseback racing at a gallop across a field of clover angling to intercept them,. The dragoons jumped a stonewall separating the field from the road and pulled their horses up in front of the docile oxen. Both of their mounts were slick with sweat. Saliva and spittle dripped from their mouths around the bits.

"Bring this wagon and follow us to the harbor. We need to cart barrels of rum to our barracks," one of them commanded.

"I regret sir, I am on the way to Huntington," Josiah replied. "I bring a gift of bread and pies to a friend and then must proceed to Searling's warehouse. There, two barrels of salted fish and one of flour await my carrying them to Jericho."

The dragoon closest to them drew his saber and viciously brandished it over Josiah's head. "No back talk from you, you scummy rascal.

You will do as I say or I will cut you down in an instant."

Matthias looked frantically around for a weapon, a heavy branch, a stick, a pitchfork. The wagon was empty, except for the basket of food between them.

"I repeat, I am unable to comply with your request."

"God damn your bloody obstinacy. One more minute and I will send you to the devil," the trooper shouted, red-faced with anger.

Josiah stood up from the wagon seat so that his head was now closer to the dragoon's sabre. He removed his hat and held it in both hands before him. "If you see anything in me worthy of my death, why then take my life."

Matthias tensed his legs, prepared to knock Josiah to the ground and spring from the wagon seat at the trooper, hoping to avoid a slashing blow and knock the man off his horse.

Josiah, with a benign smile on his face stared at the trooper and put his hand on Matthias' shoulder, not to steady himself but to restrain Matthias. The dragoon sputtered some more oaths, angrily sheathed his sabre, shouted for his companion to follow him and viciously spurring his horse, leaped over the nearest stonewall at a gallop.

"What would you have done," Matthias asked, "if the Redcoat had threatened to kill me?"

Josiah sat down and put his hand on Matthias's left knee. "You are shaking."

"And you are not?"

"I uplifted my heart to God. There was nothing for me to fear. As for your question, I would have interposed myself between you and the sabre," he said patting Matthias's now steady knee. "I would not have you die on my account."

"You would do that for me, a total stranger?" Vose asked incredulously.

"It is not so peculiar," Josiah responded with a smile. "You were prepared to launch yourself at the soldier should he attempt to strike me down." He smiled at Matthias. "I am motivated by my faith. I am not certain what moved you. Perhaps God has touched your heart as well."

Matthias chuckled and then laughed out loud with relief. "You so intimidated them, they failed to force us off the wagon and take it themselves."

"Matthias," Josiah said seriously. "I did not intimidate them. It was God's doing. We are all in His hands."

Vose remembered Caleb, his closest compatriot in the regiment, who seemed to have taken to religion after the sermon they heard near Chatham. Matthias had mocked him for his frequent comments that "God would provide" and "He is with us." In the immediate aftermath of the dragoon's threats, he at least conceded that God had been with Josiah.

Around the hearth that evening in Huntington, Searling and the other men of the house spoke in low voices of the recent reinforcement of the soldiers of the garrison at the nearby fort by a company of Associated Loyalists. The fort itself controlled access from The Sound into Oyster Bay and Cold Spring Harbor. Further east, there were supposed to be encampments of Tory raiders who crossed Long Island Sound and attacked towns and fishing villages on the Connecticut side. As he tried to fall asleep in the stifling windowless attic of Searling's low roofed home, Matthias felt trapped, surrounded by a nest of Redcoats and Loyalists. If the plan was for him to escape to Connecticut by boat how could his rescuers evade the British? He slept fitfully, waking up at odd hours sweating not from the fear of being recaptured, but of what awaited him in prison.

Josiah left the next morning with the same peaceful expression on his face. He did not express any concern for Vose, so confident was he that God would find a way to bring him to safety.

Matthias was not as calm and assured about his fate. For two days Searling kept Vose inside. Although warm and fed well enough, he became anxious with each passing hour of his confinement. The Searling home was on the eastern end of the town but close enough to the main road for Matthias to hear the occasional clatter of passing cavalry and the marching of soldiers to and fro. His story, which he rehearsed in his mind, that he was a relative from New

Jersey, here to help with the spring planting no longer sounded convincing to him.

The third day it rained, a warm spring rain that began in the morning and as the wind picked up from the northeast, chilled the body by the afternoon. The rain seemed a signal of some sorts. Late in the afternoon, after the midday meal, there was a bustle of preparation. Heavy capes were removed from trunks and hung on pegs near the fire. Searling's oldest son sat in the kitchen blackening the glass of a lantern, with only the forward pane left clear.

Shortly before midnight with the rain continuing to drum on the roof, Vose was given a pair of woolen coveralls. He put them on over his breeches.

"Keep close behind me and say not a word," Searling said, his voice already a whisper, as he proceeded through the kitchen to the back of the house.

With a cape clasped at his throat and his round hat pulled tightly down over his ears, Matthias followed Searling's dark shape out the rear door and down a cow path paralleling the road. The rain pelted them as they sloshed through pastures. As best as Matthias could tell they were heading east. The door of a tavern on the road opened, shattering the darkness with a bright rectangle of light. They heard the sound of a man vomiting, the door closed and all was dark again. The muck sucked at Matthias's feet and he almost lost the shoe with the rawhide tie. When the rain finally let up, a cold mist blew toward them from the direction of the Sound and silently enshrouded them like a blanket of cobwebs.

Searling paused, as if marking some landmark visible only to him, and veered through the shrubs into a sea of marsh grass. He stopped at the water's edge and set alight a sliver of oiled kindling with his flint. Squatting and facing the water, he lit the candle and held the lantern forward, alternately passing his hand before the light three times. Then he covered the lamp with his cape and waited. A faint light appeared in the distance through the mist and then disappeared. Searling repeated the signal and this time, when those on the water responded they were much nearer. A long dark shape glided toward them. As the distance closed, Matthias could see the shapes of two men standing at the bow behind a swivel gun. Both men were armed with muskets pointed directly at Searling and Vose.

With a rustle of reeds, the boat slid onto the marshy mud. Searling stood up and, for the first time since they left the house spoke. "Nathan," he said. The man on the bow lowered his musket. "Hale," he responded.

Several men swiftly jumped over the side, armed with an array of muskets, pikes and spontoons, and disappeared into the marsh and on to the road beyond.

"Hurry now," Searling said, pushing Vose forward into the shallow water. "And good luck to you."

A man leaned over the gunwale, offered an arm and Matthias clambered aboard. "Go aft, behind the mast and stay out of the way," the man grunted as he poled the craft back from the muck. Crouching as the whaleboat rocked in the waves, Vose did as he was told, passing eight men manning oars, four to a side. Silently, they moved away from the shore.

"Who are you?" a dark shape huddled on a bench, whispered softly.

"Private Matthias Vose of the 3rd New Jersey. Colonel Dayton's Regiment. And you?" he replied in the same soft tone.

"Corporal Ezra Morton of the Eighth Connecticut commanded by Col. Jedediah Huntington. If a Loyalist whaleboat or a British coastal sloop does not intercept us, we should back on my native shore by dawn."

"Cut your jabber," one of the rowers hissed. "Do you want to give us away?" The oars moved silently in the cloth-covered oarlocks. The only sound was the splashing of the waves against the hull. As they rowed farther from shore, Vose felt the wind pick up. Silently, two of the rowers pushed both him and Morton out of the way and hoisted the sail. The whaleboat skimmed across the water into the blackness. Matthias had no idea how they knew where to steer. He had to trust their skill and hope he would be safely in Connecticut soon.[2]

As the sky lightened ahead of them, Morton was the first to

spy land ahead. He grasped Matthias's arm tightly. "There it is," he pointed. "Connecticut. They captured me during a raid on Greenwich. I spent the last three months rotting on a prison ship in Wallabout Bay before I escaped. And now I am almost home."

Matthias was about to relate that he, too, had been a prisoner of war in New York when he was aware of a commotion in the stern. Behind them, a white sail in the distance was bearing down on them. The whale boatmen loaded the stern swivel gun and waited. Matthias hoped the distance would not close so much that they would have to fire to defend themselves. Their twenty-foot craft, smaller and lighter than the pursuing vessel widened the distance between them as they raced toward the shore. Vose saw a puff of grey blue smoke from the bow of the pursuing vessel and a large splash rose well behind them. It was a desperation shot, fired more in frustration than in hopes of hitting its target.

They landed in a small cove. "Quickly! Off the boat," one of the whalemen shouted, as he lowered the sail. "The Redcoats are coming on." Mathias and Ezra jumped over the side as one man in the bow turned the boat around so the swivel gun faced toward The Sound and the oncoming British ship.

They had alighted on a rocky coast with a thick forest that came down almost to the water line. Matthias, unsteady from the rocking motion of the whaleboat, staggered toward the trees. His ankle twisted on the smooth stones and he fell hard, banging the knee of his bad leg on a large rock. He limped up until he was safely within the trees, undecided whether to rest or continue on. He heard the light boom of the swivel gun, followed by a louder roar of another cannon.

"The Redcoats may land," Ezra said. "We had best move inland." He pointed to a well-worn trail winding through the trees.

"Neither of us look like Continentals," Ezra said, out of breath, struggling up the incline behind Vose. "We look like ill-kempt scarecrows," he added, running his fingers through his stringy hair and noting their makeshift clothes. Both men hurried on, followed by the sound of the dueling guns and the sporadic barks of muskets. They emerged from the woods on to a narrow logging road.

"Whereto now?" Matthias asked pausing and rubbing his thigh where he had been bayoneted at Yorktown.

"My family farm lies just to the north of Danbury, itself only twenty-five miles inland from here. Let us follow this road until we find a more traveled one," he said to Matthias limping beside him. "Perhaps we will find a teamster willing to take us to a nearby town."

"I escaped from the sugar house prison in New York City in December and after three long months, I am on free soil," Matthias said. "I do not wish to tarry. I seek nothing more than to rejoin my regiment and avenge my own mistreatment and the atrocities I witnessed on the Island."

"You will need food, rest and decent clothing, first. Come with me," Ezra said. "We will make inquiries in Danbury as to where the Army has assembled and then you may continue your journey."

Matthias smiled, recognizing the logic of Ezra's plan. Caleb had frequently said, "He is with us," when everything was uncertain and there was no discernible way. Perhaps it was true. After all of his travails, to have escaped the British pursuit in The Sound and be safely on this Connecticut shore, it now did not seem, to Matthias, like so much pious prattle.

—⁂—

Will rode Big Red up the Goshen Road from New Windsor to General Knox's home. He had covered the one hundred miles from Albany in five days, enjoying the solitude of the woods and the warm late spring weather. The General's headquarters were in a magnificent two story granite stone building with four red-shuttered windows on the first floor, five on the second and a simple four step entrance with a white framed door. A wide covered porch ran around one side of the house and around the back. A single level wood framed attached building for the kitchen faced the gristmill and springhouse. The headquarters guards had pitched rows of neat white tents on the broad lawn beneath a thick stand of maples and oaks. Beyond them a stone wall separated the barn and a small fenced pasture from the road.[3]

To his delight, upon entering the house, Will found Master

Sergeant Adam Cooper as the orderly for the day. Forgetting all decorum in front of the few higher ranking staff, the two old friends embraced. Adam had arrived by wagon from Philadelphia a week before. "Sarah and Emmanuel are part of Mrs. Knox's caravan," he explained. "They should be somewhere in northern New Jersey by now."

They held each other at arms length. Will noted Adam's curly hair covered most of the scar from Major Murnan's sword. His friend had gained a little weight, perhaps from staying in Philadelphia for so long and enjoying dinners at the Knoxs's residence.

"I look forward to being reunited with my family," he said, grinning at Will. "Tis a joy I never imagined I would experience. When I left them, Mrs. Knox had at her disposal four wagons laden with crates of Madeira, porter and barrels of ale, boxes of food stuffs purchased in Philadelphia, and trunks of clothing. She and her three children, including their new born baby boy are traveling by carriage, escorted by a troop of cavalry." He resumed his seat at the desk and motioned Will to a chair. "The General is inspecting a site for the artillery park a few miles from here," he said. "The Colonel and Captain Hadley are with him. You arrived alone. Where are Elisabeth and your son?"

"They are coming south from Albany to Newburgh by sloop, accompanied by my father-in-law's barge, weighed down with barrels of flour from his mill, gunpowder and other supplies for the army." He grinned at Adam, pleased their two families would be together. "My orders direct me to report here and specify housing will be provided for my wife and child at headquarters. Elisabeth and I will be together until the army marches south to besiege and take New York."

That night, the General hosted the two dozen officers of his staff to a late cold dinner of roasted chicken and lamb noting the Headquarters' cooks had not yet arrived. They sat in the largest high ceiling room off the main central hall, arrayed on both sides of two extended tables. Knox sat at the head of the table, his hair unpowdered, closely cropped in the front and cued in the back. Will had never seen the General so jovial and expansive. Instead of permitting the conversation to dwell on military matters, he spoke of how this headquarters building would be a real home, for his family and the families of his staff.

"Gentlemen. This building is only temporarily a male preserve. Soon all these rooms upstairs," he said gesturing to the ceiling, "will be filled with our beloved women and our little ones. My dear wife will soon arrive with my daughter Lucy, my son Henry Jackson and our new born babe, Marcus Camillus. Do you know His Excellency himself is our son's godfather?" he boomed out proudly.

Captain Hadley proposed a toast- "To Marcus Camillus Knox. May he have a long and healthy life." The General smiled broadly, took a sip from his glass, pleased by the gesture. "Nor will my children be the only ones to bless us with their joyful presence."

He nodded to the men around the table. "To Captain Hadley, we acknowledge the imminent arrival from Morristown of his wife Mercy and their son, Benjamin. To Lieutenant Stoner, the mighty Hudson is carrying his lovely wife Elisabeth and their son Henry to land at Newburgh and be brought here post haste." He looked down the long tables. "Where is Master Sergeant Cooper. Ah, there you are," he said espying Adam at the end. "His wife Sarah and their son Emmanuel will arrive with Mrs. Knox." He gestured with his glass to Captain Holmes. "And I hope to persuade our good Captain Holmes to bring his wife and two sons from Marblehead to our Headquarters. With those additions soon there will be at least eight children scampering around underfoot." The General's good mood was contagious and the men laughed as Knox described how difficult it would be to attend to the boring, but necessary staff work as the children ran helter skelter about the house and grounds.

Knox pushed back his chair and stood at the head of the table and raised his glass. There was the sound of chairs scraping the wooden floor as all rose. " Gentlemen, I give you a toast worthy of our shared experience on the battlefield, our valor and our honor To our dear wives and beautiful children, may we long enjoy our families in the beneficent peace we will achieve, with Providence's help, before this year is out." Shouts of "Here! Here!" rang out approvingly

Following dinner, in the cool clear evening, Captains Hadley and Holmes, Will and Adam sat on the porch steps idly watching the water wheel of the mill turn slowly. "You were with the General today," Will said to Hadley. "What does he say about the plans to take New York?"

"It is far too early to know. There are rumors the new British Commander, General Carleton has arrived with orders from London not to engage in any offensive action," Hadley replied. "General Knox states His Excellency believes this to be a ruse. Daily they improve their defenses north of the city. He may reinforce our forces in Westchester if not to protect against the enemy's incursions then to bring some semblance of order to the County."[4]

"Is the county in disarray?" Holmes asked.

Samuel sighed. "Unfortunately, as peace and a cessation of hostilities becomes more of a reality, Loyalists have become more vengeful against our compatriots, who return atrocity for atrocity and retaliate against those they suspect harbor sympathies to the Crown." He stood up, stretched and leaned against the rough stones of the house. "I, for one, yearn most heartedly for an end to this bloodshed."

"Despite this talk of peace, I do not believe the British will grant us our independence until we defeat them in New York," Will said. "'Tis better we prepare for that campaign than wait for them to strike us."

"Oh, we will prepare," Hadley replied. "General Knox has surveyed the artillery camp. Your time will be filled with training and drilling new recruits and veteran gun crews. You and Big Red will be most busy."

Adam listened impatiently as the talk went back and forth about the advisability of attacking New York or drawing the British out to White Plains, or a combined attack together with the French Navy sailing into the harbor and bombarding the British from the sea, while the Continental Army moved on Manhattan from the north. He would do his duty when ordered. However, his immediate concern was personal.

"Sarah's mother and brother are in New York," Adam blurted

out, interrupting Nat Holmes who thought Yorktown was a model for besieging New York. Adam's statement shocked the others into silence. They listened as he described how they had fled from the plantation in Virginia and now were free behind British lines.

"However, 'tis only there that their freedom is recognized. Should they venture to cross through the lines to be reunited with Sarah, they risk recapture by slave catchers and returned to their former master." Adam stomped around the porch. "I am helpless to do anything to reunite my beloved Sarah with her mother and brother. I cannot let Sarah visit them. It is too risky. Nor can I go myself. I am at my wits end what to do. I have served six years fighting for our cause and freedom. Why cannot I enjoy the simple pleasure of my wife and her mother living together under one roof in peace without fear? As all of you have done on furlough," Adam said bitterly. Immediately, he regretted his angry and accusatory tone and fell silent.

Will was the first to respond. "Adam. We are your friends and brothers in arms. We will find a way to help you and Sarah."

"Yes you are my friends, especially you, Will. Only I fight for freedom my family cannot enjoy. I thought to bring Sarah's mother and brother here, to the army's encampment," Adam continued to no one in particular. "Even if I am able to get them safely out of New York if slave catchers came here, her mother and brother would be subject to being taken." He began pacing the porch again in frustration.

"We can protect them once they are here," Will said. "We will enlist General Knox's assistance. He will bar slave catchers from the encampment."

Adam grunted derisively. "You saw the slave owners reclaim their property at Yorktown and my fellow soldiers hunt the poor souls for a guinea." He looked from one to the other until they all nodded in agreement.

"You recall correctly," Hadley admitted. "It was shameful. However, our encampment is not Yorktown. It is not open to one and all. Here, Sarah's mother could be employed to help in the kitchen and as could her brother. They would be under your watchful eye, as well as ours. 'Tis a small risk. The real danger lies in the journey from New York to New Windsor."

"Overland is too dangerous," Holmes stated emphatically. "The only route is by the Hudson River. It will not be easy to accomplish with British frigates as far up as Tappan."

Adam felt overwhelmed by their concern. "I apologize for my angry outburst. Yet, all of you being married, know the frustration that comes from being unable to provide comfort to one who loves you and looks to you for protection."

"We will find a way," Hadley assured him as they walked around the house and returned inside.

Will continued to mull over Adam's concerns during the next few days but he was pleasantly distracted by the arrival Elisabeth and Henry and surprised they were accompanied by Luykens Van Hooten, his father-in-law. His wife, showing her pregnancy looked wan and discomforted. She eagerly handed Will their rambunctious son who screamed with delight at seeing his father. Once after settling Elisabeth in their room he took Henry outside so she could rest.

"Big Red," the little boy said taking his father's hand and leading him toward the barn. "Big Red. Ride Big Red," he said happily.

"Yes. We will go see Big Red. Let me ask your grandfather to join us." Will found Luykens talking to Adam at the orderly's desk. As they walked toward the barn, his father-in-law said he had some business to attend to with General Knox. What business could that be, Will thought, slightly distracted by Henry's insistence he be seated on Big Red.

It came to him later that night, as he lay in bed with Elisabeth asleep. The General had enlisted Van Hooten once before to establish spy networks on Long Island after the British invasion in '76. Would he be engaged again and if so where? New York? No. It would be too dangerous. He would wait until Luykens spoke with General Knox and ask him for more details.

The next few days were demanding for Will. Together with Colonel Winthrop Sargent and Captain Hadley, they rode past the artillery park and scouted the terrain. They chose roads to use for the drills of the rapid transport of cannons, where to dismount and unhitch and position the guns. Then, they selected fields well away from areas used by the army for maneuvers to use as firing ranges. In the evening, he found Elisabeth tired and still weary both from her trip and the pregnancy.

At the end of the week, there was much commotion when Mrs. Knox arrived to the clatter of her escort of mounted troopers. General Knox, with apologies, terminated the senior staff meeting, to greet his wife and children. After helping Lucy down from her carriage, he cradled the infant Marcus in the crook of his arm, while lifting Henry Jackson with the other arm, as five-year old Lucy clung to his coat, chattering away.

Elisabeth was unable to find rest during the day as the house had become a great deal more lively and noisy with the presence of children. She was in better spirits with the arrival of Samuel's wife, Mercy Hadley and their eight-month old boy, Benjamin. Elisabeth was apprehensive about her pregnancy and exhausted from keeping up with Henry while Will was at the artillery park or drilling field. Henry needed attention constantly. Mercy went with the little boy as he marched determinedly from the barn to "see horses," or to the tents of the Headquarters Guards to "meet sodjurs," giving Elisabeth much needed time to rest.

One evening after dinner, Will found his father-in-law alone relaxing comfortably on the back porch, a glass of port in his hand. "Come Will. Sit with me." He pointed to the mill. "I too have a mill, larger than that one. In a good year, before '76, we produced enough barrels of flour for me to send barge loads down to New York City. They were stored in my warehouse and shipped across to England on my own ships. It was a good business even though trade was restricted to the mother country," he said, giving Will a slight shove and chuckling, "as Pieter Bleecker brusquely informed you."

Will smiled, remembering his embarrassment when Bleecker had spoken to him in a condescending manner. His father-in-law was in a good mood. Now was the time to find out.

"May I ask, sir, what business do you have with the General?"

Luykens stared at Will, his coal black eyes studying his son-in-law, as he calculated how to respond.

"Mrs. Knox has a dear friend," he began slowly, "who, like many others has members of her family who fight for our cause and some who favor the Crown. The woman's sister, has fallen ill. Her husband is a British Officer serving in the Carribean."

Will noted that Van Hooten had not mentioned any names.

"Both we and the British have issued passes to women with relatives on the other side to permit brief visits," Luykens continued, "particularly when matters of health are involved. The General is willing to do so for his wife's friend. Unfortunately, the dear lady is physically unable to travel long distances by carriage. The General has asked me, as a favor, to let my little sloop carry her to New York, wait for five days to permit her to visit her sister, and then to bring her back to Newburgh."[5]

Will's first thought was of Sarah's mother and brother. Here was a chance for them to escape by the river, the route Holmes believed was the safest. "Then you will stay with us, Elisabeth and Henry, until your ship returns. We will be most glad to have your company." He watched Van Hooten hesitate before answering.

"Sir," Will said. "With all due respect, please do not take me for a fool. Whatever mission you undertake for the General is safe with me."

"I have high regard for you Will and do not intend any disrespect. That you have seen there is more to this than transporting a woman to visit a sick relative behind British lines, further confirms my opinion of your sharp mind." He stood up. "Come. Walk with me away from the house where we will not be overheard." He left his now empty glass of port on the porch railing.

They crossed the stone bridge that arched over the mill's creek and, in the gathering dusk ambled toward the field near the barn. Big Red, catching Will's scent whinnied loudly from within.

"The General has charged me with meeting a certain person in New York and bringing him from the city to Newburgh." He held up his hand to intercept any questions. "That is all I can tell you. Do not ask for any more details. The lady will make this gentleman's presence on the sloop more credible. In addition, I plan on meeting with some persons, particularly my former warehouse manager and shipping agent. He remained behind and most likely has aided the British. I suspect," he grumbled, "now that he sees in which direction the wind is blowing, he may be inclined to aid our cause in return for strong Whig protection."

"Protection from whom?" Will asked.

"There are already broadsides being issued calling for all Tories to be expelled from the city and their property seized. Other more reasonable voices urge reconciliation for those who committed no armed offense against our cause." The dark woods loomed ahead of them. Luykens turned back toward the light of the candles in the headquarters' windows. "What good is accomplished by banishing merchants and traders, who will take their money with them, when we need to rebuild our commerce as an independent nation? I only hope that common sense rather than a spirit of revenge will prevail."

"If I were to suggest the presence of an elderly female slave and her young son on your return trip, posing perhaps as servants to the lady, would that be possible?" Luykens raised an eyebrow and nodded for Will to explain. "I will tell you what I know. We must help Adam," he said firmly. "Speak with him for the particulars of where Sarah's mother and brother are sheltered. I implore you to aid him and remind you that had he not saved my life in Boston in '76, I would not be here tonight."

"I am well aware of that Will," Luykens replied. "I will find a way. Rest assured, when I return, Sarah's mother and brother will be amongst our passengers."

That night, lying awake before Elisabeth's soft rhythmic breathing lulled him to sleep, Will envisioned his brother John accidentally encountering Van Hooten. His father-in-law had aged and physically changed somewhat since John had last seen him in '76. He sat up suddenly in bed. What if Luykens deliberately sought out John to take revenge for his brother's assault on Elisabeth? No, he whispered out loud. His father-in-law would not be so rash. Nor would he jeopardize the mission for the General. The possibility of an encounter between the two nagged at him until he finally fell asleep, only to be awoken by Henry, just before the cock's crow, demanding to get into their warm bed.

Chapter 5 - The Courtship of a Wealthy Young Lady

The gravestones in the Huntington Presbyterian graveyard all had been removed. Captain John Stoner of the Loyal American Associators took no special care to prevent his mare from trampling on the unmarked graves. He dug his heels into his horse's flanks and spurred her up the gentle slope toward Colonel Benjamin Thompson of the King's American Dragoons at the summit.

Once there, shaded from the sun by a grove of pine trees, John joined the Colonel and a few of his staff as they watched the men and boys of Huntington under armed guard, widen the ditch that would serve as a defensive perimeter for the fort. Others labored up the hill under the weight of heavy oak beams from the ceiling of their half dismantled Presbyterian Church. Judging from the ditches the locals had already dug, John estimated the fort's rectangular shape to be about 75 feet wide at the entrance with a single gate, and perhaps 150 feet long. It made sense if the intent was to teach the rebellious citizens of Huntington a lesson, but John thought it did not serve any military purpose, what with Fort Hill already located in town and nearby Forts Franklin and the East Fort in Lloyd Harbor. Thompson himself had named it Fort Golgotha, meaning place of the skull, a hill outside Jerusalem. /1

Sullen bastards, all of them, Stoner thought. Serves them right to force them to take apart their own church piece by piece. It had functioned as a meeting place for their open rebellion and perfidious treason. And now, they were whining about their sacred burial place being desecrated. He was pleased the Colonel had no compunction about respecting the gravesites of these rebels' ancestors. Thompson leaned over his saddle and pointed with his riding crop to several men pushing wheelbarrows of worn granite grave stones from the church's graveyard.

"Those stones are to serve for our field kitchen," he said. "All these treacherous scum need is a merciless sword and iron fist to beat them into submission." He gestured toward the frame going up for the gateway entrance. "Can you see the flat stone to the right of the gate?" he asked. John stood up, the leather of his stirrups creaking from his weight as he strained for a better view.

"Yes. Does it mark a special grave?"

"Oh, indeed it does," Thompson replied, grinning and breaking into a harsh laugh. "'Tis the grave of a particular scoundrel - the Reverend Ebenezer Prime of this rebellious church who long encouraged his parishioners in their treasonous acts." He motioned again with his riding crop. "Observe the location John. Every soldier entering or departing the fort will have the pleasure of treading on the grave of this God-damned Rebel preacher." /2

He chortled at the thought. Suddenly his mood became more serious.

"I fear for the good and true Loyalists on this island," Thompson said. "Damn Sir Guy Carleton and his orders to halt offensive hostilities. A major thrust up the Hudson Valley supported by our fleet on the river would smash the Rebel's army in one blow."

At the mention of Carleton's name, John scowled openly. To the detriment of John's various monetary schemes, the new commander of all British Forces in the colonies had issued orders to correct what he termed "enormous abuses." Officers were no longer allowed to own ships or wagons and were specifically prohibited from carrying on personal or contraband trade. Prices of rum, flour, molasses and coffee were already falling. /3 A timely tip from someone on Carleton's staff had enabled John to sell, at a very tidy profit, his two wagons and interest in three sloops before Sir Guy issued his orders.

Still, the climate was changing and although he remained in Judge Ludlow's employ and a very lucrative arrangement it continued to be, the days of easy money were over. He could not risk exposure and perhaps even a court martial. General Carleton had already made examples of a few prominent officers enmeshed in corrupt schemes. Their defense that everyone was similarly engaged had only increased Sir Guy's commitment to stamp it out.

Late that afternoon, John was invited to join the Dragoon Officers' evening meal taken in Widow Chidd's Tavern near the harbor. Colonel Thompson introduced him to the others, describing him as one who had served with distinction with the Queen's 17th Light Dragoons and now was a trusted and recently promoted aide to General Ruggles. John acknowledged the compliment while recalling with pleasure bidding good riddance to the Light Dragoons as they sailed from New York harbor, heading to the pestilent swamps of South Carolina. After the platters of roasted beef, venison and stews of mussels and clams had been brought from the kitchen, someone noticed, there were indented letters on the bottom crusts of the loaves of bread being passed hand to hand. The loaf John had been handed bore the name "Thomas" and the four letters "Patt," up to the edge where the bread had been broken off. Colonel Thompson, his angular face glowing from the heat of the fire and rum, summoned the Dragoons' chief baker and questioned him with mock seriousness.

"Sir. I used some of the slate gravestones from the rebels' churchyard as the floor of my oven," he explained to cheers and guffaws. "It appears the inscriptions from the stones were baked into the loaves before you." /4 He was dismissed with cries of "well-done" and "serves the scummy rebels right." Then, with great vigor, the officers tore into the bread, eagerly chewing the doughy engravings.

"We stay here one more week for the work on our fort to be completed," Colonel Thompson announced. "Drive these rebel bastards hard and tolerate neither sloth nor cheekiness. For when our work here is completed, we will ride east to John Harand's plantation for a dinner in our honor, perhaps a ball or two and definitely a day of steeplechase and hunting." The officers cheered and one rose with his glass in hand.

"I propose a toast," he shouted. "To the hospitality of Mr. Harand and all Loyalists of this Island we are sworn to protect." A drunken voice from the end of the table yelled, "And to the affections of Harand's daughters. May they be offered in abundance and reciprocated in full." Again, the men cheered the drunken statement with catcalls and whistles. "If you cannot wait, there are harlots at the back of this tavern," one officer hollared, making a mock effort to stand and rush toward the rear door.

John leaned closer to Colonel Thompson. "Sir. The reference to Mr. Harand's daughters? Are none of them married?"

The Colonel studied John, a small smile playing around his mouth. "His daughters are eligible and said to be pleasant to look upon. Their father is wealthy both in land and money. If it were not for the damned Parliament seeking peace, to wed any of them would secure a young man's future." He emptied his wine glass and raised his hand to signal for it to be refilled. "Now, all is uncertain. The value of the Harand young ladies depends on the terms of any eventual peace agreement. If he and other Loyalists are allowed to remain and continue their lives in peace, then a match would be beneficial. If they are compelled to leave, perhaps the Crown will compensate them for their losses." He shrugged. "Or perhaps not. He waved his hand dismissively. "As for me, if I must leave these shores I intend to seek a military commission on the Continent, so it matters not." /5 He stared into John's eyes. "Are you a gambling man, Captain?"

"I am Sir, but no longer at the faro tables."

"Good. Were I you, I would court one of the Harand daughters. At the present, I would wager Mr. Harand and his family will do very well no matter the outcome."

"I thank you for your advice," John replied. Indeed, I will pay court to one of them, he thought. Judge Ludlow had expressed a high opinion of Mr. Harand's business acumen. John suspected Harand was a man who planned for every contingency and such men prosper in uncertain times. If peace were agreed to and the

Rebels achieved independence, John had no intention of remaining in the colonies subject not only to their laws but the retribution of his brother. He knew not where he would go, but having a wealthy spouse would enable him to live in comfort no matter where they alighted.

Five days later, having worked the resistant rebel men and boys of Huntington on the Sabbath to complete the construction, the fort was done. The following morning, Colonel Thompson, several of his staff officers and Captain John Stoner set off in high spirits for Harand Manor. They passed several fields verdant with wheat and hay, and vast pastures with grazing beef cattle, all extending off into the distance. Thompson explained this was all part of the Harand estate. John was further impressed as they trotted up the tree lined way toward a fine Georgian three story brick structure, with two thick chimneys at either end and six tall windows on the ground floor. Negro slaves rushed forward to take their horses and saddle packs. John noted they were not liveried and seemed uncertain of their tasks but it mattered little. Mr. Harand was obviously a wealthy plantation owner. He decided sight unseen, he would court one of the sisters.

In the early afternoon, they stood in the large parlor, well furnished with mahogany side tables, black walnut cabinets and finely made book shelves of oak and maple. Mrs. Harand sat in a bow-backed Windsor arm chair, her voluminous skirts spread out around her, while her husband stood behind, one hand on her shoulder. She was a handsome woman, John thought. The oldest daughter, Eliza was playing the harpsichord surrounded by several officers casually leaning on the musical instrument, and from that vantage point, admiring the white flesh of the tops of her breasts. The other two sisters, Henrietta and Hannah, were seated on upholstered chaise lounges, Henrietta more coquettish in her pose than her sister, who seemed less interested in the attention being paid to them.

It was her standoffish attitude that attracted him to Hannah. John was repelled by the very name of Eliza, who was the best looking of the three. Too much like Elizabeth Van Hooten, the

Dutch bitch who had made a fool of him and was now married to his brother. Henrietta, with her flirtatious nature would cause him nothing but perpetual jealousy. No. Hannah with her plain name and solid figure seemed like the proper one for him. She was on the chubby side, not heavy but ample for a girl he guessed to be seventeen years old. Her full breasts did not need much pushing up from a corset. She would develop into a woman, he thought, who would obey him and say nothing if he took his pleasure with young maids and female servants as it would be his right as master of the house.

After dinner, the servants removed the long table and chairs and the windows were opened to allow the May breezes to cool the room. Three musicians, two with violins and one seated at the harpsichord that had been moved from the parlor, positioned themselves at one end of the room. After the ceremonial opening dance led by Colonel Thompson and Mrs. Harand, the officers lined up for the favor of dancing with one of the three sisters. The crowd around Eliza was the largest, but there were enough redcoats mingling around the other two sisters to ensure their dance cards would have few openings.

When it was John's turn to dance with Hannah, he initially made small talk before the honors and curtsy and concentrated on the required formal steps of the minuet. Up and down the length of the room they went, following the other couples and when it was over, John was relieved that he had danced passably well.

"This hall is spacious," he said as he escorted her off the dance floor. "At the Mischienza in Philadelphia, organized by Major John Andre, there were three dozen couples dancing at once." Hannah's face lit up with an expression of pleasure and admiration.

"And to think you danced there," Hannah said, almost breathless with delight. "I beg you tell me all about it. Mama will also be pleased to hear the details. It must have been the most marvelous ball ever given anywhere in the Colonies," Hannah said, her face flushed with excitement.

"I am at your disposal Miss Hannah and await you to only name the time," John said, bowing low before returning to stand against the wall. As another officer escorted her on to the dance floor, he was certain that Hannah was looking behind her at him. I have cast the bait and she has taken the hook, he thought to himself.

The next morning, at breakfast Hannah sent John a note suggesting he join her and Mama in the parlor for afternoon tea. He wrote his acceptance, signed his acceptance as Capt. J. Stoner, and gave it to the white maid to return to her mistress. He watched the servant girl leave the room of men, swinging her hips provocatively and thought it would be a nice to give her a tumble.

In the afternoon, John sat across from Hannah and her mother in the parlor, while some of the other officers escorted Hannah's two sisters around the grounds or enjoyed refreshments outdoors. John set the scene of the magnificent Mischienza, the boat ride from the city to the extravagantly decorated hillside and confiscated home of a Rebel merchant overlooking the river, the costumed ladies waving handkerchiefs to the jousting knights, the sumptuous dinner, the fireworks and of course the ball. He embellished his closeness not only to Major John Andre, but to General Howe in whose honor the Mischienza was held. He did not mention his obsession with the gambling tables and the hatred and anger he felt in seeing Elisabeth Van Hooten on Major Montresor's arm. When he casually let drop that he was an acquaintance of Peggy Shippen, Hannah's mother added she and her husband had dined with the Shippens in New York before the war.

"Then, as you know, Madam, their daughter Peggy is married to none other than General Benedict Arnold who has entrusted me to ensure the precious security of his wife and little son in their home in New York. I have been to the Arnolds' house many times for teas, dinners and balls. Of course, I did not let that interfere with my duty to provide protection for Prince William Henry, who, I may say, is as fine an example of a royal prince as of any royal family." As the words tumbled out, John feared he had overstated his case. Mrs. Harand looked at him a little curiously. She is thinking how many members of any royal families do I know. Nevertheless, he gushed on, describing the young prince strolling around the Battery Fort.

It did not seem to matter to Hannah. She was absolutely beside herself as John related his closeness to the Arnolds. "Oh Mama," she said, the excitement causing her cheeks to flush. "Father has talked of a week or two in our city home. We should have an intimate dinner and invite General and Mrs. Arnold, or perhaps a dinner only for invited guests and then a ball. Captain Stoner can introduce us. I am sure Captain, you know other prominent people to include on our invitation list."

He suppressed the thought Peggy Shippen Arnold would see Hannah as a plain plantation owner's daughter and take relish insulting her without Hannah even knowing she had been mocked.

"I believe General Arnold is campaigning somewhere and discretion requires me to say no more. I am certain Peggy will be delighted to receive an invitation. It will be my pleasure, if your mother requests, to assist you in planning whatever event you wish in the City," John said directing his words to Hannah. She looked at him with such trust and admiration, John thought to himself if the old lady were not here, she would hoist up her petticoat and let him have her here and now on the chaise lounge.

After a hearty breakfast, the entire troop of dragoon officers and John clattered down the road heading east for a day of hunting and a steeplechase in the broad plains to the south. John felt slightly queasy. Something in one of the clam or mussel pies did not sit well in his stomach. It would give him an excuse to avoid partaking in the steeplechase. He had no intention to risk being thrown and cracking his skull. Not now, with the promise of dinners and balls at the Harand town home in New York in one week's time. He wondered how much John Harrand would bequeath to his daughter upon her marriage. A sizeable sum he suspected, relishing the thought.

—⚜—

Jupiter watched the last of the wagons leave the barn, loaded with tents, camp chairs, cots, blankets, tables, firewood, crates containing freshly baked breads and vegetables, a barrel of rum, and bottles of wine packed tightly in a trunk lined with sea grass, as well as other supplies deemed essential for a comfortable outing. He had affected disappointment in not being chosen to go with Prince and Yast and the half a dozen other male slaves and the few women who accompanied the dragoons on their hunting and camping trip. He had put on a long face but was elated.

Mr. Marsh was accompanying the dragoons to ensure the camp was correctly established and the slaves' performed their services properly. The excursion would last two days. Jupiter vowed he would be gone by noon this very day. He ambled back to his slave hut, ducked inside the worn flap and rummaged through Yast's bag until his fingers closed around the eight-inch knife. He wrapped it in a dirty rag and thrust it deep into his pants pocket, hoping it would not come uncovered and cut his leg. Then, he joined the other slaves heading toward the fields to repair the wooden fencing and tend to the cattle and sheep.

They had been given clear and simple instructions the day before by the overseer - to straighten fence posts and replace rotten cross pieces with freshly cut rails in the fields southwest of the Manor. Marsh had threatened that he would take some flesh off their lazy black backs if the work was not completed when he returned. Other than the knife, Jupiter had nothing but the ragged, sweat stained shirt on his back, his torn britches, shoes that barely covered his feet, and a floppy hat on his head. He had left his jacket behind. It would have seemed suspicious if he wore it on this hot day. He would have to endure chilly nights until he found shelter. By midday, the heat had made he and the other slaves drowsy. With no one to force them to continue working, the four of them found respite in shade in a grove of trees. They shared some corn bread and a little jam one of the house slaves had pilfered from the Manor's kitchen. Stretching out on the soft pine needles, Jupiter pulled his hat over his face and was able to peer at the other three from under the brim.

Satisfied they were napping, he rose slowly, as if he had to relieve himself and walked deliberately into the woods. Once out of sight, he trotted through the brush, keeping the road to his right and when he thought he was far enough, angled down and crossed the road and walked in the bright sunlight into a field of wheat. He carried a small branch as a switch, not rushing, careful to convey the impression he was a slave herder, tending his masters' cattle. That would be his story. A few of the cattle had run away and rather than trample the wheat, he was walking the fence line, hoping to find them. He smiled to himself as farmers' wagons pulled by plodding oxen by passed him in both directions. The drivers, lulled by the heat and the methodical movement, paid him no mind.

By late afternoon, he left the road and crouched in a copse of trees, dragging some fallen brush toward him to conceal his hiding place. He napped until it was dark and awoke, starving and shivering. He set off at a brisk pace on the road, hoping to keep warm by walking through the night. The three quarter crescent moon bright in the night sky illuminated the road. He froze in panic when a dog barked nearby answered by another in the distance behind him. They were not tracking him. They could not be. Just dogs talking to each other in the dark, he reasoned. The renewed silence reassured him and gave him confidence. His too large shoes made a flopping noise and he took them off and tucked them under his arm. The past several weeks had toughened the bottoms of his feet and he could walk barefoot if he had to. He kept up his pace, his ears attuned to any sound of an approaching wagon or horse.

He did not hear the footsteps of two travelers coming toward him, until it was almost too late. He dove into a bush and crawled through some brambles, the thorns catching on his thin shirt.

"What was that?" he heard one of the men ask his companion. He could vaguely see both shapes standing on the road peering in his direction. The other man edged down the slope of the ditch and poked the brambles with his walking stick. Jupiter felt for the knife handle and gripped it tightly. It helped stifle his fear. He slowed his breathing and waited.

"Some kind of animal, maybe a muskrat. Long gone by now."

Jupiter waited for a while to make sure the men had not been tricking him with their talk and were circling back down the road. He was not worried about Marsh who he hoped was still far away at the other end of the Island. Slave catchers were his concern, or others who would smell a reward for turning him in.

He returned to the road and this time, instead of walking in the middle, stayed to the right side, planning to dive for cover if necessary. Ahead, he saw the lights made by a few candles glowing in the low windows of homes or taverns. He was not going to chance it. Although it would take longer, he cut through the darkened fields with only the moonlight to guide him as he skirted the town. By the time the lights were behind him he was tiring. Going through grasses, brush and mud had claimed much of his energy. He crossed a small creek and knelt to cup his hand in the water and drink eagerly. In doing so, his pants became soaked from the knees down. In the cool night air, he began to shiver anew, feeling the chill on his calves. In the waning moonlight, he could make out the shapes of farmhouses way off the road. No light emanated from them, but he knew, before dawn, these places and the road would come alive with travelers and farmers. He thought then he would have to hide in the forest and wait for nightfall. He knew every hour he hid or slept increased the risk of being tracked down by Marsh. And every hour he walked brought him closer to the river and freedom in the city. Still, he had one more day before the overseer would return to the manor.

Cold and starving he wondered if he would actually slash himself with Yast's sharp knife rather than be taken back to slavery. He was so caught up recalling Marsh punching him in the face and Prince lashing him, he did not hear the horse and open carriage behind him. He stood still, his shoes in his hand on the side of the road as the man in the driver's seat stopped and peered down at him.

"Where are you off to young man?" the voice from the carriage seat asked.

The story about looking for lost cattle made no sense in the early hours before dawn. Jupiter shrugged and replied "Brooklyn Heights," recalling the name he had overheard one of the teamsters hired by Mr. Marsh say while talking to the overseer.

"You have a fair way to go on this road," the man said. He patted the seat next to him. "Climb up and you may ride part of the way with me." Jupiter hesitated, deciding whether to run into a dark field or accept the invitation. If he ran, the man would report him and men eager for a reward would be combing the woods between here and his destination. If he accepted, he hoped at least would have a chance to escape later on.

"I am Dr. James Rawlins," the driver said, and explained he was returning from having tended to a difficult breech birth. Jupiter did not understand and did not ask. He felt himself drowsing off and clenched his fingers around his knife handle.

He must have nodded off for the doctor poked him in the ribs.

"I asked for your name."

"Jupiter Parks," he mumbled, trying to mask his southern accent.

"Where are you from?"

Jupiter did not know how to answer. If he said the Harand Plantation, the doctor would know he had run away. Unable to come up with a plausible lie, he said nothing.

"Very well," Rawlins said. "You look in need of food and more clothing than you have on. Come home with me and my good wife will see what will suffice."

Jupiter was about to murmur his thanks when he felt a violent turmoil in his stomach and an urgent need to purge himself. He jumped from the carriage and barely made it to the side of the road, pulling his pants down, before a torrent of liquid shit spurted from his ass. The doctor waited patiently until Jupiter weakly climbed up on the seat, feeling embarrassed and weak.

"How many times have you had the diarrhea," Rawlins asked.

"This is the first I have the shits."

He looked at Jupiter. "You are not carrying a canteen. Drink out of a creek, did you?"

Jupiter nodded. "Perhaps it was the water. Porridge and hot herbal tea may serve." He noted Jupiter's chattering teeth. "And a warm blanket."

Jupiter did not remember much of the rest of the journey. Later, he recalled only being helped down from the carriage and being taken into a kitchen filled with the smells of baking bread and the heat of the hearth near where they lay him down. A middle-aged woman in a drab poplin dress and a white cotton cap, hovered in and out of his view.

When he awoke, he was lying on a bed under a low-gabled ceiling. He stared at the rough hewn beams and out the open window at the blue sky beyond. He had no recollection of how he had gotten there. He propped himself up on his elbows. He was wearing a worn clean nightshirt. His clothes were nowhere in the room. His first thought was of Yast's knife. They had taken it from him. He glanced wildly around the room before he spied it lying on the side table at the far end. He thought about keeping it under the sheets but reasoned they had trusted him by leaving it in the room and he would abuse that trust by arming himself with it. How could he escape without any clothes?

Dr. Rawlins came into the room without knocking carrying a wooden bowl and spoon, and saw Yast's knife still on the table. He smiled as he pulled up a chair. He was a tall man with narrow grey eyebrows and a friendly, welcoming, expressive face.

"Let me see," he said placing a hand on Jupiter's forehead and pressing gently. Jupiter felt a calmness come over him and closed his eyes. "From my experience young people have the resilience to recover faster than my older patients." He handed Jupiter the bowl and directed him to eat. Jupiter spooned the oat porridge slowly, waiting for the inevitable questions. He still had not decided how to answer.

The doctor waited until Jupiter finished. "You spoke a little in your sleep and from your words, it is clear you are not from Long Island. I would say one of the southern colonies. Am I correct?" He waited and when Jupiter did not respond, Rawlins said gently, "I cannot help you if you do not reveal your circumstances. If you are a runaway and are anxious I will turn you in, I could have done that while you lay helpless and asleep in my house."

Jupiter considered the truth of that statement and decided to unburden himself, beginning with his and Lettia's flight from Virginia, his arrival in New York City, being sheltered by Sexton Peter Williams at the John Street Methodist Church, followed by his kidnapping and enslavement at Harand Manor.

"You are twelve to fifteen miles away from that Manor but not far enough to escape recapture, I regret to say. Your intention I take it is to rejoin your mother at the Church."

Jupiter nodded. "I will never be a slave again," Jupiter said vehemently. "I will kill myself first."

Rawlins glanced at the knife on the side table. "Let us hope there will be no need for that. I pray for God to protect you. My wife is searching for suitable clothes. You must remain inside. You are in the town of Westbury. Many Hessians are quartered in people's homes. Ours has been spared because I am a doctor and I attend to the Hessian sick when requested. Do you understand?"

Jupiter nodded.

"You endanger me and my family if you are seen. I want your word on that."

"Yes sir," Jupiter replied quietly. "I will cause you no trouble."

"Good. The ferry to New York is less than fifteen miles from here. Were we to set out early, we would make it in one night's carriage ride. The sentries will not bother me. There is nothing suspicious about a doctor being about at all hours of the night." He smiled reassuringly. "I will ask the Hessian Colonel for a safe conduct pass. He will grant it, I am sure. Then, with God's grace, we will place you on a ferry to reunite you with your mother."

Jupiter propped himself up against the pillow. He thought of how none of the other slaves had helped him. They probably had reported his running away as soon as they returned o the plantation.

"Docter Rawlins," he asked. "Why do you do this for me?"

"We belong to the Society of Friends. We ourselves owned slaves until five years ago. Our meeting decided it was against the word of God to possess another human being. We Friends of Westbury freed all of our slaves, even though our non-Quaker neighbors did not." He made a simple gesture, turning his palms up as if to say it was not so simple. "My wife and I felt the mere act of freeing our three slaves was not enough to atone for the years we had profited from their labor and kept them in bondage. We are sympathetic to the plight of any one enslaved and believe God has directed us to help them on their journey to freedom."

"I was lucky you found me on the road and not someone lookin for a bounty."

"Tis God who directed me to you in your hour of need," Rawlins replied as he stood up. "Let me attend to the safe conduct pass. My wife will bring up the clothes she has gathered. Remember to stay inside the house," he cautioned as he ducked under the low beam, closing the door behind him.

—⁂—

Peter Williams stared at the stout man seated before him in the Sexton's office. He said he was an agent for a merchant, but something about his dark piercing eyes and the man's comportment, told the Sexton he was more than a simple agent.

No white man had ever sat in his cramped windowless room before. It had been fashioned out of a storage closet underneath the stairwell, a place for the Minister and members of the Congregation to come to tell him what to do, or to leave messages if he was out digging graves in the churchyard. For a second time, Peter strained his eyes to read the letter the man had handed him. The handwriting was neat and small, definitely written by a woman. It was signed by Sarah Penrose Cooper, the person Mr. Absalom of Philadelphia had confirmed was the daughter of Lettia Parks and sister of Jupiter, and it was addressed to her mother. It instructed Peter to trust the bearer of the letter and to follow his instructions. Sarah promised, with this man's help, they would all soon be safely reunited.

The Sexton appraised the man before him. He wore a rough, brown vest with plain buttons over a linen shirt, well-used tan britches secured by buttons at the knee, and square toed boots without buckles. He decided to trust him.

"Jupiter disappeared more than fifteen weeks ago. I sent him out on an errand and he never returned." Peter did not add he thought the boy had run away, fleeing the hours of learning to read and write that vexed him so and chosen something else. Perhaps he had joined a black regiment of the army or shipped out with the British navy. At least it offered regular meals, some pay and shelter. Or God-forbid he had been kidnapped into slavery again.

He shuddered at the thought.

"I will read Sarah's letter to Lettia. She has been most melancholy since her son disappeared. Every day she implores me to pray for her son's safe return. She may prefer to stay within our church than go with a stranger, even if it means being reunited with her daughter."

The man shrugged. "It is her choice to make. You may tell her, beyond what Sarah states in her letter, her daughter is most anxious to provide comfort and care for her mother. Do your utmost to convince the old woman. She does her son no good by remaining here. Perhaps he will be reunited with the family at a later time." He stood to leave. "If you persuade her, bring her tomorrow to the third slip north of the ferry to Paulus Hook. Tis at the end of Vesey Street. I expect to be underway with the incoming tides by no later than noon. If she is not there by that time I will leave without her," he said gruffly.

Van Hooten left the Church and turned right on John Street and then proceeded north on William. His former agent of several years before the war, Andrew Brockholst, now lived on Gold Street. Luykens was staying in his stately brick home. He thought it was an appropriately named address for a man who had prospered immensely during the British occupation. Before the war, Andrew, a person with few political convictions had been a man of modest means. He said he had come by his new found wealth by trading in all manner of luxury goods from England that were much in demand amongst wealthy Loyalists. China and bone handled silverware, cambrick cloth, Irish linen, white-ribbed silk hose and large gilt buttons passed from the arriving ships through his warehouse and on to his shop for sale to those who could afford it. He boasted he acquired, at a cheap price, some fine pieces of furniture and other goods of confiscated Rebel property, which he was able to sell for a neat profit. Van Hooten suspected not only substantial bribes were paid for the privilege of purchasing these items before they were sent to a public auction house, but Brockholst was engaged in other nefarious schemes he preferred not to reveal.

A Negro servant opened the tall brown door with its ostentatious brass lion-faced knocker and led Luykens to the parlor. Andrew was seated in a straight-backed writing armchair with what appeared to be a ledger on the wide leaf on his left. He hastily closed the book and brusquely ordered the servant to bring them some brandy.

"So, Luykens. Will you be able to dine with me tonight? We have had little time together."

"I am afraid not. I leave tomorrow and there are some other matters I must attend to before I depart." Along with prosperity, Luykens thought, Andrew had put on weight and his face was red-veined. He wondered whether his former agent suffered from gout.

Brockholst accepted his excuse with a grimace of regret. "I too have matters to attend to and one in particular pertains to you and our long association and friendship."

Van Hooten's face remained impassive, his coal black eyes fixed on Brockholst, waiting for him to begin.

Andrew started nervously, talking generally about the rumors of peace and the likelihood of independence and what that might bring or more accurately mean for him when the war ended. "I am fearful my property and wealth will be confiscated solely because I remained in the city during British occupation." Van Hooten said nothing and although it was cool in the parlor, Brockholst removed a handkerchief from his sleeve and wiped his brow.

"I have read the broadsheets and reports of speeches in Congress calling for us to be imprisoned or banished from the land." His voice quavered a bit as if merely saying the words made it certain it would come to pass. "If you have any acquaintances who could offer me protection, plead my cause, for I have done nothing wrong other than trade in goods . . ." his voice trailed off.

Luykens stared at Brockholst, saying nothing until Andrew looked down at his shoes. "I have a responsibility for my wife and two daughters," he continued lamely. "I cannot suffer their being cast out, condemned to a life of destitution and homelessness."

Van Hooten leaned back in his chair. He knew Brockholst was from Poughkeepsie where his family had maintained their Loyalist sympathies until driven out early in the war by the local Whig Committee for Safety and Security. Andrew's two brothers had joined some Loyalist Regiment and fought alongside the King's troops as far south as New Jersey. No one in the family, Andrew included, would find refuge in Poughkeepsie at the end of the war.

"If and when the time comes, I would be willing to make entreaties on your behalf, provided you have not committed any offense against the Continental Army or caused the death or imprisonment of any patriot.

"I assure you," Andrew said eagerly, "it is not the case. I have never caused any patriot nor soldier any harm. I swear it is the truth." He jabbered on about helping those in extremis by generous gifts of pounds or shillings to this or that person who had been displaced by the British Army or rendered unemployed by a Loyalist through no fault of their own.

Luykens stood, disgusted with Andrew's fawning and abject pleading. "I will return late tonight and must arise early. Please arrange for me to be awakened no later than six."

As he walked out into the bright sunlight, it occurred to Van Hooten his promise to help protect Andrew from retribution was insurance against his betraying him to the British. It had been a risk to stay with Brockholst but it was that or sleep in some lice infested bed in an overcrowded tavern room.

It would be a relief to leave the city and begin the journey up the Hudson to Newburgh. From the first day he had tied up at the slip Van Hooten was eager to leave. The city, as he had known it before the war, had substantially changed for the worse. The displaced farmers, mechanics, and common laborers with neither craft nor skill, driven by the war and the incessant vicious fighting between Loyalist and Patriot militias from their towns and homes in New Jersey, were crammed together in a warren of shacks, huts and ragged tents running almost up to the planked wharfs on the river. Brothels, and taverns serving watered beer and rum were everywhere. The alleys and narrow streets were wet with excrement, either from emptied chamber pots or from being used openly as latrines. The foul smell of human waste filled the air with disease laden vapors. Rats were the only creatures thriving in this pestilent environment Van Hooten thought.

Together with his boatman, Van Hooten had visited his warehouses a day after arriving. The one between Vesey and Barclay Streets, south of King's College had been converted into an army barracks. The storage sheds for cordage and empty barrels had been torn down, he surmised for firewood. While he was tempted to see the inside of his building for himself, he dared not risk approaching the sentries or even loitering in the area for too long.

As he walked south on William and turned onto John Street again, his mind was preoccupied with plans for re-establishing his business. Once New York was liberated, he would have to expend some capital to rebuild the warehouses before he resumed shipping flour and grain from Albany. Suddenly, he was jolted from his thoughts of the future by the well-dressed crowds coming toward him. He remembered he was approaching the John Street Theater, a place he had intended to avoid for it was well attended by British Officers. There had been flyers posted about the coming performances of the play, "Tom Thumb." Red coated officers with their arms hooked around their ladies filled the sidewalks. Quickly, Luykens stepped off the curb and mingled with the flow of everyday people heading toward the river – wood carriers pushing carts, chimney sweeps with their long wire brushes carried on their shoulders, marketmen, sailors, mechanics and shoemakers with their tools in leather bags. His boots squished in the mud. He kept his head down skirting the numerous piles of horseshit and pools of filth and garbage.

Captain John Stoner listened to Hannah prattling on as she enthusiastically recounted the pleasure of seeing her very first play in a theater. "I was so enthralled when Princess Huncamunca married Tom Thumb. They were obviously in love, only to have their marital bliss destroyed by Lord Grizzle and the evil Queen. What was her name again?"

"Dollalolla," John replied succinctly, wishing this conversation would end. He was walking on the sidewalk closest to the street. Mud had splattered on his left boot. He would have his man polish them again in the morning. The play, he thought with annoyance, was a stupid low farce with silly names to garner cheap laughs. As if to echo his point, Hannah launched into a description of the comic antics of Mr. Doodle and Mr. Noodle. /6 She was surprisingly naïve and unsophisticated, more so than he thought when he first met her. He was certain she was infatuated with him, which was strongly in her favor. It outweighed any irritation he felt at her banal banter. She had displayed a sense of humor that hinted there was more to her than he had initially thought. As long as she was obedient and responsive to his wishes and did not exercise an independent mind, he was confident the marriage would be tolerable for him.

John was certain Hannah told her mother everything and with that in mind, he carefully chose where to go and who to meet. This past week he had escorted her everywhere, first to The Mall where military bands played on warm evenings and lanterns hung from every post. Officers like him promenaded their young ladies about before sitting on rough hewn benches and imbibing drinks sold by enterprising vendors. /7 He introduced her to officers of rank he knew, ignoring those he deemed less likely to impress her and indirectly, her mother. He arranged for an invitation for the Harands and for him and Hannah to attend a dinner party at General Ruggles' home. It had been a boring and staid affair but an extraordinary success for him. Mrs. Harand had praised him profusely afterwards. Tomorrow night, they would all dine at Peggy Arnold's magnificent home on lower Broadway. /8 He hoped General Carleton would attend. That would certainly solidify his standing with the Harands. The problem would be managing Peggy's sharp tongue so as not to offend poor, unsophisticated Hannah. He patted her hand affectionately, and as he looked ahead, a figure in the middle of the street, going in the opposite direction, caught his eye.

It was just an instant before the man passed. He seemed familiar even though his features were hidden by the brim of his hat. It was his gait and shape that gave John pause. He turned his head for another look. Only the crown of the man's hat was visible, his back partially obscured by others behind him. Then he was gone. Henrietta tugged at his arm.

"John. You are not listening. I asked if there are different performances this week. I would so much enjoy seeing another play."

"I will inquire but remember my dear we have a very important dinner engagement tomorrow night," he replied, still trying to put a name to the man he had seen.

That night, John awoke with a start. The Captain he shared a room and bed with cursed him for being disturbed. "God damn you, John. Stop thrashing around and let a man sleep in peace."

Stoner lay wide awake in the darkness, trying to reconstruct his dream. He had been in bed, lying on top of a naked Hannah, humping away, when her face disappeared and it was Elisabeth, his brother's wife, lying beneath him, twisting and thrashing to get away, her eyes filled with fright. Her image triggered a memory of a man walking into the Rising Sun Tavern on Long Island more than four years ago, drinking with Chatsworth and the dragoons at a long table, sending his Negro servant to bring the man's pistols to show off their workmanship, and leaving later in the evening by the rear door. It was that man, the spy Van Hooten, Elisabeth's father, who he had seen in the street. He was almost sure of it. Why was he in the city? How could he be found?

The next morning, John rose early, eager to track Van Hooten down. His man servant had not polished the boots left outside John's door. No matter. He was in a hurry and would reprimand the lazy souse later.

As a precaution against Van Hooten having confederates or being armed himself, Stoner first stopped at the barracks of the Associated Loyalists near King's College and procured a detail of a Sergeant and two Privates to accompany him. They proceeded east toward The Broadway. John intended to traverse south past City Hall before turning west and then north up Greenwich Street paralleling the piers. Before they had gone more than a block, he was accosted by packs of besotted soldiers. They were off duty, returning from a night of carousing in the streets around the College and the brothels near the river. Eagerly, they confronted every officer and gentleman of means in the street, seeking to sell texts they had looted from the College Library.

"Here, Sir," one inebriated fellow said, blocking John's way.

"Here is the book for you. Only one guinea. Look," he said leaning over Stoner and opening the book to an illustrated page. "See the fine drawing, sir. There is more of them. Them pages alone is worth the guinea." /9

John tried to push the man out of his way but the soldier stood firm. "Sir," he persisted. "A fine gentleman like you, from the Colonies," he added recognizing John's red coat with its green facing was not that of the regular Army. John turned and motioned for the Sergeant and two Privates to come forward.

"Move this man out of my way," John commanded, motioning for his escort to advance with their bayonets already affixed to the muskets.

The Sergeant hesitated and the drunken soldier seized the initiative. "One more step by these men and me comrades here will rally round and teach you a bloody lesson. It will be your head I will bash on these here cobblestones," he threatened, pointing at John, the spittle from his mouth spraying Stoner on his chin.

"Captain," the Sergeant said quietly, moving discreetly behind John. "My orders are to assist in capturing an American spy. If you choose to fight rather than bargain with this soldier, then it is between you and him." John thought he saw the Sergeant wink at the soldier but he was not sure. He was so angered by the insolence of the soldier and the insubordination of the Sergeant that all he could do to salvage his dignity was to reach into his pouch, extract a guinea, exchange it for the book and stride down the street.

In his fury, he was thinking of ways to demand the Sergeant's court martial until he realized they had walked one block and he had not looked at a single civilian passerby. Now, angry with himself and anxious to reassert his authority over the Sergeant who, he was certain was laughing behind his back, John ordered the detail into a tavern to inquire if anyone inside was from Albany. If so, they were to escort the person out into the street to be interrogated by him. After several such stops, he had questioned two and only perfunctorily. It was obvious to him from their appearance, neither was Van Hooten. He also suspected since the men in his detail stayed longer inside the taverns each time, they were partaking of the rum rather than performing their duty.

They passed some of the fine Georgian homes lining the southern part of The Broadway. He assumed Van Hooten would not be staying in one of these. Instead, John changed tactics. He led his detail one block east on Verlittenberg to the Old Dutch Church. Knowing Van Hooten was of Dutch heritage, although he did not think of him as a religious man, he entered the Church followed by his three soldiers. Once inside he ostentatiously walked up the aisle, scrutinizing the few people sitting in the pews. He questioned one man as to why he was there and received the answer –"For God's grace and peace, that you are disturbing." He heard the Sergeant snicker behind him and when he turned, one of the Privates covered his smirk with his hand.

Outside in the sunlight, he guessed it was close to noon. He turned west on King Street, crossed The Broadway again, and walked carefully through the muddy streets until he reached Greenwich. The stench both from the streets and the refuse in the river was overpowering and John covered his mouth and nose with his handkerchief. Incongruously clutching the book he had bought he passed two British cutters tied up at the pier south of the Ferry to Paulus Hook. They were small, swift river craft, with six guns each. One seemed moored with the entire crew ashore except for a watch. The other bustled with sailors scrubbing down the decks and loading provisions.

Beyond the ferry pier the wharves teemed with commercial riverboats of all types, some deep-sided carriers filled with firewood; others with barrels stacked and lashed to their decks. A forty-foot riverboat had cast off with her bow pointed up the Hudson. A burly man was unfurling a patched sail from the one mast amid ships. A lady in a bonnet, accompanied by an old Negress sat in the shade of the sail. A tall, well dressed man stood next to the lady, one hand resting possessively on her shoulder as if to calm her. John turned his attention to the man at the rudder. Although he only saw his back he was certain it was Van Hooten. He ran along the street pushing people out of his way and clomped out on to the nearest pier.

"Sergeant," he shouted "Open fire. It is the American spy.

Ho! Van Hooten. Turn about. Turn about this instant, I say."

The laborers on the pier stopped unloading cargo curious to see what excitement would ensue and watched as the Sergeant and his detail came up. The riverboat continued on its way. The man at the rudder did not turn around.

"Tis too far for a musket volley," the Sergeant said, loud enough for all to hear.

"I command you to fire."

The Sergeant took his time ordering the two Privates to load their weapons. A crowd of workmen stood idly around laughing and joking at the exercise. "I say. Turn about now," one shouted mimicking John's voice. By then, the riverboat was in midstream, its one square sail filled as it leisurely headed north, aided by the tide flowing up river. It proceeded steadily barely creating a wake.

Even John could see that a volley would be futile.

"Damn you for your insolence," he shouted red faced. Followed by hoots of laughter and suggestions from the workmen that he should jump in the river and swim after the boat, John stomped off the pier. He ran the three blocks down Greenwich to the wharf where the first British cutter lay tied up. Out of breath and sweating from his effort, he lumbered up the gangplank.

"Who is in command here?" he demanded at the first sailor he saw. The man pointed to the stern at three officers amiably chatting at the wheel. John bulled his way past several others of the crew and climbed the small ladder. Now even more out of breath he approached the officers who still had taken no notice of him.

"I want to talk to the Captain of this ship," he said gasping. "An American spy is escaping at this very moment on a boat sailing up river. I demand you weigh anchor and pursue him. Immediately!"

"And who are you to come uninvited aboard *The Cerebus* and give orders?" the tallest of the three asked, raising an eyebrow and studying John as if he were a barnyard animal who had wandered into the house by mistake.

"I am Captain John Stoner of the King's Associated Loyalists. An American spy is escaping," John repeated, flapping his arm in a northerly direction. "Get your ship underway and capture him."

"I am James Whitehead, Master and Commander of *The Cerebus*," the tall man responded, straightened his body and clasping two hands behind his back. "I will weigh anchor when ordered to do so by a superior officer of His Majesty's navy. Not a simple Captain of a Colonial militia."

At these words John lost his temper. The man's disdainful attitude and upper class accent rankled him. "Look, you obstinate bloody fool," he said, poking the officer in the chest with the book. "There is an American spy . . ."

Whitehead slapped John hard on the cheek. It seemed to John all chatter and the usual noises on the ship ceased. "Captain Stoner," he said in a loud deliberate tone. "You have insulted me in front of my officers and crew for which I demand satisfaction. Tell me where my seconds may present my demands for an apology or the terms for a duel."

John took a step backwards, rubbing his stinging cheek that had turned red from the blow, even as the rest of John's face was now extremely pale. A duel with a naval officer? The man would kill him and take pleasure doing it. He stammered out the address of his quarters, almost fell down the steps as he backed away and walked unsteadily down the gangplank to the hoots and jeers of the sailors on board.

Oblivious to the smirks of the Sergeant and his detail following him through the streets, John was in a terror. Did he or his opponent choose the weapons? What if Whitehead chose swords? John was petrified at the very thought of a duel, whether with pistols or swords. How could he couch his apology in terms that would preserve even a modicum of his dignity and honor. His life was at risk. He decided he would sacrifice anything, dignity and honor be damned. If necessary he would crawl up the gangplank of *The Cerebus* on his knees in his nightshirt to avoid the duel at all costs.

Part Two
The Army in Camp

Chapter 6 - The Hand of Providence

The maniacal laughter of the new prisoner, rocking back and forth on his stool startled the other two inmates. It was a convulsive cackle, unending and rising in pitch. Locked up in a guarded shack that served as the jail for the 3rd New Jersey Regiment, the two moved toward the farthest wall. A band of sunlight on the dirt floor, streamed through the narrow window creating an illusory barrier that separated them from him. The man had wound his arms tightly around himself. His head was lowered with his chin on his chest.

"Take it easy, brother" one of them said. "You will not be here forever. They court martial us pretty quick."

Private Matthias Vose ceased laughing, uncoiled his arms slowly and studied his two cellmates. The outburst had purged him of his anger and he felt better for it. The irony of his situation brought a smile to his stubbled face. After escaping from the wretched British warehouse prison in New York, being passed from one friendly patriot to another, evading pursuit across the Long Island Sound, and trekking in rain along muddy wagon roads for nine weeks through Connecticut and eastern New York to find the Army and his Regiment, he was challenged by the sentries at the cantonment, jailed and charged with violating his furlough.

The injustice of it again struck him as funny, except this time he chuckled more like a normal person. He had ended up where he began, in a prison, although he immediately conceded this was far,

far better than the sugar warehouse where Continental soldiers died of disease overnight and were carried away in a cart to an unknown grave in the morning. Here at least, he would be properly fed and, according to his new companions, given a trial in short order.

"Matthias. Matthias. Are you in there?" a deep familiar voice called from outside.

Vose rushed to the small window, rising up on his toes to stare out. Corporal Caleb Wade stood outside his hands on the flimsy wooden slats peering in.

"Caleb. Yes. Yes. Tis me. I am back."

Wade touched Vose's face through the slats, his meaty hand closing around the nape of his friend's neck. "You are alive. You are alive," he repeated. Tears streamed down the big man's face. "I have prayed you would survive. It was my fault. I forced you to accompany me to Middletown Point. It is all my fault," he repeated.

Matthias covered Wade's hand with his own, rubbing the large knuckles. "Caleb. We went together," he said. "It was my misfortune to be captured and your good fortune to escape. We are together again and I believe it is the doing of Providence. I truly do."

"When I heard from Lieutenant Phelps you were being held for violating furlough," Caleb said, "I told him the story of your capture at Middletown Point. When he questioned me, I told him I did not know what had happened to you between then and now. Being out of uniform turned him against you. He said all the facts will be revealed at your court martial. In the meantime, Lieutenant 'Nuthatch' said, you will remain in this jail. Tell me friend. What did happen?"

Holding on to Caleb's hand through the slats, Matthias described the prison, his escape and his efforts to find the Army and return to the Regiment. "I never even went home, although I was a mere twenty miles away. Now, all I want to do is march with the Army south to New York and liberate those who are imprisoned."

Wade patted his friend's hand. "I will speak to the Colonel. Surely there is no need to keep you in this guardhouse. Your very act of returning speaks in your favor."

The next day around mid-morning, Matthias heard Sergeant

Henderson's familiar voice ordering the guards to unlock the door and release Private Vose. As Matthias stepped out, Caleb rushed forward and enveloped his friend in a bear hug, lifting him off the ground.

"You are to report to Colonel Dayton," the Sergeant said. "He will determine whether or not to proceed with a court martial."

Caleb put his arm around Matthias's shoulder and walked with him to the Colonel's tent. Vose's ragged shirt hung loosely on his short torso. Wade thought Vose was so much more gaunt than when they had begun their six-week furlough in Trenton at the end '81. It was now mid-May. He hoped Vose would be able to satisfactorily explain to the Colonel where he had been between then and now.

A sentry admitted them. Vose was ordered to sit on a camp stool before Colonel Dayton, who sat behind a field table of planks, strewn with papers and a map. Vose thought the Colonel had aged some since he had last seen him several months ago. Lieutenant 'Nuthatch,' stood behind Dayton to his right. Wade remained anxiously beside the tent flap, fearing he would be dismissed. The Colonel paid him no mind and stared unsmiling at Vose with cold grey eyes.

"Well, Private. Begin at the beginning and leave no detail out," he said, nodding at Vose. As Matthias spoke of his imprisonment in the warehouse prison, Wade noted his friend had changed since his capture at Middletown Point. He was more self-assured, more steady and more sober in his demeanor. Gone was the drunken carouser who had been his drinking companion before Wade himself had heard Chaplain Avery's sermon and changed his own ways. He listened as Matthias described the horror of the prison and how he had rejected an offer to enlist in the British Army to escape death by disease or starvation. Vose impressed him with his modesty. He stated his refusal to serve was not unusual. No other Continental in his cell, nor as far as he knew, in the entire prison, had accepted such an offer.

"You were beaten for responding that our Army had defeated the British at Yorktown?" Dayton said rephrasing Vose's description of the event.

"Yes, Sir," Vose replied before continuing to describe the particulars of his escape and journey across Long Island. "Twas Providence that brought me to those brave men and Providence that delivered both of us from the saber of the cavalry officer. Of that I have no doubt."

Caleb now understood what Reverend Avery had meant when he preached our cause is just and the Lord is with us. His guiding hand was evident not only in Vose's miraculous escape, but in his conversion from a blaspheming drunkard, who swore frequently and foreswore attending Chaplain's services. Wade admitted he himself also had been one who took the Lord's name in vain. Caleb's heart filled with love of God and a sense of certainty – God would be with them no matter what tribulations they faced.

When Vose finished his tale, Colonel Dayton remained quiet, taking time to digest all he had heard. "You faced an enemy worse than Skinner's Greens in the woods outside Connecticut Farms or the British at Yorktown. Certain death in prison with no hope. Instead of turning traitor you chose to escape. Whether it was good fortune or the hand of Providence, I cannot say." The Colonel permitted himself a slight benevolent smile. "I commend you for your perseverance, Private Vose. Welcome back to the Regiment."

"Thank you, Sir," Matthias said. As Wade held the tent flap open, his friend turned back toward their Colonel. "It was the hand of Providence, Sir," he said with conviction.

That evening, Vose joined Wade and his old messmates as they grilled pieces of beef on their bayonets over a fire. Everyone was eager to hear of his adventures and Matthias told it in a flat, unemotional voice, unembellished by boasts or bravado that made his words more credible. The only time his emotions overcame him was when he described the horrific conditions the Continental prisoners were subjected to in the warehouse.

"I pray our Generals will have the wisdom to march our Army south, take New York and liberate those poor souls." He looked at the faces of the men around him. "Every evening when we partake of our rations we should both thank God for the food and remember our brother soldiers who imprisoned, survive on thin gruel and moldy biscuits."

In the following days, Mathias, accompanied by the bear-like Caleb, carried their rations to the cooking fires of the other men of their Company, where Mathias told his story. By the end of the week, they had met with all one hundred and thirty-eight members of the Regiment, except for those in the camp hospital. Vose's message was the same. It became more urgent in the telling. Every day was one more day of misery for the imprisoned soldiers. Every night meant more prisoners died alone to be carted off in the morning and buried in unmarked graves. "It is all true. I have seen it with my own eyes," Vose would conclude quietly.

That Sunday, Regimental Chaplain Abiel Ellis took as the text for his sermon a part of Isaiah, "Watchman, what of the night? The watchman said, The morning cometh." Matthias and Vose immediately understood it to mean that although the darkness of imprisonment of their fellow soldiers prevailed for the moment, they must have unshakeable confidence in God's promises.

Ellis stood bare-headed in the mid-morning sun on a wagon before the men of the 3rd New Jersey Regiment who had chosen to attend. With out-stretched arms he preached, "Man's extremity is God's opportunity." Despite a thin, reedy voice, he delivered his message with passion and fervor. As he reached the conclusion of his sermon, his voice rose in pitch and rolled out over the parade ground. "Our extremity has come and now is the time for Him to make bare His arm for the deliverance of His people. I proclaim over and over again my unshaken confidence in God's promises. The morning now cometh," he shouted raising his hands to the sky. "I see its beams already gilding the mountain tops and you shall soon behold its brightness bursting over all the land." He leveled his arms as if to embrace the bare-headed soldiers standing before him and exclaimed "Amen. And so let it be."[1]

No one moved. Matthias and Caleb, standing in their file, felt as if they were in some invisible presence. A few in the rear ranks began to drift away but those closest to the Chaplain remained in place as if waiting for some good news to be announced, either by

Ellis or from the heavens above.

Finally, Caleb broke the silence. "You Matthias have been urging we march south and liberate our imprisoned brethren. It may not happen this instant. The Chaplain's message told us of God's promise. I am certain our imprisoned soldiers will be freed."

Vose nodded his agreement. "I must bring my account of the misery endured in the British prisons and of God's promise to the other Regiments." Caleb smiled down at his friend. In his relatively new uniform that almost fit, he no longer looked like a teamster, peddler or some other outsider within the camp.

"I will accompany you," Wade said.

The following week, while speaking around the campfires of the 2nd Rhode Islanders, a Sergeant gave them startling news. The British had released eight hundred or so from the prison ships in Walkabout Bay. Some of the wretched men were from Rhode Island and made their way to Providence where they were now recuperating in hospitals and homes.

"My own beloved wife serves as a nurse and is providing succor and nourishment to restore these poor wretched men to health." He removed a letter from his pocket, unfolded it and held it up to the light of the cooking fire.

"She writes:

'It is enough to melt the heart of any human being to see these miserable men. Those who are able, hobble off the ships in our harbor while those less fortunate, are carried in litters borne by the concerned people of our City. The generosity of our citizens is admirable with many women assisting in the hospitals. Our Church has become a depository of donated clothing and blankets. People bring food in baskets for these living skeletons, remnants of the stalwart soldiers who left our city to serve our Cause. Most of the poor souls are sick and dying, and the few rags they have on are covered with vermin and their own excrements."

His voice broke before continuing:

"They are eaten up by lice and many I fear will be carried off by fevers. Those in their last moments take solace they will be buried in hallowed ground in marked graves. The thought that so many preceded them in death, as the survivors tell us only to be interred in the muddy banks of that accursed Bay, brings tears to our eyes. . . [2]

Wade felt Vose's hand on his shoulder. "The morning hath cometh," the big man said. "God has revealed his promise to be with us," he whispered awestruck that the promise had been fulfilled perhaps at the very moment Chaplain Ellis had been preaching his sermon.

"God has moved the hardened hearts of the British to release our men," Matthias said softly. "I pray for the recovery of all those who now reside in the comfort of their friends and relatives, as well as any who still remain imprisoned."

The Rhode Island Sergeant nodded in agreement. "Pray as well for my wife Judith and the courageous women who nurse these men back to health. I ask you to beseech the Lord the noxious vapors and fevers not be visited upon them."

A week after the Independence Day celebration at General Knox's headquarters, Elisabeth gave birth to a little girl.

They named her Agnes after her maternal grandmother. Her middle name was Sarah, the name of Will's mother who had passed when Will was only eight. For the first several days, she slept in their bed so Elisabeth could nurse and rock her so the baby's high-pitched cries would not awaken everyone in the Knox household. During the day, Will would flush with embarrassment when his daughter's wailing interrupted some officer's report at the staff meeting. Each time, General Knox would chortle and remind one and all, he preferred to have his headquarters teeming with children and Lieutenant Stoner had not only fulfilled his husbandly duties but followed his General's orders as well. Later that week, General Knox accompanied by some of his staff left for West Point to investigate the state of the fortifications and the Fort's ability to withstand a siege. He insisted that Will remain behind to be with his wife and newborn daughter.

"The orders from General Washington sending General

Knox to the Point is no indication the war is winding down," Will remarked sourly to Adam as the General and his staff, accompanied by several cavalry rode off. "A siege of the Fort would involve the British sailing up the river joined by their army marching out of New York and into the highlands."

"It would mean a major battle," Adam said, "but the gossip among the troops favors the view that the signs are for an end to it all. Their concern is with receiving their pay; not the danger of another fight."

While Elisabeth napped, nursed Agnes and had tea with Mrs. Knox and Mercy Hadley, Will and Adam took the two Henrys and seven month old Emmanuel to the pasture to ride Big Red. Everyone at Headquarters called the older boys the two Henrys. They were inseparable. One was the Knoxs' son and the other Will and Elisabeth's. Will mounted Big Red's bare back and holding the two Henrys firmly in each arm, gently used his knees to guide the horse along the fence and back to where Adam stood waiting.

"You should see Emmanuel's face," Will said. The little boy was perched on his father's broad shoulders, his eyes wide with amazement as Will and the two Henrys peered down at him. "Hand him to me and we will take a short turn about."

Adam took the two Henrys one by one and placed them on the ground behind him fearful they might run between the horse's legs, before reluctantly handing his own son up to Will. "Do not go too fast," he said anxiously.

"And do not give your son his father's uneasiness with horses," Will replied. "See how happy he is. He likes the height," he said as Big Red ambled around in a tight circle. "We will make a horseman of him yet."

"Not before I make him a fisherman," Adam answered, reaching up with obvious relief and lifting his son on his shoulders. Together they walked back to the barn and let the boys cool off by splashing their arms in the trough.

"Perhaps His Excellency is motivated more by prudence than information the British may be preparing to leave New York and provoke a major battle with our army," Adam said. Will thought of the mysterious man his father-in-law had extricated from New York City. He had seen him once at Headquarters and then, the man had disappeared from the encampment. If he were a spy and brought hard intelligence of the British real intentions, the war might not end until there was one final battle.

"I am still of the mind the British will not surrender New York City without being defeated, whether in the field or by our successful assault on their lines," Will said. He kept his thoughts about the man who might or might not be a spy to himself. The boys' boisterous laughter drew their attention. Will grabbed his son to stop him from splashing Henry Knox. It was too late. The linen shifts of both boys were wet, as was the boys' hair.

"It might be safer to face the British than the wrath of Mrs. Knox and your wife for not taking better care of their sons," Adam observed. "Let us find a sunny spot. The afternoon sun will dry them before we bring the boys inside."

The next few days were idyllic, perfect warm early summer days with not much to do until General Knox returned. With most of the staff gone, the house was filled more with the bustle of domestic activities than military matters. The schedule was dictated by the usual chores of a household with Mrs. Knox overseeing the purchase and storage of food supplies and the arrangements for the afternoon teas and evening meals. Will feared the routine and calm were merely an interlude before the war once again intervened.

Living with his wife and children after so many lengthy separations, he could envision how their life would be in the normalcy of peace. He wished for some decisive action, for the peace to be won and the war to be over. Then he chided himself for his impatience. Images of bloody and maimed bodies from the battlefield filled his mind. Better to await a negotiated peace than to eagerly desire another bloody combat.

—⚍—

Sarah Cooper wiped her wet hands on her apron as she stood in the doorway of the kitchen. Lettia, her mother sat on a bench in the bright summer sun, a tub of water between her bare feet, her gnarled hands washing the dirt off the carrots and turnips. Aprons and linens flapped from two long clothes lines hanging between tall poles set in the grassy lawn. Sarah thought how nice it would be to wear a fresh apron and shift that did not smell of wood smoke and charcoal.

Occasionally, Lettia halted her scrubbing the vegetables and rocked the crib of her grandson now seven months old and napping with arm's reach. It was the lazy kind of summer day Sarah had imagined when she had first learned her mother and brother were free and being given shelter at the Methodist Church in New York. That her husband Adam had been instrumental in helping at least her mother's escape, increased her love for him.

The other morning Lettia had accompanied Sarah to the Knox headquarters kitchen at four a.m. to begin baking. Sarah had been overcome with waves of nausea and had stepped outside to heave up the little that was in her stomach. When she came back inside, her mother looked at her knowingly and the two women's eyes met in a glance of joy. Sarah was expecting. It was extraordinary and yet ordinary after their years apart she could share this secret with her mother. Lettia would not say anything. Sarah would tell Adam at the appropriate moment. If they stayed at this house, it would be the second baby born at Knox Headquarters. Elisabeth Stoner having given birth in mid July.

All the idle talk, snippets of gossip among the kitchen help and the little her husband told her, indicated the war was winding down. She prayed the gossip was true and there would be no late summer or fall campaign. This would be the last year of the war. Then, perhaps her brother Jupiter would join them and they could live in peace in Marblehead.

Still, the parade grounds were filled with soldiers incessantly drilling. On some days, the camp was empty as Regiments left for long marches lasting over two or three days. Sarah never knew whether the army was proceeding south and smiled joyfully when the tired troops returned to the encampment. She took as a hopeful sign the growing number of wives and children who had joined the soldiers.

They would not be here, she reasoned, if the army were preparing to attack New York.

Late in the afternoon following supper she would take her mother to a cordwainer in a Rhode Island Regiment to have shoes made for her. Lettia said she had walked barefoot almost her entire life and had no need for them but Sarah, who had experienced the prior severe winters, insisted. She liked taking care of her mother who had endured so much suffering and deprivation in her life as a slave. Even now in freedom, when Lettia got that faraway look, Sarah knew she was thinking of Jupiter. She mourned her missing son. This woman, who had so much motherly love to give, had seen all her children but two, Sarah and Jupiter, torn away from her caring arms and sold to other masters.

Adam appeared around the corner of the house with the two tousle-haired Henrys. He cut a piece of washed carrot with his whittling knife for each of them and walked up to Sarah, waving an envelope.

"It came with the dispatches," he said kissing her first. "Addressed to Master Sergeant Adam Cooper, " he said bowing. "At your service. Tis from Sexton Peter Williams so it is for you to read." He kissed her again. "I have been ordered by General Knox to remove the boys from underfoot. I will take the two Henrys for an adventure along the mill creek. We will not return until we have captured at least four frogs to frighten their mothers." He kissed Lettia on the top of the little cotton cap that covered her white hair, peered in on sleeping Emmanuel, and with each little one holding his hand, he skipped with them down toward the creek, their sturdy white legs showing from under their plain linen shifts.

Even though Sarah was anxious to read the letter, she tucked it in her apron pocket and went back into the kitchen to look at the apple pies baking in the brick oven. She had made a cross-hatched design of flour strips. Mrs. Knox had asked for them for tonight's dinner with the ladies and few remaining staff. Only after she had placed the golden brown pies on the window to cool, did she sit down and open the letter. It was short.

Dear Sarah: It is with great joy that I inform you, your brother Jupiter is now safely sheltered within our Church. He was kidnapped and enslaved on a Long Island Plantation. I hasten to assure you he is in good health and spirits. Praise be to the Lord for returning him to us. He now assists me in my tasks and I am once again teaching him to read and write. Soon I hope he will be able to send you and his Mother a letter by his own hand. There is much turmoil in the City as well as hope for an end to this terrible war. I cannot Fortell what will happen when Peace arrives. It is all God's Will. I pray for your family to be reunited with God's blessing.

Peter Williams – Sexton, John Street Methodist Church

Sarah wiped her eyes with a corner of her apron and went outside to tell Lettia the good news. The old woman's shoulders shook as she cried uncontrollably with joy that her son was alive and safe.

"He must come here" she said emphatically, pointing with an unwashed carrot at the ground. "He must come here," she repeated.

Sarah's response that it was not possible right now did nothing to assuage her. Only when Sarah said she would talk to Adam and he would find a way did the old woman cease her demands.

Following supper, Adam joined them and the family walked down the road in the early evening dusk to the tents of the Rhode Islanders. Adam carried his sleeping son in the crook of his thick forearm. After asking directions they found the shoemaker, a spidery thin man, sitting at a rough hewn log bench before a fire outside his tent. He was stitching the side quarters to a shank of hard leather. Adam was surprised to see a short Negro private squatting next to him. He was cutting a thick piece of tanned cowhide spread out on a plank with a curved knife. The private seemed equally surprised to see the epaulets on Adam's shoulders indicating his rank of Master Sergeant.

"We need a pair of shoes for my wife's mother," Adam said. The shoemaker peered around his bench at Lettia's feet. "They are small and gnarled," he observed. "Leather be sure to rub those old bones raw." He shook his head. "I would fit her with moccasins, ankle high. Deerskin is softer and will not chafe. Also cheaper," he added, eyeing Adam to see how he reacted to having to spend less money.

"You and I have both served as Continentals since the beginning of this war," Adam said, noting the two inverted white V stripes on the shoemaker's blue jacket. "Were you a cordwainer before?"

"It was my small ability before I began my six years of service," he replied, noting as well the inverted Vs on Adam's shoulder. "I repair and make shoes and boots and earn a shilling or two in the bargain. It helps to pay for necessities since Congress neither pays nor provides what we were promised. You have a family so you know what I mean."

Adam grunted in agreement. Nobody on General Knox's staff had been paid for years. The General, when able, provided them with small amounts of money out of his own funds and shared his larder with the officers of his headquarters.

"How much to make a pair of moccasins for my wife's mother?"

"Depends what you have to pay me. I will not take Continentals. Nor New York paper money neither." He stood up and stretched his back. "Ten shillings even," he said with finality.

"We are brother soldiers. There must be some consideration for that."

"All who need my services are brother soldiers," the shoemaker replied curtly, driving his pegging needle forcefully through the sole.

Sarah intervened before Adam could reply. "My mother's feet are small. You will use less deerskin than for a normal pair and have some left over for other purposes. Five shillings is all we will pay, in hard coin."

The cordwainer gestured for Lettia to put one foot up on his bench and made a show of studying it. "Eight shillings and that is my final price."

"Six payable in advance. Not a pence more," Sarah responded.

"Done," said the shoemaker holding out his hand. Sarah reached into the pouch she wore beneath her waistband and counted out six shillings. Adam stood to the side, while the cobbler traced Lettia's feet with a piece of charcoal on a thick piece of deerskin.

"And what is your name?" Adam asked the private, a bit more gruffly than he intended.

"Private Gideon Hazzard," he replied not rising from his squat as he finished cutting the piece of leather with the curved knife. "Your accent tells me you are from Massachusetts."

"Marblehead, north of Boston. Are you a shoemaker too?"

"No. I was a caulker in the Providence shipyards. I am learning this trade for when the war ends. There will be more need for shoemakers than ship builders. I do not intend to work for anyone other than myself when peace comes."

Adam nodded in agreement. Gideon's answer made sense to him. A free Negro working for a white man would always be treated more as a servant than an employee, and more often than not taken advantage of to boot. He was thankful he owned his own fishing dory and nets and could sell his catch to whomever he wished.

As the shoemaker traced the outline of Lettia's other foot, Adam noticed two riflemen watching impatiently. They were both tall and lean, clothed in dirty linen shirts that came down midthigh, with fringed shoulder capes, typical of the riflemen assigned to regular Continental regiments.

"You goin to take all evenin chattin with these Negrahs," one of them said. "Wez in your regiment 'n spect speshul treatment."

Sarah moved closer to Adam and took baby Emmanuel from his arms. As she did so, she brushed her hand along her husband's shoulder in a soothing and calming manner. Her familiar gesture signaled, as she had done on many previous occasions, he should control his temper. Adam noted out of the corner of his eye, Hazzard had risen from squatting and stood one foot forward with the evil looking curved knife in his hand. It was nothing more than a moment of acknowledgment but Adam knew that it would be two against two.

"I am done. They will be ready in three days," the shoemaker said to Sarah. "Return then." He turned to the two riflemen. "Now, gentlemen, what do you need?"

In the gathering darkness, Adam and Sarah mindful of Lettia's shuffling gait, walked slowly back to Knox's headquarters. Sarah, having returned Emmanuel to her husband, placed her hand in his and entwined their fingers.

"Our son sleeps well despite the noise around him," she said, smiling at the infant's capped head.

"I could bring charges against those two," Adam said angrily, ignoring his wife's desire to calm him. "For disrespecting my rank."

"No good would come of it, Adam. I look forward to the day when you bring me, our son, my mother and brother to Marblehead. There we will settle in our own home and live as a free family in a free country."

"You may be placing too much faith on the extent of freedom we will have, Sarah." Despite his angry tone, he squeezed her hand affectionately, his thoughts wandering to being at sea once again, fishing on the open waters with his wife and son awaiting him at home.

In the early evening the day before the Sabbath, Adam, accompanied by Will, returned to the Rhode Islanders' camp to get Lettia's moccasins.

"Do not tell me that it is mere coincidence you need to inquire of this cordwainer about repairs to Elisabeth's shoes," Adam said with some annoyance, pointing at the dainty silk footwear Will clutched in one hand, "at the same time as I decide to go there for Lettia's moccasins."

Will laughed at his friend's irritation. "Adam. We both know our spouses conspire and collude to keep us safe from what they perceive as potential harm. Sarah spoke to Elisabeth who in turn has asked me to accompany you. Her shoes are but a pretext. I am not armed though. You have proven long ago, you are better in a melee than I."

"That is true, Will. However, you are white and an officer. That will deter any mischief by ignorant riflemen more than my fists and fighting prowess."

With a nod of his head, Will acknowledged Adam's point and sheepishly tucked his wife's refined petite shoes inside his jacket.

"Besides," Adam continued, "this shoemaker is a rough sort. More used to making boots and shoes for marching. He would hardly know what to do with those of Elisabeth's. You could have thought of a more reasonable ruse than that." Now it was his turn to be amused at his friend's embarrassment at being found out.

When they arrived, the shoemaker, true to his word, ducked into his tent and returned with a pair of small moccasins that he handed over. Adam made a show of studying the stitching and rubbing his hand inside to feel for rough edges. "Well done. And where is Private Hazzard this evening?"

The soldier pointed vaguely with the thick needle he held in his hand in the direction of a row of tents. "May be over there. Some papers and broadsides came in from Providence. Gideon reads them to the Negroes in our Regiment."

Adam led the way along the paths created by the neat rows of tents, past the campfires of the men until they found Hazzard sitting on an upright stump in a flat area beyond the tent line. More than thirty men sat on the ground in a rough semi-circle around him, the orange flames from a fire burnishing their intent faces.

Hazzard looked quizzically at Will, the only white in the gathering, and nodded at Adam in recognition. He folded the sheet of newspaper and continued reading. "This is from the Providence Gazette of 3rd August," he said loudly. "Only four days ago."

"Besides the account given in our last, of the evacuation of Savannah, we have the pleasure of assuring our readers, that the garrison had arrived at Charlestown before some persons (who had arrived in town yesterday having left Charlestown which was on the 11th ult.) They say that St. Augustine was certainly abandoned by the enemy."

There was a confused murmur among the soldiers.

"Let me finish reading and then I will explain it," Gideon said and the muttering died down.

"In addition to the above article our informant says, that a number of heavy cannon &c. were embarked on board some vessels in Charlestown harbour, and that every appearance indicated a speedy removal of all British forces from the quarter."[3]

"What does this mean? " a voice shouted from the darkness.

"Where is this Saint some place you read out?" another asked.

The Hand of Providence

Hazzard folded the paper under his arm and stood with one foot on the stump.

"What it says is sometime before July, the British left Savannah. Then on the 11th of July, when our troops were outside the city, the people who brought the news to Providence left Charlestown. The British were loading their cannons on their ships. That means they will be leaving Charlestown soon as well." He paused, checked the newspaper and ran his finger down the column. "It does not say when the British left St. Augustine. Savannah is in the colony of Georgia. St. Augustine is south of there."

"Where is this Charlestown?"

"That is in the colony of South Carolina," Hazzard answered. "It means the British are leaving the ports they occupied in our southern colonies. It may mean the war is coming to an end."

The semi-circle was quiet as the men contemplated the possibility of no more war and a return to their homes.

Shouted questions filled the air - would they be paid when peace comes, could they keep their muskets- what about uniforms? Adam and Will left as Hazzard responded patiently in a calm deep voice.

"Those are questions on every soldier's mind," Will observed. "As for the officers, having been promised pensions as well, there is much talk as to whether Congress will honor its commitments or simply order the Army to disband."

"For once, I hope we Negro soldiers will be treated the same as whites. The members of Congress from the southern colonies objected to our even serving in the army. Perhaps they will vote to pay only the white soldiers and not the Negroes."

Will clapped Adam on the shoulder. "Why do you always talk about Negroes and whites? My belief, having heard of some of the statements made in Philadelphia, is none of us will be paid a single dollar of what we have been promised. Congress has no need for the army after the peace is signed."

"I speak of Negroes because I am one and feel what you do not. The news Hazzard read. Did you note what is missing?"

Will slowed his walk and puzzled over Adam's question. "No," he said, shaking his head. "Tell me."

"Tis well known the British offer freedom to slaves of patriot owners who flee to their lines. What happened to those slaves in Charlestown and Savannah?" Adam asked bitterly. "Were they evacuated on British ships to continue being free? Or were they abandoned to be reclaimed by their former masters and returned to a life of slavery? You saw that yourself at Yorktown. Those are the questions I want answers to."

"The newspaper did not report on their fate," Will conceded.

"Did you not also notice an omission in our last month's Independence celebration?"

Will thought for a moment. "No, Adam. I did not. The Regiments paraded, the military bands played, bonfires were lit at night and the men, in compliance with General Washington's orders of the day, received double rations of rum."

"There was no reading of the Declaration of Independence," Adam said grimly.

"We have been together on other Fourths when it has not been read. I do not take your meaning."

"Will," Adam said in exasperation. "We are coming to the end of the war. Everyone thinks so. We will be our own rulers. And the words of the Declaration – 'that all men are created equal with certain rights including life, liberty and the pursuit of happiness' and this is not read on what is probably the last July 4th of the war?" Adam's voice rose and a few soldiers passing them stared at him. "Will, do you not see? It is as plain as your face. After the war they do not intend to extend these rights to Negroes."

"Your reasoning is strained," Will replied. "You place too much emphasis on an omission that is simply unwarranted." He raised a finger as Adam was about to interrupt him. "I have a question for you. Why would General Washington direct the Declaration not to be read to an army of more than five thousand soldiers where only a handful, say a few hundred are Negroes?"

"Because he is a slave owner," Adam swiftly replied. Will had no response and they left the dirt path that led between the tents of

The Hand of Providence

the Headquarters Troops in silence and walked rapidly on to the Goshen Road.

Will was about to defuse the tension between them when a private coming toward them on the road called out. "Lieutenant Stoner. Captain Hadley wishes to see you. Immediately."

Hadley had accompanied General Knox to West Point. If he was back, perhaps the General had returned as well. Inside Knox's headquarters, the large rooms on the first floor that had been empty, once again served as conference rooms, filled with officers meeting and drafting orders.

"Ah there you are," Hadley said as Will entered the room. "The General has been ordered to assume command at West Point.[4] The entire staff is to leave tomorrow accompanied by the Headquarters troops. Two Regiments to follow a day later."

It was an easy half a day's ride for the staff. Will calculated if the soldiers marched rapidly they could cover the roughly eighteen miles in a day's march. Hopefully, their supply wagons with tents, cots and cooking equipment would arrive before nightfall. "No families to accompany until further orders," Hadley said anticipating Will's next question.

Having been with the General throughout the war, Will was reasonably certain Lucy Knox would not tolerate being separated from her husband for very long. Will would tell Elisabeth to be prepared to travel with Mrs. Knox and the children. Hopefully, he would be reunited with Henry and baby Agnes by the end of August, if not sooner.

Chapter 7 - Tragedy at West Point

They left their muskets, with bayonets fixed, stacked twelve to a pyramid. They trooped instead with shovels and pick axes on their shoulders through the early morning heavy dew to the river below the fort at West Point. The mist on the Hudson was just beginning to burn off as the sun rose higher, shining on the fortifications across the water on the shores of Constitution Island.

"At least this time, we will not be hauling wheelbarrows across twenty foot chasms," one of the veterans remarked, as they marched along the rocky flat beach. "Twenty foot," another snorted. "More like sixty across and eighty feet down." The distance and depth became greater with each retelling by the veterans to the new replacements.

Sergeant Henry Gillet smiled to himself, recalling how he had led his men on to the narrow boards spanning the gorge on the Island. That had been in October of '80. He had overcome his fear of heights and vowed not to be placed in such a dangerous position again. He had convinced Private Gideon Hazzard to enlist with him in the sappers and miners and they ended up in front of the troops assaulting the redoubts at Yorktown. Having enough of that more dangerous duty, he and Hazzard had returned to the 2nd Rhode Islanders. And here they were again at West Point, reinforcing the fortifications in Captain-Lieutenant Tew's Company.

From the shore they could see the booms that supported the

great chain spanning the river at the narrowest point. The ends were marked by iron links anchored in rock filled rectangular wooden cribs. Nearby were the wooden windlasses used for raising the chain in late fall and laying it out in the spring. Gillet hoped by next spring there would be no need to put the chain back in the river to block British warships from proceeding further up the Hudson.

The fact they had been ordered to West Point to rebuild the fortifications, magazines and gun positions indicated to some the British might be planning a combined assault. On the other hand, Gillet reasoned, there were many other signs of a cessation of hostilities. The British had evacuated the ports they had previously taken in the southern colonies. There had been no offensive action north of New York. Since April and the arrival of the new British commander, American prisoners of war had been released. Sutlers and those who came through the lines from New York reported the Loyalists in the city were in despair. But yet, here they were preparing defenses against a major assault. It did not make sense to him.

Gillet's latest letter from his wife indicated rumors of peace were rampant in Providence. She was still attending to the released prisoners of war, reporting only a few more had arrived. Several of those had died of fevers and other ailments brought on by their imprisonment. He was worried for her health, especially now she had revealed the joyous news of her being pregnant with their second child. He knew how quickly fevers could arise and strike down even those who had been healthy the day before. He should be home attending to her needs and receiving hard money as a ship's carpenter, rather than building stone and earthen bulwarks against British cannon balls. He was envious of Hazzard who, having learned shoemaking, was now earning silver coins from soldiers in the Regiment who were able to pay for his services.[1]

That night, he wandered past the soldiers' haphazardly scattered tents. Captain- Lieutenant Tew had ineptly selected the rocky ground of an old gravel pit for their camp. At Tew's tent, he asked for and received a sheet of paper and envelope, a small quantity of ink and a quill in need of sharpening. Dispatches and letters were being sent to Providence in a few days. If he returned his letter to Judith in time, Tew would see that it was included.

Wandering back to his fire, Gillet used a borrowed bible from one of the men as his writing table and composed a letter to wife, adding a postscript to his daughter. He reminded Sally to be an obedient child and promised to be home as soon as he was able. When would that be he thought. The men resting around their fires were engaged in the same conversations they had every night – whether it was continued war or peace.

Gillet shook his head. All of these assumptions and rumors were like smoke from their cooking fires – present in the air but of no consequence. Rather than attempting to sift through scraps of news, intelligence, and gossip, Gillet thought it best to wait and see. He took the pocketknife he had used to carve the quill to a point and cut off a lock of his hair, inserted it in the envelope and sealed it with wax from his candle. He hoped it would be bring good luck to Judith and protect her and his little Sally from disease.

—⚏—

The two story wooden building with a wide porch on a bluff overlooking the Hudson served as General Knox's headquarters at West Point. It was far more modest than the solid stone mansion the General had lived in near the New Windsor Cantonment. Knox eschewed the more spacious and luxurious Robinson home on the east side of the river both because it was inconvenient and for the memories of Arnold's treason and his wife's feigned madness.

Since there was no room for the married staff to be accommodated in the smaller house, Will and Elisabeth, together with Henry and baby Agnes were quartered in a rough hewn, drafty cabin within the fort, as were Captain Hadley and Mercy with their one year old son, Benjamin.

As long as the pleasant fall weather lasted, it was but a short wagon ride to the Knox's home. Almost every morning, Mercy and Elisabeth together with their children made this trip through the surrounding woods, resplendent with splashes of bright yellows, reds and oranges interspersed amongst the patches of deep green from the conifers dotting the hillsides, to pass the day with Mrs. Knox. Once there, the two Henrys caused much mischief and disruption until Mrs. Knox recruited a young private on boring sentry duty to keep the boys amused outdoors. Little Lucy was permitted to join the ladies for afternoon teas and rock the cradle holding Will and Elisabeth's baby, while her own baby brother napped nearby. The teas were frequently enhanced by some breads with jams or even a special cake that Sarah Cooper had managed to bake in the oven at the Fort. When on occasion Sarah brought the fresh bread or cake herself, Mrs. Knox invited her to sit with the ladies and join the conversation. It always came around to when the war would be over.

At least two days a week, sometimes more, the General returned in the late afternoon "to his sweet babes," as he called all the children. He would stay for his dinner before riding back to the Fort to attend staff meetings. Elisabeth told Will he played with the boys while cradling little Marcus in his forearm. Once it was dark and the candles had been lit, Knox made shadow animals with his fingers on the unadorned wall. The two Henrys would sit cross-legged on the floor begging for more as the General conjured up rabbits, birds and dogs.

"I have never seen the General so happy," Elisabeth said, one night lying in bed as she suckled Agnes.

Will pulled off his boots and lay down next to her, stroking her blond hair. "He races through the business of our meetings, reviews reports of modifications to the fortifications in the morning and rides out to inspect them himself, before returning to deal with dispatches and correspondence."

"He works at such a pace so as to spend part of the afternoons with the children and his wife," Elisabeth observed. "His energy and strength comes from the love of his family," she continued, resting her other hand on Will's chest. As she hoped, Will grasped the thread of her thoughts.

"As is most true for me as well, my love." He turned and kissed her gently on her ear.

"Even in these drafty and makeshift quarters, I feel content with you and our dear children by my side." He sighed deeply. "I have a confession to make." Elisabeth tensed slightly, anticipating the unraveling of thoughts of family bliss and the return of talk of war and revenge.

"In idle moments, my mind wanders to what our lives will be like when this war is over. I was a simple teamster before the war. Now I am skilled in artillery, hardly an occupation for peacetime."

Elisabeth smiled and shifted on her side so she could look at her husband. "You won my heart as a handsome teamster boy. Imagine how much more I love you now as a brave officer in the army that has won our freedom."

He smiled at her. "Being loved by my wife will not put food in the larder. There is no doubt Nat Holmes and Adam Cooper will return to their lives at sea, Nat as captain of some merchant vessel and Adam as a Marblehead fisherman. Samuel Hadley's older brother is a merchant in Boston. He will leave his captaincy and join his brother in the business. What will I do? What am I capable of doing?"

"True, my love of you is no substitute for an occupation," she replied. "I am confident there will be many opportunities for officers after the war. You are trustworthy, honest, courageous and self-reliant. You have led men in battle. You have discipline and . . ."

"Stop," Will said, putting a finger to her lips. "You will make me Commander in Chief with all your exaggerated praise."

"I will cease but do not for a minute think of yourself as a simple teamster. Now," she said. "Our daughter is asleep. Get her blanket from the crib. There is a draft in our room. I want her to sleep between us to keep her warm."

When Mercy and Elisabeth visited with Mrs. Knox the following day, they found her tired from having been up most of the night with Marcus. The poor little boy had been coughing and crying, his nose clotted with snot. As the ladies took their tea, he slept fitfully, exhausted from his nighttime wailing.

"It seems like no more than a cold," Lucy said hopefully, "tho I would appreciate your opinion, Mercy."

"Let him sleep. 'Tis the best medicine for him. It will be time enough for me to examine him when he wakes." An hour later, while Lucy held her squirming eight month old son in her arms, Mercy looked into his eyes, gently pried open his mouth with her fingers to examine his throat, and placed her ear to his tiny exposed chest. "There is a burbling sound in his chest and his throat is red. Perhaps it is just from his wailing," she added reassuringly.

"What do you recommend, "Lucy asked with concern.

"A brew of sage or horehound tea, the latter mixed with honey. It should soothe his sore throat." Mercy rose from her chair. "I will boil up enough tea for little Marcus to sip and to heat and soak onto a linen and place on his chest when he falls back to sleep."

When Elisabeth and Mercy left with Henry and Benjamin in the early evening, General Knox was seated in a chair before the fireplace, his infant son cradled in his arm, with a sage tea soaked linen cloth underneath Marcus' tiny shirt.

Over the next few days, the little boy's condition deteriorated with greater swelling of the throat and difficulty in breathing. None of the herbal medicines had lessened his sore throat or the congestion. When Mercy inquired of Dr. Eustis if she could be of any assistance, the doctor shook his head. "Tis throat distemper," he concluded, "I can do no more."[2]

The following morning, General Knox did not come to the fort. Shortly before noon, one of the household guards arrived, and after meeting with Colonel Winthrop Sargent informed Elisabeth and Mercy the babe had passed and General Knox asked if they would kindly attend to his wife.

At the Knox home, the two women found Mrs. Knox in the bedroom, still wearing her night dress, her dark hair disheveled, sobbing and holding the dead infant to her bosom. Her normal blooming complexion was as gray as if she herself had died.

"I would be most appreciative if one of you would stay here with my dear wife, while the other comfort little Lucy and Henry. I myself am inconsolable, bereft of all rational thought and unable to offer any support," Knox said. He ignored the tears rolling down his cheeks and shook his head in disbelief. "Our poor little babe taken from us. The light has gone out in my heart. My mind sees nothing other than the severe anguish and suffering my beloved wife and I must endure." He stood by the window, alternately looking out at the river and returning his gaze to Lucy sobbing on the bed.

That evening, Elisabeth reported to Will. "Neither of them took any nourishment while we were there, save for a cup of tea. The General is so overwhelmed with grief he is unable to see his way from one day to the next."

"What do you mean?" Will asked.

"You are a father. Think of how the death of our precious son would devastate us. The General has gone from the highest peak of joy to deepest despair. His grief does not permit him to engage in normal human intercourse – to let any emotion in to help him heal.[3] Mercy is of the same opinion."

"I will speak with Samuel. We must do something."

The next morning, after consulting with Colonel Sargent, it was agreed that Hadley and Will would alternate, one of them attending to the General as a personal aide to provide companionship and support should he so need. Will rode to the Knox's home and found, to his consternation, he was already too late. According to the sentries, General Knox had saddled his horse and ridden off in the dull grey morning by himself.

"He went in the direction of Butter Hill," one of them said helpfully, pointing toward the yellowish hued mountain a few miles west beyond the Fort. Will rode at a gallop to the sloping base where the trail forked. The left fork continued over flat terrain around the northwestern side, the other circled easterly toward the end of the mountain that rose perpendicular from the shore. Will chose the foreboding right fork toward the huge boulders jutting from the base of the mountain into the river.

In about four hundred yards he found the General's mare loosely tethered to a tall evergreen. Will dismounted, and confident that Big Red would not wander far, left him to graze amongst the small patches of grass among the moss covered rocks. He followed the narrow path uphill between jagged boulders and soon was compelled to clamber over rocks using the roots of scrawny bushes as handholds. He began to doubt the General had come this way, but turning a bend he saw Knox ahead, seated on a flat granite slab gazing out across the river. His shoulders were hunched, his bare-head bowed with his tri-corn carelessly cast aside next to him.

Will stood frozen in place, fearing that if he approached or cried out, the General would become angry he was being spied upon in this moment of his extreme private grief.

Big Red whinnied from the valley below. The General turned his bare head toward the sound and saw Will who had stepped out from behind a grey boulder. With a slight gesture of his hand Knox both acknowledged his presence and waved him away. He clearly wanted to be alone. Will retreated down the mountain and led Big Red away from Knox's tethered horse. They waited in a glen surrounded by steep rocky cliffs where Will could observe the General's mare. Knox did not descend until the late afternoon shadows deepened and there was a chill in the air. Will followed him riding many yards behind, departing only when the General reached his home.

The next evening, Hadley compared his observations of the General's self-imposed seclusion with Will's. Knox followed the same route, leaving his horse and climbing to the isolated perch above the Hudson where he had remained for several hours.

"As far as I am able to tell, he takes neither food nor water with him. Perhaps upon his return home he does partake of some nourishment," Samuel suggested.

"Elisabeth was with Mrs. Knox, when the General returned," Will said. "She reports the two of them sat by the hearth, he holding their Henry, Mrs. Knox brushing her daughter's hair and not three words passing between them. She too, poor soul ate but the slightest tidbits during the day."

The same somber routine continued for two more days. On the fifth day following Marcus' death, with Will following at a respectful distance, Knox took the fork to the left at the base of Butter Hill. He rode slowly, with his head down and shoulders slumped, like a man who had fallen asleep on his horse. The trail ambled away from the grim granite and toward the sloping fields of grass that clothed the spaces between the rounded yellow boulders in a green mantle.

This morning, the General did not dismount but proceeded slowly around the base of the mountain and then onto a dirt wagon road that cut through the highland forest. At some point, he left his horse and walked amongst the trees disappearing from Will's sight.

After tethering Big Red near the General's horse, Will cautiously entered the forest, following a narrow muddy trail through the thick carpet of brown leaves. He found Knox sitting on a fallen log at the edge of a clearing. Beyond him, a tall barren beech, devoid of leaves, its weathered trunk and branches leaning toward the clearing, seemed to beseech the heavens for an answer. Knox sat, head bowed in the bright noonday sun, his shoulders shaking as he sobbed quietly. When his grief-stricken cries subsided, he raised his face to the cloudless sky above, stumbled forward several feet into the field and dropped his cape. Knox raised his open hands and trembled in what seemed to Will to be a gesture of both disbelief and acceptance. He picked up his cape and slowly plodded back through the clearing. He motioned to Will to join him.

They walked slowly together toward their horses through the mud from a recent rain. Will presumed to put his arm around the General's shoulder. The General did not shrug it off but reached across his own chest and patted Will's hand. "I fervently pray you never experience the loss of a precious child. The Supreme Being has prevented our dear son from ripening into manhood and becoming a blessing to me and Lucy."

Will could think of nothing to say to ease the General's grief.

"I know you and Captain Hadley have been concerned for my well-being. It is a sign of your affection for me, all the more critical to me in my time of trial," he continued. "I recognize my dear Lucy and my surviving children need me and I have failed them."

"No Sir. You have not," Will said emphatically.

"I have been absent for them, as much as a soldier who deserts his fellows in time of battle. An absence as terrible as treasonous betrayal," Knox insisted. "I have failed you and Samuel and the others of my staff as well. I am not only your commander but one who should set an example should such a disaster ever befall you."

"Sir," Will said gently. "You have not failed me, nor any of the others. You have been as a father to me. You have taught me much and placed your faith and confidence in my meager abilities. Tis you who have enabled me to develop into the soldier, husband and father that I am. Before I met you, I was nothing."

The General shrugged Will's arm from his shoulder. "Providence, not I made you who you are. I tell you Will, it has been Providence that dealt me this grievous blow, the hardest one I have received in my life. The Supreme Being is involved in all human events." Choking back tears he said, "it is a deep mystery why my precious Marcus has been taken from us. The lesson from my sorrow Will is to accept the blow even though it comes from on High, draw strength from those who love you, and persevere. Do you understand?"

"Yes Sir. I do."

"Persevere. That is the watchword. Now," he said, straightening up to his full height, "please accompany me as I ride to my dearest friend and our beloved children, to offer them the strength and comfort I have failed to provide these past several days."

When they returned, the incongruous sounds of laughter filled the field outside the Knox home. The two Henrys were romping about, playing a game of tag only the two of them understood. Elisabeth sat with Mrs. Knox on the small covered porch in the shadows, shielded from the bright fall sun. She was nursing Agnes as Mrs. Knox brushed Lucy's hair. The entire scene would have been idyllic but for the tragic loss of baby Marcus.

"I will tell the boys to cease their gamboling about. It is unseemly," Will said, apologetically.

"No. They do not understand death and mean no harm. Besides, their laughter and games are like a balm to my wounded heart." Knox stopped his mare and watched the two Henrys running through the tall grass. "You and I have seen enough death in fields like this to last our lifetimes. I pray that Divine Providence permits us to live out our days in peace and tranquility in the normal order of things," the General said softly.[4]

Will thought of the fields across from their lines at Trenton, filled with ranks of Redcoats marching toward the narrow bridge and the sound of the grapeshot from his cannon tearing into their flesh until the corpses piled up like cordwood on the cobblestones. Or the fields beyond Brandywine Creek where he and his crew had fired round after round of eighteen pound balls into the rigid lines of Redcoats, opening wide swaths in their tight ranks, until overwhelmed by the advancing Grenadiers, they were forced to retreat, leaving their own dead behind. The wounded to be bayoneted by the victorious Grenadiers. Yes, Will thought. I have seen enough and am tired of war.

"Lucy and I must leave this place if we are to return to any semblance of normal family life," the General said softly, as if speaking his thoughts outloud. "I will ask His Excellency to reassign me temporarily to New Windsor. Colonel Sargent will carry out my plans to strengthen West Point. And you, Will. You must return with us. Elisabeth is of great comfort to my poor Lucy as you are to me."

"I will obey whatever orders you give me," Will replied, thinking of how happy they had all been at Knox's headquarters and home outside New Windsor. The death of Marcus would follow them to New Windsor. That morning on the ride over, their son Henry had asked where the baby had gone. How does one explain death and heaven to a two year old? Elisabeth had tried in the simplest terms. Baby Marcus had gone away and we will all see him after a long, long time in a better place. Henry in his innocence had repeated, "baby Marcus gone," baby Marcus gone," until he mercifully was distracted by the sight of his friend Henry waiting on the porch with his mother and little Lucy.

—ːW—

The men of the 3rd New Jersey Regiment, like all the soldiers in New Windsor, were tired of the incessant drilling and marching. They grumbled while they went through the routines they knew so well – wheeling by platoons, sections and then companies to the right or left, forming up as companies, closing up platoons and columns, changing direction mid-march, quick march – all to the drum signals they now responded to instinctively.

At night, tired from the physical exertion, the men not charged with sentry duty, sat around their cooking fires chatting and sifting bits of information, attempting to separate fact from rumor. One had heard from a friend in another regiment the British had released prisoners only to spread disease among the populace and an entire town in New Jersey had succumbed to prison fever. Someone else opined a teamster who had been to New York reported the forts to the north of the city had been strengthened with many cannons. A frontal assault would be a bloody slaughter. These campfire conversations always skirted back to the soldiers' main concern – when peace came, would Congress disband the Army without paying them.

The building of the huts for the cantonment was a welcome diversion from the tedious drilling and their worries. With the weather turning colder, the men were eager to move out of their tents before the winter snows came. Each morning men trooped into the woods to fell trees with saws and axes, hewing hatchets and all manner of tools. Some dug saw pits with pick axes and shovels in the not yet frozen ground. Others hewed the rounded trunks into thick rectangular beams using adzes newly made in the army's blacksmith sheds. Still others, using froes and mauls created piles of shingles from the newly split wood. Teams of horses moved among the working parties and pulled the roughly cut beams back to the cantonment site. There, soldiers were constructing the huts in orderly rows on the flat ground encircling a low hill. A haze of blue smoke hung over the camp as blacksmiths kept their forges burning to satisfy the need for nails, hinges and other hardware, as well as repairing the axes and saws constantly in use. It was as if a horde of human beavers had been released upon the land.

As he had done for the past week, Corporal Caleb Wade led his squad of eight into the pine forest to a cleared space filled with felled trees. There, they set to work cutting and sawing the trees into eighteen-foot logs, the width specified for each of the huts and splitting the excess for shingles.

Vose bent over panting, staring down at his broad axe wedged firmly in the center of an elm log. He could see little puffs of his breath in the cold winter air. Wade came over and placed his hand on his friend's shoulder.

"You have not yet regained your strength," he said. "I can have you invalided for sentry duty."

Matthias waved him off. "No need. I have rebuilt my spirit and now must do the same for my body. Listen," he said, harking to the sounds of axes biting into tree trunks, the crash of trees striking the hard earth and the ringing sounds of blacksmiths' hammers striking anvils in some kind of clarion call urging the men in the woods to work on.

"First, let me help you. Then I will listen," Caleb said, striking one side of Matthias' axe head and then the other to loosen it. "With unseasoned wood, your axe is wedged in the middle. Strike more to the sides instead of the center to split pieces from the log," he said grunting as he pulled his friend's axe out.

"The sounds of our work are music to the Lord's ears. With so many working in a common cause, we will build our city of huts in no time. Then, our work will begin in earnest to steer our brothers from sinful practices to honoring the Lord."

Wade smiled and said nothing. He and Matthias had spoken about this before. Once the soldiers were snug in their cabins, idleness would set in. Many would turn to drink and gambling at cards and dice. And women. Already there were more than five hundred women and children around camp, many wives of soldiers but some unattached and of loose morals. It was Matthias' idea to go from hut to hut in their own Regiment first, and preach the word of God. Wade had agreed to accompany him, mostly to protect him from the wrath of those engaged in their vices. He did not believe in forcing his religious beliefs upon others, no matter how much he himself believed in Divine Will.

Vose straightened his back. Following his friend's advice, he swung his axe toward the side of the upright log, driving it deep and splitting a wooden slab almost half way down its length. Caleb smiled at Matthias, thinking how he himself had ceased his drunken and carousing ways. Now it was Matthias, who had seized the righteous path, imbued with an intense fervor, seeing the hand of Providence in his escape and the release of prisoners. There was no deterring him from his stated purpose to preach to the captive audience of soldiers soon to be snow bound in their winter quarters.

By mid-December, the men of the 3rd New Jersey Regiment, and most of the soldiers at New Windsor, were comfortably ensconced in their huts. Each was identical with a long overhang on one side, dried mud between the beams to keep out the drafts, two shuttered windows for the loft and one at ground level next to the crude central door fitted to a sill to block the rain and snow from seeping in. Large stone fireplaces, constructed by those soldiers with masonry skills, stood at both ends of the huts. Inside the men slept on two levels of roughly hewn bunk beds, twenty-six to thirty-four per hut. The huts were arranged in three rows of nine each. The latrines were behind the last row of huts.

The officers' cabins were about forty yards up the slope. Larger than those for the ordinary soldiers each housed the Regiment's Colonel, the Major, two Captains and the three Lieutenants.

At the first Sabbath following their relocation to the cabins, the Regimental Chaplain announced another building to be erected, this one to the Lord on High.

"A Temple of Virtue," Vose repeated as they left services. "Caleb, this is an act of the Divine, knowing of man's propensity to sin. He has directed General Washington to order the construction of this Temple for the salvation of the souls of the soldiers."

"It will also serve as a place for court martials, officers' conferences and concert hall, as well as a chapel," Wade observed drily, recalling the Chaplain's words.

His comment did not diminish Matthias's enthusiasm. "It will be a beacon of righteousness for the men. It will be big enough for our regiment to worship together with others. That will surely induce more to attend. And music is also good for the soul as long as it does not involve lewd dancing and drink," he observed. "We must put in our names with the Lieutenant as volunteers."[5]

"I fear, with the bitterness of a harsh winter approaching, there will be few volunteers and more conscripted labor among our fellow soldiers to erect this Temple," Caleb remarked. In the following weeks, while some in their Regiment joined them in volunteering, mostly due to the entreaties of Matthias, the vast number of soldiers returning to the woods with their axes and saws, did so under orders. As the framework of the Temple rose on the hill, it was obvious to all it was the largest building of the cantonment, more than one hundred feet long and thirty feet wide.

On a frigid day early in the new year, when it was completed and before a single service had been conducted, Matthias insisted that he, Caleb and a few others enter the Temple to admire what he declared was the work of Providence. While Wade and Vose stood in the center under the high vaulted ceiling before the pulpit, the rest crowded in front of the fireplace near one end, stomping their feet and turning this way and that to warm their frozen bodies.

"On the Sabbath, when the Temple is crowded with men, their bodies and fervor will warm this place on the coldest of Sundays," Matthias said. "This building we have constructed with our own hands, motivated by our sincere faith, makes me think of the Sinagogue of old that we read of in the Bible."[6]

Caleb looked at the rough hewn logs, mud filling chinks here and there, the plain pewter sconces and the raised platform on one side for conducting courts martial and thought it was nothing like the description of the temple in Jerusalem. The look of rapture on his friend's face convinced him to say nothing. Let Matthias enjoy this moment. He had been through much since his capture by Loyalist raiders in New Jersey. For Wade, it was enough of a blessing Vose had survived.

Bant survived the late fall and early winter, spending as little time as possible sharing a tent with McNeil and four others, and as much time hunting in the forests around their camp. His prowess with his rifle brought down deer, turkeys and once even a moose and provided the soldiers of his company with welcome meat to supplement to their meager rations. It almost made him popular, although some still referred to him as the "lunatick," and were wary of him. His troublesome dreams had become less frequent. Housed in a wood hut with thirty others, the demons he suffered returned with a vengeance. One night he awoke screaming and awakened the others. The soldier in the bunk above him jumped down, grabbed him by his jug like ears and banged his head against the wooden bedpost, threatening to cut his throat to keep him quiet. McNeil seized the irate soldier around the neck and pulled him away.

After that, Bant volunteered for night sentry duty, hoping to sleep in the hut during the day when most of the men were in the woods splitting logs to keep the fires in the hearths burning. For several nights he joined the invalids guarding the slaughterhouse where the few slabs of beef were hung, awaiting distribution as short rations to the troops. Then, on four more nights, warming himself around a pyramid of logs, he performed the useless duty of guarding an untraveled road to the cantonment, as if the British were about to march out of the darkness and take the place by surprise.

This afternoon, unable to sleep, although the hut was deserted, he wandered aimlessly through the cantonment. Smoke from the numerous chimneys wafted up toward the grey wintry sky. He found himself amid rows of huts of another Brigade. The flag flying indicated they housed the 8th Connecticut Regiment. A few soldiers were about, on the paths between the huts. Bant watched a tall brawny man with a rope around his chest, hauling a sled heavy with newly split logs up the snow covered slope toward the officers' cabin.

Suddenly, he heard a scream and a woman fled from one of the officer's cabins, her hair flying out behind her, clutching her shawl as she ran down the slope. A man in his shirt sleeves stood in the door way, hopping from one foot to another as he struggled to put on his boots, before running after her. "Stop her," he shouted to the soldier pulling the sled. "Stop her now." The soldier, encumbered by the rope was not quick enough and slipped. He skidded down the slope along with the sled as the woman skirted around him and reached the path. She looked frantically both ways before turning toward Bant. By then, some soldiers had emerged from their huts to watch the long legged officer close the distance. Realizing she could not out run him, the woman dropped to her knees in front of Bant.

"Please sir. I am a simple washerwoman. He tried to rape me. Help me."

Bant stood his ground, unsure what to do.

"Stand aside, soldier," the officer commanded.

"Are you the lady's husband," Bant heard himself ask, surprised at his own brazenness. This provoked hoots of laughter from the soldiers standing in the doorways of their huts.

"Our Captain thinks he has a way with the women," came an anonymous shout.

"That he does. It seems this woman wishes to get out of his way," another yelled.

The Captain face turned red as his men erupted in peals of laughter.

"I order you to stand aside," the Captain shouted, his voice rising. When Bant did not move, he turned to some of his men.

"Take this man." No one moved. "To assist in a rape is a grievous sin," a voice thundered. "We will not be party to it."

The Captain turned, grabbed a stout log from the sled and advanced on Bant.

Bant slid his hunting knife from its sheath and held it in front of him.

"What? You threaten an officer," the Captain shouted, undecided whether to advance on Bant and risk getting cut, or to lose face in front of his men.

Bant said nothing and kept the broad bladed knife before him, his hand firmly around the bone handle. If the Captain advanced, he intended to inflict a slashing wound across the back of his hand. If he threw the log, Bant hoped he could dodge it and wait for the next move. If he used the log as a club, Bant would side step the Captain's advance and prick him in the thigh. He heard the woman quietly sobbing behind him. He felt as calm as when he sighted his rifle on a British officer's head, held his breath and squeezed the trigger.

The Captain, sensing Bant's determination and not willing to risk a knife cut, resorted to bluster.

"What is your name and Regiment," he demanded.

"Private Peter Bant of Colonel Hand's Riflemen, assigned to the 2nd Rhode Islanders." He deliberately omitted adding "Sir."

"I will have you court martialed for this," the Captain snarled, turning on his heel and mustering as much dignity as he could, stalked up the slope toward his hut. And then he slipped on the ice and fell to one knee to the hoots and jeers of his men.

Bant saw there was no threat from any other direction. He put his knife away and followed the woman down the road. Her name was Molly Frost and she was married to a Private in the 4th New Hampshire Regiment. When they reached her hut shared by several married couples, she invited him in and introduced Bant to her daughter, a skinny little barefoot thing who stared at him from behind her mother's apron. There were several other women inside, boiling shirts and breeches in large kettles, wringing them out by hand and hanging them on ropes in front of the hearth.

"I have nothing to offer but watered bark tea," she said ladling some out of a small pot hanging over the fire." While Bant sipped the liquid and stood in front of the low fire, Molly told the other wives when she had returned the laundry to Captain Brewster, he had lunged at her before she could get out the door, insisting he was entitled to more "favors" as he put it, before he paid for her work.

Bant was uncomfortable as the women smiled in appreciation and praised him for protecting Molly from this scoundrel. With none of the bravado he had displayed in confronting the Captain, he shyly put the mug down on the planked table and slipped out the door. He took care to return to his Regiment by a different route. He told McNeil what had happened, and expressed anxiety about being court martialed. McNeil thought the Captain would not have the nerve to do so for it would expose him to the charge of attempted rape of another soldier's wife.

"His own soldiers do not seem to hold him in much affection," McNeil added.

"Who would believe me, if the Captain brought charges and testified against me?" Bant asked his friend.

"The truth will win out," McNeil said reassuringly. That night Bant was not visited by his usual demons. Instead, he dreamed of being tied to a post and lashed mercilessly. He awakened with his shirt soaked with sweat, though only embers burned in the fireplace and a draft blew down the chimney.

—⚋—

This was the third court martial of the day. Lieutenant Willem Stoner sat self-consciously in the so-called Temple of Virtue, on the raised platform, with its wooden railing and white painted uprights separating the Court from the plain planked benches below. He was the most junior of the three officers and was nervous, never having been a judge in a court martial proceeding. General Knox had assigned him, stating that many of the other officers were on personal or medical furlough and the charges did not warrant a court composed of senior ranks. It was true that Captain Nat Holmes had returned to Marblehead, having received a letter from his wife that his mother was seriously ill. Nevertheless, Will felt uncomfortable judging ordinary soldiers for what he thought would be minor acts of mischief. He was sympathetic to their plight. The men were bored during the long winter days, unpaid, underfed and underemployed, and were bound to get into trouble.

It was chilly on the platform, too distant to benefit from the heat of the large hearth at the opposite end. The guards, the prisoners and the ones who would speak on their behalf, were warmer than the officers, he thought, as he sat rigidly on the hardwood high-backed chair. The presiding officer was Major John Armstrong of General Gates' staff. The other officer was Captain Jeremiah Wheeler of the 7th Massachusetts Regiment.

The first trial ended quickly. The accused, a Sergeant admitted to plundering a farmer who had come to camp to sell winter vegetables to the soldiers. When they adjourned to the conference room behind the dais, Will deferred to the two Officers and agreed to a punishment of a public reprimand, fifty lashes and demotion in rank by one grade.

The second, involved a Private who had become drunk and surly, started a brawl in his hut and broken another soldier's jaw. The court had rendered a verdict of thirty lashes, ten per week. Will said nothing and merely nodded his head in agreement.[7]

The third case seemed more serious. Captain George Brewster, of the 8th Connecticut Line presented the case of the attempted assault and threat against him. The accused, a short jug-eared rifleman, sat before them, his head bowed as Brewster related the facts.

Major Armstrong glanced at the written formal charges in front of him. "Private Peter Bant. What do you have to say in your defense?" one of the judges asked.

Bant kept his head lowered and remained silent.

"What is your record of service?" Will asked. Like most riflemen attached to regular Continental Line Regiments, Bant wore the usual fringed hunting shirt without any markings or badges such as the inverted white Vs to indicate years in the army.

A tall, lean rifleman, sitting next to a woman who nervously clutched the rim of her linen apron, stood.

"May I speak up on his behalf? My name is James McNeil, a Private and friend of Private Bant here."

Major Armstrong nodded for him to proceed.

"Bant is shy. Never has been much of a talker. We have been together since '76. He is a good soldier and a crack shot. I have seen him kill a British officer at a distance of more than 200 yards."

"He is not on trial for his marksmanship," Armstrong snapped. "We do not have all day. Get to the matter at hand, the charges against him."

"Yes, Sir. The Lieutenant here asked for his record of service," he said gesturing with his jutting chin to Will. "Bant and I began this war with Colonel Hand's Riflemen. We protected the Army's retreat to Trenton. We were in that battle, then marched up to Princeton and fought there, as well as at Brandywine. After that we were with the Frenchie General, did much marching and ended up at Yorktown on the Gloucester side, fighting against that green coated British cavalry." McNeil paused to take a breath, this being the longest speech he had ever made.

"Bant has demons inside his head. Makes him wake up screaming at night. They come and go. He is a decent man. I have never known him to speak poorly of an officer nor assault one. He told me this Captain here tried to rape a woman and he protected her. That is all there is I have to say."

Captain Brewster jumped to his feet. "That is an outrageous lie. I left my quarters to see to the well-being of my men and saw this scruffy fellow," he said pointing at Bant, "in front of one of their huts. I did not recognize him and, thinking him up to some mischief, immediately demanded he identify himself. He refused and when I insisted, he viciously drew a knife and menaced me. When some of my soldiers emerged from their huts, under threat of their seizing him, he gave me his name, rank and regiment and then fled."

The woman seated next to Private McNeil rose. "Please sirs," she said, her voice almost a whisper. "I am the woman the Captain…" Her voice dropped so low the last words were unintelligible.

"You will have to speak louder for the court to hear you? Who are you," Captain Wheeler demanded.

"Molly Frost, sir," she said more audibly. "I am a washerwoman. My husband is Private Edward Frost of the 4th New Hampshires."

"Is the court now going to hear from a common washerwoman? Bad enough to permit an skulking rifleman to address it," Brewster sneered, standing and placing his hands on his hips in a show of exasperation.

Will interjected before either the Major or Captain could speak. "You say you left your quarters to see to the well-being of your men and they emerged from their huts when you confronted this Private."

"That is the truth," Brewster acknowledged.

"Are any of your men available to testify to support your account?"

"They are in the forest, on detail to cut trees for firewood."

"By whose orders?"

"By mine of course, Lieutenant," Brewster said, looking at Major Armstrong with a smirk as if to say this junior officer does not even know who gives orders to the men under his command.

"Issued yesterday no doubt?" Will said quietly.

"Of course."

"Yet you knew this court martial of Private Bant was to be heard today?"

"I have told you the truth," Brewster snapped back. "I did not anticipate my word as an officer and gentleman would be cast in doubt by a common servant and an illiterate rifleman."

"Nevertheless, none of your men are here to corroborate your testimony due to orders you yourself have issued," Will said pointedly. "Private McNeil may or may not be able to read but he has fought well in support of our cause, as has the accused. There is no need to belittle either of them. I favor permitting the woman to address the court."

Major Armstrong seemed to hesitate, grimaced and nodded at Molly Frost.

"No need to be nervous," Captain Wheeler said kindly, as the woman remained standing, with her bowed head covered by a worn white cap, nervously clutching her apron. "You husband is most aptly named to be posted in this winter cantonment," he added chuckling at his own joke.

Despite Wheeler's encouragement, Molly nervously stammered out her version of the events. When she recounted how the Captain's own men had jeered at him, Brewster stared at her sternly.

"Anything further to say either by Captain Brewster or Private Bant," Major Armstrong asked.

"Major Armstrong," Brewster responded. "You know me personally. I am an officer and gentleman. I appeal to this court's common sense to reject this calumny against me by those who may bear me ill will because of my rank and privilege," he said, holding out his arms to the three judges as if to emphasize he was one of them.

"It has been my limited experience," Will observed, "that wealthy men of privilege and officers, are not immune to the common conceits of all men and are just as likely to lie when their interests are at stake, as any other person. I believe Major General Knox, who appointed me to this court, would agree."

In the conference room, Major Armstrong spoke first. He was for convicting Bant of threatening an officer. "It matters not the conduct of Captain Brewster," he argued. "Indeed, the only words against him are that of the washerwoman who does not contest this Private drew a knife on a superior officer. He must be punished to ensure the discipline of the army."

Will waited for Captain Wheeler to voice his opinion and when he hesitated, spoke up for acquittal. "If my wife were to be assaulted by an officer, I would hope any man in my command, regardless of rank, would spring to protect her. Rather than ensuring discipline, punishing this Private for defending a married woman from an assault would send a message to our soldiers, as stated by Captain Brewster, that officers are superior to them merely by upbringing and rank. I do not ascribe to that view," Will said emphatically. "Indeed, he added, "since the evidence is sufficient to acquit Private Bant of the charges, it is sufficient to charge Captain Brewster. It is simply the other side of the coin."

Captain Wheeler interceded. "I agree with Lieutenant Stoner. As a married officer with my wife in camp, I would hope my own men would protect her virtue should the occasion arise." He paused and looked first at Major Armstrong and then at Will. "However, to charge Captain Brewster is to presume too much. My vote is to acquit the Private and end the matter."

With a scowl and show of reluctance, Major Armstrong changed his position. The court unanimously agreed to drop the charges against Private Bant.

The last court martial of the afternoon involved two soldiers who had stolen a goose from a nearby farm, killed and cooked it with their messmates. Although they denied the charges, claiming the theft had been committed by others unknown, feathers and entrails were found outside their hut. Will sympathized with them, arguing their hunger and poor rations had driven them to it. He was outvoted and each man was given a sentence of forty lashes, to be administered twenty lashes on the two Mondays following the next two Sabbaths. They also were fined three dollars to compensate the farmer for his loss. One of the convicted men laughed out loud when this part of the sentence was read. He stated he would gladly pay it when Congress paid the Army, unless the Court meant he was to pay in Continentals, of which he had plenty of that worthless currency. Armstrong was incensed at the soldier's impertinence and would have increased the flogging except Captain Wheeler and Will held out for letting the punishment stand.

Will returned to the General's Headquarters in the growing darkness and sought out Captain Hadley. He found him alone in a small room sorting through the General's dispatches.

"Tis a dirty business to sit in judgment on men who are ill-clothed, starving and anxious over whether they will ever be paid before the Army is disbanded. Though there was one case worthy of a court martial where the real culprit was left unpunished."

He reviewed the Bant court martial and the discussion amongst the judges. "Was I wrong to propose charges be filed against Captain Brewster? What would you have done in my stead, Sam?"

"If the goal was to achieve the Private's acquittal, I would have done as you. It led Captain Wheeler to see the compromise and agree with you on acquittal and side with the Major on not charging a fellow officer."

"Brewster should have been charged though," Will said. "To my mind, he attempted to rape the washerwoman."

"Were this to have occurred even late last year, when it was unknown whether it would be continued war or peace, I would have done as you." He waved his hands at the paper strewn desk. "By now the signs are unmistakable. The southern war is over. It is obvious from our General's correspondence with General Greene, who has occupied Charleston for more than a month.[8] Rumors that a preliminary peace has been reached in Paris are rampant, not only in our camp but are openly talked about in Congress. If the war is drawing to a close, what purpose is served by charging an officer who may have served honorably and besmirching his reputation at a time when he will return to his family?"

"Captain Brewster stated Major Armstrong knew him, from where and under what circumstances were unclear. The Major was certainly favorably inclined toward him."

Sam stopped organizing the papers on the desk and stared at Will. "I suggest you talk to the General about your experience this afternoon and your impressions of Major Armstrong. Our General has his suspicions, as does His Excellency, of General Gates."

"Why would I do that?" Will asked.

"I believe General Knox is keeping an eye on Major Armstrong and others of Gates' staff. He suspects political games are being played by some in Congress who seek to use the army's discontent to further their own policies." Seeing Will look aghast, Hadley continued in a more moderate vein. "It may or may not be true. However, tis no accident General Knox appointed you to the Board chaired by Major Armstrong."

He clapped his hands. "Enough of this talk. With all signs pointing to peace, my thoughts are already in Boston where I will be reunited with my mother and Priscilla my dear sister and introduce them to my beloved Mercy and our darling son." He gripped Will by the shoulders. "You too should be thinking of joyous reunions and a life beyond this war."

"That is precisely why I despondent," Will replied with a gloomy look on his face. "Where do I go? What do I do? You know my circumstances, Samuel. You know I cannot, nay will not, go back to my father's farm."

"Tis obvious to me you should return with Elisabeth, Henry and Agnes to Albany. To the Van Hootens' home," Hadley said beaming. "There you will make your future."

Will smiled wanly. He did not see himself in that small town, an outsider surrounded by pompous wealthy Dutch businessmen. He would be bored by their talk of money-making schemes. Nor did he think Elisabeth, with all her worldliness would fare well there either.

Chapter 8 - The Officers' Mutiny

Bant and McNeil were again hunting in the woods, bringing back whatever game they killed, to be shared among the men of their company. Although the days were noticeably longer, there was still a brisk chill to the air and a thick covering of snow on the ground. They trekked away from the cantonment leaving the smell of burning wood and the strong winds off the river behind them.

Bant as usual carried his long rifle. A borrowed musket was strapped to the sled, carrying their tent, cooking pot, ropes, a shovel, an axe and hatchet and a few other items. McNeil's rifle was slung over his shoulder and he held a musket loaded with bird shot. They took turns pulling a sled with through the powdered snow. They threaded their way under boughs of evergreen, bent low to the ground from the weight of freshly fallen snow, their eyes on the ground searching for tracks of rabbits, squirrels or birds. Because it was late in an usually harsh winter, Bant thought deer would be scarce, either picked off by wolves or dying by themselves of starvation. He kept his thoughts to himself and smiled. McNeil had said at Bant's court martial he was a man of few words. It was true.

Late in the afternoon they followed a marten's paw prints but lost it as dusk fell. The following morning, they shot a few rabbits and gray squirrels, barely enough to feed their ten messmates, let alone the rest of the men in the hut. McNeil bagged several partridges and heath hens that made them feel better about their efforts. As they came down a snowy slope, McNeil pointed ahead to the edge of a forest with tall thick trunks and bare limbs starkly outlined against the cold winter sky. There was a narrow beaten trail between the trees, probably made by deer. Beyond the woods was another slope gently inclining toward a thicker, more dense woods of evergreens. The clearing between the two was no more than forty yards, with the snow trampled down in places.

"If there are deer, they will bed down in those evergreens or beyond and forage among those oaks for acorns, twigs, shrubs, or whatever they can find," McNeil said. Bant grunted in agreement. They left the sled and stomped through the snow, following the deer trail. Once in the woods they saw fresh signs of deer tracks and droppings as well as bare spots where the deer had pawed away the snow to get at the acorns lying amidst the dead leaves.

Bant and McNeil camped well away from the site, behind a ridge they hoped would block the wind from carrying their scent toward the deer. They rose cold and stiff, before the sky lightened in the east, chewed on pieces of tough salted beef and stale bread, and trudged to the slope overlooking the two groves of trees. McNeil set about pulling some dead branches and limbs to create a place where they could crouch down and hide.

Bant wiggled his frozen toes among the rags he had stuffed in his ankle high moccasins and waited under a dull grey sky. It was difficult to remain alert and still in the frigid air. The wind continued to blow toward them as he concentrated on the edge of the trees, looking, waiting for movement. A few birds flitted amongst the low branches. All was quiet.

A large doe, leading a herd of deer, cautiously emerged from the evergreens, her nose quivering as she sniffed the air before venturing further. She pawed the ground searching for vegetation beneath the snow. Three more does and two bucks, a year or so old with small spiky horns, still covered by velvet, followed her into the open. The deer lowered their heads to nibble the matted grass beneath the snow, lifting their heads frequently to sniff the air and nervously gazing every which way for danger.

Bant raised one finger to signal McNeil he would aim for the lead doe who was the largest of the herd. McNeil nodded and sighted on another. They both fired almost simultaneously. Bant's doe went down immediately. McNeil's deer jumped and stumbled toward the oaks before crumpling into the snow and thrashing about. McNeil ran up and slit her throat. While McNeil went for the sled, Bant tugged at the dead doe until its head was uphill. He took out his large hunting knife and began gutting it. He reached into the stomach cavity and pulled out the steaming intestines and threw them to the side where they melted the snow down to the frozen grass.

Suddenly he stood up, cursing himself for his forgetfulness. He wiped his hands on his breeches and methodically reloaded his rifle. The wind blowing away from the kill would carry the scent of fresh blood to bears and wolves. When McNeil returned they placed the rifles and muskets on top of their pack, within easy reach.

Both men worked silently and efficiently in the cold, glancing tensely downwind across the snowy landscape. They stood a better chance against a single bear. It was wolf packs they feared the most. Grunting, they turned the does over so the gutted body cavities faced the snowy ground as the deer bled out.

"We have maybe two hundred pounds of meat," McNeil observed, looking first at the deer and then at the uniformly grey sky. "I think it will snow before dark. I say we head back toward camp." Bant thought it over. The remainder of the herd was spooked so he and McNeil would have to continue their hunt somewhere else. They could hoist the two deer high enough on a tree branch to keep them out of reach of wolves but not bears or martens. Better to bring back what they had than risk losing the two deer. He nodded his agreement.

They unloaded the sled and tied the two deer down with the ropes they had brought, wedging their cooking pot beneath one of the dead animals. They strapped their knapsacks containing the dead squirrels, rabbits and birds to the sled and covered the entire load with the canvas white tent. Satisfied all was secure, they reloaded their muskets with heavy lead ball cartridges instead of the bird shot McNeil had been using. Bird shot would not stop a wolf. Bant slipped the hatchet through his belt in the front and tightened the strap so it was snug against his thigh.

They set off with McNeil pulling the sled through the snow by the broad leather harness across his chest, his hands free to carry both his musket and rifle. Bant followed walking in the smoothed path created by the weight of the sled. Once when Bant turned around, he saw crows cawing noisily from their perches in the trees near where they had killed the deer. A few hawks circled above. They should have taken the time to bury the guts and take the livers he thought, but they had been in a hurry. Now, their haste might attract wolves.

They made fair progress in the woods and clearings but had difficulty crossing a stream. The snow covered rocks jutted up and the ice was too thin to slide the sled across. They were anxious to put as much distance between themselves and the kill site. They wasted some time scouting for a better crossing. Finding none, they untied the canvas and unloaded the uppermost deer, their cooking pot and knapsacks. With McNeil at the heavier end, they sloshed through the icy water carrying the sled across to the other side. Then they went back through the stream. McNeil hoisted the gutted deer on his back and Bant followed him across rifle in hand, looking anxiously back the way they had come. They lost more time reloading the sled with the deer, knapsacks and cooking pot before resuming their trek. McNeil pointed to blood staining the snow on both sides of the stream where they had laid the deer down. Bant grimaced, knowing that the scent of blood would carry on the wind that still blew in their faces. He limped along, the rags in his moccasins stiff and rubbing against his ankles. His toes were frozen beyond feeling.

It was late in the afternoon when they heard a distant howl followed by an answering cry. Ahead was an open field and beyond, the edge of the forest they had passed through after leaving the cantonment. The wolves would come after them in the open where they could spread out and try to surround them. They tried to move faster across the snow and were about two-thirds of the way across the field when they encountered drifts. McNeil grunted from the effort of pulling the sled through the deeper snow. He tugged hard and stumbled forward as the runners found thin powder. Bant walked backwards for short distances, watching for the pack to appear before running to catch up to McNeil who slogged on. After passing through another windblown drift, McNeil turned the sled sideways dropped the harness strap and bent over panting for breath.

"Better reload with dry powder," Bant said, taking McNeil's musket and leaning it against the sled. Bant removed the cartridge from his rifle, took a new one from his box and rammed it home. They both reloaded their muskets and crouched down behind the sled. The wind was blowing against their backs.

The wolves burst from the tree line running in a pack along the smoothed snow in a straight line for the sled. There were six of them, the first two larger than the others, all grey and brown with tinges of red in their neck fur. As they came closer, the wolves fanned out in a line with the younger and smaller ones attempting to flank them. The two leaders came on the run, straight at them on the packed trail carved by the sled. They were a thin and hungry lot, having survived the harsh winter when prey was scarce. Excited by the strong scent of freshly killed deer lashed to the sled, the pack leaders advanced with menacing determination, drawing Bant's attention away from the four younger wolves struggling through the drifts on either side of them.

Bant bit open the end of a cartridge and poured some powder on to the pan. "You fire first," McNeil said, "and reload." He did not have to add- as fast as you can. "I will take the other."

Bant nodded. With only two rifles and two muskets they would have to make every shot count. The wolves that survived their first round would be on them before they could reload. Bant sighted on the chest of the first wolf, less than forty yards out and hurtling toward them in long even strides. It hit a drift and plunged into the deeper snow just as Bant fired. The heavy ball creased the wolf's skull. It yelped in pain and rolled over in the snow trying to stop the burning in its head. Bant automatically went through the motions of reloading. McNeil fired and the second wolf was blown backwards and lay still. The four others were about thirty yards away, two on each side of the sled, their bodies low to the ground, slinking forward, faking a charge before retreating, working themselves closer and closer. Bant had reloaded his rifle but laid it down and took one of the muskets. He turned from one side to the other trying to keep track of the four wolves as McNeil reloaded. Three loaded guns, he thought, four wolves and one wounded pack leader. Bant tried to calculate how fast a wolf could cover the distance between them. When he turned again to look at the two on his side of the sled, the lead one was within twenty yards and weaving back and forth in the snow.

"Loaded," he heard McNeil shout. Bant laid down his rifle, thinking the musket with its heavy balls was better for close in work. He aimed at the nearest wolf's chest and fired. The wolf tumbled backwards from the impact and lay still, bleeding heavily in the snow. Bant heard the loud bark of McNeil's rifle. He turned to see a wolf jump into the air biting at its shoulder. McNeil finished it off with a musket ball as the two remaining wolves slunk away, retreating toward the tree line behind them.

Bant took his rifle and approached the pack leader he had wounded. It lay on the snow snarling at him as he approached. At less than ten feet, Bant pointed the gun at the center of the wolf's skull and fired. All he heard was a dull click of the hammer flint striking the pan. The powder must have gotten wet. The wolf leaped to its feet, bared its teeth and lunged. Bant dropped his rifle and was barely able to unsheath his knife as the wolf jumped for him. He thought he had buried the blade in the wolf's throat as he was knocked over, smelling the stink of the wolf's breath and then hearing the thwack of McNeill bringing the axe down on the wolf's neck. He struggled to his feet shivering from the cold snow under his collar and down his back. The front of his hunting shirt was covered with blood.

"It had better be from the wolf or else I will have to pull you on the sled back to camp," McNeil said, not looking particularly alarmed. Bant ran his hands over his chest and legs making sure he had not been bitten. He shook his head and knelt in the cold snow panting for air. McNeil dislodged the axe from the dead wolf's spine and stomped off, axe in hand, checking each wolf they had shot to make sure all were dead. Bant stood up, a bit wobbly, and after a minute stooped and wiped his knife on the dead wolf's fur.

"We could skin the wolves and sell the pelts," he said thinking of their constant need for hard currency to buy food from local farmers. They made quick work of two of them and then with a light snow beginning to fall, camped deep within the forest and built a large fire for warmth and to ward off any other predators. They took turns keeping watch and sleeping beside the sled that served as a wind break. When it was his turn, Bant built up the fire and spent the time staring into the black darkness beyond, with his rifle across his knees and a loaded musket leaning against a tree within reach. With the war almost over, after all the dangers they had endured in battles to numerous to count, it would be strange he thought, to be killed by a bear.

The snow was falling in heavy wet flakes by morning when they broke camp. They followed a deer trail through the woods until they came to an area recently cleared of trees by the troops. They quickened their pace passing the snow covered stumps on a wide path made for hauling logs out and toward the encampment. Bant had to admit even he was eager to return to the warmth of their hut. The other soldiers would be decent toward him for a while, grateful for the fresh meat they were carrying.

They proceeded on the road through part of the cantonment. As they passed a parade ground, Bant recognized the flag of the New Hampshire Regiment of Private Frost.

"I would like to give some of our kill to Molly Frost and her daughter. They need food more than we do."

McNeil nodded his agreement. "Those are more words than you have spoken for the entire hunt," he chuckled. "If she were not married, I would venture you are sweet on her." Bant blushed. "Their little girl is as skinny as a sapling," he said in reply to justify his gift.

They found the washerwomen's hut. When the two entered, Bant first, carrying two partridges by their frozen legs in one hand

and a rabbit in the other, several women screamed. Molly put her hands to her mouth and peered at him. "Is that you Private Bant? You look a fright all covered in blood." Bant looked down at his hunting shirt. "'Tis the blood of a wolf we killed," he mumbled by way of explanation, holding out the rabbit and two partridges. "These are for you and your daughter," he said, shifting from one foot to the other waiting for Molly to take them. It was hot and uncomfortable in the washing hut. He wished to be outside again.

"This is very kind of you," she said pointing at the two birds and rabbit. "Have you been gone from camp for long?"

"Four days," Bant muttered looking to McNeil for help.

"Well," one of the other washerwomen chimed in. "You will find much changed. For one, the officers now gossip amongst themselves and fall all silent and guilty-like when anyone else is around."

"Like washerwomen," another yelled provoking loud cackles of laughter.

"We know they are up to something secret," the first one said boastfully, "as we go throughout the camp taking their dirty shirts and returning them clean."

"It means nothing to us," Bant said, hoping McNeil would say something and they could leave.

"Private Bant," Molly said. "I will come by your Company and take your hunting shirt for washing. The wolf's blood will come out with a good scrubbing."

"I cannot pay."

"No need," Molly said, taking the rabbit and the partridges from him.

As they left, Bant realized he had only this one bloodstained hunting shirt. He would borrow one from McNeil who owned two. It would come down below his knees and those in the hut would ridicule him. If it got too bad, he would do nighttime sentry duty and sleep in the daytime when most of the men would be out. It was what he had done before. He could do it again.

The high-ceiling long room of Knox's headquarters, the scene of many a boisterous and cheerful dinner was quiet. Instead of a comforting roaring fire, only a few logs and embers burned low in the cavernous fireplace. The table was completely bare – no food nor drink - save for several sheets of paper stacked in front of General Knox who, as usual, sat at the head of the table, with Colonel Sargent to his left. The twelve officers of his staff remained silent, wondering at the reason for their being summoned to what promised to be a somber and grave meeting.

Will had never seen the General so grim and serious. His lips were tightly compressed as if to prevent some terrible secret from escaping his mouth into the cold air of reality. His eyes glanced from one officer to the next, assessing the character and loyalty of each. Will held his breath when the General's piercing gaze skewered him, and exhaled slightly when his eyes passed on to Captain Hadley seated to Will's right. Satisfied that all he had summoned to attend were present, Knox hoisted his large bulk from the wide-backed chair and lumbered to the room's door. All eyes followed him and Will caught a glimpse of his friend, Master Sergeant Adam Cooper, seated at a desk blocking the doorway, flanked by two armed sentries.

"Master Sergeant Cooper," Knox thundered, as Adam jumped to his feet. "No one is to enter this room without my permission. If any officer presents himself, the sentries are to bar his way. You are to knock and announce his name. I will give you an order to permit or deny entry. Is that understood?"

"Yes Sir," Adam replied.

"My order applies to anyone regardless of rank. Generals included," he added for emphasis. The officers within the room gasped. "I guarantee there will be no adverse consequences for your following my orders," Knox said before stepping back into the room and firmly closing the door.

The General resumed his seat and shuffled the papers in front of him. "Gentlemen," he began in a loud voice before lowering it to what he deemed was a confidential tone. "Upon your oaths of allegiance to our cause you are sworn to maintain the secrecy of what I am about to discuss with you. It involves no less than a call to refuse to disband if the Army's demands are not met. T'is a threat to subvert the Congress and cause we have fought for together. If any among you cannot abide by the demands of complete secrecy, you are free to depart and no approbation will attach to your action." Knox paused and again scanned the faces around the table. Not a man moved.

"Very well, gentlemen," he said taking a deep breath.

"An anonymous letter from one signing himself 'Brutus, a fellow soldier' has been circulating amongst the officers of the different regiments. Are any of you aware of this?" Will shook his head as the others in the room murmured they had no knowledge of such a writing.

"Tis as I suspected. The fact that you, my officers, were not recipients of this treasonous missive speaks words about the author's nefarious purpose. I take pride that this Brutus, and those more senior," he added ominously, "who instigated his action did not deem you to be fertile soil for a general mutiny." The room buzzed with shock at the thought of an army rebellion led by its officers. "Nay, wait till you read this for yourselves to see the perfidy in the suggestion. I admit Brutus puts forth many cogent arguments. However, he has made a veiled assault on the integrity of His Excellency, General Washington. The letter has been widely distributed. Some one's clerical staff worked through the night, cloaking the perpetrators' deeds in darkness, to disburse this missive throughout the Cantonment."

With that, Knox shoved copies of the letter down each side of the table and encouraged his officers to share and read it for themselves. Will moved his chair nearer to Hadley who placed one of the candleholders closer so they could read the cramped writing. This copy had apparently been passed through many hands for stains obliterated the ink in a few places. A paragraph midway down the page held Will's attention and he reread it to make certain he understood it correctly:

Having shared your misery for so long, my own faith in Congress is no more. Faith has its limits as well as temper – and there are points, beyond which neither can be stretched without sinking into cowardice. Suspect the man, who would advise more moderation and longer forebearance. If Congress treats us such this way when we are still under arms, what treatment may we expect from peace? Many prospered at home while we fought and starved, ill-clothed, surviving on broken promises of provision of clothing, rations and pay. Will you consent to be the only sufferers by this Revolution, and retiring from the field, grow old in poverty, wretchedness and contempt? Let us meet in unity on the 11th of March, draw up one final remonstrance to a Congress that has remained deaf to our prior pleas with coldness and severity, and if their response to our valid claims be nothing but complete agreement to our just demands, then act we must, by force if necessary, to obtain what is our just due.[1]

"This is a call for mutiny," one of the Majors blurted out in a shocked voice. "A meeting not authorized by General Washington. How can that be?"

A Captain, his face red with indignation shouted angrily, "This request to suspect the man who urges more moderation is an indirect reference to General Washington himself. Why it is no less than a direct affront to his integrity and reputation." He looked toward the head of the table. "His Excellency has evinced extreme zeal in pursuing our cause before Congress, as have you General Knox," he said, pointing at their commander.

Knox let them voice their complaints and opinions before signaling for silence.

"Tis true General Washington has pled the army's cause with firmness and consistency. Congress has at least given the impression by its inactions having found us useful during the war, it now wishes us to disband with the coming of peace and would rather see the men starve than pay a penny in support." He cleared his throat and spit the phlegm into his handkerchief tucked in his sleeve. Will recalled the first time he had seen Knox, then a Colonel use his handkerchief to hide his missing fingers. That was more than seven years ago, he thought. And after all the retreats and battles, with victory and peace so near at hand, . . . He did not complete his thought.

General Knox stood and angrily slammed his thick hand on the hard wood table. "This call for general mutiny puts at risk all we have fought for and could cause the British to reverse course and seek our annihilation. Even worse, it would thrust our country into the horrors of civil war from which there may be no receding."

He leaned forward on the table, his fleshy palms spread out. "This is the moment when we either take appropriate action or risk losing all – even our very independence from the Crown. I tell you this in strictest confidence. General Washington will issue general orders tomorrow prohibiting this irregular and mutinous meeting. He will acknowledge the just concerns of the army and authorize a regular meeting of all officers on March 15th to be presided over by the Army's ranking officer, General Gates, and direct him to report the results of the meeting."[2]

Will wondered why General Gates would speak to the assembled officers when Hadley had told him of Knox's suspicions of both Gates and Major Armstrong. When Will told Knox of his encounter with Major Armstrong on the court martial board, the General had smiled and said it was more evidence of what they already surmised.

"You are all to attend the March 15th meeting at the Temple. Do not sit together but spread yourselves around the hall. At the appropriate moment, which will be obvious to you when I speak, you are to loudly proclaim support for what I say." He straightened up into his full height with his hands upon his lower back. "Gentlemen, this meeting is as important as any battle we have fought together. The fate of our glorious cause rests on the outcome. The issue is whether we survive as a country or sink into the horrific abyss of either tyranny or civil war."

He motioned for the officer closer to the doors to open them. "Master Sergeant Cooper," he called. "Notify the kitchen to provide us with ale, cider and some good Madeira."

When the tankards and bottles arrived and the men's glasses were filled, General Knox raised his.

"I propose the army's two favorite toasts in one," he said as all the officers stood ready. "A hoop to the barrel and cement to the union," he cried.[3] The men cheered the call for unity and disbursed into small groups, talking agitatedly amongst themselves.

Upon leaving the room, Hadley took Will's arm and led him outside on the porch and down across the grounds toward the well house. "If it does not go well on the 15th, there will be no promise of a peaceful life. Some of the officers will stand with General Washington. I hope it will be the majority, but others, like this 'Brutus,' will rebel and incite the regular troops. We will be fighting amongst ourselves with the British not yet gone from our shores."

"No matter what happens, even if it means taking up arms against our former brothers in arms, we will follow General Knox," Will said vehemently. He was overcome by the vision of Continentals fighting against one another, arrayed on opposite sides of fields of wheat shimmering in the summer sun. He envisioned his cannon balls mowing down the advancing ranks of soldiers with bayonets fixed, whose Regimental colors he knew.

"It will be truly terrible," Hadley said as if sharing Will's vision.

"Sam?" Will asked. "You are always the hopeful one, who sees good and brightness ahead. Now I sense you fear for the future."

Hadley clasped Will by the forearm and looked directly at him. "Will. I place my faith and trust in His Excellency and General Knox. I believe they will see this through to a successful conclusion." He removed his tri-corn and shook his head in the cool night air, as if to clear away darker thoughts. "Tis a strange business being both a soldier and a family man. My sense of duty is to the army though my heart leads me to protect my own. I so much yearn for peace and a return to a normal life," he sighed. "Perhaps, all our dreams of an imminent peace have obscured the conspiracy amongst of our fellow officers. I had no inkling they would go so far as to threaten the Congress for pay and pension."

"I too would like the pay owed and a pension as well. Tis for the financial security of my young family," Will admitted. "However, the failure of Congress to act would never drive me to threaten mutiny and civil war."

"I believe many think as you," Hadley said. "General Washington has wisely provided a few days for cooler heads to prevail, which I believe they will and turn the situation about."

Will nodded in agreement. For the past seven years, the army had held together and endured more than ordinary men could be expected to suffer.

"Sam, I hope you are right in placing your confidence in His Excellency. Yet it is one thing to instill in men the courage to fight an invader of their homes and land. Another to have them hold the line against real injustices and broken promises by their own government."

Hadley turned and looked at Will with a mixture of surprise and admiration. "You have phrased the problem exactly. I am sure it is as General Knox sees it as well. Knowing our General well, as we both do, let us go through the next four days with our anxiety tempered and confidence in a favorable outcome."

Will found that argument as thin as a powder quill to rely upon. Yet, smiling he thought of his experience as an artillery man. The slow match always lit the powder in the quill in the touch hole and ignited the powder charge.

The morning of Saturday the 15th dawned bright, clear and crisp. The meeting of all officers was to begin at twelve noon. Elisabeth seemed surprised as Will fussed over which uniform to wear, trying on first the one his father-in-law had purchased for him from an Albany tailor, the jacket deep blue with clean facing and shiny brass buttons, and then the tattered old one he had worn throughout the campaigns and battles.

"It matters not which one you wear," she said, cradling Agnes in her arms. "Tis what you think and say that will have bearing on the outcome." He had told her nothing about the meeting of General Knox's officers but knew she had a general sense of the significance of this meeting. Lucy Knox had taken her into her confidence.

Will acknowledged she was correct. Still, he felt self-conscious in the pristine new uniform, almost as if he were going to a dress parade or a ball. In the end, he selected the breeches and stockings from the new uniform, both clean and white, and his blue regimental coat that had been with him since his promotion to Lieutenant at Valley Forge in '78. He strapped on his sword and tightened the worn leather strap with its tarnished brass buckle as Elisabeth brushed his frayed and patched tri-corn. Even though it would be warm in the Temple Hall, with all the officers present, he asked Elisabeth to button his neckstock above his clean linen shirt. It presented a neater appearance.

"You remember when I sent this to you from Philadelphia."

Will nodded and kissed her lightly on her head, taking in the clean smell of her blonde hair.

"That I do, my love," he whispered, planting his lips on their baby daughter's forehead. "Where is Henry?"

"Our son is with Adam and their little boy this morning. I will spend my time with Mrs. Knox. We both pray Providence will bless this meeting with a positive outcome."

Despite his uncertainties over his uniform, he had no doubts as to how Big Red should look. The day before he had brushed the horse until his coat shone like burnished copper and the leather bridle and saddle glistened with an inner glow. Will rode the two miles from Knox's headquarters to the Temple of Virtue on the sloping hill overlooking the cantonment. An orderly took the reins as he dismounted and led the horse to a paddock already populated with the mounts of other officers who had arrived earlier. Will entered the sunlit vaulted hall. A pulpit had been set up on the raised platform where Will had sat as a member of the court martial board just days earlier. The rough hewn benches closest to the platform were filled, mostly by higher ranking officers. Will recognized Major Armstrong among them, talking excitedly with those around him. He assumed they were also part of General Horatio Gates' staff. He was not surprised to see Captain Brewster among them.

Will looked around the room filled with hundreds of officers. From midway back in the hall Hadley waved to him. Will threaded his way through the narrow space between the benches and squeezed in a few places in from the narrow aisle on the opposite side from Samuel. There was a commotion at the front and General Gates entered, followed by Generals Knox, Lincoln, and Von Steuben, prominently wearing the sash bearing the Star of Prussia across his chest. Gates stood behind the pulpit, slightly stoop shouldered, his hair fully powdered and curled and waited for the hubbub to die down.

"Pursuant to the Commander-in-Chief's General Orders of March 11th, this assembly of general and field officers and staff, with one officer from each company in attendance, I call this assembly to order. The sole purpose of this meeting . . ."

Gates paused hearing a noise behind the platform. General Washington entered through the narrow door of the conference room and strode toward the platform in his highly polished, knee-length-riding boots. His presence was completely unexpected. The entire body rose to their feet to the sounds of scraping of benches and the rattling of swords and scabbards. General Gates immediately yielded the podium.

Washington acknowledged the standing officers and gestured for them to sit down. The room was completely silent. Not a cough nor sneeze, no clearing of throats as the men waited expectantly for Washington to begin. The General stood tall and erect before them. The difference in height and bearing between him and Gates was obvious to everyone. Unlike Gates, Washington's uncurled hair was only lightly powdered, the brown grey color showing through. The gold colored epaulets emphasized his broad shoulders. His cheeks and nose were ruddy as if he had ridden a long distance in the cold, instead of the short way from Newburgh. He surveyed the assembled officers with his blue eyes before removing a few papers from his waistcoat.

Washington cleared his throat and began to speak in a firm tone, his mouth clenched in a tight grimace, his eyes occasionally raised from the page before him to look out at the officers. Will, who had only seen the General on the battlefield and then from a distance, was excited to be addressed directly. He hoped others would be similarly moved and accepting of Washington's words. First, like an aggrieved, stern father whose sons had misbehaved, the General rebuked them for calling an irregular and unauthorized meeting and accepting the argument Congress was deliberately ignoring their just demands. He reminded them he had been with them from the very beginning of the war. He intimately knew their sufferings and the hardships they had endured for they had endured them together. The General's eyes scanned the assembly, brightening with familiarity when he recognized an officer here or there as if to emphasize their common experiences.

"Who amongst you believes I am indifferent to your interests after all we have suffered, struggled and accomplished together. Who believes I have not fervently pled your case before Congress with all my being and abilities. Trust in Congress to take action and to recognize your sacrifices and to satisfy your country's debt to the Army. It is not deaf to your pleas."

Will sensed an uneasy shifting on the benches around him and a low muttering, initially indistinguishable until he was able to discern a few words. "More moderation and forbearance just as Brutus predicted," the man next to him said, looking down at his feet. "What has trust in Congress gotten us to date?" the officer to Will's left asked Will directly. "We cannot feed our families on trust," a Captain in front of Will said in response.

Washington clearly heard the murmuring and raised his voice to quiet the growing dissent. "Have we reached the moment when we seriously discuss taking up arms against our country. The writer who proposed this is no friend of the Army. Nor to our country. By sowing the seeds of discord and separation between the civil and military powers he is plotting the ruin of both."[4] He spoke more forcefully, having seemingly abandoned his prepared remarks. Will suspected the General was simply more familiar with the argument to be made and making it appear he was speaking extemporaneously.

"I implore you to give Congress a chance to address your grievances and I will, as I have consistently done so in the past, do everything in my power to achieve a just result." He paused and lowered his voice so those in the middle and back of the Temple leaned forward to hear his words. "If you trust Congress to take action, you will give one more distinguished proof of unexampled patriotism and patient virtue, rising superior to the most complicated sufferings."[5]

There were scattered cheers but it was obvious to Will that Washington's words had not carried the assembly. Most of the officers remained unconvinced, despite their General's appeal to their patriotism and loyalty to the cause. There was an uncomfortable shuffling of feet and embarrassed coughing.

Washington remained standing tall and erect at the podium surveying the assembled officers before him. He reached into his regimental coat and held up one page of writing. "This is a letter from Congressman Joseph Jones of Virginia, written to me in response to my pleading the cause of the Army. Permit me to read it to you as evidence of the Congress's willingness to address your grievances."

Washington smoothed the folds and laid it on the pulpit, stumbling over the first few sentences. He held it closer to his face but still seemed unable to read the words. A whisper of sympathy filled the hall. The General reached into another pocket and withdrew a pair of spectacles. There was an audible gasp as the officers saw their invincible leader, the General who had led them into every battle and shepherded them through every retreat, don reading glasses and look down at the paper before him.

"Gentlemen," Washington said as the assembled officers murmured in shock. Washington thought their muttering indicated their impatience. "You must pardon me. I have grown gray in your service and now find myself growing blind."[6]

Some of the officers near Will had tears in their eyes. Many had been in the field with the General for the entire eight years of war. "If our General places his trust in Congress, how can we do otherwise," a Captain said quietly, blowing his nose in a handkerchief. Will barely heard the words of Congressman Jones' letter praising the army and promising all of his efforts to address their grievances.

The emotional support for their aged, vulnerable commander was palpable. When Washington finished reading the letter and took off his glasses, the officers erupted in cheers. Many had tears on their cheeks, others waved their tri-corns wildly, declaring their affection and support for their Commander-in-Chief. Others stood about, shocked at what had transpired until Washington left the room.

Will heard General Knox's voice, the same voice that had thundered out orders for loading the Durhams to cross the Delaware

The Officers' Mutiny

that stormy night in '76, asking the officers to thank His Excellency for his presence and speech. It was unnecessary for Will to shout in favor as the call was resoundingly supported from every corner of the cavernous hall. A second call for a Committee chaired by General Knox to propose a resolution for the officers to consider was also approved by shouts of agreement.

Will found Hadley in a crowd of officers milling about, who were recounting the times they had seen or been in close proximity to General Washington during the war. They talked how he conducted himself nobly, his wise decisions and his steady hand, the instant calming influence he had upon the men in battle. No one spoke any longer of their grievances nor of rebelling against Congress until all of their demands were met.

In what seemed an incredibly short time, General Knox stood at the podium and in his booming voice read the resolution proposed by the hastily convened committee he had chaired. It called for the officers to reaffirm their unshaken confidence in General Washington and faith that Congress would resolve their grievances in a timely manner.

"Vote to support the Resolution," Will shouted out as similar cries came from throughout the hall. It was clear they were not only coming from General Knox's staff. The officers from all companies were caught up in the emotion of the moment.

"All those in favor of the Resolution signify your approval by Huzzah," General Knox boomed out. He was answered by a resounding chorus of huzzahs accompanied by tri-corns being tossed in the air and loud claps of approval. He waited until the hubbub had subsided.

"Any opposed, signify by stating nay," Knox thundered, staring directly at General Gates' staff officers in the front benches. Not a single voice was heard. "As Chair of the Committee I will report the results to His Excellency. With the permission of General Gates," he said nodding to the senior ranking officer in the room, "I hereby declare this Assembly dismissed." And with that, Knox stomped off the podium, his fleshy face containing no expression of gloating or the joy he and his staff felt at the successful outcome.

Will and Hadley rode slowly back to Knox's Headquarters. "His Excellency planned all along to attend this Assembly," Will said.

"True," Samuel agreed. "Think of the many times he outmaneuvered the Redcoats, surprising them by being somewhere else than they thought we would be. I suspect the hand of some in Congress in General Gates' activities." He laughed out loud. "His Excellency has applied the strategy of the battlefield to the field of politics. I admit it was close but our faith in General Washington, with the assistance of our own General Knox, was not misplaced. So now, Will, we may return to our dreams of peacetime bliss and life with our families undisturbed by war and separation."

Will pretended to be as pleased as Samuel. The uncertainty of his future gnawed at him since he had neither plans nor even a glimmer of an idea of how to support himself, Elisabeth and their two children.

Chapter 9 - The Army Disbanded

The men of Captain Lieutenant Tew's company of the 2nd Rhode Island Regiment stood in loosely disciplined ranks in front of the wooden huts which had protected them from the frequent snows of the preceding harsh winter. Now, in mid-April with evidence of spring all around, the men had nothing to do. Their quarters stank of the fetid air of living close together. They were plagued with scabies and the itches and bothered by the ubiquitous flies attracted by the latrines and offal. The men knew of the noon proclamation of the cessation of hostilities to the assembled officers. Rumors ran through the camp for the rest of the afternoon. It meant discharge was imminent and with it, the promised pay they were due.[1] That could be the only explanation for this evening's assembly, company by company for all Regiments.

Sergeant Henry Gillet stood amongst the men of his platoon, thoughtful and listening to the wild talk of what the men would do with their accumulated pay. It was true Congress had voted five years full pay to the officers but not a word had been said about the pay due to the soldiers. He thought even the promise of pay to the Officers was just that - a promise. No one had seen any hard specie brought to the cantonment. No rumors of a paymaster's visit to give the men their due.

The men listened restlessly as Captain Olney read the Proclamation of Cessation of Hostilities. He was followed by the

Regimental Chaplain who, in an uninspiring and hasty manner, anxious to be gone from the parade grounds, asked for a rendering of thanks to God for all His mercies and for causing the wrath of war to end among nations.

"I would rather give thanks to God for the pay that is due us," a soldier shouted out. "And our discharge," another called. The Chaplain scowled and retreated behind Captain Olney. Cries of "Discharge!," "Discharge!" were taken up by soldiers throughout the Regiment.

Gillet made certain none in the ranks near him joined in. He felt sorry for Captain Olney, a brave officer and one who had earned the respect of his men on the battlefield. Olney held up his hands for silence and ultimately, the tumult died down.

"I understand your frustration and eagerness to return to your hearth and homes. I too feel the need as keenly as you."

"Promises will not buy food for our families," a soldier shouted out. Cries for "Discharge! Discharge!" again rang out.

Seeing no benefit in trying to talk to the soldiers who were becoming more rowdy by the moment, Captain Olney ordered the Lieutenants to dismiss their companies. As the men disbanded, they insolently marched in step toward their huts, but instead of shouting out one-two-three-four, yelled "Discharge" on every fourth count.[2]

That night, around every campfire, the talk was of being discharged and going home. Gillet thought of his wife Judith, their daughter Sally and another babe on the way. He had been a ship's carpenter before enlisting. Unconsciously, he touched the two inverted white Vs on the sleeve of his jacket, indicative of his more than six years of service. He hoped to earn a living in the Providence shipyards. What if there were no work? What if he had to sell his carpenter's tools for food? He would need money to pay the mid-wife for the baby. The comradeship with his fellow soldiers offered some small measure of security, despite the constant hunger, threadbare uniforms, and fear of disease. Life on his own now seemed fraught with uncertainty.

Over the next days, little of the comradeship of the Army was in evidence. With nothing to do, some of the idle soldiers stoked their anger, gathering in irate clusters and heatedly discussing whether or not to seize supplies from the commissary and leave for home. Others turned to gambling with cards and dice, resulting in numerous brawls. Officers walking through the camp were met with boos and derisive hoots. If they dared to issue an order it was met with sullen looks and a slowness to respond that bordered on insolence. Gillet could sense the atmosphere worsening with each passing day as the men brooded over the lack of pay, broken promises and news of discharges.

The usual night-time strolls of officers talking to the men around the campfires decreased. Only Captain Olney appeared regularly. Gillet was sitting with some of the soldiers from his hut when he saw the Captain approaching. "Here comes the Captain to lord it over us," one of the men muttered.

"I was with the Captain when we captured the stone redoubt at Yorktown," Gillet replied sharply. "He led us into battle and is a brave man. He deserves our respect."

"Yes," another agreed. "That is true. Besides, our fight is not with him but with the Congress- bloody dickweeds every last one of them," he added hastily as the Captain approached.

Gillet attempted to set a tone of respect. "Good evening, Captain," he said and several of the men chimed in. Gillet made room on the log where he was sitting and Olney joined them.

"Any news, Sir? The men are anxious to go home," Gillet said. "My own wife is nearing her time, if the babe has not been born already. She will need me. None of us are doing anything of worth here," Henry concluded. "Except starving on half rations," one of the men added. "And getting into each other's business and way," another said.

Olney stared around at the men, their worn, thin faces illuminated by the flames, his gaze coming to rest on Gillet.

"It is Sergeant Gillet, is it not?" Henry nodded in reply.

"You and one of the Negroes were in the miners and sappers. At Yorktown, was it not?"

Gillet nodded. "Yes. With Private Gideon Hazzard."

"I was bayoneted four times at Yorktown." He paused as if

remembering the sounds of the siege cannons, the casualties and the wounds he suffered. "Our Regiment has been through fire and brimstone together. And now, as peace is within reach we are fighting amongst ourselves."

"We only want our pay," one of the men said quietly. "To be discharged and to return home," another added.

"The only advice I may give you is to wait, as our Colonel must await for orders from General Washington." He paused until the groans around the fire died down. "His Excellency has again written Congress and urged you 'war men' those who have served for the duration, be discharged. We all can only hope Congress sees the wisdom of such advice and acts promptly."

With no letter from home, Gillet found it harder to wait. Each day he hoped for news from Judith. When none came, he began to fear the worst – she had died in childbirth. This horrible thought so obsessed him, he could not sleep. He would leave his hut and pace the parade grounds, ignoring the few sentries still obeying orders and manning their posts, and gaze up at the night sky as if he could find a favorable sign amongst the constellations. He forgot the gnawing hunger and instead only felt an ominous foreboding. Mentally, he calculated the distance from the cantonment at New Windsor to Providence and how long it would take him to walk there. He estimated it was more than two hundred miles, maybe three. If he averaged twenty miles a day he could be home in ten to twenty days, assuming he encountered no bad weather and no major obstacles to delay him. As each day passed, he would say to himself, well, from today, I will be home by mid-May; then the third week in May; then by early June. Then he stopped counting and simply prayed for a letter from Judith bringing him good news.

On the first Saturday in May, the entire Regiment was convened on the parade grounds. Their Colonel sat erect on his horse as he read to them the General Orders. They were not to be discharged but only furloughed, which meant they were subject to being recalled. Gillet was certain that would never come to pass. All soldiers would receive a furlough paper. They also would be given a note, signed by the Congressional Superintendent of Finance for the pay due them, and permitted to take their muskets and cartridge boxes with them.[3]

"A promise is better than turning a deaf ear to our right to pay," a Private near Gillet muttered. "Although it does not buy us anything to eat."

"It might induce merchants to extend credit," Gillet said loudly enough for the men in his file to hear.

That night, Captain Olney was again present talking to the men, gauging their mood and answering their questions.

"When can we go home?" Gillet asked, voicing the thought on everyone's minds.

"In truth you should receive your furloughs and 'Morris notes,' on Monday, tomorrow being the Sabbath. You may then leave the cantonment when you wish." He smiled at the men around the campfire. "I assume none of you will tarry too long," he said to chuckles from the soldiers.

"That is right, Captain. I will set out as soon as I have tucked the papers in my jacket." Others cried "Me too," and "I am for that."

Gillet knew once he left camp there was no possibility of receiving any letter from Judith. He would travel as fast as he could. He would hope and pray that when he arrived in Providence he would be greeted by the sight of his wife, their daughter Sally and a newborn, healthy babe.

Early Monday morning, he joined a stream of soldiers walking briskly down the road from New Windsor toward West Point. While some stopped to rest in the shade, or turned off to seek food at nearby farms, Henry continued on with a few others from his old Regiment. They reached the ferry at West Point well before noon. As he anticipated, the crossing, still controlled by the Army, was free. Once on the other side of the Hudson, he glanced at Constitution Island. There, after experiencing such fear of heights he had impetuously joined the newly created regiment of miners and sappers.

Gillet headed southeast on one of the narrow wagon trails that cut through dense pine forests. By nightfall, he and a few others bedded down in a tavern situated on wagon road that ran south to New York City and north toward Poughkeepsie. It was not even a crossroads, a lonely place with two or three out buildings surrounded by hardwood trees just beginning to show the light green of early spring. The owner, a man named Tompkins, was as eager for the company as he was for the opportunity to make money.

Henry used a few of his precious coins to pay for a bowl of venison stew, a piece of bread and some hard cider, and the privilege of sharing a bed in one of the lofts with two other soldiers. It was more crowded than the bunks in the huts back at the Cantonment but it was dry and warm. That mattered for something.

Anxious to move on, Gillet was up at dawn. As he descended the stairs, he was met by Tompkins who was hastily trying to load a rifle. His oldest son stood by him with what looked like an antique musket that had not been used since the French and Indian War.

"There is a bunch of armed Negroes in my yard," Tompkins said grimly, ramming a ball down the muzzle. "I intend to run them off before they do me or my family any harm."

Gillet heard footsteps on the narrow porch, a knock and then Private Gideon Hazzard appeared in the doorway. Behind him were two others from the 2nd Rhode Islanders. "Gideon," Henry shouted in greeting, stepping between Tompkins and his friend. Hazzard's familiar face broke into a gap-toothed grin. "You remember Privates Mingo Power and Jeremiah Warmsley," he said gesturing with his head toward the two soldiers behind him.

The three crowded into the tavern, stacked their muskets against the wall and sat down on both sides of the table.

"What do you want here?" Tompkins asked warily, still holding his rifle.

"Breakfast," Gideon replied curtly, noting the tavern owner's uneasiness, and enjoying his discomfort.

Tompkins stared at the three newcomers. The thought of more money overcame his distaste of having to serve them. "Only if you can pay," he said, waiting until Hazzard nodded.

"For the each of you, some porridge, bread and cheese, ten

shillings. All I have is cider at forty pence a mug."

Gillet looked up at Tompkins. "That is more than you charged me for dinner and the bed upstairs," he said with an edge to his voice.

"A man has got to make a living," Tompkins replied. "Why you siding with them anyway," he added in an aggrieved tone.

"Because we are of the same Regiment and have fought alongside each other for the past four years."

"Not used to seeing armed Negroes in uniform," the tavern keeper muttered by way of explanation.

"We did not come here for trouble," Gideon said, rising from the bench. "We are hungry." He turned to Gillet. "Sergeant. We will abide by your judgment. You set a fair amount to pay and we will pay it. If the tavern owner here does not accept your price, then," he paused looking around the room and back at the inn keeper "after Sergeant Gillet leaves, there is no telling what may happen."

"No need to get so stirred up," Tompkins said. "I can be accommodating. Say five shillings for each of you."

Gillet shook his head. "I was thinking three shillings for the breakfast and cider would be more in line with what you charged me."

"Done," said Tompkins, "but only if your Sergeant stays here and you all leave together."

Gillet had wanted an early start. However, he realized that if he left, Tompkins might still cause trouble. He was confident Hazzard would not start a fight but knew he was entirely capable of finishing one to his advantage.

"I will stay," he heard himself say reluctantly. "However, I look for Mr. Tompkins to give me true advice on how to proceed toward Danbury over the Connecticut line."

As the men ate, Tompkins explained he had been hired, two years ago, by a farmer to deliver barrels of flour to Danbury by wagon. It had taken him more than twelve days heading due east "Nothing but deer tracks and old Indian trails, thick forest, some lakes you have to go around, and once in a while a house or two."

Henry thought on this, weighing whether he would be better

off taking a less direct route. "What about the road heading south."

"I would guess it is forty or so miles to the Connecticut line." Tompkins shrugged. "I do not know how far from there to the coast. Where in Connecticut are you heading?"

Gideon and Henry laughed simultaneously. "Providence, Rhode Island, where our homes are," Gillet responded.

"All I can tell you is that if you take the road south, there will be wagoners doing the same. If you put in a full day marching, you could walk it in two or three days, If someone gives you a ride shorter than that."

"And you say it took you twelve days to get to Danbury from here by going due east."

"Not a day less," Tompkins affirmed.

Gillet turned to Hazzard. "What do you think?"

"Even if it takes us two more days from the line to reach the Connecticut coast, we could ship out and sail up to Providence. That may take another day or two depending on the weather." Henry agreed. The southern route offered the best chance for him to return home the soonest.

The four set out south on the muddy road a little after ten in the morning. By noon they fell in with soldiers from New York Regiments, and some from Connecticut heading toward the coast. That night, camping in the woods, in answer to Gillet's inquiries, a few of the Connecticut men said there was a good road just north of White Plains to the Sound. It was less than ten miles. From there one could take the Boston Post Road north or sail up the Connecticut coast.

"You will not find much left in the way of towns from Greenwich Harbor to New Haven," one of the Connecticut soldiers said as he turned a rabbit roasting on a spit over the fire. "The Redcoats raided up and down the coast from '79 onwards burning everything in sight. My youngest brother was in the militia. Took a ball in the leg defending Norwalk and was almost burned to death by the bloody Hessians when they set fire to the Presbyterian Church." He stared into the fire and fell silent.

Gillet had seen enough of burned towns and farms, ruined

churches and decimated orchards. Besides, the sea was more familiar to him. He resolved once he arrived at the Long Island Sound, he would rather proceed by water than the Post Road.

The next day they marched through a pouring rain from morning until dusk. The air was warm and Henry did not mind being soaked through. It was the mud that dampened his spirits because it slowed them down, sucking at their shoes, seeping in the seams and squishing between his toes. By nightfall, when they reached a burned out frame of a barn and took what little shelter it offered, the men were worn out. They lit a small fire, more for comfort than warmth, and slept fitfully.

When Gillet arose the next morning, the wind brought the smell of salt air and with it, the promise of the nearby coast. In less than an hour, they reached the junction with the Post Road. The Connecticut men turned north, leaving Gillet, Hazzard, Power and Warmsley to continue due east. By early afternoon they saw the choppy waters of the Sound. They stacked their muskets against some pine trees on the edge of a rocky shore. Eagerly, they stripped off their clothes raced down to the water and washed themselves. Renewed and hopefully free of the lice that had infested their hair and armpits, they continued up a narrow trail through the forest. The trail broadened as it sloped down toward a river. There amidst the ruins of Norwalk and the few remaining buildings, were two ships, one a brig, the other a two masted coastal trader, riding at anchor.

As they got closer, Henry made out the name Nancy on the trader. His mother's name. After all the piles of amputated limbs following a battle, the stinking, bloated corpses of the dead, the dangers he had endured from cannon balls, musket fire, a fever he had almost died from and the constant cold and starvation, he took it as a sign. He was certain the *Nancy* would carry him home, or as far up the Connecticut coast the ship would go until he could find another to carry him to Providence. I am not superstitious, Henry acknowledged. However, sailing on a vessel bearing his mother's name was reassuring. His deceased mother's spiritual presence could only mean he would safely arrive home, to be met by Judith, their little Sally and a healthy newborn babe. Of this he was certain.

—⚜—

"Tis better we leave as individual soldiers without a fancy parade and ceremony," Private Matthias Vose said as he marched down the road from the Cantonment.

"Why do you say so?" his friend, Corporal Caleb Wade asked.

"So the men recognize our victory is attributable to God and do not forget He was with us always, during this long war. It was as you said on the way to Yorktown," he reminded Caleb.

They were part of the 3rd New Jersey Continentals streaming south from the Cantonment on the familiar way to West Point. The road was clogged with boisterous soldiers, furloughed and heading home to the towns and farms above New York City, and southwest toward Bergen and Essex Counties and beyond. Some had already sold their muskets and cartridge boxes to the sutlers who waylaid them and paid a pittance to the cash strapped soldiers as they left the camp. Then, tempted by the rum offered by the same sutlers, they returned the coins for full canteens and drank from them frequently as they continued on their way.

Many of the men had shed their worn blue jackets, strapped them to their haversacks and walked carefree in their shirts. Instinctively, they marched in loose ranks, having had the pace and formation drilled into them. It was early June and the sun was warming, the air fragrant with the smell of flowers and the blossoms of apple trees. Soldiers lounged under shade trees by the side of the road, having succumbed to the rum and heat of the day.

"I am afraid most of our fellows are less ready to attribute victory to God and are more eager to celebrate their freedom from discipline by drinking themselves into a stupor," Caleb observed as they passed a cluster of soldiers sprawled out on the grass next to the trunk of a tree. "Freedom to return to their homes seems to mean freedom to imbibe to excess."

"I look back on the manner of my sinning and how it was only a close encounter with death that caused me to turn away from my own life of drunkenness and blasphemy," Matthias responded. He clasped Caleb's big hand in his two. "I acknowledge your example of finding God and gently teaching His presence is with us. You contributed to my change in character." He released his friend's hand. "When I escaped from prison in New York, it was God's hand that led me to those on Long Island who guided me to freedom. I learned from Josiah Oakley, a true man of God who never sinned in his life, to trust in Him, even while a British cavalry sabre was poised to cleave his skull."

"So you have told me," Wade replied, a bit wearily. "I believe this Oakley is a godly man but no one is devoid of sin." He paused, looking ahead down the road as if he were divining the future. "As soldiers we have done our share of killing. We must struggle against our violent tendencies taking hold again and overcoming our best intentions," he added soberly.

"True. 'Tis well said," Matthias responded, as they continued on in silence thinking of the hand to hand combat and fighting they had experienced.

That night, they camped on the parade grounds at West Point along with some two hundred other furloughed soldiers. The regular troops on duty, mostly from Massachusetts, who had not yet been given their papers looked on with obvious envy, as the newly released soldiers rose late and with no officers to order them about, leisurely ambled around the grounds. They left in small groups, laughing and waving goodbye to those still under arms.

Wade and Matthias saw no need to tarry and were among those setting a faster pace. They left behind others who preferred to walk a few miles and then bask in the sunlight in soft grassy areas alongside the road, simply to enjoy the novelty of being able to stop when and where they wanted. Or to drink and gamble under a blue sky as a diversion from marching.

Two days later, the two friends together with a half a dozen or so of their original regiment took shelter at Coe's Tavern. They were drenched by a warm summer downpour and covered with mud, from having forded a narrow river and clambered up its slippery banks.

The small tavern, a low planked building, able to accommodate perhaps a dozen travelers was crowded with almost forty men from other regiments, who had arrived earlier. The soldiers sat on the few available benches and against the walls or stood almost shoulder to shoulder filling the only room. Pools of water accumulated on the floor from leaks in the roof. The dominant smell was of wet wool and unwashed bodies, with an occasional whiff of stale vomit. Some had passed out from too much drink and lay sprawled on the dirty floor.

Caleb and Mathias shook the water from their tri-corns. Wade, whose height and size caused men to give way rather than chance a fight looked over the heads of the men packed closely together. Spying a possible space against a wall, he pushed through the crowd with Vose tucked in his wake. They plunked down against a wall, elbowing others to clear a small area for the two of them. Wade apologized and thanked them for their consideration. His words and disarming smile appeased their new neighbors. An offer to share a bit of cheese sealed the bargain. He and Vose had their little piece of floor and wall for the night.

A man in a leather apron approached and they ordered two bowls of beef stew and mugs of hard cider.

"I need to see the coins first," the tavern-keeper said gruffly, bending over them. "Three shillings each for the stew and two for the cider." Caleb grunted as he reached into the pouch he kept in an inner pocket of his breeches and paid for both of them. The owner saw the bulge of the pouch. Immediately his attitude became friendly. "John Coe at your service," he said in an ingratiating tone. "A gill of rum would warm your insides up and ward off the chill from the rain. Only four shillings each."

"We prefer the cider," Wade responded. When the stew and cider arrived, it took only a moment to know they were watered. Vose shook his head in disgust. "One would think the owner would be satisfied making an honest living instead of cheating soldiers who have starved for much of their service." They spent the night trying to sleep propped up against the wall with the noise of drunken shouts and arguments around them. Sometime in the early morning hours, the din died down. Before drowsing off, Matthias whispered to Caleb, "We sleep in a den of iniquity amongst sinners. May God enable them to see the light."

"They are men who have endured much – fear of battle, arbitrary orders, the lash for minor infractions - are now free of discipline. Some boisterousness is to be expected."

"We have endured as much if not more and yet we are not gambling or drinking so much rum as to spew our vomit on others."

"Matthias," Caleb reminded him gently. "We both were once like our brothers here- blind drunk, ready for a fight and with a dull head all the next day." He put his arm around his friend. "Let us try to sleep. In the morning we will have fresh air and an open road to revive us."

Caleb awoke first. The rain had stopped and the day promised to be clear and warm. They took turns at the well outside, one keeping their space and guarding their muskets and haversacks while the other washed his hands and face in the yard. The tavern keeper, mindful of their ability to pay, offered them hot porridge and bread. "Only if there are no weevils in either," Caleb replied and withheld payment until he and Matthias had found their breakfast satisfactory.

As they ate, three men came down the stairs from the attic. The first was a gentleman with a brushed brown double-breasted coat, over a clean buff colored waistcoat. He was followed by a short thin man, dressed not quite as elegantly, whose nervous eyes darted about the room, like a rat emerging from its hole and testing the air for danger. The third man, stout and taller than the other two, wore a pair of rough breeches and a simple linen shirt that revealed thick muscular arms. Two heavy saddlebags hung from each of his shoulders. The husky man pushed two sleeping soldiers off a bench and sat down with his companions. Coe ran up to them immediately, and returned with a platter of cheese and bread and what smelled like hot coffee. After the three had finished, the gentleman placed a large heavy leather pouch on the table. The metallic clink of the coins within immediately drew the attention of those awaiting their breakfast.

The rat-faced huckster placed a sheet of paper, ink-well and quill in front of him in anticipation.

"My good soldiers. Give me your attention for but a moment and it will profit you immensely," the gentleman declaimed loudly. "You have been given these Morris notes which you cannot cash. I have seen your dire need for hard specie last night when some went without food or drink," he said expanding his arms to embrace the crowd of soldiers before him. "I will buy two rounds of rum for the first ten men who sell me their Morris notes at a small discount. Why" he said smiling as if he were a benevolent uncle bestowing unexpected wealth on a favorite nephew, "depending on how much your notes are for, some of you will leave here with as much as one hundred dollars. All in coins- shillings, crowns, guineas, or" he paused dramatically, "even pound notes." He hefted the bag and shook it hard so the coins jingled inside, before dropping it with a satisfying clunk on the table. "Think of how your loved ones will welcome you home when you return in new clothes and coins in your pocket." He paused to let the men envision the picture he had painted.

"It appears this tavern keeper is not the only one who intends to cheat soldiers," Caleb said with disgust, gesturing toward the gentleman and the little huckster at the table. He returned his spoon to his haversack and rose from the floor. He approached the soldiers who were talking amongst themselves whether to cash in their notes for the real money being offered and recognized a few from their New Jersey Regiment.

"My fellow soldiers. Remember all we have been through together," he said loudly in his deep voice. "You have earned every dollar specified in the notes with your blood and your time away from your families and farms." The soldiers who had been charmed by the gentleman and entranced by his talk, turned their heads, like sunflowers along a pasture fence to listen to Caleb. "When you return home, the merchants who know you will extend credit on the basis of these Morris notes. In that way, you will receive full value. Do not let this man who, by his dress and manner appears never to have served a day on the line, or marched a mile on a muddy road, or withstood a bayonet charge, profit by offering you a pittance of what you are due for your sacrifices."

"You give a pretty speech," the little huckster sneered, motioning with his head to the heavy set ruffian behind the table. "These men will need hard specie for food and drink and lodging. Many are still days away from home." Wade saw the big man making his way around the edge of the group of soldiers. He moved one foot a little behind and shifted his weight for better balance. "We offer them a service, coins in hand to tide them over when they arrive home. The merchants you speak of may not be so eager to extend them credit." He stood up and pointed at Caleb. "This man's advice is . . .

Wade did not fall for the huckster's attempt to distract him. The thug was a few steps away, a small hard wood club in one hand, with his arm extended to grab Caleb. As the man lunged forward, one of the soldiers extended his leg and tripped him. The man stumbled. Caleb seized the opportunity. He smashed his fist into the man's face breaking his nose and a split second later hit him hard on the side of his head. The ruffian went down as if he had been pole-axed and lay still.

Caleb motioned for Matthias to bring their muskets and haversacks. "I have said what I think," he said addressing the soldiers. "You may take this gentleman's coins or my advice."

At the door frame, Matthias turned toward the soldiers' upturned faces. "Remember the bible passage," he shrieked with religious fervor, pointing at the gentleman and the little man at the table. "Jesus overturned the tables of the money changers and drove them from the Temple."

"Tis hardly a temple," a drunken voice bellowed from a far corner of the room. "Tavern keeper. Another gill of rum," someone else called out. The soldiers continued to argue back and forth as to whether to take the money or not, as Matthias and Caleb stepped out into the sunlight.

"If only one of our fellow soldiers keeps his note for full pay, you will have done well," Matthias said as the two of them followed the road away from the tavern.

Caleb shook his head. "I have reverted to my old ways of violence. As soon as I saw the man move from behind the table, I knew I would fight him. Why did I not restrain myself or better, leave to avoid having to hit him?"

"You defended yourself. The man had a club," Matthias responded.

"Unlike Josiah Oakley, the man you have told me about, I resorted to violence instead of shunning it. He placed his faith in God. I, who am of lesser faith, placed my trust in my fists." Matthias sought to console him and took his friend by the elbow. Caleb shook it off. They walked on in silence, and when they stopped to rest, Vose pointedly buried his face in his bible, silently mouthing the words he was reading.

"I am not mad at you, Mathias," Caleb said quietly. "I have found myself wanting and am ashamed for it."

"There is nothing for you to be ashamed of," Vose said, closing his bible. "Had you not spoken out, some poor soldier may have been cheated out of his pay. You acted with a generous heart." Wade accepted the words but was still brooding when they continued on their way.

By the end of the day, after seeing only an isolated farm or two, they arrived at a small village. All that remained of the church that had stood just beyond the junction with the wagon road, was the brick foundation and a makeshift hut, made out of the charred timbers of the steeple and roof. The main street was flanked by one story planked homes. Brambles grew where fences had stood marking now empty pastures. A ruined mill with the waterwheel askew on its old shaft, marked the river that ran through the west of town. As they passed the churchyard they saw an old man, on his hands and knees, weeding an overgrown patch of garden. Matthias left the road and wandered over while Wade waited under a broad branched oak.

"Caleb," he called. "Come meet Reverend Pomeroy." The man was thin as a rail, not in a wiry strong way but emaciated and weak. The leathery mottled skin visible on his hands and neck gave him a desiccated appearance. Tufts of white hair sprouted from his ears and nostrils, matching his unkempt hair and wayward eyebrows.

Pomeroy squinted up through rheumy eyes. Wade politely moved so the sun was not shining in the Reverend's eyes. "You are not the first soldiers to come through here. We keep hoping some of our own have been furloughed and will return. I need help in rebuilding my church," he said gesturing to the ruins behind him. "I pray every day our young men are alive and whole and the Lord will bring them home."

It was obvious the Reverend could not offer them any lodging. However, he accompanied them to the home of a matronly widow and vouched for them. Caleb and Matthias slept on her kitchen floor. In the morning, when Caleb awoke, Matthias was gone. Caleb washed, chopped some firewood for the widow and stacked it and was eating porridge when Matthias returned.

"I went to talk to the Reverend," he said by way of explanation. "Tory militias have savaged this town and its environs. Some of the young men who stayed were captured and rumored to be imprisoned in New York. Heaven help them if they were," Vose said with a shudder, recalling his own incarceration in the Sugar Warehouse. "The cattle, hogs and oxen have all been driven off, the horses impressed in Tory service. All these people have to live on is turnips and corn, and a meager apple crop from ill-tended orchards. The only meat they have comes from the squirrels and rabbits they trap in snares," he said.

Wade grunted in response.

"The Reverend says there are a few young children, maybe a dozen in need of schooling, and the church needs rebuilding."

"Speak your mind, Matthias," Caleb said smiling at his friend.

"We could do some good here, the Lord's work helping these people."

"You mean to stay?"

"I feel the Lord has called me to this place. I could learn more of the scriptures from the Reverend, repair the church so it is fit to hold services again. Work for my keep," he added as his voice trailed off.

"Matthias. You neither need to persuade me nor gain my

approval. If you wish, I will stay a day or two more. Then, I will return to my own farm and family."

"Caleb. I did not mean for you to remain. My older brothers manage our farm, their wives the households and marketing." He shrugged his shoulders. "There is more need for me here. I feel it in my soul."

They parted two days later on a mild June day, both agreeing it would seem strange not to be in each other's company. The last Matthias saw of his friend as he stopped at the bend in the road, was a final wave goodbye before heading further south into Bergen County. Vose turned. The little village was bathed in early morning sunlight. He walked toward the Reverend's hut with its makeshift roof askew. Soon we will have a church and a proper parsonage, he thought. The Lord is with us, he muttered to himself.

—⚜—

It did not bother Will he was not being furloughed. He was with his family and the General's staff at West Point. If I am truthful with myself, he thought, I welcome the opportunity to remain in service. I have nowhere else to go. General Knox had said it was only until the British finally evacuated New York City. That had been in August and now it was the middle of October and still the Redcoats remained in the city.

Despite the beauty of the fall foliage in the Hudson Valley, the General's headquarters was a somber and difficult place. The Knox family had returned, due to necessity, to the modest wooden building where they resided before. Where his infant son had died almost a year before. Little Lucy now almost eight years old and Henry Knox, Henry Stoner and Adam and Sarah's son, Emmanuel frolicked in the yard. Yet, the adults were overcome at moments that crept up on them by surprise, an image here, a sound there, triggering thoughts of the death of little Marcus. Elisabeth spent most of her mornings with Lucy Knox, outside on the wide porch overlooking the river, when it was warm, inside in the parlor when it was not. Once a week she would accompany Lucy to a grove of trees set back from the plateau. It was there the Knox's little boy was buried, in a small grassy plot underneath a maple tree, whose bright golden orange leaves contrasted with Lucy Knox's black shawl and dress.

Elisabeth awoke as Will buckled on his sword and buttoned up his jacket. It was a little before midnight and he had night guard duty. She sat up in bed, careful not to wake their son sleeping next to her and peered at Agnes in her cradle. "Do you know what little Lucy said today?" Elisabeth whispered as Will pulled on his boots. "She said her little brother and sister Julia were in heaven and some day" Elisabeth's voice broke and her eyes filled with tears as she sat up in bed. "She hoped soon, she would be with them so as to take care of them." Will sat down next to her and put his arms around his wife and rocked her gently. "How did you respond?"

"I said her mother and father are here on earth who love her dearly and would very much like her to stay with them. And she can play with her little brother Henry and all the other children." She shook her head sadly. "It is so difficult to explain death to little ones. Our Henry overheard and asked me if we would go to heaven together."

Will waited for Elisabeth to continue. "I told him we will, but first we must enjoy each day God has given us on earth." She cupped her hands in front of her mouth and stifled a sob. "Oh Will. I am so fearful with winter coming on, and we living once again in this drafty wooden cabin within the Fort, our Henry or little Agnes will sicken and . . ."

Will kissed the top of her head, smelling the lavender she used and feeling her body against him. "The General believes we will be in New York soon. It is only a matter of the British obtaining enough ships to evacuate those who wish to leave." He did not add as more and more Loyalists fled to the city, it was more likely the British would delay their departure until they procured more ships. Nor could he guarantee his family would have a solid brick house where they would live and firewood for the hearth.

"The river is not yet frozen. You could write your father and ask him to send a sloop to take you and the children to your parents' home in Albany."

She put her hands on his chest and looked up at him. "After all our separations during this cruel war, I could not bear to be apart from you. Not for a week. Not even for a day," she added fervently.

Will leaned over and kissed her passionately. She stifled a cry of pain and pushed him away. "Your sword hilt pressed against my stomach," she said by way of explanation, laughing at his surprise. "Now go and do your duty this cold and dark night and no more talk of my leaving you."

Will walked across the yard. The moon was obscured by clouds and there was a crispness to the night air. Adam Cooper had assembled the thirty men for guard duty and they stood in two lines before the main ladder leading to the main battery. Damn, Will thought to himself. Of all the ways to end this long and seemingly interminable war, he never foresaw it would be protecting the army's diminished food supplies, rum and firewood from ill-disciplined soldiers. Yet, he consoled himself, he was serving out his time with a few old friends. He first met Adam, a soldier in the Marblehead Mariners, in '76 when Will was just an unemployed teamster. There were a few of the original gun crew who had survived the battle of Brooklyn, and many others – Isaiah Chandler, Levi Tyler, John Baldwin. All men he could trust to follow orders in dealing with a rowdy and ill-disciplined mob of resentful soldiers.

Loud singing and drunken shouts came from the surrounding barracks. The soldiers at West Point, apart from those in the artillery regiment, were seething with anger at not being furloughed as the others had been. They were eager to return home to Massachusetts. Many of their officers shared the men's resentment and did nothing as discipline deteriorated. Fights frequently broke out as the men gambled and drank more.

"A relatively peaceful night," Captain Hadley said as Will relieved him. "It remains to be seen whether they drink themselves into an intoxicated stupor, or the rum provokes them to engage in mischief," he added handing Will the six foot long spontoon. "If needed, fire a volley and we will come on the run." Will watched the earlier guard detail disappear into the darkness. Master Sergeant Cooper ordered the men to fix bayonets, divided them into details and marched them off to their stations. There were three -the long, low shed adjacent to the Fort's main kitchen, housing the barrels of flour, salted pork, beef, and some vegetables, an open sided shingled roof structure covering six foot high and twelve feet long stacks of firewood, and the padlocked stone building within which the barrels of rum, port and cider were stored. Although General Knox had prohibited it, the neighboring farmers sold cider and beer to those soldiers who could pay for it. Since paper money was worthless, the soldiers intensified their gambling to earn hard coins at cards or stole food and firewood to sell to other soldiers who wanted more than their rationed share.

The raucous singing, drunken shouts, loud oaths and curses of soldiers losing at cards or dice died down shortly after the watch called out at two in the morning. Will guessed many of these soldiers would not make roll call at reveille.

On the third night of guard duty, Will was surprised to see Captain Hadley join them. "I have been sent to find Adam," he said with some urgency. "Sarah is in labor and Mercy and Sarah's mother are with her now." Will pointed toward the kitchen. "He is on detail over there. Tell him he is relieved from duty." As Adam rushed by, Hadley returned. "Mercy tells me a man is no good at all during a birth, much like a fifth leg on a chair. Supportive, but useless, are my wife's very words."

Will recalled the birth of his son while he was snowbound in Morristown. His wife was at General Washington's headquarters at the Ford Mansion more than three miles away, when it was attacked, during a blizzard by Tory raiders. It was Adam who had sounded the alarm and saved the General from being kidnapped. Little Henry was born the day after the raid was foiled.

"Is Sarah in difficulty?" Will asked, wishing the best for his friend's wife.

"Mercy did not mention any trouble when she told me to alert Adam. She has delivered both of your children and Sarah's first one. With Elisabeth and Sarah's mother to assist, I am confident all will be well."

"Let us hope so," Will replied, thinking of the stories he had heard of women dying in childbirth. Throughout the remainder of the cold night, Will nervously scurried from one station to another, talking to his men on guard detail, alert to any change in the sounds coming from the soldiers' barracks. Yet when all was quiet, his thoughts were with his friend Adam and his wife, Sarah.

At six when they were relieved, he returned to their room in the Fort. Elisabeth was dozing in their bed, both children asleep beside her. She opened her eyes when he sat down to pull off his boots, feeling the bed sag under his weight. "What news?" he whispered, lying down next to her. "A beautiful baby girl," she replied smiling. "Sarah is doing well and Adam is beside himself with pride."

"Poor Adam," Will murmured. "His daughter has already captured his heart as surely as he hooks a fish."

Elisabeth stifled a giggle. "As if our little Agnes is not the source of your fatherly pride. Henry is rough and tumble and you adore him. But I see the way you look at Agnes. There is some precious bond between you," she said, rubbing his arm but he was already asleep.

There was more than the usual merriment at the General's staff meeting a week later. Held in the General's dining room, the officers stood crammed around the long table. First they drank a toast to General Washington, then to Knox himself, then to the army with the usual toast of "a hoop to the barrel," and finally to Master Sergeant Adam Cooper and his newborn daughter.

"What is her name, this newborn babe of yours?" General Knox asked in his booming voice from the end of the table.

"Priscilla is her first name. A proper New England one at that," Adam added. "The same as my beloved sister," Captain Hadley said, raising his glass in Adam's direction.

As the murmurs of approval died down, Adam said softly in a voice tinged with sadness, "Her middle name is Sabinah, named after my mother-in-law's second daughter. She was sold off the plantation at age twelve and never heard from again." There was shocked silence. Some of the officers looked away from Adam, embarrassed by his raising the reality of slavery in their presence.

Will seized the moment and raised his glass of ale. "To my god-daughter, Priscilla Sabinah Cooper. May she live a long, healthy and happy life."

"To Priscilla Sabinah Cooper," Knox said in his deep baritone and the other officers joined in, some less enthusiastically than others.

Knox settled in his chair and waited for the noise of scraping and rattling of swords to subside. "His Excellency, in response to my letters describing the situation at West Point of disgruntled soldiers on the verge of mutiny and their officers refusing to do their duty, has given me permission to furlough as many as I deem necessary. I will issue orders tomorrow, sending most of the men of the Massachusetts regiments home. /4

"We will maintain a garrison of some two hundred or so at West Point. As for you, my trusted officers and the artillery regiment," he paused looking around the table, "His Excellency has given us the honor and duty of securing New York City after the British leave and before he, the Governor and other officials enter." Will smiled at the announcement. It would further delay his having to confront the uncertainties of civilian life. Others around the table did not seem as keen at the prospect. "We will march to Tappan this Friday, make temporary camp and await our English cousins departure," Knox continued. "His Excellency anticipates, with fair winds and good will on their part, the British troops will evacuate New York City by early November. The artillery regiment, together with New York Militia under my command will maintain order, until civilian authority is established,"

Will noticed Knox did not offer a date when that may happen. He guessed it might not occur until the new year.

"I am aware," Knox said, looking deliberately around the table, "many of you wish to follow others of my staff who have already been furloughed and returned to their families. You have served your country long and well and are entitled to leave now if you so desire." There was some shifting in chairs and protestations of continued loyalty to the General, followed by a few officers and then others, voicing personal considerations of the urgent need to return home.

Will did not doubt the truth of their reasons – a seriously ill wife or family member; diminishing funds to sustain the family and the need to ask for credit on the basis of Congress' promise of half pay for five years; businesses failing or homes falling into disrepair with winter coming on. The General listened patiently, with a benevolent look on his face, like a father hearing the just complaints of his children. "Those of you who have expressed the need to be furloughed now, are free to go. My clerks will prepare the necessary papers." He rose from his chair and raised his glass. "I propose one last toast while we are all in this room - to the suffering we have endured together, to the battles we have won and to the blessings of the peace to come."

As the officers filed out, Knox gestured for Will to remain. He stood until the General motioned impatiently for him to sit down. "Will, there is no need for such formality." He poured more Madeira in his glass and leaned back in his chair. "I am pleased you have not chosen to be furloughed."

"To be honest, Sir, as you know my family is here and I have nowhere else to go."

Knox chortled. "When we march to New York, our wives and children will remain at West Point. I do not have to tell you how Lucy and I detest being apart," he said with a sigh. "I swore to her this will be the last time. It is a comfort to me your Elisabeth and Captain Hadley's Mercy and child will keep her and our children company. Once the city is ours," he motioned toward the second floor, "I will send for Lucy, your family and that of Captain Hadley. I propose they travel on a river sloop provided by your father-in-law and I have written him to have a ship standing by at the Point."

Will nodded, thinking of how he would tell Elisabeth he must go south without her and the children. The General's promise of a swift reunion would help persuade her to accept his decision but perhaps not assuage her anxiety.

Lost in his thoughts of rehearsing the words he would say to his wife, Will was surprised to hear the General add, "I am promoting you to the rank of Captain Lieutenant."

"Sir, I truly have done nothing to deserve this. My duty at the

Cantonment in New Windsor and West Point has been so routine as to barely amount to any service whatsoever. I am honored you. . ."

"Nonsense," Knox interrupted. "You have served me and your country through this entire war in exemplary fashion." He laughed. "Although you seem not to have learned a mere Lieutenant does not contradict a Major General." He wagged his finger. "As Captain, you will command more authority in New York." He pointed at Will's left shoulder. "Ask your wife to remove that epaulet and transfer it to your right shoulder. Please have her do it before tomorrow when you and she, the remaining staff and their wives will do Mrs. Knox and me the pleasure of joining us for dinner."

As Will strode across the grounds toward his quarters, he was pleased to be promoted. However, he thought I will soon be a discharged Captain of the artillery and my higher rank will no more assure employment at which I may provide for my family than my present one.

Part Three
Peace and Its Aftermath

Chapter 10 – Panic in New York City

Andrew Brockholst sat against the high windowed wall on a long bench at Merchant's Coffee House on the corner of Wall and Water Streets. Many of the merchants, traders and gentlemen present who dealt in leases and even sales of fine houses, were, if not his friends, at least his acquaintances or business associates with a common purpose. As recently as six months ago, there would have been an pleasant atmosphere in the room, a loose association of men of wealth, making deals, talking politics, trading news of the latest arrival of a British ship of the line, or the published general orders of Sir Guy Carleton. Now, an anxious air filled the cavernous coffee house. The East River and a forest of masts were visible through the windows and shafts of sunlight of this warm April day illuminated the room. Despite the promise of spring, the atmosphere within the room was one of gloom, verging on palpable panic brought on by uncertainty and indecision. The preliminary provisions of the peace treaty had been published in James Rivington's Royal Gazette.

"Tis that bloody Fifth Article," a merchant named Talbot grumbled, returning to a complaint they had all made before. "Who would have thought the Parliament would compromise their honor and relinquish their duty to us," he said angrily. Brockholst grunted in agreement. The preliminary peace treaty contained no guarantee of Loyalist property. Just a promise by Congress "to recommend" to the various states they return and protect Loyalist property. That promise is as worthless as a Continental paper dollar, Andrew thought.

"Have you read the latest broadside from Albany," another dealer asked glumly. "It arrived yesterday by river packet. Signed by someone called "A True Patriot," it calls for the banishment of all Loyalists and the seizure of their property."[1]

Brockholst did not consider himself a Loyalist unlike the prominent New York DeLancey family who had much more to lose than he. Yet, he was certain the victorious Rebels would treat him as one, when they entered the City, in order to get their scheming avaricious hands on his town house, his land holdings, his warehouse and goods, not to mention the thousands of pounds in hard currency he had hidden away. His confidential conversation with Luykens Van Hooten gave him little comfort. His former employer had only given a vague assurance to intervene on his behalf to protect what he had garnered. He had not been completely truthful with Luykens. On the basis of false affidavits, affirming that Van Hooten was a Loyalist residing in Albany, and that he Brockholst continued to serve as his agent, he had rented the Van Hooten warehouse to the British Army for One Hundred Pounds per year. True, it was not all profit for he had to pay a substantial bribe to the Deputy Quartermaster responsible for soldiers' housing to accept the affidavits. Would Van Hooten remain willing to intercede to protect Andrew's wealth if he learned of this? Would he demand Brockholst disgorge the wealth he had accumulated over the past five years? Whether he lost all his wealth by decree of the new Whig Government or having to pay Van Hooten, the result would be the same. He would be almost destitute with few prospects to make money in a Rebel occupied city.

"I, for one, do not intend to wait until the rapacious scoundrels arrive to sate their desire for revenge on innocents such as us, who have merely made a living under the occupation," Talbot stated. "We have done no one any wrong, yet it is clear we have no future here." He held his meerschaum pipe by the small bowl and scowled at it, as if it were the pipe's fault it had gone out. "The lowest sort of people will rule and the woe-begotten States will crumble in short order under their enormous debt and the even greater taxes they must impose. No, gentlemen, it is time to leave this blighted land. I have booked passage to London for myself and my family in two months time. The weather will be most pleasant then for crossing to the other side of the water."

"And what do you propose to do with your property, furniture, leases and the like?" another merchant asked. Brockholst leaned forward with the others, all sensing an opportunity.

"I will appoint an agent to manage my land and leases. If they be seized by these Rebels, I will petition the Crown for recompense. Furniture and other disposables I will ship some and regretfully sell off the rest, at auction for a certain loss. However," he waved his pipe at them, "the loss I face will be insignificant to the loss I would sustain if I stayed. You would be well advised to follow my example."[2]

Brockholst thought perhaps he could use the same agent as Talbot to manage his own leases and land, and thus save on fees. But what would he do in London or anywhere else for that matter? That was the question. And how would his wife and two daughters manage. What would their prospects be?

"You speak nonsense, Talbot," a merchant and trader named Lawlor responded. "I intend to stay and take advantage of the pent up demand these Whigs will have for English goods. Rather than fear their coming, I intend to boldly seize the market opportunity. To this purpose I have recently corresponded with various London merchants eager to do business with the newly independent republics."

"Mark my words," Talbot replied testily. "Yes, profits flow to those who take greater risks but only a fool risks all for nothing."

"Tis you who are the fool," Lawlor answered. "Why, I have received letters of inquiry from no less than four reputable London merchant houses, anxious to resume a vigorous commerce with their former colonies, untrammeled by Crown regulations necessitated by war."

This does not affect me, Brockholst thought. I have profited from the occupation and done well but I am no merchant trader.

Van Hooten handled those arrangements. *I would do well to make inquiries as to availability for summer passage on a sound ship bound for London. Then again,* he thought, *maybe summer will be too soon. Perhaps I should wait and see the lay of the land.*

"Rather than stay and risk all, it is Nova Scotia for me," another merchant chimed in. "There is good soil, a spacious harbor and the weather in St. John's is milder than here."[3]

"Posh, Edward," Talbot said dismissing him with a wave. "You sound like one of those glowing promotions published for a price in the Royal Gazette. The place is no more than a wilderness surrounding a desolate port. What business will you engage in? Selling timber? Or fish? I hear rocks are plentiful. Perhaps you can offer them at a cheap price as ballast to the few ships that put in to St. John's." There were chuckles around the table.

Lawlor agreed with him. "Only the lesser sorts, the small farmers, mechanics and Negroes to whom the British promised freedom will settle there. They will have a hard time eking out a living in that harsh land." He clicked his tongue. "Tis not a fit place for a gentleman to settle. And the dearth of eligible women to marry would condemn a man to a life of celibacy or pox ridden strumpets." He grinned lasciviously, looking at the other merchants. "Now that gentlemen is indeed a gloomy prospect."[4]

Brockholst listened carefully to the competing arguments, vacillating between staying in the hope he could mollify Van Hooten and retain most of his wealth, or leaving with his family and money before the major evacuation and making his way in London.

By May his mind was made up. The atmosphere of the city changed, much for the worse from his point of view. Joyful Whigs, who had fled to Philadelphia, and safe havens beyond, returned and flocked the streets. They greeted one another loudly and bumped long faced Loyalists off the sidewalks in passing. Presbyterian Ministers resumed their duties and the sounds of construction echoed from within as they repaired their churches. Brockholst heard rumors of fiery sermons on Sundays calling for expulsion of all Loyalists from the city as God's retribution for their sins. There was an alarming increase in street brawls with Loyalists, especially well-dressed ones singled out by gangs of toughs armed with clubs. In response, the British posted sentries on almost every corner to maintain a modicum of order. Andrew fearfully went about his usual business. His wife was compelled to do her own marketing after their two ungrateful Negro servants ran away, taking some of his candlesticks and silverware. The only place he felt safe, other than his home, was at Merchant's Coffee House where the atmosphere had become increasingly gloomy.

Talbot, whose departure was imminent, read solemnly from the Royal Gazette of reports of Loyalists in upstate New York attacked by angry mobs and notices from various cities warning that Loyalists were not welcome back. Brockholst left the Coffee House despondent, firmly resolved to book his passage that week for the earliest departure date possible. He discovered, to his consternation, that he was not alone in that desire. Now, it was the shipping agents and captains who took advantage of the panic and desperation of Loyalists like himself and seized the opportunity to benefit from their situation. For what he knew was an exorbitant fee, Andrew booked passage on a large merchant ship scheduled to depart for London on the earliest date available, the second week of July. He, his wife and two daughters were compelled to share a cabin with another family of three. They were allowed to bring aboard only three trunks. Andrew thought himself shrewd in cutting out the shipping agent and negotiating directly with the Captain, an additional price for two pieces of furniture. The Captain pocketed the money and declared if Brockholst and his family presented themselves with any more than the agreed upon and paid for baggage and furniture, it would be thrown into the harbor.

When he returned to the coffee house later in the week, satisfied with his decision to leave for England, he found Talbot holding court and fuming. "This shipping agent, with whom I have dealt with over the years and to whom I provided with a fine profit, informed me that my reservation to leave on the Richmond required an additional twenty pounds. He had the audacity to tell me to my face that if I did not pay, he could readily find new passengers anxious to fill the space who would meet his price." Talbot's face flushed with anger. "Why Twenty Pounds is what the ungrateful scoundrel normally earned from my business for half a year's work in regular times."

"And what did you do?" one of the other merchants inquired.

"I paid his extortionate fee and we are ready to embark as scheduled," Talbot replied, his voice quivering with anger. "Fortunately, I have booked my essential household goods and furniture on a ship that will carry few passengers and is connected with a trustworthy merchant house in London I am engaged to do business with."

Later when Talbot left the coffee house, Brockholst accompanied him, obtaining the name of his agent in New York who would manage his properties and also the merchant house in London. Talbot promised to put in a good word for him in London and request they receive Brockholst's household goods and warehouse them for a reasonable fee. Andrew would have to make his own arrangements to have them shipped.

Brockholst feared his shipping agent would renegotiate the price of passage although, like Talbot, he had paid in hard currency in advance. It worried him tremendously but there was much to do before their ship departed in July. First and foremost he purchased three stout wooden trunks with sturdy locks, at a price he knew was inflated by the panic spreading among the Loyalists of the city. He mulled over carpenters he had worked with as Van Hooten's agent, determined he could reasonably place his trust in one man he believed he had dealt with fairly, and contracted with him to build false bottoms in all three pieces. Then, thinking these precautions were insufficient, he hired a carter to bring a plain oak desk he owned, along with his wife's much fancier dresser to the carpenter's shop for refitting also with hidden compartments.

The carpenter shrewdly gauged Brockholst's desperate state and charged him Half a Pound per trunk and an additional Two Pounds and Twenty Shillings for modifying the desk and dresser. Tis more difficult work, he explained. Bloody thief, Brockholst thought, handing over the notes and coins in advance.[5]

Two weeks later, when he inspected the carpenter's work and

was satisfied, Brockholst was shocked to find a dearth of carters to bring the trunks and furniture back to his home. All of the Negroes who had plied their trade in the streets, charging six pence a load were gone. "Slave catchers and bounty hunters have driven them off," the carpenter explained. "The lucky ones have gone into hiding. The less fortunate have been shipped down south to their masters."

"What am I to do," Brockholst almost wailed.

"I know some wharfmen, strong lads of a rough sort. They probably will charge you double or triple the Negro carters' rates but there you have it."

Andrew let the carpenter make the arrangements. He ended up paying a Pound and a Half for delivery of two carts. The men gouged him for another Half a Pound to unload the cart and carry the pieces inside. They left them in the downstairs parlor, refusing to carry the trunks upstairs. Brockholst had to do that himself, and then deal with his wife and daughters fretting and crying over how many fine Holland bed sheets and various dresses, coats and frocks to take with them and which linens and clothes to leave behind to be shipped after they departed. He did not care what they decided, only that there was enough clothing to conceal the hidden compartments in the trunks and dresser, now filled with large denominations of pound notes.

The week before they were scheduled to leave was one of frenzied activity. His wife and daughters made the rounds of friends and acquaintances, promising to reunite in London or unrealistically comforting each other their stay in England was only temporary. Once matters stabilized they would all be back in New York and life would return to normal, they reassured each other.

Andrew alternately spent most of his remaining time at the coffee house where he commiserated with others who had decided to leave and heard the increasingly dire news that reinforced his own decision. Occasionally, he would bustle out to visit the warehousemen, shipping agents and his newly retained property manager, to confirm for himself that all the arrangements he had made were complete. He was in constant fear of additional extortionate rates being charged and was thankful when the day of departure finally arrived.

He overpaid the carriage man who brought them to the dock and the porters who carried their three trunks, and the desk and dresser aboard, the trunks being stowed in the cabin and the furniture in the hold below. As the *Lord Townsend* weighed anchor and put out into the Bay, Andrew breathed a sigh of relief while his wife and daughters on deck were weeping and commiserating with each other. He thought he had enough money to live well enough in London for a few years if they watched their expenses. By the time the *Townsend* had cleared the lower bay, Brockholst had convinced himself he was leaving because he was an avowed Loyalist, persecuted for his support of the Crown, and not because he was a simple businessman afraid of retribution from a vindictive Whig government. Surely, he thought, with a smug grin on his face, if the cursed Whigs seized his home and properties, the King would adequately and promptly compensate him for his losses. Perhaps even an annual pension. Then he could live worry free and fairly luxuriously in the mother country.

―⁂―

It was the last Wednesday of September. Since April, the British-American Board of Inquiry had been meeting weekly to review evidence and take testimony of slaves claiming to be free and entitled to be evacuated from British occupied New York.[6]

A chill wind blew off the East River. The mass of Negro men, women and children, huddled for warmth against the walls of the buildings. They waited nervously and quietly, loosely grouped in two lines for entry into Fraunces Tavern on the corner of Pearl and Broad Streets. The Board was meeting upstairs in the Long Room. British soldiers admitted them three to five at a time and maintained order along the rows that stretched north up Broad, where those waiting were at least sheltered from the wind.

Sexton Peter Williams was there as he had been every Wednesday since the Board began hearings, to provide comfort and advice to those waiting anxiously in line. Today, he was here to support Jupiter's claim he had arrived in the city more than a year before and should be deemed free and no longer property of his former master in Tidewater, Virginia.

Jupiter wore his slouch hat low on his forehead to cover the telltale scar branded into his flesh when he had first tried to escape. There was no telling when some slave catcher would accost him in the street, based upon his master's description and throw him in chains on a ship, along with other unfortunates, bound for the cotton plantations of Virginia. If it were not for the British soldiers keeping order around Fraunces Tavern, the white men prowling the street beyond the line of Redcoats would have plunged into the crowd of Negroes and seized their prey like wolves descending on a flock of sheep.[7]

"It will go well," Peter assured Jupiter in a confident soothing voice. "I will vouch for you, as I have done for others. The Commissioners know me and my position as Sexton. They give credit to my word." Jupiter nodded and looked fearfully across Broad Street as a lean white man wearing a planter's hat strolled by accompanied by two toughs. The Sexton followed Jupiter's glance. "I trust you have no second thoughts. No doubts of not joining your mother and your sister Sarah."

"They cannot protect me from slave catchers," Jupiter said bitterly. "You yourself are still a slave," he said accusingly, as if Peter's status reaffirmed the injustice and danger of remaining in New York.

The Sexton arched his high eyebrows. The expression on his round face was placid. "My fate is in the hands of the Lord, not a Board composed of men," he replied amicably.

"No, I have not changed my mind. New Yawk or wherever my mother and sister go, are not . . . " His voice trailed off. "The only safety for me is away from heah. You say this Board will give me permission to travel on a ship to Nova Scotia?"

"Yes, I have seen the certificates myself. Once it has been issued, you are assigned to a ship, you present the certificate on boarding, the Master of the vessel verifies your name against a list of Negroes he has been provided by the Board and you sail for Nova Scotia."

Jupiter smiled for the first time since they had stood in line in the early morning. "I pray it will be as simple as that. I am eager to leave this place. Been kidnapped once and enslaved again is more than enough. More than I am willing to bear." His Virginia accent softened the bitterness in his voice, somewhat diminished by the Sexton's tutoring.

Jupiter fingered the knife hidden in the pocket of his tattered brown coat. It hardly reached Jupiter's mid-thigh and had undoubtedly been donated by a white parishioner of the Sexton's Church. What kind of church would keep a slave as a Sexton, he thought? Or for that matter, require the Negroes to worship in the gallery, forbid them places in the pews down below and only administer to them their Methodist rituals after all whites had received them. He had seen all of this demeaning treatment and wanted no part of this religion or anything else in New York. He hoped things would be better in Nova Scotia. At the very least, he would be a free man and also free from fear of being enslaved ever again.

The Sexton tugged at Jupiter's coat sleeve. "Judging by the length of the line in front of us, we will not reach the entrance for at least another hour or more." Peter's kindly face broke into a smile. "I will distribute some food to the souls who wait behind us," he said, patting the large woven sack hanging by a rope handle from his shoulder. "Remain close to the wall and do nothing to call attention to yourself."

Jupiter watched nervously until Peter's head with his closely cropped hair disappeared among the taller of those in line. He moved closer to the wall, thankful that others were between him and the open street, clenched his teeth and waited.

The Sexton moved among the crowd, listening to the soft voices of the women who clutched their children to warm them. They were bundled up against the unaccustomed northern chill they felt in their bones, in a hodge-podge of coats over jackets over shirts and blouses and layers of mismatched skirts, their heads covered in caps, under bonnets under hats. These women, their backs bent from hard labor in the plantation fields, had not been given much respite, he thought. They had been put to work in New York as cooks and laundresses and general laborers for the British, carrying firewood or pulling loads on barrows or carts like beasts of burden. Still, the British were honoring their promise of freedom. They would soon, God willing, be working for some wages, however pitiful an amount it would be and living free in Nova Scotia. He favored the women with the few pieces of stale bread and hard cheese he had in his bag. The women instinctively gave the meager portion to the children and even shared with the young ones of other women, before taking a bite for themselves.

Most of the men acted more selfishly, not that he could blame them. They also were hungry, anxious and afraid. They felt obligated not to show their fear but Peter recognized it in the way they shifted their feet, or spoke too loudly. By virtue of wearing a piece of a uniform or the way they held themselves more erect, Peter knew some of them had served in the British Army, either in Black Regiments or as laborers supporting the troops. To such men, he offered strong reassurances they would have an easier time proving they were entitled to leave.

"You who have served with the British military – remember any details of your service – the names of your commanding Officers or Sergeants, the towns or places you marched to, where you dug fortifications, built roads, carried supplies, the months and years when you did so if you remember – they will support your claim. I urge you to tell the truth, the Lord will be with you and the truth will prevail."

Prompted by Peter's urging, the men began rehearsing among themselves the facts as they recalled them, triggering others to recall more particulars. Smiling to himself, the Sexton left the hubbub he had created and made his way down to the Pearl Street corner. Jupiter nervously waited for him, worried that his turn would come and the Peter would not be there to support him. They were about twenty people back from the colonnaded entrance. The three-story building with its sloping roof loomed above them, as formidable to Jupiter as a fortress.

With Williams leaning on him for support, they climbed the steps to the second floor. Jupiter licked his lips, his mouth dry as the cotton he had last harvested so many years ago on the Tidewater plantation where he had been born. A British sentry opened the door and they were ushered in and directed to stand before six men, who were seated at one long table with two large ledger sized books before them. Three of the men wore their British Regimental jackets. The other three wore the blue of the Continental Army.

Jupiter instinctively stood with his head turned toward the three Redcoats. "State your name, age and where you were born," one of the red-coated officers demanded. "And remove your hat immediately," he barked.

Jupiter did as he was told, holding his slouch hat in front of his groin. "My name is Jupiter Parks. I was born on the Tidewater Plantation of Willis Parks in Virginia. I believe I am seventeen years or so." He concentrated on pronouncing as Sexton Williams taught him, although there were hints of his southern accent.

"When did you leave the Plantation?"

"I do not know the year. I left with my mother and came to this city and met the Sexton. I have been here ever since."

"Sexton Williams," one of the British officers said. "You have appeared several times before this Board. What year did Jupiter arrive at your church?"

"Sir," Peter responded, bowing deferentially. "He arrived with his mother in the late summer of '81."

"How convenient," one of the American members said sarcastically.

"The Sexton has testified this Jupiter Parks has been in New York for more than one year. He qualifies as a free man pursuant to the 1779 Proclamation of Sir Henry Clinton." The other two Redcoats nodded in agreement. One took up a quill, dipped it in an inkwell and began to write in the ledger before him. Jupiter watched as the American did the same, the two quills scratching away across the columns of paper. "I will describe him as a strong black young man, seventeen years old with a branded scar on his forehead," the British member said. "I will do likewise," the American responded.

"He will be assigned," the Redcoat consulted a list to his right, "to the *Lehigh* that is scheduled to depart on October 7 for Port Roseway, Nova Scotia. Sexton. You will see this young man is delivered to the dock on that day. Otherwise, there will be no other place for him on any other vessel. Do you understand, Jupiter?" he asked as if addressing a child.

Jupiter nodded. He would change his name in Nova Scotia. No longer would he be called by the hated names given by his master.

"The clerk will issue a Certificate."

And with that, Williams and Jupiter were directed to another table where a clerk, with blank certificates filled in his name, the date and they were out of the room, down the stairs and into the street. It was dark as they hurried back to the Church. In the candlelight of the sanctuary, Jupiter sat with the precious certificate in his trembling hands and struggled to read the words. The words danced before him until he steadied his hands.

"New-York - the 24th of September 1783

THIS is to certify to whomfoever it may concern, that the Bearer hereof, Jupiter Parks - a Negro, restored to the British lines in consequence of the Proclamations of Sir William Howe, and Sir Henry Clinton, late Commanders in Chief in America; and that the said Negro has hereby His Excellency Sir Guy Carleton's Permission to go to Nova-Scotia, or wherever else he may think proper. By Order of Brigadier General Birch."[8]

"What does this mean?" Jupiter asked pointing to the last sentence of the precious certificate.

"It means," replied Peter, "you must be on the *Lehigh* to Nova Scotia on the 7th of next month. You have no choice of another destination. However, you will be a free man in Nova Scotia and as such, have the freedom to travel anywhere else. You will not need this certificate to do so." He beamed at Jupiter. "You will be a free man. Think of that and praise the Lord for his beneficence."

"I will and do," Jupiter said overcome with emotion, still

holding his certificate with both hands. "You have been kind to me. You have taught me to read and write and helped me to begin a new life."

The Sexton's round face broke into a broad smile. "I am extremely pleased you now recognize the value of an education. It would please me more, if you would write and leave with me a letter for your mother and sister. I will see it is delivered to them. Perhaps in your new life, you will be able to reunite with your family, if it so please the Lord."

"I will write you also from Nova Scotia so you can tell me where my mother and sister are." Jupiter bowed his head, his eyes filling with tears. He had gained his freedom and lost his family. He cursed the men who had kidnapped him and separated him from his poor mother. She had seen so many of her children sold away and now she would lose another. He doubted he would ever see her again but vowed he would live a life so she would be proud of him.

—⚜—

Lieutenant John Stoner left the stately Georgian residence of Brigadier General Timothy Ruggles on Princess Street near the Royal Governor's House, smirking to himself. The old fool planned to embark on one of His Majesty's ships reserved for senior officers, not for London but for Wilmot on the Bay of Fundy and the wilderness of Nova Scotia. He had been granted 1,000 acres of what he claimed was prime land, a reward for his unwavering loyalty and service to the Crown since '75 and compensation for the confiscation of his estate in Hardwick, Massachusetts by the Rebels. He had been banished from that Colony and had no prospect of ever returning. Ruggles had offered John a position to be determined in his barely civilized and yet undeveloped fiefdom. John had to admit that Ruggles still cut a physically vigorous figure, standing over six feet tall. At more than seventy years old, he had waxed eloquent about his plans to clear the land, establish an estate, with breeding horses and prize cows, and cultivate fruit of every variety and crops to feed the nearby towns.[9]

More likely, John thought, Ruggles would drop dead before

the first tree was cleared. Probably, the land grant was of infertile, barren rocky soil. He had heard descriptions of Nova Scotia that were less than complimentary. True, there was timber, but John had no intention of serving as some supervisor over a group of laboring louts.

No. His plans included Ms. Hannah Harand and her substantial dowry, a London townhouse, a life of leisure and acceptance, into London society, by virtue of his money and hers. He had courted Hannah attentively while she and her family resided in their home in New York City. In early September, when her father took the family back to the plantation on Long Island, he welcomed, without any remorse, the respite from her cloying presence and inane and unsophisticated questions. As soon as the Harands had left, John repeatedly but discreetly relieved his sexual desires in one of the better class of brothels.

He and Hannah exchanged weekly affectionate and modestly worded letters throughout September. She begged him to visit the Plantation but John, pleading the press of business and military matters in the City, declined. It was too much trouble to ride out to the middle of Long Island and besides, he did need to get his affairs in order before his anticipated departure for London. Of course he would travel with the Harands and hoped Hannah's wealthy father would book passage on a comfortable and uncrowded merchant vessel, or even better, use his prestige and influence, to obtain accommodations on a ship of the line. When Hannah had written John the family was returning to the City and would be at their townhouse by October 1st, he had immediately responded with as many caring and warm expressions of his devotion as he could muster and signed it, "your loving and lonely Lieutenant, John."

Confident that his letter had reached her, John rode up The Broadway past St. Paul's church and turned east on Franklin Street. Tonight, he would formally ask John Harand for Hannah's hand in marriage. He would not bargain for the dowry but damned if he would depart the house without knowing the amount he would receive as her husband. He tied his mare to the Harand's post, instructed the servant who opened the door to attend to his horse and was directed into the parlor.

Harand was seated before the fire. Opposite him John recognized the spindly, crane-like figure of Judge George Duncan Ludlow, Master of the Rolls and Superintendent of the Police of Long Island. This will go well, John thought. The Judge had benefitted from the work John had performed to ensure Ludlow's schemes of kickbacks, fees, and extortion redounded to his own coffers. Why, John recalled with a slight smile, the trusting fool had even praised John for the meticulous records he kept of rents and fees collected, licenses issued and paid for. Not to mention the host of undercover informants employed to ferret out those men on the payroll of the Master of the Rolls and Police who were skimming off the Judge's profits for themselves. John had doctored the ledgers so that John himself was receiving almost twenty-five percent of what the Judge was entitled to and who never suspected a single figure was out of order.

Something in the way the Judge cocked his head sideways on his thin, frail neck, like a heron poised to strike a fish, gave John pause. He greeted Harand warmly, feeling a coolness in the response. He noted the absence of an offer to sit down and join them before the fireplace.

"Judge Ludlow has paid me a visit in preparation for our mutual departures to London," Harand said frostily. "Upon my advising him of your courtship of Hannah, my youngest daughter, the Judge has provided me with more information about you, your character and activities."

"I am certain his opinion will further enhance your own view of myself and you will look favorably upon my request to ask for Hannah's hand in marriage," John replied, hiding his puzzlement at his reception behind a broad smile.

"Do not be certain of anything, you duplicitous scoundrel," Ludlow snapped. He pointed a boney finger at John, his hand shaking with anger. "Your stealing from me succeeded only as long as you paid my employees." His voice rose in a cracked pitch. "But now we are to leave this City, and the payments from you will cease, those men I hired and you suborned, look to me for what they call severance pay or a bonus." He shook his head in disbelief as to how he had misplaced his trust in John and leaned further forward in his chair.

"Initially, I responded to their demands harshly. They have been well compensated for services rendered and deserved no more. That was when several, nay most of them, offered to expose nefarious schemes they participated in at your behest to steal from me." He snorted in disgust. "I paid for such information even though I was rewarding them for their dishonesty. In return, I have caught you sir, the master thief. By exposing you I have prevented my friend here from, in ignorance of your low character, permitting his innocent daughter to marry a scoundrel." Ludlow's eyes set deep in their sockets of his skeletal head bore into John.

"I will have you arrested and imprisoned until the last British ship has sailed from New York harbor unless you repay all you have stolen from me."

Craftily, John thought the Judge's threat was an empty one. The British military ruled the city and had no time or interest in prosecuting cases of corruption. Not at this late stage of the occupation. It was more than enough to maintain order in the face of the daily influx of Whigs, eager to reclaim their property, and of Loyalists selling off what they could before embarking.

"You dare not have me arrested," John replied as confidently as he could. "You would expose yourself to accusations and proof of your own corrupt schemes which I only facilitated," he replied with more conviction than he felt.

"Who would believe the word of scoundrel like you against my own. Or of an officer," Ludlow continued maliciously "who is such a coward as to stand on board the *Cerebus* in broad daylight before the entire crew and passerbys on the wharf and abjectly apologize to its Master and Commander."

John's face turned red, as flushed as the day when he had been slapped by Commander Whitehead and challenged to a duel. He would have to bargain for time with this wizened spiteful Judge.

"I will repay the amounts I have skimmed," he agreed, putting on an obsequious air. "It will take at least a week for me to liquidate some properties and merchandise I acquired."

"Spoken like a true coward and thief upon being exposed," the Judge said smirking and gesturing to Harand to witness John's capitulation. "We will meet here in this very house a week from today and not a day later. At eleven o'clock. If you fail to appear with every pound and pence you have stolen from me, I will keep my promise to have you arrested. Now, get out of our sight," he directed. "Your very presence reminds me how I was taken in and duped by your false protestations of loyalty and honesty."

John stormed out of the house and found his mare tied where he had left the horse. Cursing the servant who had ignored his instructions and smarting from the tongue lashing he had just received, he rode down The Broadway. No marriage to Hannah he thought. Well, she was a cow anyway. He was already displeased being in her presence. Imagine how it would have been seeing her day and night. The cool air cleared his mind. He did not intend to pay the Judge anything. So where to go and what to do? He still had his fortune in pounds, more than enough to enable him to live well for many years. He would ship out to Halifax before the week's end. Pay whatever was the exorbitant price for passage. The Judge's reach would not extend to Nova Scotia and even if it did, he could bribe his way out of any situation that might arise.

Early the next morning, John visited one of the main shipping agencies and discovered there were three ships, with available berths for Army officers, leaving for Nova Scotia in a few days. They were to be part of a convoy of "Negro ships" as well, carrying those with certificates to leave. He paid the Twelve Pounds in advance for a portion of a cabin to be shared with four other officers on the *Duchess of Gordon*, departing on the 7th of October for Halifax . With that accomplished, he returned to his quarters and busied himself sorting what he would take with him. He did not own any civilian jackets or coats. Only one uniform would be necessary and he would wear it. He would buy a serviceable coat, waistcoat and several shirts, some breeches and stockings befitting a gentleman, a pair of shoes with buckles to replace his boots and some more blankets, sheets, bedding and the like. There was plenty to be purchased in the markets as Loyalist families sold off the clothing they were unable to take with them. John thought he could pack all his possessions in two trunks, in which he would hide his banknotes, some in the false bottom of one trunk, some wrapped in linens and the like in the other. The rest of the pound notes would be on his person. For additional security, he had a money pouch to wrap around his waist underneath his clothes. That afternoon, he sold his horse, to be delivered to the buyer the afternoon of October 6th , the day before his departure.

He returned to his quarters, planning to go to a nearby tavern for dinner and then a visit to one of the brothels. A note in a familiar handwriting had been shoved partially under the door. It was from Hannah. She was writing him in secret. She professed her love for him and begged for John to meet her that evening at 7: 00 pm at the home of a discreet friend on Williams Street.

He returned home close to midnight, having extracted his exquisite revenge upon John Harand and by association, Judge Ludlow. He had not only deflowered Hannah Harand in her friend's bedroom, but left her with the heartfelt promise, one he never intended to fulfill, of sending for her to be his wife once he established himself in Nova Scotia, thereby destroying the poor girl's chance of marrying any suitor in London for some time to come.

—⁂—

The closer they came to the East River docks, the more crowded the streets became. Sexton Peter Williams held firmly on to Jupiter's arm as they shoved past horse drawn wagons and carriages, men pulling carts or pushing barrows and throngs of people on foot, laden down with heavy boxes and bags. The scene was more chaotic once they entered Water Street and could see the quays. There were ships tied up to every available pier, slip and dock. Towers of furniture of every type were stacked willy nilly, creating narrow corridors for boarding passengers to thread through. Men argued with the carters, the crew and even the captains as the passengers sought to squeeze one more trunk or chair, another barrel or box on board, all to seemingly no avail. Women cried out in anguish as their precious possessions were denied permission to be carried up the gangplanks.

Out on the river, a host of ships heavily laden and low in the water, wallowed in the gentle swells, their masts bare of sails, awaiting orders to weigh anchor and form a convoy in the upper bay. After making inquiries, the Sexton and Jupiter found the *Lehigh*, tied up at the end of the Fish Market Dock, surrounded not only by other ships but trawlers and small craft bringing their catch to market. Swarms of sea gulls swooped overhead, heading for the killing and cleaning tables. There were no piles of furniture, trunks or valuables here. This was the Negroes' boarding dock and most of them had few, if any, possessions.

Jupiter swung his cloth bag over his shoulder. It contained all he owned in the world – a worn but clean shirt, a pair of extra breeches, a rag for a towel, and some bread and cheese for rations. He embraced the Sexton. "Stay until you see me boahd," he pleaded. Williams reached beneath his coat and handed Jupiter a bible. "Read and learn this, as I have taught you and the Lord will watch over you." Jupiter slipped the bible into his bag. He thought, how can the Sexton have such faith in a religion that permits him to be owned by the very men who pray and attend his church? He said nothing. Clutching his Certificate of Permission, he strode up the gangplank and presented the precious paper to the First Mate. The man consulted his list, nodded and waved Jupiter on board. "Find a hammock in the hold," he said gruffly.

Jupiter preferred to remain on deck, watching and still fearful despite Sexton Williams' assurances, that some slave catcher could still come bounding aboard and haul him off to be sent south back into slavery. The good Sexton had left, apparently confident in the authority of the certificate or that the Lord would protect him. Jupiter watched as other Negroes presented their certificates and boarded. None were turned away. Some went below deck while others remained, looking over the side at the turmoil on the docks.

The first mate waved to a sailor standing under the mast who nodded and ran up a plain, powder blue flag. Some kind of signal, Jupiter thought. Shortly thereafter, two men in uniform, one in Continental Blue and the other a Redcoat, marched up the gangplank. Jupiter watched as the first mate presented them with the list he had used to check off Jupiter's name.

The Captain, a stout man in a black long coat and a tri-corn with a white plume joined his first mate.

"Are there no other Negroes on board other than those on this list," the Continental Officer demanded.

"None," the Captain responded curtly.

"You have permission to leave this dock. Anchor in the river and await further orders."[10]

Jupiter breathed a sigh of relief at they untied from the quay. He remained on deck as the *Lehigh* rocked gently in the river's waves, staring out at the city he longed to leave behind. He amused himself by counting the number of ships waiting to set sail. There were at least thirty he could see easily. Most, judging by the passengers on deck, were carrying former slaves like him to freedom. Toward the middle of the day, a few of the larger ships, crowded with white Loyalists joined the line of vessels in the river. Here and there, Jupiter noticed some of the whites were attended by Negroes, most probably their slaves. This puzzled him until he recalled his time on the Harand plantation. None of the slaves of white Loyalists had been freed. Only those of the Rebels. Did this mean there would be slaves and free blacks in Nova Scotia? Was he at risk of being kidnapped and made a slave again to serve some white master whose male slave had died? He had a solution for that, he thought as he fingered the long bladed knife in his coat pocket.

He tried to remember Sexton Williams' explanation. With his certificate he would be a free man, free to travel and live anywhere outside of these hostile former colonies. As the ships weighed anchor and proceeded down river into the upper bay, Jupiter bolstered his flagging spirits with images of how he would make a new life, perhaps learn to ride a horse, apprentice to a mechanic and learn a trade, find a wife. He wondered whether taking a new name would invalidate his certificate.

By the time the *Lehigh* was in the lower bay, pitching and

yawing in the rougher waters, Jupiter had hurled over the side the hot breakfast the Sexton had provided him and then dry heaved up nothing but sour acidic liquid. He felt so sick he did not even see Long Island, the wretched place where he had been unjustly enslaved, receding in the distance.[11]

Chapter 11- A Liberated City

Captains Will Stoner and Samuel Hadley, together with the men of the Artillery Regiment arrived at Kingsbridge and the Harlem River after a series of short marches from West Point to Tarrytown to Tappan. As they came into sight of the towering angled fortress, ringed by abatis and ditches, the British lowered the Union Jack flying from the flagstaff and trooped south. The muffled boom of a light cannon signaled their departure.[1]

Two companies of the Fourth and Fifth Massachusetts Regiments crossed the Harlem River on ferries as the advance guard. The rest of the contingent followed and by mid-day, the six-hundred or so soldiers were across and encamped in tents in the barren brown cornfields south of the British fortifications.

Once their tent was erected, Will and Hadley returned to the now abandoned British fort.

"It would have been a difficult crossing and assault under the cannons of the Redcoats," Samuel observed as they rode slowly around the fortification, pointing at the multiple gun embrasures. The rectangular openings looked far less menacing absent the muzzles of eighteen and twenty-four pounders.

Will realized how exposed his battery of cannons would have been on the flat land across the Harlem. He imagined the ferocious fire from the British guns, the smell of gunpowder and bursting of shells, the shrieks of wounded men and the stacks of amputated limbs outside the field hospitals. He shuddered with relief of knowing there would be no more battles. Their duty now, once the British confirmed they had left New York, would be to secure the city and await General Washington's arrival.

They returned to camp as the soldiers on the side of the road cheered upon seeing a herd of cattle flanked by drivers passing by. They were on the way to slaughter at the far end of the camp, away from the tents. With most soldiers furloughed, the supplies of meat, flour and rum were more than sufficient for those remaining in service.

"The men will be pleased tonight to be feasting on fresh beef," Will said. "I have lost my taste for salted beef and pork and hope never to see it on my plate again."

Sometime before midnight, having made the rounds of the campfires of the Artillery Regiment, Will returned to the tent he shared with Captain Hadley. The men were in a festive mood, not only thankful for the roast meat and rum, but anticipating brief duty in New York and returning to their homes and families. Will pulled his blanket close up to his neck against the winter chill, hoping in a few more days to be sleeping inside a warm brick barracks with news his wife and children would be arriving soon. General Knox had promised all the wives and families left behind at West Point would sail down the Hudson to New York once the British had left.

Three more days passed without an order to advance to the city. General Knox was headquartered south of their camp at a tavern in Harlem. On the afternoon of the 24th, Colonel Sargent ordered the Artillery Regiment to be prepared to march the following morning.[2] That night was cold with a wind blowing from the city north toward their encampment. It brought the smell of thick and acrid smoke, although it was difficult to know whether it was the campfires of Redcoats or something more ominous.

Will and Captain Hadley were standing on a small hill looking at the occasional twinkling of lights in the distance. "If we could see New York more clearly from here, what could we perceive," Samuel mused. "Would it be a city in flames or in quiet anticipation of the Redcoats' evacuation and our entry?"

"You are thinking of the night in '76 on Dorchester Heights," Will replied. "When the Redcoats destroyed parts of Boston and their sailors went on drunken rampages before they sailed away to Nova Scotia."

Hadley nodded. "Do you think seven years of war will have improved the manners and behavior of the British Navy? They may not have torched the city. Yet I suspect there is much havoc being wrought on good patriotic citizens."

The next morning, the soldiers of the two Massachusetts Regiments and the gun crews of the Artillery Regiment marched south through Harlem to Bowery Lane, an unpaved hard dirt road. A barrier of logs and an empty sentry's hut marked the dividing line between the British forces still in the city and the Americans eager to enter. The clear blue sky promised the weather would not interfere their march into the city.

General Knox joined them. After waiting impatiently for two or more hours, three British officers galloped up Bowery Lane. The lead officer approached Colonel Sargent who smiled broadly and trotted his horse up to where the General was standing. He leaned down and passed along the message. Knox took off his tri-corn and waved it vigorously above his head. "The city awaits," he shouted in his booming deep voice. There were orders to form up and prepare to march. Several soldiers ran forward and removed the log barrier as the British officers disappeared down the road to the south.[3]

Will mounted Big Red who held steady as the artillerymen clambered aboard the wagon. With General Knox leading the way, accompanied by Colonel Sargent and their other officers, the Artillery Regiment was in the forefront, followed by the marching Massachusetts Regiments.

The fields on both sides of Bowery Lane were bare, the crops of hay and wheat long since harvested. Occasionally, they passed imposing mansions, well set back from the road, not quite hidden by the tall trees oaks now devoid of their fall foliage. By the time they reached cobblestoned Queen Street, closer to the East River, Will could see the charred doors and smashed windows of some of the row houses, some still defiantly flying American flags. A few men were on the streets cleaning up broken glass and boarding up windows.

By the time they got to the heart of the city, there were more people cheering and waving in welcome. They rode a few more blocks down Broadway and passed the burned stone structure of all that remained of Trinity Church. The artillery men jumped out of the wagons and formed up in ranks. The men of the Massachusetts Regiments continued marching down Broadway toward Fort George at the Battery.

"Captains Stoner and Hadley," Knox called. "Unhitch your wagons and ride with me." Together they galloped north through the city to the Bowery where they stopped outside The Bull's Head Tavern. The road in front of the tavern was crowded with civilians and officers in pristine, clean uniforms. Knox dismounted in front of the tavern and strode up the porch. Shortly after an orderly ran down the steps and led Will and Samuel, past the shed on the side of the tavern where four highly polished brass cannons rested in front of the barn.

"General's orders. You are each to hitch up your horses and pull one of the guns as part of the parade into the city."

Will swung out of the saddle, dropping the reins in front of Big Red, confident he would remain still and walked over to the six pounders. The first was engraved beyond the raised heraldic emblem of the Crown - "Captured at Yorktown." Will patted it affectionately, as if the six pounder were an old friend. "We were both at the siege of Yorktown," he said bowing in a mock salute. With the orderly's help he turned the gun carriage around and firmly lashed it to the traces behind Big Red. /3

They rode around and waited under the sign of a black snorting bull as the procession formed up. Will recognized General Washington in the lead on his grey mare. Next to him was a well-dressed civilian, behind them were more civilians on horseback, waiting eight abreast. They were followed by General Knox and other officers. Will and Samuel, together with two other mounted officers pulling six pounders, were directed behind a crowd of civilians on foot, loosely lined up eight abreast.[4]

When the procession reached the pavement of Queen Street, the parade of civilians on foot had lost most of its cohesion, despite the spirited beat of the drums and the high pitched tune of the fifes of the military bands, It was nothing more than a happy mob of men, waving vigorously to the people crowding the sidewalks and cheering them on.

"Tis as if they had won the war single handed," Samuel said to Will, "though I would wager not many served either as Continentals or militia." The civilians were following the lead of General Washington and the other leaders, doffing their hats and brandishing them in the air. Will noticed the windows and balconies of the second floor of the houses were packed with women, holding colorful scarfs over the sills and railings. Here and there, a few American flags flew from makeshift poles hastily attached to iron gratings or open shutters. Small boys and stray dogs darted from one side of the street to the other, disrupting the pace of the civilian marchers. A few of the older boys, more daring than the rest, ran behind the cannons, touched the polished brass, and raced away as if they would be punished for their actions.

By the time they turned west on Wall Street and were nearing Broadway, many of the marching civilians had dropped out of the procession, tired from their walk. Those who remained took advantage of the welcoming sign of Cape's Tavern at Broadway to seek liquid refreshment inside.

The four horsemen pulling the six pounders closed ranks and were now behind the mounted civilians. The crowds were thicker and more enthusiastic the further down Broadway they went. More women were in the balconies looking down at the procession, their feminine cheers adding a more melodic pitch to the deep throated "huzzahs" from the men on the sidewalks. Occasionally, they passed a burned out building with charred bricks and missing window frames.

Nearing the tip of the Island the parade came to a halt. Cries of disappointment and anger drifted back. Will stood up in his stirrups. "The British flag still flies over Fort George," he shouted in consternation "Make way, Make way," he yelled urging Big

Red forward through the mounted civilians. General Washington and the other dignitaries were sitting calmly on their horses in the square before the fort. Thirteen eighteen pounders were in position, manned by the men of Knox's artillery regiment. Knox rode impatiently behind the guns, eager to fire a salute to honor the arrival of the Americans but unable to do so as long as the enemy's flag flew over the fort.

The General called out to the two Captains. "They have nailed their Ensign, cut the halyards and greased the pole. The last perfidious act of Albion before they leave our shores," he said angrily.

Will recalled that when the Army had been in New York, there was a blacksmith shop as part of the fort. "Sir. With your permission, may I take Corporal Levi Tyler with me?" he said, pointing to one of his old gun crew. Levi had always been the one to climb the trees to scout the Redcoats' positions from afar.

"Take anyone you want but get that damn flag down."

Will and Levi ran into the fort and opened the doors of the abandoned wooden sheds beneath the battlements. In one they found an anvil and a few discarded tools. Will got down on his knees and moved his hands through the dirt. "Help me search for nails," he cried to Tyler. They found a few, enough to serve the purpose Will had in mind. Directing the Corporal to take off his shoes, Will hammered the nails from the inside so that two or three inches stuck through the soles.

"Can you climb the bloody greased pole in these?" he asked.

"Yes, sir." Levi replied grinning as he ran barefoot out of the shed in the direction of the flagpole. At the base, he slipped into his cleated shoes, slung a haversack with the American flag over his shoulder, took a leg up from one of the soldiers and began to climb the fourteen-foot high oak pole. He slide once on the way up, dug the nails in deeper and made it to the top. There, he unceremoniously ripped the British flag from the pole and let it flutter to the ground. He tied the American flag to the remains of the halyard and made sure it was secure. Then, in a series of sliding jumps of two or three feet at a time, he descended to cheers and shouts of "well done."[5]

After the thirteen gun salute, General Washington, accompanied by Generals Knox, McDougal, Von Steuben and the civilian leaders rode back up Broadway. The men of the Artillery Regiment took over the recently abandoned barracks in a two story brick building near the fort.

The celebrations of Evacuation Week continued throughout the next few days. One night, Will and Captain Hadley wandered the crowded streets, filled with celebratory crowds. There were veterans, wearing their black and white cockades on the left breast of their civilian coats. Fashionably dressed women, their hands stuffed in fur lined muffs, passed by, escorted by men in tight-sleeved coats with embroidered cuffs, strutting with their brass topped walking sticks under their arms.

The two friends stood pressed against a brick wall by the crowds staring up at the fireworks display in the sky.[6] Will wished Elisabeth were with him to enjoy the festivities. His mind turned to the fireworks they had watched together near the wharves in Philadelphia on Independence Day. Soon after, he left for the battlefield and she remained behind, during the British occupation of the city.

"You realize, we are among the few men in uniform on the street," Samuel commented, breaking into Will's recollections. "Soon it will be time to exchange our Continental blues for a more tailored brown dress coat with narrow tails at the back," he said pointing at two nearby gentlemen. Will grunted, not ready to relinquish the indicia of the only life he had known for the past six years.

"I, for one, am eager for it," Samuel said. "It will be several more days, a week or two at the most, to accomplish our orders. Then it will be back to Boston for me and Mercy and Benjamin." He tipped his tri-corn to a gentleman he had accidently bumped. "It is my strongest desire to have her safely in Boston before the winter sets in. I hope the voyage will not unduly upset her."

"Elisabeth has relied on Mercy as the calm and clever one in all situations. Why would traveling to Boston by boat upset her?"

"Oh," Samuel said with a wave of his hand. "I meant her

physical well-being. We are expecting another child."

Will grabbed his friend by the elbow and clapped him on the shoulder. "That is good news. A child to be born in time of peace and the start of your civilian life." He was genuinely pleased for his friend yet sad thinking of how he would miss his company when he left.

The next morning, Will, led a detail, including two of his old gun crew to the warehouses on the Hudson River. They stayed close to the wharves avoiding the muddy alleys and the makeshift shacks and shanties constructed of planks and scrap wood. The piers themselves and the shallow waters surrounding them were filled with discarded furniture, trunks and crates, the abandoned possessions of Tories left behind when they boarded their ships for London or Nova Scotia. Despite the chill wind off the river and the late November temperatures, destitute people were diving into the muddy water and salvaging anything they could use or refurbish and sell later. Men fought over teapots and mugs. Women bartered on the piers for bedding and clothing, shirts and shoes. Others smashed up any abandoned furniture to use either to shore up their shanties or for firewood to keep warm.

It was not for him, Will thought, to try and bring order to the scavenging mob. His orders were to take inventory of any supplies abandoned by the British Army and to secure the buildings until civilian authority was restored. Corporal Tyler, sporting a new pair of shoes given him by some patriotic civilian in a moment of drunken friendship, forced the padlock on the first warehouse with a crowbar and slid the bolt back. The doors creaked open and a shaft of light shone from a high window down on to an empty dirt floor and rows of barrels against the far wall. Isaiah Chandler, with a ledger under his arm, set up a makeshift table, removed his inkwell and quill from a pouch and began writing as the men pried open the barrel tops and shouted out their contents – Indian corn, sugar, flour and saltpeter. There were not that many barrels and the process did not take long.

Will's mind wandered as he watched Isaiah writing with his quill, thinking of another time when Corporal Chandler inserted a different quill, one filled with gunpowder, in the touchhole of an eighteen pounder at the Battle of Brandywine. Will had been running between the cannons of his battery as the Grenadiers advanced up the hill. Samuel had been shot and in falling, hit his head on a rock. All had been confusion; rescuing Hadley and the others of the gun crew; no time to spike the cannons; Big Red pulling a wagon of wounded; the fear of being outflanked and ambushed as they retreated. He shook his head in wonder at how he had survived essentially unscathed throughout the war. He thought of the thunderous cannonade as they bombarded Cornwallis' troops and the counter fire of the British mortars. Adam had saved his life and the lives of the gun crew from an unexploded mortar shell at Yorktown. Adam would definitely return to Marblehead when they were all discharged. Will would miss him and the others as well.

"Captain, Sir? We have finished here," Chandler said.

Outside the warehouse, the cold wind cleared Will's head of memories of past battles and gloomy thoughts of the imminent departure of friends. He left two men to guard the place and proceeded with the rest of his small detachment north past Crown Street. A flotilla of small boats was approaching from the Jersey side of the river. He guessed they were bringing goods to trade in the city. Hopefully, Elisabeth and the children would soon come down from West Point. He would have to move out of the barracks and find suitable quarters for his family. When his discharge became effective, paying for the lodging would be his first immediate problem.

The next warehouse had little stored within — a small pile of coal and firewood, not enough to fill one wagon. Still, Chandler entered it into the ledger, noting the warehouse was just north of the intersection with Crown Street.

"Will they change the street names?" Chandler asked as they proceeded to the next warehouse.

"It will be up to the civilian authorities," Will replied, covering his nose at the stench that emanated from a nearby alley.

"It may be confusing. My entries identify the warehouse by the nearest street."

"Whoever receives this ledger will be tasked with distributing the supplies. I feel certain they will know how to find them."

They approached a building, more substantial than the others. An empty sentry post was tilted over and blocked the muddy entrance. Remnants of a wooden planked fence ran the length of the street. Some of the boards had been pried loose for firewood, leaving gaps like missing teeth amongst the others. Dark pits in the yard and pieces of charred wood indicated this warehouse had held soldiers who cooked outside. The double door hung askew. Instead of forcing it open, the men simply pried the door off its hinges and slipped through the opening. Inside, empty musket racks stood to the side of each door and two tiered wooden bunk beds littered with dirty straw were lined up in neat rows, stretching toward the darkness at the back. A few birds, disturbed by their entry, fluttered from the rafters and flew through the open windows high up near the roof beams.

"Bring some lanterns," Will ordered. In the back they discovered a rectangular pile, four feet high and more than twenty feet long, of white woolen British standard issue army blankets, all bearing the Royal symbol of the King's arrow and the initials GR for George Rex.

"Well. Those will serve to keep some patriotic citizens warm this winter," Tyler said, bending down to feel the wool. "If it t'were mine," Chandler said, "my wife would stitch a patch over the King's initials or sew a bed cover for the entire blanket." He set up his table as the soldiers began counting the blankets and restacking them on the bunk beds to keep them off the dirt floor.

The decreasing piles revealed three–foot high columns of neatly folded four man tents. As the tents were removed and tallied, they revealed rows and rows of barrels initially well hidden from view, lined up across the entire width of the back wall. There was no need to pry open the lids to determine the contents. Each barrel emitted the telltale smell of rum, wine or port.

"Aha," Tyler said triumphantly. "This will be far better than blankets to keep one warm in winter months. 'Tis a shame we must leave it all behind for the New York patriots to enjoy and not take some with us back to our barracks."

"Tally the barrels carefully," Will cautioned. "I will speak to the Colonel and see if there is a possibility of obtaining one or two for our Regiment." The soldiers grinned appreciatively, confident of their Colonel's known willingness to provide for his men. It took them the rest of the morning and a good part of the afternoon to complete the inventory of the warehouse. Chandler reported the count as six hundred and twenty two tents, one thousand seven hundred and eighty five blankets, two hundred and three barrels of rum, one hundred and thirty six barrels of wine and seventy-seven barrels of port.

Will took the ledger and left Corporals Tyler and Chandler in charge of a guard of ten men to protect the warehouse. Upon returning to the barracks he had a detail assigned to relieve them. But first he obtained the Colonel's approval to requisition one barrel of rum and one of wine for the officers and men, and a barrel of port for General Knox.

The following morning Will continued inventory duty. After inspecting several more warehouses between Dyes and Weasyes Streets, just below King's College, Chandler added to the ledger a specified number of barrels of wheat, corn and flour, one hundred hogsheads of sugar, fifty hogsheads of molasses, twenty casks of coffee, seventeen casks of assorted medical supplies, ten barrels of saltpeter, fourteen barrels of tallow and seven of tar, and miscellaneous quantities of ordinance, tools for carpentry, blacksmithing and shoemaking. Surprisingly, in the last building they checked, they found a complete but dismantled printing press.

By mid-afternoon, Will and Corporal Chandler returned to General Knox's headquarters at Number 1, Broadway. It was this very same building that Knox, then a Colonel, had occupied in '76 as the British Fleet sailed into the lower bay. It had not changed much from the outside in the five years of British occupation. Once inside, Will approached the orderly and asked to report and deliver the ledger to General Knox or Colonel Sargent.

"The General and Colonel are both with His Excellency at Fraunces Tavern. A messenger has been sent to inform the General that his wife and family have arrived."

"Here," Will blurted out. "Here at Headquarters. Were there other ladies with Mrs. Knox? Where are they?"

The orderly pointed up toward the second floor. Will left Chandler clutching the ledger under his arm and bounded up the stairs. The sound of womens' voices came from within one of the rooms, followed by a deeper masculine one inquiring where to place the trunks. Will pushed open the door without knocking.

"Why Captain Stoner," Lucy Knox said, extending her hand. "What a pleasure to see you." Little Lucy, who was at the open window looking down at the street below and pointing out sites to her brother Henry, turned and squealed with delight. She ran to Will and hugged him around the knees. Henry squirmed around her begging to be picked up.

"My how you have grown," Will said, throwing the little boy in the air and cradling him in one arm.

"I am certain you would like to greet your own children," Mrs. Knox said taking Henry from Will. "I believe you will find them down the hall." As Will left, she added, "Mercy Hadley and little Benjamin also are here. Master Sergeant Cooper, Sarah and family are one floor above."

So intent was he on finding Elisabeth, her words made no impression on him. He burst into a broad sunny room to find Elisabeth trying to unpack the bedding while holding Agnes on her hip. Her back was to him. Three year old Henry saw him first.

"Pappa," he screamed running barefoot across the wooden floor. Will bent down with open arms and grabbed Henry and tickled his ribcage as the little boy giggled with delight. "We came by boat. A big boat. With grandpa," he said in his little sing song voice. "We saw big birds up in the sky." Holding him in the crook of his arm, Will embraced Elisabeth and planted a kiss on Agnes' forehead.

"We are together at last," she whispered.

"Yes. We truly are." He wanted to say more but Henry, demanding attention, pulled on his father's ear and begged him to listen his recounting of the voyage on the "wide river to the big city."

That evening with Agnes asleep in her crib and Henry snuggled between his parents for warmth, Elisabeth grabbed Will's hand and held it tightly. "With peace, I pray we will never be apart again," she said fiercely.

"I promise to do all in my power to make it so," he replied kissing her gently on her temple.

Will awoke shortly after midnight, confused and unsure what had awakened him. The building shook slightly. Elisabeth felt the tremor and sat up in bed. Will put his hand over her mouth to stifle a cry. "Shh. Lie still." The building shook one more time. Will held his breath, waiting for additional shocks. There were none. Through the open windows they heard shouts of panic and cries for God to save them as some people streamed into the streets. After a while, as people realized the earthquake was over, they retreated from the cold back to the warmth of their homes.[7] Will and Elisabeth lay in bed clinging to each other for comfort. Will suppressed a laugh, almost choking with the effort, before letting out low spasmodic guffaws.

"Will. Hush. You will wake the children. What is so amusing?" she asked sharply.

"I thought after all the dangers I have been through, to die by earthquake after the war has ended . . ." his voice trailed off. "I suppose it is not that funny," he admitted.

"It would be an unusual way to die." She sighed and snuggled closer. "Do you think my dear husband, married couples in peacetime speak so often of death? I suspect not and vow to relish thoughts of nothing but calm and harmony." Their whispers were interrupted by Henry's thrashing about in his sleep and waking with a wail. "So much for calm and harmony," Will said, as Elisabeth comforted their son by rocking him in her arms.

The day after the earthquake was Sunday. Many more citizens of New York attended church that morning, certain that God had sent them a signal to abandon their sinful ways. While the Hadley and Stoner families rode in carriages up Broadway to St. Paul's, Adam, Sarah, Lettia and the two children hurried on foot to the John Street Methodist Church. Lettia, despite her age and infirmities, led the way, using Adam's arm for support. Bent forward, her chin jutting out, she strode ahead, her lips tightly compressed, her determination driving the family on. Adam held Emmanuel on his shoulders, the boy clasping his father's epaulet with one hand and pounding on his tri-corn with his little fist. Sarah trailed behind carrying baby Priscilla bundled up and close to her bosom. They joined the crowd of white and black worshipers arriving at the blue stucco building for the morning's service. Lettia let go of Adam's arm and hobbled off toward the Sexton's office. Finding it empty, she stood confused until Adam, pushing through the crowd filing into the narthex took her by the hand.

"We will see him after services," he said reassuringly.

"Must find my boy. Must find Jupiter," she mumbled.

"We will," Adam said, guiding her toward the entrance.

A gaunt faced Negro in a tailored jacket raised his palm toward Adam as they were about to enter the main hall. "Negro people sit upstairs in the gallery," he said genially, pointing with his outstretched arm toward the stairs on the side.

"This Negro fought for his country," Adam said indignantly, pointing to his chest. "For the right of these white people to be able to worship free of British rule."

Sarah swiftly came to his side. "Come, Adam. We are here for mamma to see Sexton Williams. Do not create a disturbance. For her sake and mine. Please," she implored.

Upstairs in the gallery, crammed in on narrow, uncomfortable benches, Adam seethed through the long sermon by a white minister and watched with increasing fury as the minister, assisted by the Negro who had directed them to the gallery, gave communion to the white congregation. He felt his wife's hand on his thigh, attempting to soothe him. It did little good. The Negro congregants were invited down to receive communion only after all the whites had left the main hall. Adam was so angry that he had no intention of receiving even a blessing from the minister.[8]

Sarah held his hand tightly as they crowded into Sexton Williams' tiny cubicle of an office.

"I am thankful you were instrumental in reuniting my mother

with my family," Sarah said after they had introduced themselves. "What news of my brother, Jupiter? We are all most anxious to learn of his whereabouts?"

"I have a letter from him for you and your mother. He is free and well but a far distance from here."

Lettia seemed confused by the Sexton's statement.

"Where is he? Where is my boy?" she repeated as Sexton Williams took out a folded piece of paper from his bible and handed it to Sarah. It was a brief letter from Jupiter he before he boarded a ship for Nova Scotia, he explained. Sarah read it out loud.

Dear Mother and Sister: I write this the evening before I leave by ship to Nova Scotia. I am not afraid to go. I am eager to live as a free man in St. John's. I do not know what I will do there. I will write you care of Sexton Williams once I am settled. I can read and write because of Sexton Williams. He is a good man. I do know I will rid myself of my slave name Jupiter Parks and take a free man's name. I will not even sign this letter by that name and only end,

Your loving son and brother.

"Where is he now?" Lettia asked. "Where is he?"

Adam took her hand in his. "He is in Nova Scotia, a place closer to Marblehead Massachusetts where we are going. It is a different country, ruled by the British. We cannot go there but perhaps he could come to Massachusetts." He felt anguish at lying to Lettia. Jupiter could not live free in Massachusetts unless the commonwealth abolished slavery and banned slave catchers.

He put his hand under his mother-in-laws' chin and lifted her head. "Your son is a fine young man. He has done what is necessary to live as a free man, like me and your grandchildren. You should be proud of him."

Lettia grabbed Adam's hand with her two and nodded her head. "All I want is to see my son for I die."

"The Lord willing," Sexton Williams said, "you will do so."

At these words, Adam could no longer contain himself. "How can you tell this old woman the Lord cares about her when whites and Negroes do not worship together in this very church?"

"Adam, please," Sarah said.

"In Marblehead we worship in our one story church, sit in the same pews, are buried in the same graveyard and join and fight in the same regiment to protect the lives of those whites who force us to be in the gallery." He brushed off Sarah's hand. "No, Sarah. I will not calm down."[9]

"You are frightening the baby," she said as Priscilla whimpered softly. "At least lower your voice."

"Sexton," Adam said, in a softer tone. "You have helped my wife's brother and I am grateful for that. However, neither I, nor any member of my family, will set foot in this church on any Sabbath and suffer the indignities we have endured today."

Sexton Williams smiled, his round face unperturbed by Adam's outburst. "Perhaps you will agree to come to our church during the week to simply bring comfort to Lettia. She can hear from me how her son spent his days here, after she departed."

The old woman stared through her rheumy eyes at the Sexton. "My son, Jupiter. He was fine when he left here?"

"Yes, Lettia. Come back tomorrow and I will tell you all about him."

The next day, Adam brought Lettia to the church. Sarah had been up since dawn baking dessert for the dinner Mrs. Knox had arranged for General Washington, Governor Clinton and some of the other civilian leaders and their wives. Lucy had been fussing about arrangements, nervous as a hen minding her chicks. It was no time for Sarah to be away.

They sat in the office of James Varick, who had assisted in administering communion to the Negroes the day before. It was a bit larger than the Sexton's closet but not by much. Peter started his account with Jupiter's escape from being enslaved on Long Island, his renewed attention to learning to read and write and his helpfulness around the church. Varick chimed in, noting how bright Jupiter was and how diligently he studied the bible.[10]

"Where is he now?" Lettia inquired and upon hearing again he was in Nova Scotia, looked uncomprehendingly to Adam.

"Tis two day's sail from Boston," Adam explained, "if the

winds be right and the weather good." He shook his head. "Tis not the distance, Lettia. He will not be free in Marblehead and we cannot go to a British colony."

Lettia bowed her head. "I want to see my son," she said, adding her familiar phrase "for I die."

Varick leaned forward in his chair and placed one hand on Lettia's head in a gesture of benediction. "I will pray the Lord to grant your wish."

"Why do you both remain in New York," Adam said in disgust. "In this church, subject to weekly if not daily indignities. I assume it is the white trustees that have made these rules to separate the Negroes."

There was a long embarrassed silence, broken by Varick clearing his throat and nodding to Williams to respond.

"I cannot leave now," the Sexton said quietly, running his fingers through his closely cropped hair. "My master, a wealthy Tory, was evacuated with the British Army. The good Church Trustees bought me at a private sale, to spare me the embarrassment of a public auction."

"What? Adam bellowed out incredulously. "You are a slave owned by this very Church. Good lord man," Adam said. "Do you not see the contradiction between your faith and your condition? You live in bondage instead of as a free man."

"My former master was a tobacconist and taught my father," Williams responded matter of factly. "I learned from my father how to make cigars. I make and sell cigars in addition to my duties as Sexton. In another year, maybe two, I will have earned the Forty Pounds to buy my freedom."

"This is nonsense," Adam shouted, banging his hand on the Varick's worn desk. "I will raise the Forty Pounds from my friends by the end of this week so you can buy your freedom immediately."

Peter slowly shook his head. "You are angry. That is not my way. My former owner lived on Beekman Street, not far from here. I was born in his barn in a place as lowly as our Lord Jesus. I am a man of humility and patience." He gripped Adam's arm in his. "I do appreciate your sincere offer to purchase my freedom. I will place my faith in the Lord who will set me free."

"You should take matters into your own hands to help God help you," Adam said gruffly.

Once outside the church, Lettia held Adam's hand tightly as they walked back toward Broadway. She was afraid of the many stray dogs that wandered the streets. Occasionally, he would wave his free arm to drive them away. When they reached One Broadway, Lettia stopped in the central hallway, looking up the staircase toward their quarters on the third floor.

"These stairs are too much for me," she sighed shaking her head.

Adam looked at the two sentries and the orderly behind the desk. He picked Lettia up in his arms, ignored their sly smirks, and strode up the stairway, taking the steps two at a time. The sooner they left for Marblehead and home the better, he thought. *I do not feel free here.* Traveling by ship to Boston in December was risky. The weather could turn nasty. He would speak to Sarah. For him, any discomfort was worth the price to be back in Marblehead.

—w—

Slouched in a comfortable armchair before the fire, Will was still wearing his uniform although he had relinquished his commission as had most of the officers of General Knox's regiment. The warmth felt good on this cold December night. His father-in-law, Luykens Van Hooten sat in the other chair, his legs stretched out toward the flames in the hearth.

"I must apologize Will for being unable to meet with you sooner. There were and remain many business matters to attend to." Van Hooten glanced around the room, his eyes resting on mahogany side tables, cherry and ash cabinets, artfully carved wing back chairs and ornate brass sconces on the walls.

"My former agent, Andrew Brockholst did very well for himself during the British occupation. Do you not think so?"

Will nodded in agreement.

"I stayed here in this very house," he continued, "when I came to the city at General Knox's request."

"When you returned, you brought Adam's mother-in-law to West Point."

"Precisely. I was pleased to be of assistance. Sarah baked me a special cake in appreciation."

He chuckled quietly. "At the time, Brockholst expressed every intention of remaining after the liberation. I wonder what deeds he had committed that persuaded him to flee to London with his wife and daughters."

"My former agent," Van Hooten continued, "has hired a manager of this house who wishes to charge me rent. I, in turn, have promised to pay, once I have examined Andrew's accounts of managing my properties. It seems Brockholst's ledgers are no where to be found."

Will shifted in his chair and stared at his boots. The only clothes I own are my uniforms, he thought. "So you are at a standoff, so to speak," he said.

"Yes," Van Hooten replied. "In the meantime, my two warehouses on the Hudson are in need of major repairs. Parts of both roofs need to be replaced. The British used one as barracks. There is human filth from their latrines in that one, bird shit all over the rafters and floors, stray dogs, cats and rats from the waterfront have made their homes in every nook and cranny," he threw up his hands, "I could go on and on. There is much work to be done before I will ship any flour and other food stuffs down from Albany."

He put his brandy glass down on the side table, clasped his hands together under his lips and studied Will. "I would like to make you an offer. Tis not for the reason you are married to my daughter. You are intelligent, trustworthy and able to gain the respect of men. This will be beneficial in supervising workers and seeing a project through to timely conclusion."

Will sat up in his chair and edged forward. "Sir. You have already done more than. . ."

Luykens held up his hand. "None of that Will. I am not offering you employment solely to help you. I am doing so for it will also benefit me. I need an agent in New York. One who initially will see to the work of repairing my warehouses. Someone I can trust with my money to pay the workers and not pad the payroll and skim off the proceeds."

"After the warehouses are ready, then what would be my duties?" Will asked, thinking what employment he could find in a few months time.

"Why to manage my business – to see to it the flour from my mills and other food stuffs are promptly delivered to ships on the wharves, that payment is received and deposited and my river sloops are loaded with the supplies I have ordered and return to Albany."

Will shook his head. "I believe I am capable of overseeing the rebuilding of your warehouses. I do not have a mind for business, nor numbers. It is beyond my capabilities."

Van Hooten let out a loud guffaw. "Beyond your capabilities," he hooted. "You were a mere teamster lad when I first met you. Hungry all the time and not an extra shirt to clothe you." He rose from his chair and paced back and forth before the fire, now and then pointing his finger at Will. "Now you are a Captain of Artillery, a man who has commanded others in battle, calmly faced enemy fire and performed with distinction. No, you will do well. Of that I am certain. Besides, I have explained my idea to General Knox. He approves wholeheartedly."

"Sir. I am honored by the trust you place in me. I will do my best as I have always done for the General."

"Your acceptance relieves my mind of a great burden. I shall leave for Albany within the week. The Hudson is not yet frozen here but I fear I will not be able to proceed any further than West Point by boat."

Will looked shocked. He had assumed Luykens would remain in New York to instruct him in the intricacies of his business affairs.

His father-in-law read his thoughts. "Besides the repairs and dealing with the problem of Brockholst's missing ledgers, no need to concern yourself with shipping of goods. I will return with the spring thaw and together we will make the rounds of the bankers, buyers representatives and shipping agents." He waved his hand dismissively. "You are a quick learner, Will. I wager you will be among the best in the city within a matter of months."

"Sir. You honor me with your confidence in my yet unproven abilities."

"Call me Luykens in private. Before our employees, refer to me as Mr. Van Hooten."

"Yes sir."

Van Hooten raised his eyebrow in admonition. "You are no longer in the Continental Army. End your habit of calling me sir. That is an order," he added, laughing at his own jibe.

Will left the house and ran almost the entire way back to One Broadway. He rushed up the stairs, eager to tell Elisabeth the good news. Not only was he to be employed as her father's agent at the munificent salary of Eighty Pounds for the first year. Within a few days they would move into the house on Gold Street, sharing it with her father until he returned to Albany. It would be their home in the city, at least until the rent and ledger issues were resolved. The floorboards creaked under his booted feet as he slowed his pace. He opened the door to their room. Both children were asleep, Agnes in her crib and Henry lying across their bed, his dark hair peeking out from the quilt edging.

Elisabeth was seated at a small table, reading her book of poetry by candlelight. She put her finger to her lips and motioned for him to stay in the hall. She left the door slightly ajar and reached up to kiss him. Will could not keep himself from disgorging all the good news at once and poured out the details of the offer. "I now have employment and we will have a home. It has been weighing heavily on me as you know."

"This is such good news. Father never gave me any hint of his plans." She entwined her hands in his. "It will be a good beginning for our life here. Many of our mutual friends will be leaving," she sighed. "Lucy Knox told me she and the General will be departing for Boston by the end of this month. With His Excellency's leaving, General Knox has been appointed general in chief of the army."[11]

"I could ask to stay on as an aide de camp for no pay," Will said. When he saw Elisabeth's look of surprise and disappointment, he quickly added, "I am simply teasing my dear."

"Time enough for that once we are settled," she said crisply.

"There is the move to father's house and Mrs. Knox is in need of my assistance in preparing for the Christmas and farewell dinner for her dear Harry and our friends, a guest list to be prepared, the menu to be planned and . . ." Will put his finger to her lips. "Hush," he said. "Let us enjoy a quiet moment of the beginning of our new life."

Elisabeth kissed his finger and removed his hand. "Not to mention you need to visit a tailor and purchase new clothes."

As Christmas approached, Elisabeth scurried from home to home in Mrs. Knox's service, arranging for borrowed china from this house, linens from another, extra glasses and goblets from a third. Will was dragooned into overseeing the carters hauling barrels of wine, beer, ale and port, all of which were stored in the basement of One Broadway for the big event. He felt self conscious riding Big Red wearing his new tailored overcoat instead of his old blue Continental with the familiar buff facings and buttons.

Christmas Day began overcast with the threat of snow. By the time the forty guests had arrived, light flakes were falling and the fireplaces in each of the parlors and the main dining room were ablaze. General Knox, in his Major General's uniform at the head of the table, his face flushed from the heat and excitement of the occasion, welcomed all with a toast to freedom and liberty, followed by his observation his former officers present would soon admit that no officers's mess ever offered a feast like tonight's. Will and the other invited officers heartily agreed.

"It is difficult for me to recognize my former officers in their civilian clothes," Knox said loudly, raising his glass to the men and women assembled around the table. "The ladies are as beautiful as ever," he added with a bow of his head to Mrs. Knox, whose hair was a towering structure adorned with red, white and blue ribbons. "I confess my powers of utterance are unequal to the strength of my feelings. In a few days time, Mrs. Knox and I will leave for Boston. We deeply lament this separation from my officers and their wives. Many have been part of my official family since '75. I need not detail the hardships and difficulties we have endured to come to this point. They are all familiar to you who have lived them."

Will heard the roar of the cannons and the screams of the wounded. He recalled the fever that consumed him after Yorktown and almost killed him and the panic he felt at the thought of never seeing his wife again. He was overcome by emotion and felt Elisabeth squeeze his hand under the table.

"I offer the hope in peacetime that all around our table this night may enjoy the good health and quietude they deserve." As he raised his glass, first the former officers and then the civilian invited guests stood, faced the General and saluted him.

"Now having unwittingly introduced a somber note to this festive occasion, I seek to lift your spirits with another matter of different weight." Knox remained standing and placed one hand on his expansive stomach. "There is a scale at West Point. In August, eleven senior officers, including His Excellency agreed to record our respective avoirdupois. It was on this occasion, and on this occasion alone, I ever surpassed our beloved General Washington in any manner." Knox held up his hand to stifle the laughter. "I weighed at 280 and His Excellency at 209 pounds." The room erupted in cheers as Knox exaggeratedly lowered himself heavily in his chair.[12]

Dinner began with the usual platters of roast meats and freshly grilled fish, along with bowls of vegetables brought from the kitchen. Mrs. Knox beamed with pride when, to a fanfare by the musicians on the temporary dais at the far end of the room, the Christmas pie was presented. The General called for silence as his wife explained the recipe was Mrs. Washington's and the bulging pie with its hard crust was stuffed with turkey, goose, duck, partridge and pigeon, all properly seasoned with nutmeg, mace, cloves, black pepper and salt and four pounds of butter.

General Knox helped himself to a generous portion and as the guests filled their dishes, his voice boomed out down the table, "I will endeavor to maintain my position as the heaviest of the senior officers in the Continental Army." He began to laugh so hard, tears ran down his ruddy jowls. "In truth, I am now the only senior officer in the Army."

Mrs. Knox raised her glass in the direction of her husband. "My dear Harry, unable to eschew the patriotism that has governed his life, accepted this position until Congress in its wisdom, determines to recognize his talents and elevates him to a more prestigious post."

The recollection of the warmth and camaraderie of the farewell Christmas dinner did little to lift Will's spirits as he stood on Hudson pier on the last day of December, and watched one of the sailors untie the thick worn rope around the capstan. The General was on deck, his cloak wrapped around him against the blustery wind, encasing his son Henry in it folds. Will supposed the women, Lucy, Mercy and Sarah were down below in their cabins. Samuel Hadley stood bare-headed, his black tri-corn raised in farewell, the strong breeze blowing his brown hair across his forehead. Benjamin Hadley held his father's hand and waved with the other to Will. Adam Cooper stood gripping the railing. His son, perched on his shoulder, eyes turned toward the grey sky, pointed at the seagulls as they darted above the masts.

Will waved back at his three friends and then, solemnly saluted. His eyes filled with tears as the General gave him a farewell salute in return. His closest friends and his mentor, nay the man who was like a father to him, were leaving to begin their lives anew. It was his task to do likewise -to fulfill the trust Luykens had placed in him, to provide for his family, and to adapt to life outside the army. As he walked toward the Van Hooten warehouses, his mind was already wrestling with the problem of how to replace one of the main beams in the roof. He would fasten two pulleys to the adjacent beams and hoist up the new sound one. Once it was in place they could begin the work on new shingling.

Chapter 12 - The Blessings of Peace

The Presbyterian Church, located not far from the Stoner's home on Gold Street, was a recognizable landmark with its incomplete steeple. It was known to residents as the Brick Church so named for its red brick exterior in the Georgian style.

It was a chance meeting that brought Will here. One of his workmen had fallen from the warehouse roof and shattered his leg. Will brought him to the newly named Columbia College, formerly King's College. There, he met Dr. Charles McKnight, recently appointed as professor of surgery. The doctor was also on the Advisory Board to the Brick Church. Upon learning that Will was in charge of repairing the warehouse, he asked him to survey the church and offer an opinion on the extent of repairs necessary to restore its structure.

Will hurried along on foot, thinking that these brisk March winds would soon give way to April and the return of his father-in-law. One could already see the beginnings of a thaw in New York but he knew from being posted at West Point during the winter, the Hudson would remain frozen solid near Albany for at least another few weeks.

Dr. McKnight was waiting for him in the narthex. Several months after Evacuation Day, the stench from the imprisoned sick and dying American soldiers still filled the empty hull of the Presbyterian Church. He had a thin, angular face, ending in a sharp, almost jutting chin, and dark arched eyebrows. His bristly hair was brushed straight back, leaving a pinnacle in the middle that accented the receding hair line on both sides of his head.

Will kept his overcoat on to ward off the draft coming in under and around the temporary ill-fitting doors to the main worship hall. The originals along with the pews, railings and altar had long since been consumed for firewood. The bare brick walls bore scratch marks in places where the prisoners had etched their names, the number of days of their ordeal, or plaintive pleas for God's mercy.

"We do not know how many of our soldiers were imprisoned here, nor how many died of disease or starvation," Dr. McKnight said. He had the flat accent with little modulation of someone born in the mid-Atlantic colonies. "The British first used it as a hospital. Later, after they had burned all the wood to keep their sick soldiers warm, they converted it to a prison for ours, leaving them to freeze in the winter and swelter in the summer."

Will walked slowly around the interior, staring up at the thick oak ceiling beams and occasionally stooping to read the scratched words in the bricks. They were at the height of where a man lying on his pallet would be able to reach and carve his message. What did these men hope for, he thought. Was it the expectation of being remembered?

"Were our soldiers who died buried in the church yard?" Will asked.

Dr. McKnight shrugged. "The ground would be too hard to dig a grave for those who died in the winter. There are some fresh unmarked graves. I shudder to contemplate others were given neither a decent service nor a proper burial."

The two men somberly walked the length and width of the hall. "I am impressed Mr. Stoner you take the time to see the human tragedy that occurred in this sacred space. The others we have consulted hastily surveyed the area, quoted an exorbitant price with the caveat that it would increase once they were better able to examine the conditions and left as if to attend to more important business."

"I suspect none of them served in the Army as I have," Will

responded. "The bond with brother soldiers provides the knowledge of the hardships endured and the compassion to imagine the horrors of imprisonment."

"Well said. I too was with the Army, as a surgeon of course," McKnight said. As he related his duties as Senior Surgeon for the Middle Department, the two men discovered they had both been at Jockey Hollow in the terrible winter of '79.

"It was the worst winter of the entire war," Will replied. "My son, Henry, was born in Morristown at General Washington's headquarters in February '80 while I was snowbound at Jockey Hollow." He smiled at the thought of first seeing Elisabeth and their baby and his reunion with Adam who had thwarted the raid to kidnap His Excellency.

"My father was a Presbyterian Reverend. He was arrested in '77 and held on the prison ship Jersey on the East River. When he was released his health was broken. He died on the journey to our home in New Jersey," McKnight said. "I intend, when we restore this church, to leave the inscriptions of these desperate prisoners in place to remind generations of parishioners of the suffering that occurred here." /1

They finished their perambulation of the interior. "I propose to erect scaffolding," Will said, gesturing with his hands toward the ceiling, "and inspect the roof and beams from the inside. Then, we will look at the condition of the shingles on the roof from the outside. I assume there is no plan to complete the steeple."

McKnight shook his head. "Not at this time."

"I will employ four men, at five shillings six pence per day. I anticipate the inspection will take no more than three days. I will not charge for my own services," Will added. "If you accept our recommendations we will then agree on a price for such."

"That is most generous of you," McKnight replied extending his hand.

They parted on the steps of the Brick Church. It was mid-afternoon and there was no need for Will to return to the warehouses, the work having been completed for the day. He walked up William Street anxious to return home for dinner with his family. He was pleased at having struck up a friendship with the doctor. Their shared military service created their affinity for each other. As he approached Gold Street, Will realized how much he missed Samuel and Adam. He hoped they were well. He would ask Elisabeth to write to Mercy Hadley for news.

Three days later, a liveried servant delivered a written invitation to Mr. and Mrs. Willem Stoner to dine at Dr. and Mrs. Charles McKnight's residence on the grounds of Columbia College, the first Saturday in April.

It was too far to walk from their house on Gold Street. Will rented a carriage for the event. He and Elisabeth thought owning one would be an extravagance, yet both desired to arrive in style. "If cost is an issue, you could ride sidesaddle on Big Red with my arms around you," Will teased, when Elisabeth asked how much the rental had cost.

The McKnight's home fronted on Berkeley Street which ran from the Hudson River to Broadway, the western boundary of The Common. Behind the few neighboring houses with their ample fenced yards, loomed College Hall, a huge four story stone building, set on a flat green field of several acres.

Their arrival was unusual, for Will was both the driver and the escort of the lady in the open carriage. He jumped down from the seat, took the footstool from the interior of the carriage and offered Elisabeth his hand as she descended in the carriageway of the McKnight's residence. A stable boy took Big Red's reins in hand and led the horse and carriage to the barn behind the mansion.

Other guests arriving at the same time gaped at the uncommon spectacle. With Elisabeth's arm on his, they walked confidently up the stairs and into the grand entrance. Elisabeth wore a rich, dark maroon low-necked gown with sleeves ending at her elbows. Her neck and bare shoulders were covered by a gauze scarf with a flowered pattern.

"I fear my gown is out of fashion," she whispered to Will, directing his gaze to several ladies in front of them, waiting to be introduced to Dr. McKnight and his wife. Their dresses were looped in the back over a quilted petticoat and puffed out behind them.

"Nonsense," Will whispered back. "If that is the new fashion, I want none of it. These women look as if they are mother hens hiding their flock of chicks under their voluminous tail feathers." Elisabeth giggled at the image. "Yet, I feel much as when I attended dinner parties at the Shippens in Philadelphia," she said. "A pretty adornment though seen as lacking in upbringing and education of the fine young ladies of that city."

Will patted his wife's hand. "The men here will admire your beauty. The women, who on first glance, seem pampered to me, will be in awe of you. You are the only lady here who served our nation as a spy. You are a friend to Lucy Knox and have not only met His Excellency and Martha Washington and given birth in the General's headquarters, but also attended General Howe's extravagant farewell party. You may regale them with all of this, not to mention your account of Mrs. Arnold's madness at West Point." He squeezed her hand affectionately. "My dear. I suspect we will receive many dinner invitations in the future if you but modestly speak the truth of your adventures."

As they were presented to Dr. and Mrs. McKnight, the doctor's wife remarked she understood Will and Elisabeth had spent time at New Windsor and West Point. "My husband was at a hospital in Peekskill, a most inhospitable place in the dreariest of winters." Elisabeth, recalling the drafty wooden quarters at West Point agreed. "We were fortunate at New Windsor to be housed in General Knox's headquarters along with Mrs. Knox and their children. And other officers and their families as well," she added, anxious to avoid the misconception that she and Will had been the only ones sharing the home of the General and his wife.

Mary smiled at Elisabeth and turned her gaze to Will. "Perhaps, as a military officer, you know my father, General John Morin Scott." /2 The doctor's wife had thick curly black hair that hung loosely around her ears. Like Elisabeth, she had eschewed powdering her hair.

"I regret I have not had the pleasure of meeting him," Will replied.

"I will introduce you tonight. I suspect the two of you will enjoy one another's company," she said glancing meaningfully at her husband.

The dining room table was set for twelve couples, among them, Dr. Samuel Bard, a colleague of the host and a trustee of the newly named Columbia College, Mr. Hugh Gaine, a book publisher, Nicholas Low, a merchant and trader, Frederick Rhinelander, another merchant and sugar importer, and a few others whose names Will did not remember. General Scott was the only person at the table in uniform. Will felt a twinge of remorse for wearing his newly tailored clothes. He was the youngest of the men seated around the table and besides making him more comfortable, his uniform would have added some gravitas to his presence.

The long dining hall was ablaze with candles. Negro liveried servants stood attentively along the paneled walls. Will wondered whether they were freemen employed by the Doctor and his family or slaves. Perhaps a combination of both. He thought how furious Adam would be were he attending this dinner.

True to Mary McKnight's word, Will found himself seated opposite General Scott and on his left, Mrs. Gaine, to whom out of politeness he conversed about Elisabeth's interest in poetry and the possibility of her visiting her husband's shop. Unfortunately for Will, Mrs. Low was on his right for his hearing was worse on that side. She spoke in such a soft voice and with all hubbub around the table, Will had difficulty understanding her and could only nod appreciatively once in a while.

After fulfilling his gentlemanly obligations, Will leaned across the table and asked General Scott where he had seen service. The General was over fifty, a stout man with a broad nose and thick curly hair streaked with white across the crown. While his daughter had inherited her dark curly hair from her father, her more delicate features and figure obviously came from her mother's side.

They discovered they both had been at the Battle of Brooklyn in '76, although at different parts of the field. While Will had been involved in slowing the British flanking movement crashing down from Jamaica Pass, General Scott and the 1st New York Battalion had been guarding the Gowanus Road opposite the infamous General Grant.

"I confess, it is much more pleasurable to be discussing this over a fine dinner on a mild spring evening, then retreating for my life across Gowanus Creek and the muddy banks beyond. I believe I owe my escape and that of my men to the holding action of your artillery unit," Scott said raising his glass to Will.

"In truth General, we both owe our lives to General Stirling and the brave stand of Smallwood's Marylanders."

Scott raised his glass higher, acknowledging Will's reply and took a sip from his crystal wine glass. They were about to continue to reminisce when Mr. Gaine, seated two down from the General, interrupted their conversation.

"What think you General, of the debate raging in our papers of those who condemn Whigs who socialize and invite so called 'Tory vipers' to their dinner tables and advocate for the seizure of all Tory property and their expulsion them from our state, and those who prefer to let every man, regardless of Tory inclinations, proceed with his business unmolested."

Conversation around the table came to a halt. Some, discomforted by the question, stared at Dr. McKnight, deeming the question an affront to his hospitality. Others were eagerly poised to hear General Scott's reply.

"I ask it," Gaine added hastily, "as a former publisher accused of supporting Tory tyranny and now a simple book publisher seeking to make a decent living in a city known for its citizens' love of reading."

"Before General Scott responds," Dr. McKnight intervened, "my wife and I have invited all of you tonight after due consideration. We both believe stimulating discussion among those of differing views will serve to promote greater harmony amongst us all. It will redound to the prosperity of New York City." He smiled graciously at his wife and the seated guests.

The General cleared his throat and spoke loudly enough for all to hear. "I have had the honor of participating in our righteous struggle to free our country from the British Crown. Having seen so much blood spilled on the battlefield, my desire for revenge is tempered against those who never raised a sword against us." Scott spread his hands broadly before him. "My inclination is to permit those individuals who wish to remain to contribute their efforts toward our mutual prosperity, so I am opposed to those who call for seven year expulsions and proscriptions against Tory businesses. However," he raised his index finger as a caution, "interests of stability and continuity should not outweigh the rights of those who fought for liberty from reclaiming their properties nor the sale of estates owned by those Tories who chose to flee."

"You refer to your own property?" Gaine inquired.

"Yes," Scott replied. "I am now in possession of my home, located north of the Common. It is as it should be for others who went into exile rather than remain under British occupation. In addition, our Legislature has recently released confiscated Tory properties for sale to new owners, that is patriots of means. I wholeheartedly support such efforts."

"The establishment of a Bank of New York, particularly the appointment of General McDougall as President and the composition of its Board of Directors gives me cause for concern," the merchant, Nicholas Low said. He was seated near the end of the table across from Dr. Samuel Bard. "Perhaps General Scott, you can reassure me and others of General McDougall's propensities to foster stability."

"As for me," Dr. Bard added in a thick Scottish brogue, "my concern is the opposite of Mr. Low. The New York Packet reported the names of the new Directors. Three at least known to me are Loyalists who not only profited from their association with the British but espoused their cause as well. Why should men such as these serve on this new and powerful institution vital to our State's prosperity?"[3]

Frederick Rhinelander, sensing the General needed some support offered a response to Bard's question.

"There is little cause for concern for those named as the Bank's Directors. The overall composition is sound." He raised one hand and counted off his fingers. "On this important Board are one, Alexander Hamilton, two, Isaac Roosevelt, three, John Vanderbilt and four, William Maxwell. All men of substance, strong convictions and the intelligence to pursue and enact their ideas, with which I totally agree." He lowered three fingers and kept his index finger in the air. "The one appointment I would question is that of Joshua Waddington. He is currently engaged in litigation brought by a widow for the payment of rent and restoration of her property she was forced to abandon in '76 and occupied by Waddington throughout the war."

"Yet, Waddington is represented by our very own Alexander Hamilton who you have praised as a newly appointed Director," Dr. Bard responded.[4]

"Perhaps, Mr. Hamilton has found a personal road to prosperity by representing Tories in their property disputes against widows," Dr. McKnight said with some bitterness. "My father saw his church burned and gave his life for our cause. It is my opinion, a person such as Joshua Waddington has no place on the Board."

"Leaving aside discussion of the appointment of Mr. Waddington," General Scott said, "I would refer again to General McDougall, the President. No one may impute to him an improper motive. His patriotism is well known as is his lengthy service for his country. I have absolutely no doubt that General McDougall will see to it the bank is managed in an appropriate manner for the benefit of all and steer a moderate course to enable our economy to prosper."

"Gentlemen," Gaine said. "We bore the ladies to tears with our talk of bank management. Surely, we can regain their interest and fond attention by finding another less serious topic."

Will was surprised to hear Elisabeth's clear voice. "Sir. With all due respect, perhaps many of the ladies present have endured this long and dreadful war as participants and friends to their husbands and do not wish to relinquish their intellectual capabilities in peacetime."

A few of the men smiled condescendingly and looked at Will, silently blaming him for her outspokenness.

"I for one," she continued, "take an active interest in the

business climate of the city and remind you, many women managed their husband's businesses while they were away at war. This accumulated wisdom and experience did not vanish from our heads with the arrival of peace," she concluded, relishing the stares of the men around the table.

"Perhaps you will share your knowledge of trade with the rest of us and advise as to what goods to sell and what to buy," a man at the end of table said sarcastically.

Elisabeth took his question with good grace. "My dear sir. As a woman I am well aware of the rising interest for luxury goods, not only from England but from the continent. As husbands and merchants you will be well served to select such goods wisely and in quantity. As for your exports," she continued with a teasing lecturing lilt in her voice, "I suggest you seek to sell your grains and flour, timber and minerals to the entire European continent which lies before you as a lucrative market. I need not remind such astute men as yourselves, you are no longer limited by London's unjust restrictions to trade only with England." She glanced around the table. "Those merchants who remain tied to their traditional relationships with only British trading houses will not prosper in our new economy."

"Mr. Stoner," Nicholas Low called out. "Your lovely wife's opinions on the state of trade are, shall I say, both interesting and unique. What say you to our city's prospects after the late unhappy commotions?"

Will bristled at both the tone and the description of the war. He saw Elisabeth smiling at him with a look cautioning him to be measured in his response.

"My wife's own opinions mirror those of her father, a grain merchant and trader who chose to provide flour and services to our cause, for promises to pay in the future rather than," he said with a more severe tone in his voice, "to continue to supply the enemy for the gain of hard currency." He did not have to add more. Those around the table knew that Low's brother, Isaac, had sold essential food supplies to the British and enhanced his position and wealth before being forced to flee the previous November.

"I do not know you personally Mr. Low and will not ascribe to you the behavior of your brother." He hesitated and added in a lower voice, "I too have a brother who dishonored our family by plundering those with patriotic sentiments and serving as an officer in a Loyalist Regiment." Will glanced at Elisabeth, saw a flicker in her eyes and decided not to mention John's assault on her in Philadelphia. "Thus, I am sympathetic to the proposition brothers should not be blamed for the acts of their siblings."

"That being said," Will added, his voice rising, "I have served since '76 in the Continental Army and survived more bloody battles and seen more carnage and death than I wish to remember. I will not tolerate the demeaning of the sacrifice and courage of our soldiers to win our freedom, nor the current suffering of the maimed and widows, and the destruction evident around us in this city, by a vindictive and beaten enemy, with a reference to this long war as 'the late unhappy commotions.' It was not a 'commotion,' Mr. Low. It was a war in all its horrific slaughter, with men dying from being bayoneted or blown apart by shot and shell." Will took a breath as he heard inside his head the cries of battle once again.

"I regret if my words have offended you, Mr. Stoner," Low replied quickly. "They were ill chosen without any intent to diminish the sacrifices made to bring us to this moment of victory and peace."

"No offense taken Mr. Low."

After dinner the ladies and men adjourned to separate rooms, the women presumably to talk about their interests, although Will thought Elisabeth would steer the conversation more in the direction of substance than fashion.

The men retired to a separate room to sip their brandy and port. Will joined Dr. McKnight who was leaning on the mantle, in earnest discussion with General Scott.

"What think you Mr. Stoner of this new Society of the Cincinnati? Our New York chapter is in need of members," the Doctor inquired.

"Our President for our State Chapter is none other than General McDougall," Scott added.

"I confess I am ignorant of its purpose or provisions."

"Why, Mr. Stoner. You surprise me," Dr. McKnight said. "Your General Knox is the originator of the idea. He drafted its charter and it was adopted a year ago this coming May at Fishkill. I was there on an inspection tour of the hospital and was privileged to be present at the initial conference"[5]

"Tis an organization with a noble purpose," General Scott added. "We are a fraternal organization of Continental officers with the purpose of perpetuating our wartime friendships."

"If General Knox initiated and supports it, I assure you of my heartfelt commitment." He felt his face flush, embarrassed he was ignorant of the Society's existence. "After the army was disbanded and my close brothers in arms left for Massachusetts, I must admit I have found myself somewhat adrift in this new civilian world."

"A natural reaction," General Scott replied. "You will find new bonds of fraternity within our State Chapter. Either General McDougall or I will be convening a meeting of our chapter within a fortnight. First, if I am to be the host," Scott smiled, "I must replenish my wine cellar, entirely depleted by my former uninvited British guests. I do regret," he said with a touch of anger, "their appropriating for themselves some books from my library." He looked across the room at Mr. Gaine. "Excuse me, gentlemen. I must consult with our former Tory publisher turned bookseller as to the possibility of replacing some volumes."

As Scott left them, Dr. McKnight observed ruefully, the British also had decimated the college library. "Even today, I find pages from torn books blowing down the streets like leaves in autumn, or see scraps wedged into chinks and spaces between logs in the poorest of homes."

When Will and Elisabeth returned home and compared their experiences, it seemed the evening had been a success. "The women were most intrigued about the extravagant Mischienza for the departure of General Howe. I could only tell them so much detail in one sitting. I am sure to receive several invitations to teas to describe who wore what, the splendidness of the dinner, the fireworks and most importantly to them, the scandalous costumes the ladies wore for their so-called knights."[6]

Will paused in unbuttoning his dress shirt and grinned. "I am certain many of the gentlemen would also desire to hear the details of the gauzy dresses. Perhaps you could prepare a lecture series on the Mischienza to be delivered in various parlors around town."

"No, my dear," Elisabeth said, giggling at the thought. "I am afraid I already spoke too much in public at tonight's dinner."

"Nonsense. You and I have attended many dinners when Lucy Knox has offered her opinions on the issues of the day." He lay down and kissed her gently on her brow. "Never do change my darling wife. Do no succumb to what others think or convention requires your role should be."

"I shall do my best to obey my husband in this regard," she replied, mischievously.

"Come Papa. We go find grandpa," Henry said, taking Will's hand and pulling him toward the door. "We go find grandpa." Will tried to recall when Henry had lost the sing-song lilt in his voice. Now, he truly acted like the little boy he was, full of curiosity, chattering constantly, even sometimes beginning sentences with "I think" accompanied by a serious expression.

"Please Will, be careful. The neighborhood near the wharves is populated with many rough types," Elisabeth implored as Will lifted his son on to his shoulder. "You know I do not like you taking Henry there. Remember. He is only four."

"Do not worry," Will said waving goodbye. In the carriage house behind the mansion, Henry sat patiently on a mounting stump as Will cinched the saddle on Big Red and adjusted the bit. The little boy watched as Will talked to the horse in a calm voice, patted his neck and fed him a large piece of carrot. "I want to feed Big Red," Henry cried.

"Hold your hand flat, like this," Will said placing a carrot in his son's hand while holding the reins in the other. The boy giggled with delight as the carrot disappeared into the horse's mouth followed by crunching noises.

Will took the route he had taken every day to see if Luykens' sloop was sailing down river from Albany to New York. Henry sat in front of his father, his little legs spread across the saddle, his father's hand on his tummy to steady him. Will had to admit, in a few short months, the civilian administration under Mayor James Duane had done much to improve the city. There were fewer stray dogs and cows no longer wandered the streets unattended. Magistrates presided over functioning courts, issued licenses and collected fees. Nothing could be done about the stench and filth in the narrow alleys that ran between the crowded shanties.

The most obvious improvement was the return of river commerce. The wharves teemed with carters and day laborers, all manner of mechanics repairing ships and sails, ropes and hawsers, and food vendors in makeshift stalls selling all manner of cheap goods.

Henry sat up high on Big Red, taking in the noise and commotion, first looking at the sloops, brigs and small river craft tied to the piers and then up river at the grey sails approaching. Big Red stood on the main north-south road that serviced the wharves, solidly planted as people and wagons flowed around them.

"I look for grandpa," he yelled, pointing to the north. "Is grandpa coming? " he asked excitedly as a ship approached, only to be disappointed when no one on board waved to him. As his son's interest waned, Will turned Big Red away from the water. They rode up Broadway to the Commons, where Will let the horse graze freely while he and his son sat under a tree and watched the flocks of sheep and goats. Henry fell asleep in his father's arms and, when he awoke, as a special treat, they rode until Broadway turned into an unpaved road. They turned off the main way and stopped at a fresh water pond.

Will watched as his son scampered bare foot along the pond's edge, finding sticks and rocks and tossing them into the water. He felt an immeasurable sense of peace and realized with a start, he no longer dwelled on the war, or his brother or any of the experiences that had marked his life the past several years. He was content in his work and with his family. The sun was no longer high in the sky and he realized Elisabeth would be worried. He wished her to find the same contentment he felt and vowed to himself to do his best to help her achieve it.

—⁂—

After inspecting the sloop Mary Ellen near Murray's Wharf on the East River, Luykens and Will hurried to Merchant's Coffee House where an auction was about to begin.

"She seems sound to me below decks," Van Hooten said. "What do you think Will?"

Will wished he knew more about ships. The beams and keel seemed solid enough. As for the joints and tarring, he had no idea what to look for.

"I am no seaman as you know. If you intend to buy her, perhaps you should have a shipwright inspect her on your behalf."

"I already did. He opined she was solid enough if I only intended to use her for river service. If the price is right," Luykens said, "I will buy her. She will carry iron bar from furnaces in the Hudson Valley down river to the city. There is a good market for iron goods and many forges in the city to make them into hinges, locks and other items much in demand."

They found seats at one of the long tables in the main room on the first floor of the Coffee House. It was crowded with all manner of people, some well-to-do merchants, others shopkeepers seeking to buy odds and ends on the cheap and resell them for a profit. Will squeezed in on Luyken's right to hear him better. He was overwhelmed by the clamor of many voices in anticipation of the auction and shouts of patrons ordering coffee and meat pies. He knew his hearing failed him in large crowded rooms. He had stood too many times with his right side toward eighteen pounders near the touchhole. The command "Give Fire," echoed in his brain. Even now, with the strong aroma of coffee wafting from the brewing pots on the granite shelves over the hearth, he could almost smell the acrid odor of gunpowder.

"I said," Van Hooten repeatedly loudly leaning his mouth toward Will's left ear, "does not the rich smell of coffee excite the senses?"

Will nodded in agreement and made a show of sniffing from his porcelain cup.

The auctioneer, aptly named Mr. Tongue, stood on the temporary platform, as his clerk took his seat at a table next to him. "They say William Tongue performed this very same service during the British occupation and has returned to practice again," Luykens' neighbor said.

"The new law requiring auctioneers to be licensed does not prohibit former Tories from engaging in the business," Van Hooten replied. "If he is good at his profession, I say, let him practice."

"Yet he is taking work away from good Whigs," his neighbor persisted.

"If the good Whig auctioneers surpass his abilities, they will take the work away from Tongue. In the meantime," Luykens said amiably clapping his neighbor on the back, "we as buyers benefit from their competition."

The auctioneer began with odd lots of broad cloth and flannels, twelve hogsheads of Indian corn and five hogsheads of what Tongue characterized as 'excellent' Muscovado sugars. These were followed in rapid order by sixty five tierces of new rice, forty hogsheads of tobacco, 'of the bright yellow kind called Kytefoot,' the auctioneer added to induce greater interest and higher bids, and a quantity of household furniture, consisting of tables, chairs, beds and bedding and two dozen or so portmanteaus, leather trunks with brass fittings. Next were thirteen hogsheads of Claret, twelve barrels of anchovies and two hogsheads of Taunton Ale in bottles. /7

"Van Hooten looked around the room, noting others who might be waiting for more substantial items. Will followed his gaze and recognized the tall thin figure of Frederick Rhinelander making his way, with three well to do merchants to a separate round table. A small terrier crouched underneath, sniffing for scraps.

"I believe there sits our competition," Luykens said. "Any one or all of the four."

After William Tongue returned from soothing his throat with some liquid refreshment stronger than coffee, the auction resumed with the sale of land and leases. The first were two houses with lots described as being on Bayard Street, off from the intersection with Kyndert Lane. Will had ridden with his father-in-law to the fresh water pond and crossed the Lane to inspect the houses. Both were simple clapboard structures, one with a large keeping room with a fireplace for cooking, but in the main not noteworthy and certainly not as imposing as their brick mansion on Gold Street. At the time, Will had thought it was nothing but idle curiosity, a way of prolonging a pleasant afternoon in the countryside.

Rhinelander bid first and again when a second bid was shouted from across the room. The price was still low when Van Hooten raised his hand and acknowledged a Ten Pound increase over the last bid. From there, the bidding went back and forth between Rhinelander and Van Hooten with Luykens finally prevailing at One Hundred and Eighty- Five Pounds.

Will looked at his father-in-law in astonishment. To make a purchase of two rather plain houses for that amount, more than twice Will's own yearly salary seemed a reckless act of extravagance. He began to doubt the wisdom of accepting employment with Luykens, thinking if disaster befell Van Hooten's business, he too would be taken down.

Apparently his face betrayed his disapproval for Luykens laughed at Will's concern. "Withhold judgment until the end of the day," was all he said, nonchalantly observing the bidding on sales of other properties and leases for seven lots here and ten lots there.

When the bidding opened on the sloop Mary Ellen, Luykens bid early and earnestly, foolishly betraying, Will thought, his eagerness to purchase the vessel. He was not surprised when Rhinelander entered the chase and rapidly bid the cost of the ship up to where, with an obvious show of disappointment, Van Hooten dropped out.

Following the auction, Luykens with Will following him, circulated among the merchants and gentlemen who remained. They stopped at the Notice Board near the doorway to read the posted advertisements appearing in the local newspapers of various meetings scheduled to be held at Merchants.

"There is one we must attend," Van Hooten said, pointing to an announcement from the New York Packet, of a meeting of The

Whig Society in two weeks time. Will's eyes focused on another for the organizing meeting of the New York Society for Promoting Useful Knowledge. It seemed innocuous enough but provoked his interest. What would the well-educated gentlemen of the city consider useful knowledge?

His thoughts were interrupted by Frederick Rhinelander who greeted Will familiarly and Luykens a bit more stiffly. He was accompanied by one of the merchants who had been seated at their private four-person table.

"I am sorry to have disappointed you in your pursuit of the Mary Ellen," he said loudly. "It is I who have slipped ahead and captured the sloop." He laughed, a bit too loudly at his own strained witticism. His companion snickered. "However, all is not lost Mr. Van Hooten. If you still desire the vessel I will sell it to you for a small profit, say," he paused for effect, "Forty Pounds over what I paid for her."

Luykens smiled broadly and put up both his hands. "You are most kind Mr. Rhinelander. However, I must decline your generous offer. You are aware, I assume," he said still smiling, "there are accumulated wharf fees of Seventeen Pounds that must be paid before taking possession. Unfortunately, these fees continue to accumulate at Five Pounds per week. I am certain you plan to put the ship to immediate good use so it should not cause you any concern." Rhinelander appeared taken aback by Van Hooten's response. It was clear he had acted spontaneously and from spite at having lost the two houses and lots to Luykens.

"I suggest," Van Hooten continued, "we discuss the matters between us in a week or two. If you wish to meet sooner, I plan to enjoy the social atmosphere of this coffee house in the afternoons the coming weekdays."

Over dinner at Fraunces Tavern, Van Hooten explained he had seen an opportunity in Rhinelander's eagerness for the houses and lots. True, it was a high price to pay. However, if he held the houses as an investment, they would appreciate at least twofold in time and pay rent in the interim. Rhinelander was a real estate speculator and knew the value of the properties. He was not in shipping and had no interest in owning vessels.

"He will take my offer of selling me the Mary Ellen and paying the wharf fees, all of them, in return for purchasing the two houses and lots from me with a small increase over what I paid." Luykens cut a piece of beef on his plate and chewed slowly. "I wager he will make back the premium I ask and the wharf fees within the year. The trick Will," he said pointing with his fork, "is not to make an enemy of Rhinelander but to give him a fair arrangement so he is satisfied."

"Which is why you did not propose a deal at the Coffee House," Will said. "So he would not lose face in front of others."

Luykens nodded.

"I do not understand," Will asked. "Why not simply bid on the Mary Ellen and pay the price. Why the subterfuge of purchasing houses and lots and then reselling them?"

"Men attending auctions behave in predictable ways," Luykens explained, leaning back in his chair. "I say this based on experience and observation. There are the honest bidders who come solely with the intention to buy. Then there are those who think they are smarter than the rest, and with secret arrangements amongst themselves, bid in appearance against on another and drive up the price. The hapless honest buyer pays a far higher price and these sharp practitioners receive a payment from the auctioneer or his employer." He paused in his lecture. "You know of course, the higher the price paid, the greater the fee the auctioneer makes?"

Will shook his head. "No. I did not."

"I sensed this was the case with Mr. Rhinelander and his friends. Particularly when they were afforded a private table and spent time familiarly in the company of the estimable Mr. Tongue." He grinned at Will. "So. To thwart their bidding up the price I would pay for the Mary Ellen, I bid and purchased the houses and lots, property they indeed wanted. There was little risk for I am certain property values in the City will rise as more and more Whigs seek to live here. Mr. Rhinelander ended with a sloop he does not want. A trade to our mutual advantage, but with more advantage to me is the solution." He raised his glass of port. "To prosperity and improved commerce," Luykens said exuberantly. Will joined in the toast, uncertain whether he would ever be as astute a businessman as Elisabeth's father.

The early summer months brought an outbreak of the pox as well as oppressive heat. The wind blew west to east, bringing the stench from the accumulated filth of the shanties and shacks clustered along the Hudson River. People in the streets covered their noses and mouths to ward off the foul odors and the air many believed spread the pox.

"Nonsense," Dr. McKnight said to Elisabeth and Will as he prepared to inoculate Henry and Agnes. He had come to their home on Gold Street at Will's request. "Both of you were inoculated to prevent small pox. It is proven medicine. The bad air does not spread the disease."

"Please answer a concerned mother's question, Doctor," Elisabeth pleaded, clutching two-year old Agnes in her lap. "Is inoculation of our children the only way to prevent their getting this dread disease. I want to do it but am so afraid the fever will carry Henry and Agnes away. They say sometimes infecting little ones gives them such a terrible case of the pox. . ."

"Tis that or catching a mild case from an infected person," McKnight responded gruffly. "It will all go well. Little ones are most resilient," he added more gently as an after thought. He removed a lancet from his black medical bag and a glass tube filled with pus. He cut a black thread from a spool, inserted it in the vial. Henry, now four and a half, sat on the window seat bravely biting his lower lip and fighting back tears. The doctor made a shallow incision on his forearm, ran the pus-laden thread in the cut, and then bandaged it up.

"Good boy, Henry," Will said, kissing his son on the top of his reddish brown hair.

"Do not cry, Agnes," the boy advised. "It does not hurt."

Nevertheless, his sister scrunched against her mother, her

face buried in Elisabeth's bosom and whimpered as Dr. McKnight inoculated her.

"Three weeks quarantine for they can infect others," Dr. McKnight instructed. "I will return in two days simply to inspect the incision. The pustules will appear in ten to twelve days time, perhaps a day or two more," he said as he carefully closed the vial with a cork. "There may be fever and headaches as well. Have your servants been inoculated?" he asked as he stood to leave.

"Our cook has," Elisabeth answered. "Our maid refuses to undergo the procedure and will return when you advise there is no longer a need for quarantine."

"Foolish woman," McKnight snorted. "We had a terrible outbreak of the pox among the soldiers in '76. I must have inoculated an entire battalion and the burial detail interred at least one hundred."

Elisabeth gasped.

"I am truly sorry," Dr. McKnight stammered, embarrassed at his slip. "In most instances, inoculation results in only a mild case. The soldiers who died," he said, trying to repair the anxiety he had instilled in Elisabeth, "were infected from others, not from the inoculation procedure."

Will escorted McKnight to the door. "I do appreciate your attending to my children personally. If you are able, please visit us often. It will reassure my wife."

"I will most certainly do so. I will leave some powder when I return should either child develop severe headaches and pains. In my experience, the most difficult part will be restraining your exuberant son indoors for three consecutive weeks."

The doctor's prediction was correct for the first week and a half. By the twelfth day, Henry's red sores had developed into bulging, oozing pustules, some on both arms and his chest and mercifully only a few on the smooth youthful skin of his face. He complained of pain in his head, lost his appetite and developed a fever. Agnes too had a few pocks on her arms and body and some on her ears and cheeks. Although her case appeared to be much milder than

Henry's, Elisabeth was fearful the pocks would spread to her eyes and mouth.

As Agnes recovered and became more lively, her pocks dried out scarring her permanently here and there. However, Henry's condition worsened. The second night of the fever, he tossed and turned on the mattress on the floor of their bedroom, his face flushed, his skin hot to the touch. He begged for water constantly and moaned as he tossed his head from side to side trying to rid himself of the pain.

Elisabeth and Will took turns sitting up with him, applying wet cloths to his forehead and wiping his arms and chest with linen soaked in water from a tub cooling in the vegetable cellar. Although some of the pustules had begun to scab, Henry's fever and headaches had not abated.

Will was with his son at dawn. The heat so early in the morning promised another stifling summer day. Elisabeth, exhausted from lack of sleep nevertheless awoke early. She hurried down to the kitchen and returned with a pot of tea made of rosemary, mint, marigold, all grown in their kitchen garden, and the powder Dr. McKnight had given them made from shredded bark of a willow tree. /8

"It should help both his thirst and his headache," she said holding Henry's head up as he sipped at the homemade brew.

Will left her and, after rummaging through his army trunk, returned with his old canteen. "He needs to feel fresh air and cool breezes," Will said. "Fill this with your herbal remedy. I will saddle Big Red and take Henry for a ride."

"Will," Elisabeth responded with alarm. "He is under quarantine. He cannot go out. Besides, he is all aches and pains. The ride will harm him."

"I will ride slowly and take him where there are few people." Elisabeth gave him a worried look. "To the fresh water pond north of the Common. The breezes off the water will cool him far better than lying here in this heavy heat."

"We should consult with Dr. McKnight first," Elisabeth replied. Will shook his head. "I believe it will do him good. We used to lay the soldiers with the pox on the grass on pleasant days to let them breathe fresh air. Elisabeth. Please do as I say."

Without telling his wife, Will took a heavy linen cloth and a thin blanket and stuffed them in his saddlebag. With his canteen full, and Henry moaning softly in his arms, Will rode Big Red at a steady pace, so as not to jar his son too much, north on Nassau Street until they came to the pond. Ducks and geese swam placidly along the shore, quacking and honking noisily at the intrusion. A few fishermen sat motionless slouched in the shade of distant trees. Will judged they were far enough away to satisfy any requirements of Henry being quarantined.

He sat down on the grass and removed his boots and stockings. He undressed Henry and holding him in his arms, waded into the water up to his knees. It was cool and refreshing. Gently, with his arms supporting Henry's naked body, he held the boy in the water, supporting his head with one hand the other on the small of his back, so he floated on the surface. Henry smiled weakly in pleasure. "It feels good pappa." After a few minutes, Will retreated to the shore. He dried his son with the linen and wrapped him loosely in the blanket. He sat against a tree trunk and cradled the boy in his arms, feeling the coolness of his skin against him.

"Drink some of your mother's tea. It is good for you and made with all her love for you."

Henry took a long draught. "Is this your canteen from the war?"

"Yes," Will said. The boy stroked the worn wooden rim with his small hands and then gripping the leather strap in his fingers, nodded off.

As Henry slept, Will talked to him. He recalled his own fears as a boy, terrified of his father and the arbitrary beatings and incessant ridicule. He promised he would never treat Henry in such a manner. "Your godfather, General Henry Knox is a man of warmth and compassion, well read with sound convictions and principles," he said, "who, together with Mrs. Knox have been most generous to me and your mother." He told the sleeping boy of the General's commanding presence, his booming voice during the nor'easter when they crossed the Delaware at night and attacked the Hessians at Trenton, and of the great siege at Yorktown.

He voiced his hopes that his son would be as fortunate as Will had been to find good men who would become his friends for life - about how he and Adam had first met at the Mariners' barracks in Cambridge, how Adam had saved Will's life not once but twice and protected Elisabeth in Morristown. "He was a spy for his country and for the love of Sarah now his wife, who was a slave at the time and freed by Adam's bravery. He is the most steadfast of friends. He has taught me to respect the dignity of all regardless of their color. I hope to teach you to do the same." Will continued to speak of Samuel and Mercy Hadley and the hospital in Morristown, of Nathaniel Holmes of the Marblehead Mariners who first befriended him on the noble train of artillery in the winter of '75, of Sergeant Merriam, Isaiah Chandler, Levi Tyler and others of the gun crew.

"Although these friendships were forged in war," Will told his sleeping son, "I fervently pray you will never have to take up arms and endure the horrors of battle. If you do, I also pray you will be fortunate to have men as brave, patriotic and resolute as those who are my friends. I hope you will in peacetime make friends as good as those I made in war."

He had no more to say. He looked at his son lying in his arms with his eyes closed, breathing peacefully, and thought of future times when they would visit the battlefields in Brooklyn and the nearby Jersey Palisades, Boston and Dorchester Heights and be with the Hadleys and Nat Holmes and his family in Marblehead. And especially with Adam and Sarah Cooper and their children.

Will leaned over and kissed Henry's forehead. It was cool to his lips. He placed his palm on his son's forehead, then his arms and chest. The fever had broken. He let Henry sleep, staring at his son's placid face, marred here and there by scabs, at his long narrow body and his strong wiry legs. Yes, he thought. I will tell you these stories again and again. We will visit these friends and you will know such good and decent people exist to be emulated by you as an adult. When your mother and I are gone, you will pass on these stories to your children and your children's children – so they will know ordinary men and women performed extraordinary deeds to gain our freedom.

The boy stirred, opened his eyes and smiled weakly at his father. Will whistled for Big Red. Mounted on the aging warhorse, Will and Henry rode home together in the warm late afternoon sun.

Note to the Reader

My grandfather, Captain Willem Stoner, passed away in his sleep on the 18th day of November, 1831, at the age of 71. He was a remarkable man – a member of the Society of the Cincinnati, a prominent businessman in New York City and a Federalist member of the New York State Legislature for fourteen years. He prospered first as an agent for my grandmother Elisabeth's father, then as a merchant and agent for others. In 1789, Secretary of War Major General Henry Knox introduced my grandfather to a man who planned to manufacture glass in central New Jersey but lacked the financial means to do so. Grandfather Stoner became his partner. The business of making glass for all purposes but especially windows for the new homes in our rapidly growing city is the basis of our family's fortune today.

My father, Henry Samuel Stoner married my mother, a cousin of the Schuyler family of Albany and distantly related to the wife of Alexander Hamilton. He took over the management of the glass manufacturing in 1822. I was born in 1803 and by the time I was ten, we moved from my grandparents' home on Gold Street, to a fine Georgian style brick house surrounded by a few acres of green pastures and orchards. My father loved the new home and the nearby fresh water pond. It was later filled in and the area developed into estates and mansions for the wealthier residents of the city.

I, William Stoner II, am one of five children, the only boy

born to my parents and thus named after my grandfather. My first name has been Anglicized although I myself would have preferred Willem. I grew up literally at my grandfather's knee, listening to his stories of the marches, the battles, and especially of his friends from the War for Independence. He spoke often of General Henry Knox, who died in 1806. Thus, I never met the great man. Yet, I learned a lot about his character and integrity, first from my grandfather, then from my own father, who was the General's godson and was fortunate to have been in his company on several occasions when the General was a member of President Washington's Cabinet and lived in New York City.

My grandmother Elisabeth, with some prompting from me, related her experiences as well, vividly describing the time spent in Philadelphia as a spy, lying abed on the verge of giving birth to my father in snow-bound Morristown in February of 1780, during a Tory raid on General Washington's headquarters, and of meeting General Benedict Arnold's wife at West Point after the dastardly treason was discovered. She spoke of the close emotional ties with General and Mrs. Knox. She too spent time with Mrs. Knox when she and the General were in New York City. My grandmother passed away two years before my grandfather.

Having been raised on my grandparents' accounts of the people and battles of our War for Independence, much as an infant naturally is nurtured by his mother's milk, and having lived in New York and enjoyed many a raucous Evacuation Day celebration commemorating the British departure from the city, it is only natural I developed a keen and abiding interest in the Revolution.

It became a compulsion when I entered the College of New Jersey in Princeton, in 1820. My grandfather visited me several times. Together we toured the very battlefield, where he had manned his cannons and soldiers had fought and their spilled blood flowed down the slick ice that covered the fields, where General Mercer was killed and where my grandfather had left the main army to transport the sick and wounded to Morristown. It was there he first met Mercy Van Buskirk who became the wife of my grandfather's good friend, Captain Samuel Hadley.

Initially, I was studying law and philosophy and finding neither of great interest, availed myself of the library in Nassau Hall, the very building where my grandfather showed me the damage from a cannon ball fired at the south side of the building by another artillery unit. There, I read voraciously. After completing "The Life and Strange Adventures of Robinson Crusoe," by one Daniel Defoe, a work of fiction, presented as an autobiography by the fictional character, the thought occurred to me to write an account of my grandfather's own true adventures in the form of a novel. My grandfather had envisioned I would write his memoir. I explained to him the purpose of my project was to attract a wider readership through the popularity of novels, as a means to educate more of the public about the real struggles of ordinary people in our war for freedom. He reluctantly gave me his blessing on the condition nothing be published until after his death.

Both my grandfather and my own father gave me letters of introduction to friends and compatriots. My father had met many of them as a young boy, traveling on visits with his parents and added some helpful advice as to who might have specific details about some of the events about which I hoped to write. From 1823 until 1830 - I admit with the luxury of inherited wealth - I traveled often, meeting those who had survived, or their children who like my own father were raised with their parents' stories of their roles in our Revolution. When I returned with vivid descriptions of encounters, events and battles, I would spend many a pleasant afternoon with my grandfather, testing his recollections against the accounts of those I had met. Then, I would sit in the sunlit room of our home and write, sometimes for most of the day and well into the night.

Fortunately, the plan I formulated was to begin in Maine with Mrs. Knox and travel south from there to Marblehead and Boston. I say fortunately because I spent almost two full weeks with Mrs. Knox in 1823 and although I planned to visit her again, she passed away the following year at the age of 68. She was vivacious and friendly and gave me meaningful insights into the youthful courtship of my grandparents. She shared with me much of the correspondence between her and her beloved Harry. It enlivened our evenings together and she taught me to play whist. But she lapsed into somberness and grief when she spoke of the untimely death of the General. She and her husband were dealt a harsh hand in life with only three of their thirteen children surviving to adulthood. I believe I repaid her kindness and hospitality with my companionship and talk of my grandfather, and my father whom she remembered as a youthful scamp at West Point and later as a handsome boy in New York City.

From the Knox's mansion near Penobscot Bay, I traveled comfortably on a coastal trader to Marblehead. I met with Master Sergeant Adam Cooper with some trepidation, for he had saved my grandfather's life on at least two occasions. I wondered how to strike the proper attitude and feared he might think some of my questions presumptuous. He was seventy some odd years old when we met, his arms still thickly muscled. I could easily envision him carrying my grandfather away from the mob intent on tarring and feathering him, or lugging barrels of nails to be used as grapeshot. He agreed to relate all he remembered but only if he could take me fishing as he had done with grandfather. The sea does not bother me and I willingly agreed. We spent several pleasant days within sight of the coast with one of his sons doing most of the rowing. I helped with the nets and Adam told me his recollections of serving in the Marblehead Mariners and on General Knox's staff. While he could not recollect some details, the incident at Yorktown when the plantation owners came to reclaim their slaves after the British surrender was particularly etched in his memory. By some fortuitous circumstance, I mentioned the year of his feigned desertion. That brought forth detailed descriptions of the raids with Colonel Tye on the farms and businesses of Patriots, accounts he had never told my grandfather. I detected a lingering sense of pride in freeing the slaves of Whig masters who professed freedom and liberty for themselves but not for those they kept in bondage. At night, so as not to loose a single fact, I stayed up into the early morning hours in my rented room in a boarding house, writing down detailed notes of our conversations.

He and his wife have three sons and two daughters. Emmanuel, the oldest is married and resides in Boston where he works at his trade as a cooper, the name Adam's father had taken when he became a free man. He has children of his own. The two other boys were fishermen like their father. Adam and Sarah's daughters are both married and live in Salem.

Sarah, Adam's wife, is a local baker of some renown, as she had been in her youth. It was she who described the dinners General Knox and Lucy gave for the officers and their manner of entertaining. Her mother, Lettia died of pneumonia the first winter they were in Marblehead. Her brother was still in Halifax, having taken the name of Thomas Scott and learned the craft of ship carpentry. They correspond and although Massachusetts has effectively outlawed slavery and is the center of a robust abolition movement, Sarah's brother has declined to visit.

Sergeant Cooper's inability to become a member of the Massachusetts Society of the Cincinnati is a continual source of bitterness. Although he rose to the rank of Master Sergeant, that rank was not deemed an officer under the Society's Charter. Had he been white, I have no doubt he would have been promoted at least to Lieutenant during the war, a fact he emphasized to me when I stated I would also be meeting with Captain Nathaniel Holmes, himself a member of the Society. The two men meet at the annual reunions of the Marblehead Mariners and still attend the same church.

Captain Holmes lost his wife, Anna in giving birth to their third child, a girl, who died a few weeks after her mother. Holmes remarried a wealthy widow with two children of her own. He returned to the sea as a captain on a ship trading in the Caribbean and remained in Marblehead, managing his shipping company and enjoying the company of the surviving members of the Marblehead Mariners. Unfortunately, General Glover died in 1797. Now approaching seventy-five years of age, Captain Holmes is the senior surviving officer of the remaining Mariners. They meet yearly and toast General Glover's memory on Independence Day. Of the one hundred and sixty four members of the Mariners who fought in the Revolution, he told me only forty-three were alive in 1827 when I interviewed him.

Captain Holmes recalled his first meeting my grandfather and the rigorous efforts to haul the cannons from Lake George to Cambridge. He gave me many details of the noble train of artillery and I owe him a great debt for adding authenticity to that account. His narrative of the rescue of my grandfather by the Mariners was vivid with the detail needed to make the scene come alive in my novel.

In Boston, I stayed with Captain Hadley and his wife Mercy in their mansion on Beacon Hill. The Captain and I visited Dorchester Heights, Nooks Hill, Lechmere Point, General Washington's former headquarters in Cambridge, and the wharves of Boston Harbor. Having a modest talent as an artist, I made a few sketches for later reference and took extensive notes of Captain Hadley's descriptions of the gun emplacements. He helped me to better understand the battles of Brandywine and Germantown, with the aid of his library of military maps of the Revolutionary War.

I asked him of the whereabouts of Sergeant Merriam and Corporals Levi Tyler and Isaiah Chandler. The good Sergeant had passed away from consumption shortly after returning to Boston in '77. Tyler died a few years ago. Chandler lived in a modest area of the city and I insisted on taking him to dinner. He was stooped with age, being closer to eighty and no longer working as a bookbinder. He survives on his pension from the Commonwealth and Congress and seems content to live his remaining days in peace and quiet. He has lost some of his memory and frequently repeats himself. However, his account of the retreat at Brandywine before the onslaught of the menacing British Grenadiers was so clear I could hear the quick march of their steps and their fierce shouts above the din of battle.

From Boston, I travelled to Providence, again by ship, not to interview anyone in particular but to talk with some veterans of the Continental Army who had served in the Rhode Island regiments. After some brief inquiries, all I consulted referred me to Brigadier General Israel Angell, living in Smithfield. The old gentleman and his much younger wife, who I was given to understand, was his third, received me most graciously and insisted I stay at their home. He was eighty-seven at the time, with a long white mane of hair. He had not heard of my grandfather. It was he who described the Battle of Springfield and the role of the Rhode Islanders in holding the vital bridge. The Colonel generously gave me letters of introduction to some officers living in Providence, among them, Captain Stephen Olney. The good Captain recalled General Knox and some of the artillery officers at Yorktown but could not state with certainty he had met my grandfather. My interviews with the General and Captain in turn led me to meet with some surviving soldiers of the two former Rhode Island Regiments.

I found in interviewing ordinary soldiers, many felt they had been treated shabbily when the army was disbanded in '83, having been granted only the right to keep their torn uniforms, their muskets, cartridge boxes and canteens. No pay was issued and many sold their final settlement certificates to obtain money to buy clothes and pay for their journey home. Unlike many of the officers of means, they could not afford to wait until the Federal Government issued them bonds for their accrued pay with interest at six percent.

Some of these brave soldiers now praised the Government for the pensions to support them as they approached the twilight of their lives. Others were bitter in their extreme poverty. Still others preferred to say nothing of money and instead spoke glowingly of living together as a family of brothers, sharing the hardships, dangers and sufferings common to a soldier's life. I took these sentiments to heart and employed them in my descriptions of the ordinary soldiers depicted in the novel.

Had I begun my research efforts in New York City, I would have met with Sexton Peter Williams. Unfortunately, he died by the time I returned to the city. However, I interviewed his son, Peter Williams Jr. who has the distinction of being the second African American Episcopal Priest ordained in America. It was he who described his father's efforts to help freed African Americans apply for transport to Nova Scotia and thus become inscribed in the Book of Negroes. He expressed no bitterness in the fact that it took his father until November 4, 1785 to purchase his own freedom and receive a formal paper of emancipation from the Trustees of the

John Street Church.

I completed my novel of more than one thousand pages in 1833 and presented it to my publisher Harper & Brothers, located at 331 Pearl Street. The very wise John Harper, a printer by trade, suggested the novel would sell better if it were divided into segments or separate books, each presented to the public a month or so before Evacuation Day in November and in May or June before Independence Day, when interest in our Revolution would likely to be high. Thus, my novel was published in six separate books from 1833 to 1836.

The custom at the time was for the author to underwrite most of the cost of publishing, which I did for the first two volumes. However, I am proud to say, the public was so taken with my writing and the demand for copies was so great, Harper & Brothers agreed, beginning with "Blood Upon the Snow," and any reprinting of the prior two segments, to bear the full costs of production and to pay me fifteen percent of all sales. I, in turn, agreed to travel and give lectures to drum up further sales. Not that I need the money. My purpose is to expand the reading public's knowledge of our Revolution, devoid of the mythology that has been fed, in my opinion by homegrown nativism and excessive patriotism. To hear some of the accounts today, one would think the Minutemen of Massachusetts and the ragtag militias won the war almost singlehandedly with the Continental Army playing a minor role and all without the participation of a single woman, Negro or Indian.

The astute reader of this Note will observe, I did not interview John Stoner, my grandfather's brother. Other than the manifest listing him as a passenger on the Duchess of Gordon bound for Halifax, Nova Scotia in 1783, I found no trace of him. My grandfather believed his brother became dissatisfied with life in Nova Scotia and sailed to London. Perhaps, he died at sea. Given the final decree of expected life, he is certainly dead now. Whether he died sooner or later is irrelevant. My grandmother swore me never to discuss with my grandfather the details she provided of her encounters with John Stoner. I never mentioned these specifics to him, although he knew some of them from her own lips. It was she, not my grandfather, who informed me of my grandfather's vow to kill his brother for assaulting her.

The other secret my grandmother revealed concerned Captain Montresor's pearl necklace, the one he gave her to wear to the Mischienza. When my aunt Agnes married, at the age of 17, my grandmother gave her the necklace as a wedding present. It has passed down through Agnes' side of the family although I doubt they are aware of its origin. I must remember to tell my aunt or perhaps one of her descendants reading my novels will discover its significance.

When my grandfather died, my father requested two personal items. One was his army canteen, with its dried out and broken leather strap. The other was his sword. I assume, as my parents' only son, these will someday come into my possession. I will wear the sword to the first session I attend of the New York Chapter of the Society of the Cincinnati and offer a toast in honor of my grandfather, Captain Willem Stoner of General Knox's Headquarters Staff and Artillery Regiment.[1]

William Stoner, II, October 25, 1836
New York City

End Notes

Part One – The Limits of Liberty

Chapter 1 – Family Matters

1) The following is a typical document freeing a slave:

"City of _____ Date

Release of Slave
These may certify that I (name of master) of ___ in the county of ____ in the State of ____, for diverse causes and consideration, have remised and released and set free this Negro whose name is (name of slave), the bearer of this instrument who has been my lawful servant from (date) to this day (date) so that now he/she hath full power to conduct and act for himself/herself.
Witness my hand

(signature of master)"
(Boston Blog 1775, April 29, 2018)

2) The second edition of Forgotten Patriots – African American and American Indian Patriots in the American Revolution, (2008)

produced by the National Society of the Daughters of the American Revolution, identifies over 6,600 names of African Americans and American Indians who contributed to American Independence.

"Over the course of the war, about five thousand blacks fought as rebels – including at any given time, about six to twelve percent of Washington's army." (Glickstein, Don, After Yorktown – The Final Struggle for American Independence, p.86.)

There are a few official counts at various times throughout the war. One for example, states:
"An official return of Negroes [in service in the Continental Army] dated August 24, 1778 . . . totaled 755, scattered over fourteen brigades. The detachment with the highest percentage was General Samuel Holden Parson's brigade, which had 148 Negroes, most of them from Connecticut." (Quarles, Benjamin, The Negro in the American Revolution, pp. 71-72.)

3) The John Street Methodist Church, originally known as The Wesley Chapel, was built in 1768. It is the oldest Methodist Congregation in North America, founded in 1766 as the Wesleyan Society in America. Today, it is still a functioning church, located at 44 John Street in New York City, although the current structure was built in 1841.

Peter Williams was a slave, a member of the Church who became its sexton in 1778 and held that position for the duration of the war. His master fled to England at the end of the war and Williams was bought by the Trustees of the Wesley Chapel in a private sale. He purchased his own freedom for Forty Pounds and was one of the original founders of the African American Methodist Episcopal Zion Church.

4) Although Pennsylvania banned the importation of slaves into the colony in 1767, it was not until 1780 that it passed the Abolition Act that ended slavery through gradual emancipation. (Vermont

abolished slavery by its Constitution in 1777.) Basically, this meant that Negro and Mulatto children born after the effective date of the Act, were born free but had to serve as indentured servants to their mothers' masters until they reached the age of 28. The Act did not free approximately six thousand people who already were slaves in Pennsylvania. Slaveholders among the State's Founding Fathers included Benjamin Franklin, John Dickinson and Robert Morris. Franklin and Dickinson later became supporters of abolition.

There was a racially mixed Quaker school founded in Philadelphia in 1770 by Anthony Benezet. In 1773, Dr. Benjamin Rush wrote: "Anthony Benezet stood alone for a few years ago, in opposing negro slavery in Philadelphia; and now three-fourths of the province, as well as of the city, cry out against it." (Quarles, Benjamin, pp. 35-26.)

5) John Murray, Earl of Dunmore, the last royal governor of Virginia, formed what was misnamed "Lord Dunmore's Ethiopian Regiment" in the fall of 1775 from the several hundred slaves who escaped their servitude to join him. Their uniforms were embroidered with the slogan "Liberty for Slaves." Dunmore's proclamation promised freedom to servants and slaves able to bear arms.

In June 1779, General Clinton, the British Commander-in-Chief, issued a proclamation promising freedom to slaves who fled to British lines, regardless of whether or not they took up arms against the Americans. They were free to pursue "any occupation which [they] shall think proper. . ."

Half-a-million blacks lived in the thirteen colonies – about twenty percent of the population. An estimated 80,000 to 100,000 slaves escaped during the war." (Glickstein, Don, p.76.)

6) Adam Cooper is referring to the slaves who had fled to British lines to gain their freedom and were captured at Yorktown. They were restored to their masters. "Washington retrieved two young

house slaves – twenty-year old Lucy and eighteen-year old Esther – who had been among the seventeen who had escaped aboard the British sloop *Savage*, six months earlier, thinking their freedom assured." (Chernow, Ron, Washington – A Life, p. 419.)

7) The current town of Matawan, N.J. was known as Middletown Point during the Revolution. A major raid on May 27, 1778 by Loyalist Militia burned the Scots Presbyterian Church to the ground and destroyed the substantial corn mills, storehouses and the waterfront buildings belonging to John Burrowes, Sr. an open and avowed supporter of the Revolution. He and the Reverend Charles McKnight, were captured. The Reverend died after being released from a British prison ship in New York harbor in 1778.

For purposes of the plot, I have described the raid as more recent, occurring a few months before Wade and Vose arrive in the winter of 1781.

Chapter 2 – New Opportunities

1) On September 4, 1781, General Benedict Arnold, with 1,700 men, many of them Connecticut Loyalists, attacked New London and Groton, Connecticut. New London was the main American privateering port and served as a base for raids on British held Long Island. The attack was successful, resulting in the burning of the town and many of the ships on the river, and the capture of Fort Griswold. Many of the American prisoners were bayonetted by the victorious British soldiers. (Randall, Willard Sterne, Benedict Arnold, Patriot and Traitor, pp. 586-590.)

2) On September 26, 1781, sixteen year old Prince William Henry, King George's son and third in line to the throne, arrived in New York City on Admiral Digby's 98 gun flagship the *Prince George*. Washington entertained plans to kidnap not only the Prince but Admiral Digby as well. (Chernow, Ron, Washington, A Life, p. 425.) The British, vaguely aware of a plot to kidnap the Prince and senior

military officials, took "great precautions ... for the security of those gentlemen by augmenting the guards, and to render their persons as little exposed as possible." (McBurney, Christian, Abductions in the American Revolution-Attempts to Kidnap George Washington, Benedict Arnold and Other Military and Civilian Leaders, pp. 160-164.)

Prince William became King William IV in 1830.

3) Judge George Duncan Ludlow was appointed Master of the Rolls and Superintendent of the Courts of Police of Long Island by James Robertson, the Royal Governor of New York. Martial law remained in effect in New York, a city of about 26,000, comprised mostly of die hard Loyalists who fled to the city as the British lost battles and territory. Despite a proclamation in 1780 promising civil government the city remained under martial law until the British evacuated it. The Courts of Police functioned as military courts without a trial by jury. Robertson himself clipped pieces of metal from the coins in usage commonly known as "half-joes." They were Portuguese coins worth between eight and nine dollars. The clipped coins became known at "Robertsons."

4) James Rivington is a fascinating and mysterious character. Ostensibly a notorious Loyalist printer in New York before and at the outbreak of the Revolution, he was forced to flee to England and only returned in 1777 when the British were securely in control of the city. In December 1777, he began publication of The Royal Gazette with the words on the masthead, "Printer to the King's Most Excellent Majesty."

Historians now believe that Rivington was a spy for the Americans and a member of the Culper Spy Ring that provided significant information to General Washington. His secret messages were written and bound in the covers of books carried to the Americans by unwitting messengers. When the British evacuated New York City in November 1783, Rivington remained behind, unusual conduct for a prominent and avowed Loyalist but suffered from his public reputation as a supporter of the Crown.

5) There is no doubt that General Clinton should have sent a force to reinforce Cornwallis at Yorktown and assist in lifting the siege. Arnold served under Cornwallis in Virginia in June 1781 and urged him not to "fortify the indefensible spit of land at Yorktown, but, if he must have a permanent base in Virginia, let it be far up the James River, at Richmond, and out of reach of the French fleet." (Randall, Willard Sterne, p. 586.) Cornwallis contributed to his ultimate defeat by ignoring Arnold's advice.

6) There were plenty of opportunities for corruption by Judge Ludlow and he took advantage of his position to enrich himself. The schemes listed are some of those detailed in a dissertation by Frank Paul Mann entitled "The British Occupation of Southern New York During the American Revolution and the Failure to Restore Civilian Government," (History-Dissertations, 2013, Paper 100, Syracuse University.)

7) While the British offered freedom to the slaves of rebels, they did not free the slaves of Loyalists.

8) Livingston's Sugar House, called the Old Sugar House, was on Crown (now Liberty) Street, just east of Broadway in lower Manhattan near the Middle Dutch Church. It was used by the British as a prison for American soldiers (not officers) beginning in 1777.
"[It was] a dark, stone building, with small, deep porthole looking windows, rising tier above tier; exhibiting a dungeon-like aspect. It was five stories high, and each story was divided into two dreary [rooms.] On the stones and bricks in the wall were to be seen names and dates, as if done with a prisoner's penknife or nail."
(Dandridge, Danske, Three Rivers: Hudson-Mohawk-Schoharie -American Prisoners of the Revolution, Chapter XV – The Old Sugar House-Trinity Churchyard.)

Besides the Old Sugar House, American prisoners were held in city jails, churches converted for the purpose and the buildings of King's College (now Columbia University.) However, the worst, most vile and deadliest of places where American prisoners were kept were the prison ships, *Jersey*, *Good Hope* and *Falmouth* moored in the ship channel in Wallabout Bay, today, the site of the Brooklyn Navy Yard.

9) The conditions in the prisons were abominable. "Words cannot describe. . . 'the misserys that attend the Poor Prisoners Confined in this Horrid place, they are dying dayly with (what is called here) Gaol fever [typhus] but may more properly be called the Hungry fever.'" (Captain Nathaniel Fitz Randolph in a letter to his wife, quoted in Burrows, Edwin G., Forgotten Patriots – The Untold Story of American Prisoners During the Revolutionary War, p. 91.) Rations were a meager allotment of raw pork and wormy sea biscuits, which in the absence of fuel forced the prisoners "to eat the meat raw and our biscuit dry. Starved as we were, there was nothing in the shape of food that was rejected or was unpalatable." (Burrows, Edwin G., p.92.) Twenty-five years after the end of his second imprisonment, Captain Coffin asserted that, "I can safely aver, that both the times I was confined on board the prison ships, there never were provisions served out to the prisoners that would have been eatable by men that were not literally in a starving situation." (Getty, Katie Turner, "Walking Skeletons- Starvation on Board *The Jersey* Prison Ship,"All Things Liberty, March 11, 2019.)
However horrendous conditions were in the prisons of Manhattan, they were many times worse on the prison ships.
"There was only one passage to go on the deck in the night, . . .and the guards would only allow two men up at a time. Many of the prisoners were troubled with dysentery and would come to the steps and not be permitted to go on deck, and was obliged to ease themselves on the spot, and the next morning for 12 feet around the hatches was nothing but excrement. . ." (Burrows, Edwin G., The Prisoners of New York, Long Island History Journal, 2011, Volume 22, Issue 2; Getty, Katie Turner, "Death Had Almost Lost

Its Sting" Disease on the Prison Ship *Jersey*, All Things Liberty, January 10, 2019.)

The description of conditions below deck is even more appalling. Silas Talbot, a prisoner on the *Jersey* wrote years afterwards:

"There were no berths or seats, to lie down on, not a bench to sit on. Many were almost without cloaths. The dysentery, fever, phrenzy and despair prevailed among them, and filled the place with filth, disgust and horror. The scantiness of the allowance, the bad quality of the provisions, the brutality of the guards, and the sick, pining for comforts they could not obtain, altogether furnished continually one of the greatest scenes of human distress and misery ever beheld." Burrows, Edwin G., The Prisoners of New York.)

Philip Morin Freneau, known as "The Poet of the American Revolution," himself imprisoned on a British ship in the Hudson for several months, wrote a stirring poem called "The British Prison Ship." The first verse of Canto II begins:

These Prison Ships where pain and sorrow dwell; Where death in tenfold vengeance holds his reign, And injur'd ghosts, in reason's ear, complain;

This be my talk - ungenerous Britons, you, Conspire to murder those you can't subdue;

Why else no art of cruelty untry'd, Such heavy vengeance and such hellish pride? Death has no charms his empires barren lie, A desert country and a clouded sky; Death has no charms except in British eyes, See how they court the bleeding sacrifice!

See how they pant to stain the world with gore,

And millions murdered, still would murder more; . . .

One prisoner, Captain Thomas Dring, horrified upon seeing other prisoners infected by small pox, inoculated himself and incurred a light case of the pox and recovered fully. Four decades later, the scar on Dring's hand where he had inoculated himself "served as an immutable memento of his imprisonment." (Getty, Turner Katie, Death Had Almost Lost Its Sting.)

10) Faced with the misery of their conditions, surrounded by disease, starvation and death, the fortitude and resistance of American prisoners to British efforts to recruit them is nothing short of amazing. While there are no solid statistics, anecdotal evidence suggests that most prisoners did not buy their freedom by enlisting in the British army or navy. Ethan Allan opined that "Many hundreds, I am confident, submitted to death, rather than to enlist in the British service." Of the 800 prisoners who surrendered at Ft. Washington, fewer than twenty enlisted in the British Army, "and these were Irish or English who were generally servants whose masters had sent them with the Militia to show their Whigism and patriotism." And "Major Abraham Leggett likewise rebuffed 'Very Flattering offers if I would Join the British. . .My answer was . . .I shall stand by my Country." (Burrows, Edwin G., Forgotten Patriots, p. 112-113.) Others enlisted to get out of prison and then deserted at the first appropriate opportunity.

The end result of these horrific conditions of imprisonment is "more Americans lost their lives in the prisons of New York, and the prison ships of Brooklyn, . . . between two and three times as many as those who died in combat." (Burrows, Edwin G. Forgotten Patriots, p. 201.)

More than 11,000 prisoners held captive on the ships in Wallabout Bay died "which averages out to around 230 per month, fifty to sixty per week, or between seven and eight per day. That falls comfortably in line with contemporary testimony, which ranged from five or six fatalities every day. . ." (Burrows, Edwin G. Forgotten Patriots, p.199.) This places the mortality rate between fifty to seventy percent (as compared to thirty-five percent among Union prisoners at Andersonville and a little more than thirty-seven percent in Korea.) Applying the Revolutionary War percentage for the prison ships to the prison population of New York, the total number of American prisoners of war who died in British hands is in the range of 15,575 to 18,000. This compares to American battlefield casualties, that is those killed in action, of 6,824. Another

10,000 succumbed to wounds or disease afterwards. (Burrows, Edwin G., Forgotten Patriots, pp. 200-201.)

Chapter 3 – Home in Albany

1) General Knox was in Philadelphia for the birth of his son, Marcus Camillus, born on December 10, 1781. Instead of remaining with his family, by March 1782, Knox was in Elizabethtown, New Jersey, together with New York Congressman Gouverneur Morris negotiating an exchange of prisoners of war with the British commissioners. The negotiations were lengthy but unsuccessful. Knox did not leave Elizabethtown until April 16, 1782. (Hamilton, Phillip, The Revolutionary War Lives and Letters of Lucy & Henry Knox, pp. 146, 163-165.) Prior to doing so, he was informed that Congress had promoted him to Major General, retroactive to November 15, 1781, that is after the victory at Yorktown. (Drake, Francis S., Life and Correspondence of Henry Knox, pp. 74-75.) Knox did not rejoin the army at the New Windsor cantonment until May 1782.

2) Alexander Hamilton and Elisabeth Schuyler were married on December 14, 1780. It was a small family wedding in the Schuyler home, named The Pastures, followed by a ball and dinner for invited guests. At the time of the wedding, Elisabeth's mother, aged 47, was seven months pregnant with her twelfth and last child, Catherine. (Chernow, Ron, Alexander Hamilton, pp. 147-148.)

3) This melancholy verse is from Edward Young's The Complaint, or Night-Thoughts on Life, Death and Immortality. It was a very popular poem in the late 1700s.

4) Julia Rush was the wife of Dr. Benjamin Rush, signer of the Declaration of Independence and for a time, Surgeon General of the Continental Army. She also was the daughter of Richard Stockton of New Jersey, who also signed the Declaration of Independence. Julia Rush and other prominent wives, including Martha Washington,

embarked on a campaign to raise money for the troops. By June 1780, they had collected more than $5,600, the equivalent of $100,000 today, from 74 donors. (Fried, Stephen, Smithsonian, September 2018, A New Founding Mother, pp. 16-22.)

I have changed the chronology so that Lucy Knox's letter to Elisabeth Stoner sent in the winter of 1781-1782, appears to report on Julia Rush's successful efforts as if they had occurred a few months before.

5) Slavery and plantations were common on Long Island. In the 1771 census, one third of the 3,623 people in King's County were black and most of them were slaves. In Queen's County (including present day Nassau County) of the 10,980 people, one fifth were black. Of the 13,128 residents of Suffolk County, eleven percent were black.

That same 1771 census of New York City reported fourteen percent had African ancestry. Blacks were employed as chimney sweeps, carriage drivers, worked on the docks and performed artisanal trades such as shoemaking. (Van Buskirk, Judith L.,Generous Enemies – Patriots and Loyalists in Revolutionary New York, p. 131.)

There was a famous slave on Long Island named Jupiter Hammon. He was born in 1711 on the plantation known as Lloyd Manor and remained a slave there for his entire life. In 1760 he became the first published African American poet. In 1787, he published "Address to the Negroes of the State of New York" in which, referring to the American Revolution he wrote, "I must say that I have hoped that God would open their [white] eyes, when they were so much engaged for liberty, to think of the state of the poor blacks, and to pity us." (Wagner, Stephen, Slavery on Long Island, p. 11, Hofstra University Library, Special Collections Department.)

The Price of Freedom

Chapter 4 – Escape to Connecticut

1) Many of the characters, descriptions and events in this Chapter are taken from a Journal kept by a woman named Mary, the wife of a Continental Officer living on Long Island, "a region of the country which was taken early, and held by the enemy during the war. . . (Leopold Classic Library – Personal Recollections of the American Revolution- A Private Journal Prepared From Authentic Domestic Records, Barclay, Sydney, Editor.)

The Preface to the Journal states the citizens of Long Island "were subject to the depredations, insults and levies of the British, and to robbery, incendiarism, and brutal assaults from a class of outlaws, between the armies; the refuse of both parties, called Runners, Rangers, Cow-boys, etc." The incident involving the fictitious Josiah Oakley and the British cavalry is described in detail in the Journal.

2) The Long Island Sound, even as the war wound down on land, was the site of frequent raids back and forth, between Americans from Connecticut attacking British strongholds on Long Island and kidnapping prominent Loyalists, and Loyalists raiding the Connecticut shore for the same purpose.

Whaleboats (not to be confused with boats launched from a New England whaler to hunt whales) were generally thirty feet long, pointed at each end and "manned with 8 to 10 oars. Some had removable masts . . . and each was crewed by about seven to ten men. . . some Patriot whaleboats had a swivel (firing half pound shot). . ." (Kuhl, Jackson, Journal of the American Revolution, November 1, 2013, The Whale-Boat Men of Long Island Sound.)

3) General Knox's headquarters today is a State Historic Site, located just outside Vail's Gate, New York, one mile from the National Purple Heart Hall of Honor and the New Windsor Cantonment. Knox and his family resided there from May until sometime in the summer of 1782 when Knox went to West Point to

inspect the defenses. Subsequently, he was appointed Commander of West Point on August 29, 1782.

An interesting side note is the celebration at West Point on June 1st of the birth of a son to King Louis XVI. At the ball, General Washington, described as being "unusually cheerful," led the dance with Mrs. Knox as his partner. (Brooks, Noah, Henry Knox, A Soldier of the Revolution, pp. 167.)

4) General Guy Carleton arrived on May 5, 1782 to replace General Clinton who was blamed for the defeat at Yorktown. Prior to Carleton's departure from London, Parliament voted to end all offensive military action against the Americans. More importantly, captured rebels were to be treated as prisoners of war and not treasonous subjects of the Crown. While Carleton wrote General Washington on May 7th about Britain's new "pacific disposition," and offered to match "conciliarty acts in kind," he also set about strengthening the fortifications protecting New York City. (Glickstein, Don, pp. 204, 345-346.)

Washington in his correspondence wrote "Notwithstanding all the pacific declarations of the British, it has constantly been my prevailing sentiment [that their] principal design was to gain time by lulling us into security . . .and in the interim to augment their naval force and wait the chance of some fortunate event to decide their future line of conduct." (Glickstein, Don, pp. 349-350.)

5) Because women were deemed non entities in the political sphere, they were allowed to cross the lines and enter and leave New York City for visits of mercy to visit sick relatives or even social calls. Also, the custom of the times allowed for distinctions between "the public domain of political allegiance and the private realm of family." (Van Buskirk, Judith L., pp. 61-62.)

"While women of a wide spectrum of socioeconomic backgrounds could enter and exit the city, those with connections could cross the military lines for a simple visit to family or friends [even those] who were in no dire need of their succor." In fact, women were "so successful . . . in moving about the war zone that male spies sometimes dressed in women's clothing to improve their chances." (Van Buskirk Judith L., p.57.)

Chapter 5 – The Courtship of a Wealthy Young Lady

1) The British occupation of Long Island was particularly brutal in 1782, when excessive force was unnecessary. The war was winding down. Yet Fort Golgotha was essentially built for spite by the forced labor of the residents of Huntington, Long Island who were compelled not only to tear down their church to be used as timber in the fort but to destroy the cemetery of their ancestors as well. (Mann, Frank, Paul, The British Occupation of Southern New York During the American Revolution and the Failure to Restore Civilian Government; Griffin, David, M., Lost British Forts of Long Island, pp. 65-67.)

2) The story of Colonel Thompson placing the gravestone of Reverend Ebenezer Prime at the gate to the fort so that it could be stepped on may be apocryphal. It appears in Griffin's Lost British Forts of Long Island on p. 67. Ebenezer Prime was the Reverend of the Huntington Presbyterian Church from 1723 until his death in 1779. He was a strong supporter of the Revolution.

3) General Carleton moved quickly after his arrival to eliminate the rampant corruption that kept prices of flour, rum, molasses and coffee artificially high. In the words of Reverend Ewald Gustav Schaukirk:

"The new commander-in-chief makes many wholesome changes to the great saving of public expenses . . . . A couple of hundred deputy commissioners in different departments have been dismissed, hundreds of carpenters and other workmen have been turned off [apparently there was payroll padding] . . . .No officer will be

allowed to have vessels, wagons etc. to carry on any [personal or contraband] trade. We rejoice that the chain of enormous, iniquitous practices will at last be broken. . . ."
(Glickstein, Don, p. 346.)

4) The use of Presbyterian headstones in the British troops' ovens did in fact result in the inscriptions being transferred to the loaves of bread. (Griffin, David M., p. 66.)

5) Before the Revolution, Thompson himself married a rich heiress. He was a man of considerable property and sided with the Loyalists. After the war ended he returned to Britain. He was knighted by King George III, spent eleven years in Bavaria as Bavarian Army Minister, reorganized their army, and was made a Count of the Holy Roman Empire. Later he focused on his scientific interests. He devised a method for measuring the specific heat of solids. His work in heat led him to invent improvements in chimneys, fireplaces and industrial furnaces. His redesign of fireplaces improved the flow of air upwards through the chimneys and eliminated the backflow of smoke into a home's rooms. In 1799 he, along with Sir Joseph Banks, established the Royal Institution of Great Britain that developed into a premier research laboratory. Thompson's second wife was the widow of the noted French chemist, Lavoisier.

6) Henry Fielding wrote the play "Tom Thumb" in 1730. It is both a farce and a low tragedy about Tom Thumb who is both small in size and status and is given the hand of the princess. Their marriage angers the queen who attempts to bring ruin upon the newly wedded couple. Frank Paul Mann in his dissertation on the British occupation of New York notes that this specific play, in addition to other comedies and tragedies, was performed at the John Street Theater with all profits being given to the poor

7) The British created a Mall around the ruins of Trinity Church, severely damaged in the great New York City fire of 1776, and removed gravestones for a broader area in which to promenade

A poem of the time, attributed to Hannah Lawrence, a Quaker member of a New York City literary society, went:

"Enlarge the walk to which the fair
In shining nightly throngs repair.
The female Size by hoops increased,
Demands a tomb or two at least."

She allegedly posted the poem at the Mall at Trinity Church. (Van Buskirk, Judith, L., p. 35.)

Other churches of New York suffered or survived depending on their political persuasion. St. George's and St. Paul's, both Anglican Churches, were spared but were so crowded, services were held in the large courtroom of City Hall. Others, like the Dutch, Presbyterian, French Baptist, & Quaker churches were converted to hospitals, barracks or prisons.

8) For purposes of the plot, I have placed Mrs. Arnold in New York City while General Arnold was campaigning in the field. The Arnolds actually had left the colonies and arrived in London in January 1782.

9) The library of King's College, now Columbia University, which contained some 60,000 volumes was plundered by British soldiers who sold the books on the streets for extra money.

Part Two – The Army in Camp

Chapter 6 – The Hand of Providence

1) The text of this sermon is taken from one preached by Reverend Cotton Mather Smith to his congregants in Sharon, Connecticut as they waited for news of the outcome of the battle between the Americans and General Burgoyne's Army at Saratoga in October 1777. Reverend Smith's sermon ended with his prophesizing -"The

morning now cometh. I see its beams already gilding the mountain tops, and you shall soon behold its brightness bursting over all the land." This was followed by the statement – "Amen! So let it be," and congregation fell silent.

At that point, a messenger rode up to the meetinghouse, strode into the hall and up to the pulpit to deliver a letter to Reverend Smith. The first words the Reverend saw were "BURGOYNE HAS SURRENDERED."

"The arrival of such news at the close of that sermon was a strange coincidence, but the Revolution is a history of just such coincidences." (Headley, J.T., - The Chaplains and Clergy of the Revolution, pp. 312-315.)

2) Sir Guy Carleton ordered the parole of about eight hundred prisoners in May,1782. Those that were able made their way back to their towns and villages. By the end of the year, the population on the prison ships had been drastically reduced. One prison ship officer wrote there were "700 miserable objects, eaten up with lice, and daily taking fevers, which carry them off fast." (Glickstein, Don, p. 347.)

3) The words fictional Private Hazzard reads to the soldiers are the actual words published in The Pennsylvania Packet, dated Philadelphia, August 3, 1782. The article also contained the guarantee by General Anthony Wayne not to attack the British troops as they evacuated Savannah. (Andrlik, Todd, Reporting the Revolutionary War, pp. 348-349.)

4) In September 1782, Knox took command of the fortifications at West Point, and Lucy and their children followed.

Chapter 7 – Tragedy at West Point

1) Silver and gold coins were called "specie" or "hard money." The

colonies were prohibited by Britain from minting their own coins and the exportation of coins from England was also banned. Thus, the hard coins in circulation during the American Revolution were mostly of Spanish and Portuguese origin – the peso, the pistole, the guinea and doubloon, Spanish reales or pieces of eight. (Barbieri, Michael, All Things Liberty, The Dollar in Revolutionary America, September 27, 2016.)

2) Doctors in Revolutionary America called both scarlet fever and diphtheria "throat distemper," not knowing they were two different diseases – scarlet fever caused by a streptococcus infection and diphtheria by a bacillus. (North Louise V., Wedge Janet M., and Freeman, Landa M., In the Words of Women – The Revolutionary War and the Birth of the Nation, 1765-1799, p.170.)

3) Knox was greatly distraught by the death of his son. He wrote General Washington on September 10, 1782:

"I have the unhappiness, my dear General, to inform you of the departure of my precious infant, your god son. In the deep mystery in which all human events are involved, the Supreme Being has been pleased to prevent his expanding innocence from ripening into such perfection, as to be a blessing to his parents." (Callahan, North, Henry Knox – General Washington's General, p. 197; Hamilton, Phillip, p. 146 and note 22.)

Indeed, Knox was so depressed by the death of his son, for several weeks he neglected writing to anyone else. His friend, General Benjamin Lincoln, worried because Knox had not responded to several of Lincoln's letters, wrote Knox asking what was wrong. Knox finally replied and apologized for not answering "but saying it was due to the death of his son." (Callahan, North, pp.197-198.)

It is reasonable to assume that Knox not only neglected his correspondence, but also isolated himself from his staff who would have been concerned. The compassion shown to him by Samuel

Hadley and Will Stoner, who had been with him almost since the beginning of the war, is in keeping with their characters.

4) There is some confusion about the identity of Knox's deceased infant son. Several facts are seemingly indisputable.
- Lucy Knox gave birth to a boy on December 10, 1781 in Philadelphia.
- General Washington was the boy's god-father.
- Knox wrote his friend, General Greene, he would name the infant "after some fine Roman whose character I think you may like."
- The infant died in September 1782 when the Knoxes were at West Point.
- Knox wrote General Washington by letter dated September 10, 1782 informing him the boy, Washington's god-son had died.

All this points to the conclusion that the infant, named Marcus Camillus, born on December 10, 1781, died in September 1782. Philip Hamilton, in The Revolutionary War Lives and Letters of Lucy and Henry Knox concludes after the family was reunited at West Point, "sadly, little Marcus Camillus died soon after they had all arrived at that posting." (Hamilton Phillip, p. 146.) Hamilton drops a footnote citing Knox's letter to George Washington advising of the death of his god-son. Similarly, William Fowler, Jr. in his book "American Crisis –George Washington and the Dangerous Two Years After Yorktown, 1781-1783, refers to Marcus Camillus' birth on December 10, 1781, his invitation to George Washington to be the boy's god-father and Knox's letter to "my dear General," informing him of the death of "my precious infant, your Godson." (Fowler, William M., Jr., pp. 160-161.)

Then the confusion begins. On pages 197 and 198 of North Callahan's biography of General Henry Knox, he quotes Knox's letter to George Washington, informing him his god-son had died. In Callahan's index, however, listing the children of Henry and Lucy Knox, he states Marcus was born in 1781 and died in 1790.

And then there is this caption to a portrait of a young boy, hanging at the Knox Museum in Montpelier, Vermont:

"Portrait of Marcus Camillus Knox by Joseph Wright, ca. 1791 Marcus Camillus was the second son of Henry and Lucy Knox, and was regarded by the family as a promising young lad who would follow in his father's footsteps. Unfortunately his death at the age of 8 on September 8, 1791 intervened. Apparently the grief-stricken parents immediately commissioned a posthumous portrait, probably sketched while the boy was laid out. On October 5, 1791 Knox noted in his account book, now at the Maine Historical Society, "Paid Joseph Wright painter for a picture of my dead son Marcus $32.66/ 7 Guineas." Wright had moved to Philadelphia shortly before the commission, and was one of the most prominent American artists of his time."

If the boy in the portrait died at age 8, he was born in 1783, not 1781 as Callahan states. Biologically it is certainly possible that Lucy was again pregnant after delivering a child on December 10, 1781 and if the boy, described as the Knoxes' second son (after Henry Jackson Knox, born in 1780) then it must have been a girl born in December 1781 who died in September 1782. Yet, Knox in his correspondence clearly describes the deceased as his son and Washington's god-son.

I have not solved the mystery. Nor have I been able to locate a complete accurate listing of the twelve or thirteen children of the Knoxes, only three of whom survived to adulthood. I have proceeded on the assumption the child born after the victory at Yorktown who died as a nine-month old infant at West Point was Marcus Camillus Knox, George Washington's god-son.

5) One of the plaques at the replica of the Temple of Virtue at the New Windsor Cantonment states it was proposed by Israel Evans, Brigade Chaplain to the New Hampshire Regiment who thought, "the army could worship together rather than attend separate services around town or ignore the Sabbath completely." He also

believed the Temple could be used as a meeting place for the officers to assemble.

The Temple was constructed of 5,000 feet of finished timber, 21,000 shingles and fieldstone sufficient to build the cantonment's largest building.

6) The reference to the "Sinagoge of Old," is a direct quote from another plaque at the site which states:

"To day we meet at the temple whare there is a temple pulpit maid and a Gallery for the Musick – it is a building which is converted to Many Uses Which Makes Me think of [the] Sinagoge of Old that we Read of." Private Thomas Foster, 7th Massachusetts Regiment."

General Heath described the building as "handsomely finished with a spacious hall, the vault of the hall was arched; at each end of the hall were two rooms, conveniently situated for the issuing of general orders, for the sitting of Boards of Officers, Courts Martial etc."

7) The United States Articles of War were adopted in 1776 and specified the punishments for various offenses, if the accused were found guilty. Among those, the most serious was death for desertion. Other punishments were demotion in rank, public reprimands for Officers and Sergeants, and for other offenses, a maximum of one hundred lashes.

8) Knox had written Greene a letter effusively praising him for accomplishing the British evacuation of the South.

"It is acknowledged by all that you have had innumerable difficulties and you have overcome them by your judgment, fortitude and perseverance. Your country will ever preserve a lively memory of you." (Callahan, North, p. 198.)

Chapter 8 – The Officers' Mutiny

1) The background for the Brutus open letter, in essence calling for mutiny, is as follows:

The Officers and soldiers of the Continental Army had gone without pay for years. The cause was the structure of the loose confederation of the colonies. Under the Articles of Confederation, Congress had no authority to demand money from the states or collect taxes on its own. The nationalists in Congress, such as Alexander Hamilton, James Madison, and Robert Morris, sought to solve the problem by a national impost duty, proposed in 1781 and not yet ratified. In December 1782, General Knox, with the approval of General Washington, sent another petition to Congress demanding the overdue pay and urging that the request for half pay for life be changed to a one-time lump-sum payment.

Knox's petition, signed by almost all of the officers at the New Windsor Cantonment, stated: "We have borne all that men can bear...our property is expended... our private resources are at an end...our friends are wearied with our incessant applications... any further experiments on their [the army's] patience may have fatal effects." (Wensyel, James W., The Newburgh Conspiracy, American Heritage, 1981, Volume 32, Issue 3.)

Around the same time, Washington wrote to "his friend Congressman Joseph Jones of Virginia; 'The dissatisfactions of the Army has arisen to a great and alarming height...
Hitherto the Officers have stood between the lower order of the Soldiery and the public and . . . have quelled very dangerous mutinies.[I]f their discontents . . . rise equally high, I know not. . .the consequences.'" (Wensyel, James W., The Newburgh Conspiracy.)

Before Knox's petition was delivered, Virginia basically killed the legislation calling for a national impost duty by repealing its earlier ratification. The nationalists in Congress, in particular Alexander

Hamilton, believed that the prospect of an officer mutiny might "represent a handy lever with which to budge a lethargic Congress from inaction, leading to expanded federal powers." (Chernow, Ron, Washington-A Life, p.432.)

The nationalists' basic idea "was extortion, pure and simple. Let the states yield power to raise funds and satisfy the army, or face mutiny." By countenancing mutiny, the nationalists "played a dangerous game. Without risking [enough of a mutiny to move Congress] they risked continuing erosion of the Confederation. If they tried it, they risked anarchy, civil war, a violent end to the Confederation. They decided to chance it." (Wensyel, James W., The Newburgh Conspiracy.)

Hamilton first wrote Washington proposing that he exploit the officers' discontent to influence Congress, but pointed out the obvious difficulty of keeping the mutiny "within the bounds of moderation." Washington responded that the officers would listen to reason. He rejected the proposal to have the military "encroach on the prerogatives of Congress." In later correspondence to Hamilton he warned that the army "was a dangerous instrument to play with." (Chernow, Ron, Washington – A Life, p. 433; In his equally excellent biography of Alexander Hamilton, Chernow states: "Hamilton was coaxing Washington to be a lofty statesman while covertly orchestrating pressure on Congress." Chernow, Ron, Alexander Hamilton, p. 177.)

The nationalists wrote to General Knox soliciting his support for a "limited mutiny." Knox did not respond, probably based on his own convictions and knowing that Washington would not permit the use of the army as an instrument to move Congress.

Next the nationalists turned to General Horatio Gates who was second in command at the Cantonment. Historians are uncertain as to the roles played by different officers but generally agree that Gates cooperated with the nationalists. Colonel Walter Stewart arrived in the Cantonment from Philadelphia and met with Gates and some of his staff on March 8, 1783. Brutus' letter, dated March 8th and circulated Monday, March 10th called for a meeting of officers on Tuesday to send a resolution to Congress seeking agreement to their demands for pay and pensions. Well after the events, Major John Armstrong of General Gates' staff admitted to writing the Brutus letters to the officers. Major William Barber and Captain Christopher Richmond, also on Gates' staff copied and distributed the letters throughout the New Windsor Cantonment. (Chernow, Ron, Washington – A Life, pp.432-433; Wensyel, James W., The Newburgh Conspiracy.)

2) Washington's General Orders of March 11 banning the unauthorized meeting stated as follows:

"Head-Quarters, Newburgh, Tuesday, March 11, 1783.
The Commander in Chief, having heard that a general meeting of the officers of the army was proposed to be held this day at the new building [Temple of Virtue], in an anonymous paper which was circulated yesterday by some unknown person, conceives, although he is fully persuaded that the good sense of the officers would induce them to pay very little attention to such an irregular invitation, his duty, as well as the reputation and true interest of the army, requires his disapprobation of such disorderly proceedings. At the same time he requests the general and field-officers with one officer from each company, and a proper representation from the staff of the army, will assemble at 12 o'clock on Saturday next, at the new building, to hear the report of the committee of the army to Congress. After mature deliberation, they will devise what further measures ought to be adopted as most rational and best calculated to attain the just and important object in view. The senior officer in rank, present, will be pleased to preside, and report the result of the deliberations to the Commander in Chief." (Library of Congress, The Newburgh Conspiracy, December 1782-March 1783.)

3) In correspondence following the distribution of the Brutus letter, Knox wrote that the army had always disliked the concept of "thirteen armies," and desired a unified command. "It is a favorite toast in the army. . .A hoop to the barrel or cement to the Union." (Callahan, North, Henry Knox, General Washington's General, p. 200.)

Callahan observes that Knox, in a letter to Gouverneur Morris in mid February 1783 about the failure of Congress to find the revenues to pay the Army had written:

"America will have fought and bled to little purpose if the powers of government shall be insufficient to preserve the peace. . . As the present constitution is so defective, why do not you great men call the people together and tell them so; that is, to have a convention of the states to form a better constitution?" This was far-sighted of Knox. (Callahan, North, p. 200.)

4) Washington's staff had prepared his written remarks "on nine long sheets." The number of pages was not due to the length of his speech. His "aides mindful of his dimming vision. . .had copied his notes in large script." (Chernow, Ron – Washington- A Life, p. 434; Wensyel, James W., The Newburgh Conspiracy.)

5) I have audaciously modified Washington's actual words to make them more understandable to the reader.

What he read to the assembled officers, at this point in his prepared remarks, after counseling moderation and patience was:

"By thus determining and thus acting, you will pursue the plain and direct road to ... your wishes...[Y]ou will give one more distinguished proof of unexampled patriotism and patient virtue, rising superior to the pressure of the most complicated sufferings; and you will, by the dignity of your conduct, afford occasion for Posterity to say . . . had this day been wanting, the World would have never seen the last stage of perfection to which human nature is capable of attaining." (Wensyel, James W., The Newburgh Conspiracy.)

6) When Washington attempted to read the letter from Congressman Jones, the writing was too small for his deteriorating vision. He extracted his spectacles and for the first time, the officers, outside of his immediate staff, saw their Commander in Chief wearing eyeglasses. The words quoted are Washington's exactly. They "exerted a powerful influence" [on the assembled officers.] The disarming gesture of putting on the glasses moved the officers to tears as they recalled the legendary sacrifices he had made for his country." (Chernow, Ron, Washington – A Life, p. 436; "When he stopped, the officers crowded around him in reassurance and contrition. Some wept. Others simply stood, stunned and silent, as the general left the room." Wensyel, James W., The Newburgh Conspiracy.)

As one historian has observed "what is important about the Newburgh crisis is what did not happen. There was no mutiny, no coup, no military dictatorship... The precedent that was set was that the first national army of the young republic totally rejected military interference in the government and affirmed its subordination to civil authority. America stood at a real crossroads in March of 1783. That Washington, by personal leadership, persuaded his officers to civil obedience ranks as one of his greatest achievements." (Wensyel, James W., The Newburgh Conspiracy.)

Chapter 9 – The Army Disbanded

1) It was impossible to keep the news of a general peace from the rank and file. On April 18, Washington issued the following General Order:

"The Commander in Chief orders the cessation of hostilities . . . to be publicly proclaimed tomorrow at 12 o'clock in the Newbuilding, and that the Proclamation which will be communicated herewith, be read tomorrow evening at the head of every regiment and corps of the army. After which the Chaplains with the several Brigades will render thanks to almighty God for all his mercies particularly for his over ruling the wrath of man to his own glory, and causing the rage of war to cease among nations." (Fowler, William M., pp. 191-192.

The men's expectations of pay were ill-founded. The officers were to be paid in money or "securities on interest at six per cent per annum." Nothing was yet said about the back pay owed the soldiers.

2) Washington himself was concerned he could not "hold the [soldiers] much longer," as they were angry and refused to obey orders. Congress by the end of May granted Washington permission to "furlough" the war men, that is those who had enlisted for the duration. (Fowler, William M., p.193.)

3) Washington had attempted to get Congress to pay the soldiers three months' back pay, but Congress had no money. Instead, they provided the soldiers with certificates payable in six months. These so-called "Morris notes" after the Superintendent of Finance were sold at steep discounts by the cash starved soldiers. (Fleming, Thomas, The Strategy of Victory – How George Washington Won the American Revolution, p. 250-251.) Congress did vote to give the men their arms as a farewell gift. Many sold their certificates to "procure decent clothing and money sufficient to enable them to pass with decency through the country and to appear something like themselves when they arrived [home.]" (Martin, Joseph Plumb, Private Yankee Doodle: Being a Narrative of Some of Adventures, Dangers and Sufferings of a Revolutionary Soldier, George E. Scheer, Editor, pp. 280-281.)

4) Knox was authorized by General Washington to grant discharges to any officers, noncommissioned officers or enlisted men as he saw fit. He did so, noting in a reply to the Commander in Chief, the

"men were in a wretched condition for want of warm underwear, having only the remnants of their overalls and uniforms. . ." (Callahan,North, p. 206.)

Part Three – Peace and Its Aftermath

Chapter 10 – Panic in New York City

1) The preliminary articles of the peace treaty between the United States and Britain were published in James Rivington's Royal Gazette in March 1783. The Pennsylvania Packet, a Philadelphia newspaper, on April 10, 1783, published the "Authentic Copies of the PRELIMINARY ARTICLES OF PEACE, between His Britannic Majesty . . .and the United States of America, Signed at Versailles, the 20th of January, 1783." (Andrlik, Todd, pp. 344-345

A broadside from Poughkeepsie, signed by someone calling himself Brutus, was addressed to ". . . All Adherents to the British Government and Followers of the British Army commonly called Tories who are at present with the City and County of New York." It promised "blood or banishment of all Tories who dared to stay," and "anticipated Loyalist appeals to the American government or to influential friends, labeled these tactics as delusional and hopeless. A free people, explained Brutus, would quash any bribery or flattery or special 'contracts.'" (Van Buskirk, Judith L., pp. 165-166.)

2) As thousands of Loyalists made plans to leave New York City they had to "consolidate their belongings, collect debts, and sell off what they could not take with them. Every day, incoming Whigs, could attend auctions for items as varied as Chippendale sidechairs, horses and books. . . Given that the evacuation was imminent, New York was definitely a buyer's market. Americans looking for a more advantageously situated store, home upgrade, or investment rental property could purchase Loyalist estates for as low as one-twentieth of their value." (Van Buskirk, Judith L., p. 172.)

End Notes

3) In 1783, St. John or St. Johns, Nova Scotia was indeed the destination of many Loyalists from New York. In 1784 the colony of Nova Scotia was partitioned and St. John, on the Bay of Fundy, became part of the new colony of New Brunswick.

4) There was both optimism and despair amongst the Tories of New York. English merchants and some of their American counterparts anticipated renewing the "unimpeded flow of goods and credit between Britain and America." Others, fearful of retribution, or unwilling to risk the uncertainty, fled as soon as the harbor and bay thawed in the spring of 1783. In May, General Carleton informed General Washington 6,000 Loyalists had already been evacuated. "By June, 3,000 more shipped out, and in August, 8,000 Americans including many men from the provincial regiments stood on the decks of their ships and watched New York disappear from view." As of November 24, 1783, a grand total of 29,244 Loyalists had departed for Canada. (Van Buskirk, Judith L., pp. 176-177, 231, note 44.) Glickstein gives the total as 35,000 Loyalist refugees and 20,000 soldiers. (Glickstein, Don, p. 360.)

5) Several experts agree that it is tricky business to try and establish the equivalency of pounds, guineas, crowns, shillings and pence to today's money. The English pounds in the 1770s were printed, by the Bank of England, in various denominations from Ten Pounds all the way up to Five Hundred Pounds.

Instead of conversion rates, perhaps a better measure would be the daily or yearly wages paid to different categories of workers to determine what people could buy then for what they earned. For example, a male servant received Twelve Pounds per year; a female servant, Seven Pounds. An unskilled working man's wages for a year were about Twenty Six Pounds. A carpenter's daily wage was between Two Shillings, Six Pence to Five Shillings per day (Twenty Shillings, Twelve Pence equaled One Pound.) A skilled carpenter, after working five full days, may have earned a little more than One Pound for his week's work.

Generally, Fifteen to Twenty Pounds a year would be a low annual wage. A family of four probably needed Forty Pounds per year to live modestly. The rich would be those living on more than Five Hundred Pounds per year.

I have taken the usual wages for services of a carpenter and others and inflated them, given the panic of those fleeing. The prices for booking passage must have changed from week to week if not day to day as the Loyalists' desperation increased. Price gouging, the rule of supply and demand and human nature probably were no different in 1783 New York City than they are today, as evidenced after a natural disaster by the sharp increases in gasoline, food and motel and hotel rates in the surrounding area.

6) The British American Board of Inquiry was formed as a result of a dispute between General George Washington and Sir Guy Carleton over the meaning of Article 7. At a meeting between the two Generals in May, 1783 at Washington's temporary headquarters at Tappan, New York, Washington claimed the Americans were entitled by the Treaty to take possession of all Negroes and other property. Carleton took the position that the Treaty could not be interpreted to mean the British would renege on their promise to free slaves who had joined their ranks in response, first to Lord Dunmore's proclamation of November 1775 which offered freedom to those blacks who served the British Army, and then the 1779 Philipsburg Proclamation of Sir Henry Clinton which stated in part,

"To every Negro who shall desert the Rebel Standard, full security to follow within these [British] lines, [and to work at] any occupation which he shall think proper." (Chernow, Ron, Washington – A Life, pp. 440-441; Hill, Lawrence, Canada's History, Behind the Book of Negroes,)

Of course, there was no British proclamation freeing the slaves of white Loyalists, many of whom were evacuated with their masters in 1783 to remain slaves in England or Nova Scotia.

Sir Guy Carleton seized the high moral ground and in effect argued that Article 7 referred to Negroes as property but those who had succeeded in reaching British lines were now free and thus no longer "property" within the meaning of the Treaty. The parties agreed to form a Board of Inquiry and the British would keep a register of those former slaves who were free and were being evacuated. This register became known as the "Book of Negroes," and exists in two original versions. The British original is in the National Archives (Public Records Office) Kew, England. The American original is in the National Archives of the United States, in Washington, D.C.

The Book of Negroes contains the names, ages, sex, brief physical description, (sometimes brutally blunt and insulting) and origins (who had been their former masters or what plantation they had escaped from) of approximately 3,000 black men, women and children who were evacuated from New York, as well as the names of the vessels they embarked on and the destination of the ship (and sometimes the Captains as well). The Book of Negroes covers the period from April through November 1783 and includes 1,336 men, 914 women, 339 boys, 335 girls and 76 children of unidentified gender. (Hodges, Graham Russell, Editor, The Black Loyalist Directory – African Americans in Exile After the American Revolution, Introduction, p.xix.)

Among the men listed in the Book of Negroes is one Henry (Harry) Washington, described as age 43, "fine fellow.[Formerly the property of General Washington; left him 7 [years ago.]" Hodges, Graham Russell, Editor, pp. 111-112.) He was evacuated to Port Roseway, Nova Scotia and eventually voluntarily went to Sierra Leone. (Chernow, Ron, Washington – A Life, p. 441.)

7) Black Loyalists in New York City were terrified when they read Article 7 of the Peace Treaty. It provided:

"All Hostilities both by Sea and Land shall from henceforth cease; all prisoners on both sides shall be set at Liberty and His Britannic

Majesty shall with all convenient Speed and without Causing any destruction or carrying away any Negroes or other Property of the American Inhabitants withdraw all its Armies, Garrisons, and Fleets, from the said United States." (Hill, Lawrence, Canada's History –"Behind the Book of Negroes, February 10, 2015.)

Boston King as quoted by Lawrence Hill wrote: ". . .rumour prevailed at New York, that all the slaves, in number 2,000, were to be delivered up to their masters, altho' some of them had been three or four years among the English.

This dreadful rumour filled all of us with inexpressible anguish and terror, especially when we saw our old masters coming from Virginia, North Carolina, and other parts, and seizing upon their slaves in the streets of New York, or even dragging them out of their beds. Many of the slaves had very cruel masters, so that the thoughts of returning home with them embittered life for us. For some days we lost our appetite for food, and sleep departed from our eyes." (Hill, Lawrence –Behind the Book of Negroes.)

Boston King was among those evacuated and became a minister in Nova Scotia and subsequently in Sierra Leone.

8) The wording of Jupiter's Certificate is taken verbatim from a Certificate issued to Cato Ramsay, dated April 24th, 1783. The italicized words in Jupiter's Certificate were most likely filled in by the Clerk of the Board. (Hodges, Graham Russell, Editor, Illustration # 3, following p. 172.)

9) At the age of 72, Brigadier General Timothy Ruggles sailed to Nova Scotia and settled in Wilmot on a land grant of 1,000 acres from the Crown. He was followed by his three sons. His wife and three daughters remained in Massachusetts. When Massachusetts published a list of the top 300 Tories who were unwelcome to return, Ruggles was third. Ruggles did develop a fine estate of orchards and animals. He died in August, 1795 at the ripe age of 83, almost

making it to his 84th birthday in October. He is buried in the Old Trinity Church cemetery in Middleton, Nova Scotia.

10) A typical certificate of inspection, clearing a vessel to evacuate Blacks who were deemed to have been freed by the British, signed by representatives of the United States and Great Britain read as follows:

"In pursuance of two Orders from His Excellency, Sir Guy Carleton, K.B. General and Commander in Chief of His Majesty's Forces, . . . We whose names are hereunto Subscribed Do Certify that we did carefully Inspect the aforegoing Vessels on the [days of the month], 1783 and that on board of said Vessels we found the Negroes mentioned in the aforegoing Lists amounting to [number of men, women and children] and to the best of our Judgement believe them to be all the Negroes on board the said Vessels. . . And we further Certify that we furnished the master of each Vessel with a Certified List of the Negroes on board his Vessel and informed him that he would not be permitted to land any other Negroes than those mentioned in the List and that if any other Negroes were found on board his Vessel he would be Severely punished and that we informed the Agent of Transports of this matter and desired him to use means for returning to this place all Negroes not mentioned in the List.

[Signed -Name on the Part of the United States; Name on the Part of the British Government]
(Hodges, Graham Russell, pp. 140-141.)

11) In addition to the 3,000 blacks listed in the Book of Negroes and evacuated from New York City in 1783, approximately 4,000 blacks were evacuated by the British from Savannah and another 5,000 when the British left Charleston in 1782. Some were freemen and women who had fled to freedom behind the British lines. Others were slaves of British officers. Many of the blacks ended up in Jamaica or St. Augustine, Florida with a few managing to arrive in

New York or reach Halifax, Nova Scotia. (Quarles, Benjamin, pp. 163-167.) Including the numerous slaves who fled their masters and were not recaptured, the years 1782 and 1783 were probably the greatest migration of African Americans until the Civil War.

Chapter 11 – A Liberated City

1) Washington, met with New York State Governor Clinton on the 19th of November at Tarrytown and the two subsequently rode together to Day's Tavern in Harlem, "where they waited for the final word from Carleton." (Fowler, William M. Jr., p. 229.)

2) On the 24th of November, Sir Guy Carleton sent a message to Washington. It stated,

"I propose to withdraw from this place to-morrow at noon, by which time I conclude your troops will be near the barrier."

To prevent any accidental incident occurring between the two armies, "Carleton asked Washington to hold his troops in place until [a British] officer was sent to give information to [the American's] advance guard." (Fowler, William, M. Jr., p. 229.)

3) By one p.m. on the 25th, after receiving word from the British that the last of their soldiers were leaving for their transports, General Knox led the American troops into New York and secured the city. Knox then rode back to the Bull's Head Tavern on the Bowery and rejoined General Washington and Governor Clinton. Washington had previously ordered the artillery companies, when they rode into the city, to pull "four six pounders, all trophies engraved with the times and places of their capture from the enemy. (Fowler, William, M. Jr., pp. 229- 230.)

4) General Washington and Governor Clinton rode side by side, followed by the Governor's mounted advisors and then Washington's officers. Citizens followed them but "[n]oticeably missing in the

parade accounts were representatives of the rank and file of the army. . . the low-ranked were not highlighted as featured players in the newspaper or personal accounts." (Van Buskirk, Judith L., p. 181.)

5) Fowler attributes the removal of the offending flag to a Sergeant named John Van Arsdale who "slapped on a pair of cleats, climbed to the top, and ripped the Union Jack away, replacing it with the American flag." (Fowler, William, M. Jr., p. 230.) Chernow does not mention how the Union Jack was removed. (Chernow, Ron, p. 449.)

I cannot conceive a good reason why any soldier would be carrying around a pair of cleats, ready to be used to climb a greased flagpole and tear down a nailed flag. Accordingly, I have imagined Will improvising and driving nails into shoes to make them cleated.

6) There was an impressive fireworks display one week later, with "[t]he houses on the city's major thoroughfares . . . packed and 'the Street itself was scarcely capable of containing another Spectator. The 'prodigeous concourse' roared their wonderment and approval, the sound of which (and the illuminations that inspired it) wafted out into the harbor and onto the Loyalist ships waiting for a good wind." (Van Buskirk, Judith L., p. 183.)

7) The earthquake, unusual for New York City, occurred after midnight on Saturday, November 29, 1783. Although some panic stricken people ran into the streets, General Washington slept through it in his quarters at Fraunces Tavern. (Chernow, Ron, p. 451.)

8) A description of the John Street Church states black worshippers prayed from the gallery and received communion after the white parishioners.

9) For purposes of the plot I have assumed African Americans in Adam's church, in the small community of Marblehead, worshipped

with whites in the main sanctuary and were not confined to the gallery, if there was one. This assumption may not be accurate. In 1800, the African American Easton family, living in Bridgewater (now Brockton), Massachusetts was forced to sit in the gallery of the Congregationalist Church. (Boston 1775, Forging a Future, May 17, 2007.) In 1787, at Philadelphia's St. George's Methodist Episcopal Church, a white trustee ordered African American communicants "to get themselves to the gallery." (Quarles, Benjamin, p. 193.)

10) James Varick was instrumental in forming the African Methodist Episcopal Zionist Church and became its first Bishop.

11) Washington designated Knox as general-in-chief of the Army, to go into effect on December 23, 1783.

12) Of the eleven officers weighed at West Point in August, 1782, eight of them were over 200 pounds. Knox's friend, Colonel Henry Jackson weighed 230 pounds. Presumably, the weigh in was all done in good fun, and fortunately recorded by Colonel David Cobb, who weighed 186. (Callahan, North, p. 205.)

Chapter 12 – The Blessings of Peace

1) Charles McKnight was ordained a Presbyterian Minister in 1742 and was one of the founders of the College of New Jersey, now Princeton University. He had two sons, Charles and Richard. Reverend McKnight was an outspoken opponent of British rule and his church at Middletown Point was burned in 1777. He was arrested, imprisoned on the British prison ship, , released and died January 1,1778. His son, Charles McKnight was a surgeon with the Continental Army at the battle of White Plains in October 1776.

2) General John Morin Scott born in New York City in 1730, was a lawyer by profession. During the Revolutionary War he commanded the 1st New York Battalion, the 2nd New York County Battalion and other New York militias. After the war he ran for Governor

of New York but lost to George Clinton. He did become New York Secretary of State and was a delegate to the Continental Congress.

3) The people of New York, at the end of the war, were divided between those who either wanted to drive out their Tory neighbors or at least deprive them of positions of power and influence, and those who wished to reintegrate those Tories who had remained into business and society. It was a class thing, and "like-minded, similarly educated, finely clothed people sought out their own kind with a vengeance. Such prompt reconciliation, hardly surprising given the degree of civility during the war, rubbed salt into the wounds of those who thought a New World would result from the Revolutionary crusade." (Van Buskirk, Judith L., pp. 186-187.)

The New York State Legislature took a moderate approach to the Loyalists in the State. To appease the hue and cry of radical Whigs, the State released more land formerly owned by Loyalists for sale although certain prominent Loyalists were allowed to buy back their forfeited lands. The prominent Loyalist DeLancey family was not so fortunate. The Commissioners of Forfeiture resold their land holdings at auction.

Loyalists who served in pro-British military units were barred from voting or holding any public office. Yet the harsher measures called for by radical Whigs, such as expulsion, seven year banishment or prohibition of Tories owning businesses, were not enacted. The Legislature "sent a strong message to the community that stability, continuity, and prosperity were its priorities." (Van Buskirk, Judith L., pp. 188-189.)

4) The case of Rutgers v. Waddington involved a widow, Elizabeth Rutgers, who had fled British occupied New York City, abandoning her brewery which was subsequently taken over by Joshua Waddington. He ran the brewery from 1778 until 1783. New York State passed the Trespass Act that restored property owned by Patriots who had left the City. In 1784, Rutgers sued in the Mayor's

Court under that Act for back rent. Hamilton argued the statutory law of New York (the Trespass Act) was trumped by the Laws of Nations and the New York State Constitution that incorporated English common law. In addition, he claimed the provisions of the Treaty of Paris pertaining to Loyalist property prevailed over State law and barred application of the Trespass Act to Waddington. Since Waddington had paid rent to the lawful British authorities at the time, the widow Rutgers had no claim for him to pay rent to her. Hamilton prevailed. The case had broad implications for claims against Loyalists for property belonging to Patriots. While Hamilton only received Nine Pounds for his successful legal services, Rutgers v. Waddington provided him with many more clients being sued under the Trespass Act.

(Rogers, Alec D., Journal of the American Revolution, March 8, 2016, "Rutgers v. Waddington: Alexander Hamilton, The End of the War for Independence, and the Origins of Judicial Review.")

5) Henry Knox actually put forth the concept of the Society of the Cincinnati as a fraternal organization of Continental Army officers in the spring of 1783. The name came from the example of Lucius Quintus Cincinnatus, a farmer who became a successful general in 458 B.C. and upon winning the war against the Aequians, returned to his life as a farmer.

George Washington was elected its first President and Henry Knox the first Secretary General. The organization was criticized as undemocratic and not befitting the new country because it created a hereditary membership of descendants of Officers of the Continental Army, deemed by some to be a hereditary aristocracy. There was fear the Society would control general elections and military men would take the reins of power. Thomas Jefferson, at one point urged that the Society be abolished.

Whether or not the Society as an institution exerted influence on the newly emerging country, at the Constitutional Convention, 27 of the 65 Delegates were members of the Society and 23 of them voted for the new Constitution.

J.W.S Campbell, President of the New Jersey Chapter, attended every meeting of the Society beginning in 1885. In 1910 he addressed the members and noted that at every meeting there was a toast to General George Washington and none to General Henry Knox. He noted: "It is especially difficult to understand why, in the written history of this country, the commanding character, pre-eminent abilities and incalculable service of General Knox are almost as inconspicuous." (Callahan, North, pp. 210-226.)

6) The Mischienza was a lavishly bizarre festival in Philadelphia to honor and say farewell to General Howe who was departing for London. Attended by four hundred guests, it had a medieval theme, the ladies chosen by their "knights" wore scandalous "exotic Turkish costumes." Following an elaborate dinner there were fireworks, dancing and gambling until dawn. (For a more detailed description of the Mischienza, see "Spies and Deserters, Chapter 7, End Note 2, p. 322.)

7) During the British occupation and after liberation, an auctioneer named William Tongue worked at Merchants Coffee House. The description of the auction and the goods being sold is taken from an account of auctions after the British evacuation. Merchants Coffee House became a place for daily meetings, a mercantile center and a place of prominence in the city's social life. (Bayer, Jonathan, Journal of the American Revolution, "Society At Auction: Coffee-House Culture in Occupied New York, November 10, 2016.)

8) Most women used their herb gardens for preparing medicines as well. In the absence of established apothecaries, some Doctors provided pills, balms, salves and ointments. I have presumed Dr. McKnight was one who did so.

Note to the Reader

1) As the author, it is my imagination that determines what happened to my fictional characters- Will and Elisabeth, Henry and William Stoner, Adam and Sarah Cooper, Samuel and Mercy Hadley, Nathanial and Anna Holmes, Levi Tyler and Isaiah Chandler, and yes even John Stoner- after the war.

The references to the historical characters are factually correct.

General Knox died in October 1806. Lucy outlived him by many years, dying in 1824 at the age of 68. Unfortunately for the Knoxes only three of their thirteen children lived to adulthood: Henry J. Knox who died in 1832 at the age of 32, Lucy Knox who died in1854; and Caroline Knox who died in 1851.

Colonel Israel Angell of the Rhode Island Regiment died on May 4, 1832 at the age of 91 in Smithfield, Rhode Island. He was married three times and fathered seventeen children.

Captain Stephen Olney lived in North Providence, Rhode Island after the war and died on November 23, 1832.

In 1771, three hundred and eight Marblehead Mariners voted and at least one hundred and sixty four fought in the American Revolution. Colonel John Glover, later promoted to Brigadier General, died in Marblehead, Massachusetts in 1797 at the age of 64.

Peter Williams, Jr., the son of Sexton Peter Williams of the John Street Church, was the second African American Episcopal priest, ordained in America. His father died in 1823 and was one of the founders, along with James Varick, of the African Methodist Episcopal Zion Church, which was located on the corner of Church and Leonard Streets. Sexton Williams purchased his freedom from the John Street Church trustees, making the final payment on November 4, 1785.

Author's Notes and Acknowledgements

"*The Price of Freedom*" is the sixth and last novel in my series on the American Revolution. Over the course of the war my characters have evolved from when they were first introduced in "*Cannons for the Cause.*" This is especially true for Will Stoner who, at the beginning of this saga, was a poorly educated fifteen-year old teamster. By the end of the series, he is a seasoned artillery Captain, married with two children, and attached to General Knox's headquarters staff.

I have tried to portray the development and maturation of his friendships primarily with Adam Cooper, who saved Will's life, not once but twice and was instrumental in thwarting a raid on Washington's headquarters. The fictitious characters of Samuel and Mercy Buskirk Hadley, Nathaniel Holmes and Sarah Cooper were early acquaintances of Will and continue to be part of his life. John Stoner looms throughout as the evil brother. I created him, not just to include a villain, but to enable me to tell the Loyalist and British Army's side of the war. That I made him a coward as well, in contrast to cavalry he rode with who were always seeking honor on the battlefield, made him a bit more despicable.

For me, after Will and Elisabeth, Adam Cooper is the most interesting of all the characters. Peter Bant runs a close second. Adam is a free African American, fighting for liberty from the Crown. Yet, throughout the war, he is confronted by the cruel reality that the freedom he is risking his life for, is not for everyone. It is not for the slaves of Patriots nor even the slaves of Loyalists who are evacuated at the end of the War. He witnesses slave owners prowling the battlefield of Yorktown looking for their escaped property. He is disrespected by white patriots, even though he is protecting them from the British and Hessian troops. He is torn by his support for the rebel cause and the satisfaction he gets from freeing slaves of New Jersey Patriots as part of Colonel Tye's Loyalist band of raiders in New Jersey. He has to buy the freedom of the woman he loves, barred from courting her because she is considered the property of her master.

This contradiction between the high principles of the Revolution and the stark reality of his every day existence as a black soldier, makes him the most interesting character psychologically. I added Private Gideon Hazzard and the other African Americans of the Rhode Island Regiment to highlight there were other integrated units in the Continental Army besides the Marblehead Mariners. One could conclude African American free men, serving as soldiers, had an even stronger commitment to the Revolution. They enlisted for the duration despite the lack of respect and denial of promotions because of their race.

Peter Bant, suffered from what today we would recognize as PTSD. He witnessed a horrific act of murder by British cavalry, blames himself for the death of the victims and suffers from survivor's guilt. In every war, there must be those who have PTSD. In the Revolutionary War, his strangeness, nightmares and hallucinations merely made him in the eyes of other soldiers, a "lunatick." There was no treatment for his condition. He simply has to endure and suffer.

Elisabeth Stoner, Mercy Hadley and Mary Lewis epitomize the active women who not only supported the patriotic cause, but played major roles as spies, nurses and business women managing their husbands affairs. They are modeled on real women of the period such as Abigail Hartman Rice, a nurse at a hospital near Valley Forge, Lucy Knox and Mary Otis Warren who, by their correspondence and writings voiced their views and established themselves as the intellectual equals of their husbands. Peggy

Shippen Arnold is another strong woman, who, according to some historians, most likely persuaded General Arnold to commit treason. If so, she certainly deserves to be classified as an influential member of the so-called weaker sex.

The real historical characters, primarily Henry and Lucy Knox, are fascinating. Lucy Flucker Knox, daughter of the Royal Secretary of Massachusetts chose her love for Henry Knox, at the time a modest bookseller, over loyalty to family and the Crown. Together, they cast their fate with the revolutionary cause and never look back. Their correspondence is full of their deep affection for each other, their despondency when they are apart and their fervent hopes for living together in peace when the war ends. Much of the dialogue of both General Knox and Lucy is based on the actual wording of their letters.

I have consciously avoided a plot giving General George Washington too much prominence. He appears where necessary to the story. For example, steadying the troops at the first battle of Trenton. At Newburgh, New York he dissuaded the Continental Army Officers from marching on Congress to demand their pay. The words that appear in "*The Price of Freedom*," attributed to him are in the main taken from his address to the officers. To his great credit, Washington resisted using the Army and a "little mutiny" as a lever to strengthen the hand of the nationalists in Congress. He maintained the principle of subordination of the military to civil authority and thereby prevented a mutiny, coup or even possible civil war.

However, I have also attempted to accurately depict Washington's warts, particularly with respect to slavery. He did reclaim two of his escaped slaves when the British surrendered at Yorktown. He also argued, in negotiations with General Sir Guy Carleton, the British were obligated under the Treaty of Paris to return all Negroes to the Americans as confiscated property. The British took the high moral ground that the clause in question could not and did not apply to freed slaves behind British lines. This gave rise to the Book of Negroes.

I am deeply indebted to the real soldier, Private Joseph P. Martin of the Eighth Connecticut Continental Regiment and his memoir, "Private Yankee Doodle." My fictitious characters of Privates Levi Tyler, Isaiah Chandler, Henry Gillet, Caleb Wade and Matthias Vose are based upon Private Joseph Martin's experiences, emotions, sufferings, deprivations, bravery and fidelity as an ordinary soldier. He was an extraordinary person, an excellent observer of human nature and a good writer. In recognition of his abilities, I have given him the last word on the back cover of the last book in the series. The excerpt does not do justice to his description of how the soldiers were given nothing they were promised when they enlisted for the duration, were discharged with barely the clothes on their backs and worthless paper promises to pay what was owed them, and had to endure "vile" criticism when, many years afterwards, Congress finally provided them with some compensation for their service.

When I first started writing in 2014, I did not lay out the plot and actions of the characters for the entire series. Characters and scenes developed without any pre-planning, almost haphazardly in some cases. Instead of having great prescience in foreseeing plot and character development as I wrote these novels over the course of three, four and five years, it was pure luck.

For example, when I first introduced Elisabeth to Will, in Cannons for the Cause, I had no plan to have her become a spy in Philadelphia and part of Peggy Shippen's social circle. Nor had I yet done the research to know Peggy Shippen became Mrs. Benedict Arnold, or when Arnold's treason was discovered and he fled West Point, Peggy would engage in an academy award performance, recognized by historians as her "mad scene" to protect herself from being accused of complicity. Yet, because Elisabeth and Peggy were acquaintances in Philadelphia, it was a credible plot development in *Treason and Triumph* for Elisabeth to offer to help Mrs. Arnold when she apparently had lost her mind.

Similarly, Adam's early expressed anger as a free African American, fighting for liberty yet aware of the patriotic slave owners around him, logically led to his demonstrating, in "*Spies and Deserters,*" in front of General Washington's headquarters at Valley Forge and pretending to desert, all for his love for Sarah Penrose in order to buy her freedom.

The one constant theme I stumbled upon was the role of "invisible minorities" in our Revolution, minorities being defined as African Americans, Native Americans and women. I hope the characters I have introduced, based on accurate historical facts, will help the reader to better understand the diversity of soldiers and civilians who supported the war. Despite all the heroic paintings depicting the war, our independence was not won by only stalwart looking white men.

Over the past five years, I have had the support of many friends who have critiqued drafts, offered advice based on their individual areas of expertise, and in general simply supported my efforts to write a saga about the Revolution. Dan Edelman brought his own perceptive eye to the manuscript and, as usual, caught errors, both major and minor that I missed. More importantly, he questioned plot developments and paths I had taken as well as compelling me to think through whether my depictions of historical characters were factually accurate. I could not have wished for a wiser and more understanding friend to help me along the way.

Without Glen Baquet's knowledge I could not have accurately described any aspect of a horse's behavior, digestion, illnesses, strength or speed. Big Red is based on a horse of the same name on his horse farm. In addition, Glen's advice, drawing on his professional expertise as an audiologist, provided me with the details for the temporary and permanent loss of hearing likely to be experienced by the artillery men. I highly recommend watching a short video of Revolutionary War re-enactments of volleys of musket fire and cannons, to realize the deafening noise they created.

Don Crane helped me understand deer hunting. It was he who suggested a wolf pack would be a great danger to hunters in winter time. That added drama to an otherwise mundane hunting scene.

My friends have taken a keen interest in my characters and encouraged me with their comments on my writing and research. To a person, they have favored the use of End Notes. This leads me to wonder why more authors of historical fiction do not do so. I am convinced good writing coupled with thorough research, referred to in End Notes, enhances the readers' enjoyment and understanding of historical events.

I could not have written these six novels without the unstinting efforts of my son and wife. My son has done both the formatting, which is time consuming and tedious, and the internal artwork. More importantly, the covers are all attributable to him. His perceptive advice on selection of paintings for all the covers has been spot on. His sensitivity and knowledge of the social currents have saved me from some embarrassing mistakes. We have made the journey together and it has brought us closer. It is truly a wonderful experience to collaborate with one's son and share the pleasure of seeing all the hard work transformed into an actual book.

My wife's contributions are immeasurable. Besides providing moral support and constant encouragement, she has tolerated not only my immersion in the writing process, but the stacks of historical books, magazines, maps and printouts that have made our coffee table unusable for any other purpose for almost half a dozen years. Our frequent discussions about "invisible minorities" kept me focused on this underlying theme. Her caution about including too many battle scenes have made the novels more balanced and I hope more interesting. She has a keen editor's eye and the writing is far better due to her efforts.

All remaining errors, including those of fact, grammar, spelling and punctuation, are my responsibility.

The saga ends with *"The Price of Freedom."* The characters live on in my mind and I hope in yours too. Should you have the occasion to visit any of the sites described in these novels; Trenton, Morristown or Princeton, New Jersey; Albany, Newburgh, or Lake George, New York; or Cambridge, Boston, or Marblehead, Massachusetts, I hope you will discover my novels have added to your understanding of the historical events that took place there.

Martin R. Ganzglass
Washington, D.C.
July 2019

Bibliography

The following are the books, blogs and websites I have relied upon for historical accuracy. The Journal of the American Revolution and its blog, All Things Liberty, as well as Boston 1775 were especially helpful.

My research about American prisoners of war led me to Edwin G. Burrows' book, "Forgotten Patriots –The Untold Story of American Prisoners During the Revolutionary War," and his paper, "The Prisoners of New York," published in the Long Island History Journal, and Katie Turner Getty's articles about the prison ships. Both were shocking for two reasons. First, the graphic recollections of the survivors depict such scenes of filth, disease and deprivation as to call to mind images of concentration camp inmates in the 20th century. Second, the statistics of the numbers of prisoners who died while in British captivity surpass the death rate percentages of any American prisoners in any war, including those held by the Confederacy at Andersonville. The mortality rate of those imprisoned by the British was between 50% and 70%, as compared to 35% at Andersonville. On the prison ships in Wallabout Bay, approximately 11,000 American prisoners died, at the rate of fifty to sixty per week or seven to eight per day.

I also found much of the material on the Newburgh Conspiracy described by Ron Chernow in his biographies of Washington and Hamilton, as well as James Weynsel's account most helpful in understanding the political machinations of Hamilton and others in Congress.

Finally, while much research is dry and unexciting, it was a particular thrill to see the actual entry in the Book of Negroes for Henry (Harry) Washington, described as age 43, "fine fellow. [Formerly the property of General Washington; left him 7 [years ago.]"

As always, Private Joseph Plumb Martin describes the thinking of the ordinary soldiers, their suffering and to me their inexplicable commitment to the cause of freedom, despite being deprived of promised pay, clothing, food and land in return for their steadfast service.

Since it is easy enough to search a book or article on line by author and title, I have omitted the customary reference to publisher and date of publication.

Andrlik, Todd,
Reporting the Revolutionary War – Before It Was History It Was News

Barbieri, Michael,
The Dollar in Revolutionary America, All Things Liberty, September 27, 2016

Barclay, Sydney,
Personal Recollections of the American Revolution- A Private Journal Prepared From Authentic Domestic Records, Leopold Classic Library

Bayer, Jonathan,
"Society At Auction: Coffee-House Culture in Occupied New York, All Things Liberty, November 10, 2016

Brooks, Noah,
Henry Knox, A Soldier of the Revolution

Burrows, Edwin G.,
Forgotten Patriots – The Untold Story of American Prisoners During the Revolutionary War

Burrows, Edwin G.,
The Prisoners of New York, Long Island History Journal, 2011, Volume 22, Issue 2

Callahan, North,
Henry Knox – General Washington's General

Chernow, Ron,
Washington – A Life,
Alexander Hamilton

Dandridge, Danske,
Three Rivers: Hudson-Mohawk-Schoharie -American Prisoners of the Revolution

Drake, Francis S.,
Life and Correspondence of Henry Knox, Major-General in the American Revolutionary Army

Fleming, Thomas,
The Strategy of Victory – How George Washington Won the American Revolution

Fowler, William, Jr.,
American Crisis – George Washington and the Dangerous Two Years After Yorktown, 1781-1783

Fried, Stephen,
A New Founding Mother, Smithsonian, September 2018

Getty, Katie Turner,
"Walking Skeletons- Starvation on Board The Jersey Prison Ship," *All Things Liberty*, March 11, 2019.
"Death Had Almost Lost Its Sting" Disease on the Prison Ship Jersey, *All Things Liberty*, January 10, 2019.

Glickstein, Don,
After Yorktown – The Final Struggle for American Independence

Griffin, David, M.,
Lost British Forts of Long Island

Hamilton, Phillip,
The Revolutionary War Lives and Letters of Lucy and Henry Knox

Headley, J.T.,
The Chaplains and Clergy of the Revolution

Hill, Lawrence,
Canada's History, Behind the Book of Negroes

Hodges, Graham Russell, Editor,
The Black Loyalist Directory – African Americans in Exile After the American Revolution

Kuhl, Jackson,
The Whale-Boat Men of Long Island Sound, *All Things Liberty*, November 1, 2013

Library of Congress,
The Newburgh Conspiracy, December 1782-March 1783

Mann, Frank Paul,
The British Occupation of Southern New York During the American Revolution and the Failure to Restore Civilian Government

Martin, Joseph Plumb,
Private Yankee Doodle: Being a Narrative of Some of Adventures, Dangers and Sufferings of a Revolutionary Soldier, George E. Scheer, Editor

McBurney, Christian,
Abductions in the American Revolution – Attempts to Kidnap George Washington, Benedict Arnold and Other Military and Civilian Leaders

North Louise V., Wedge Janet M., and Freeman, Landa M.,
In the Words of Women – The Revolutionary War and the Birth of the Nation, 1765-1799

Quarles, Benjamin,
The Negro in the American Revolution

Randall, Willard Sterne,
Benedict Arnold – Patriot and Traitor

Rogers, Alec D.,
"Rutgers v. Waddington: Alexander Hamilton, The End of the War for Independence, and the Origins of Judicial Review," *All Things Liberty*, March 8, 2016

National Society of the Daughters of the American Revolution,
African American and American Indian Patriots in the American Revolution

Van Buskirk, Judith L.,
Generous Enemies – Patriots and Loyalists in Revolutionary New York

Wagner Stephen,
Slavery on Long Island, Hofstra University Library, Special Collections Department

Wensyel, James W.,
The Newburgh Conspiracy, American Heritage, 1981, Volume 32, Issue 3

Made in United States
Cleveland, OH
01 June 2025